The voice in her head grew to a roaring, and a winter-white sunburst exploded all around her, like the brightest spotlight she'd ever stood in. Kelley's wings burst forth, and she could see them at the edges of her vision—furling outward like silver lace, edged with purple flame. She leaped and they swept her up through the crumbling rafters of the derelict theater and out into the night sky.

LESLEY LIVINGSTON

Tempestuous

a novel

An Imprint of HarperCollinsPublishers

For John. And for Jack.

HarperTeen is an imprint of HarperCollins Publishers.

Tempestuous
www.epicreads.com

Library of Congress Cataloging-in-Publication Data
Livingston, Lesley.
    Tempestuous / by Lesley Livingston. — 1st ed.
        p.   cm.
    Sequel to: Darklight.
    Summary: Sonny Flannery joins a group of underground Lost Fae as he
struggles to recover from his heartbreak over Kelley Winslow, while Kelley
tries to uncover who is hunting Sonny's Green Magick so that she and Sonny
can be together again.
    ISBN 978-0-06-174002-2
    [1. Fairies—Fiction.   2. Actors and actresses—Fiction.   3. Fantasy.]
I. Title.
PZ7.L7613Te   2011   2010015902
[Fic]—dc22   CIP
                                                                              AC

Typography by Sasha Illingworth
12 13 14 15 16   LP/RRDH   10 9 8 7 6 5 4 3 2 1
❖
First paperback edition, 2012

HIPPOLYTA: How chance Moonshine is gone before Thisbe comes back and finds her lover?

Reenter Thisbe

THESEUS: She will find him by starlight. Here she comes; and her passion ends the play.

The antique black carriage sped through the night, its tall spoked wheels whirring, skimming the surface of the river as though the spectral horse that pulled it followed a paved track. In the distance, along the banks, the city lights shimmered, but there, in the middle of the river's wide expanse, all was darkness. As the carriage approached the black, hunched shape of an island, it picked up even more speed, thundering through the crumbling arch of the abandoned coal dock like it was a gateway to another realm.

The finger of a smokestack thrust up into the sky above the treetops, crowned with a nest of birds that took sudden flight as the carriage horse's hooves clattered along the remnants of the pier and onto an overgrown avenue. Fallen leaves left over from the previous autumn danced in the wake of the passing carriage.

The driver hauled on the reins, pulling the horse to a stop in front of the gaping doorway of a moldering stone building. Years of neglect had left the surrounding foliage free to grow thick and lush, climbing up the walls almost to the roof. The profusion of vines and moss had softened the building's contours but was unable to disguise the elegant lines of its original design.

As the driver's feet touched the ground, a wave of iridescent illumination washed outward from the carriage, transforming the abandoned building, altering its rough appearance like a mirage. By the time the driver had thrown open the carriage doors, there were several cloaked figures standing by to receive the occupant of the coach.

The only surviving son of the Greenman lay on the velvet bench seat like a broken toy that had been thrown against a wall. His limbs were splayed at odd angles. Greenish bloodstains marked the skin at the corners of his mouth. There was a dark scorch mark in the shape of a four-leaf clover at the base of his throat, and he looked to be barely breathing.

The driver nodded curtly at him. "Bring him inside."

As two of the attendants moved toward the coach, the driver turned to the stone edifice and the steps leading up to it—which now appeared smooth and gleaming like marble in the light that spilled from the windows on either side of the open, carved-oak doors. The shadowy figures lifted the unresponsive body and carried it through into the hall. Sounds of merriment and feasting came from within, and the scent of flowers was heavy in the air, seductive and beckoning.

But before ascending the steps, the carriage driver looked up into the night sky and said, in a voice like a whispered death sentence, "Find the Green Magick. And bring me the one who bears its burden. . . ."

The dark air filled with darker shadows as the remaining cloaked figures swirled into a frenzy of action: throwing back their cloaks, they shed the smokelike bodies hidden beneath and grew wings. Dark feathers coalesced out of the fabric of the night, and a flock of screeching, red-eyed herons took to the air.

I

The crowd of onlookers had largely dissipated once the New York City Fire Department had finally gotten the blaze under control, though the entire block remained cordoned off with yellow police tape and the gutters ran full with soot-blackened water. Fortunately the structure had been stand-alone, unlike most of the surrounding shops and apartment buildings, and so the damage had been confined to the Avalon Grande Theatre—damage being wholly inadequate to describe the devastation wrought upon the old converted church by the fire that had started there in the early hours of that morning. Just before dawn.

Just before . . . what?

Sonny Flannery stood in a shadowed doorway across the street from the ruination and struggled desperately to remember. He knew that he had been inside the Avalon in the moments before it had been consumed by fire—holed up, waiting for morning, held under siege by malevolent Fae— and he knew that there had been fighting. Vicious Green Maidens and their leprechaun brothers. Sonny and his friends had been short on odds. And then . . . something had happened. Something bad.

And for the life of him, Sonny couldn't remember what that was.

All he kept coming up with was that one minute he'd been fighting for his life. The next, he'd woken up in his apartment with a head full of cotton wool and hobnails—only to discover that the one place in all the worlds that Kelley Winslow, the girl he loved, had truly called "home" was gone. Destroyed.

Now, standing in front of the smoking remains of the Avalon Grande Theatre on Fifty-second, Sonny had the horrible gut-twisting feeling that it was entirely his fault.

One brick wall still held bits of broken, rainbow-tinted glass in its window frames, but most of the rest of the building had been reduced to rubble when the bell tower collapsed. Over near the side alley where the stage door still hung awkwardly inside its sagging frame, Sonny saw the shattered remnants of mirrors and burned and blackened costume racks. On the end of one rack, a pair of sparkly fairy wings hung from a cord, barely singed.

Sonny turned abruptly and stumbled blindly down the sidewalk—almost knocking over a middle-aged woman in overalls and half-glasses who stood staring at the wreck of the theater, tears streaming unheeded down her face.

It began to rain, a few spattering drops swiftly turning into a downpour. Head down, shoulders hunched, Sonny walked without having a destination in mind. The wind that pushed the rain against him, soaking his T-shirt and plastering it to his chest, held a biting chill. But there was also the hint—just a taste—of green, growing things, spring buds and blossoms, that reached Sonny's nostrils, and he breathed in deeply, almost gulping the air, in an attempt to steady himself. Green things . . . and smoke? No. The smoke was in his head. A memory of . . . of what? Of a fight he couldn't remember. A battle that had set Kelley's theater ablaze, apparently. That was, at least, what he had gathered from the images on the television—video footage shot earlier that morning of the Avalon Grande collapsing in on itself, disappearing in a thick column of inky smoke, gutted. Like Sonny had been in the moments after Kelley Winslow had uttered those words.

"I don't love Sonny Flannery."

Green things and smoke . . .

He looked around, the need to run, to hide, to escape almost overwhelming. His chest ached—inside and out—as though he'd swallowed seawater into his lungs or been thrown against treacherous rocks, battered by waves.

This must be what it feels like to be shipwrecked, Sonny thought. *Clinging to a hope for rescue that isn't coming . . .*

Sonny turned and stumbled backward, off the curb and into the street, ignoring the outraged protests of car horns and screeching brakes.

"I don't love Sonny," she had said—unaware, it seemed, that he was standing right there. Behind her. Close enough to step through the door. To reach out a hand and touch her bright hair. He didn't know why she'd said such a thing, but he did know that it had to be true. One of the universal truths in Sonny's world was this: Faerie couldn't lie.

Kelley was Faerie.

"I never did and I never will," she had said.

The memory of her words seared through Sonny even as the teeth of the wind tore at him. He'd grown up in the court of the Winter King and rarely felt the cold, but now he was shivering so hard his teeth rattled. In front of him the yawning maw of the subway station entrance at Fiftieth and Eighth beckoned him. He staggered blindly toward the shelter of the stairwell and then on down, traveling underground like Orpheus in search of his beloved in hell. Only Sonny knew with bitter certainty that *his* Eurydice didn't want him.

She'd said so herself.

II

"She's leaking," rumbled the ogre.

"She's not 'leaking,' Harvicc." Tyff shushed him.

"She's . . . *crying*. And crazy."

Kelley barely felt her roommate's hand on her shoulder, shaking her gently.

"Kelley . . . why are you suddenly a crazy person?"

Under any other circumstances, Kelley would have laughed at Tyff's question. Why was she "suddenly" crazy? Why was she acting as if the world had just collapsed all around her? Probably because it had.

Through a blur of tears, she watched as the French doors

leading into Sonny's apartment flew wide and the tall, lanky shape of the Janus Guard Maddox came tearing out onto the balcony. "What in seven hells is going on around here?" he shouted, a thundercloud frown darkening his face. "Where's Sonny? I want some bloody answers!"

Tyff opened her mouth to say something, but Kelley shot to her feet and turned a blazing look on her roommate that made the Summer Fae put up a hand and back off.

"Somebody had better tell me what happened," Maddox said, looking back and forth between the two girls. "Kelley?" There was a dangerous note of warning in his voice.

The pain from the iron knife blade that had slashed across Kelley's ribcage throbbed mercilessly. Tyff had dressed and bound the wound, but still, only the four-leaf clover charm Kelley wore around her neck kept the pain from being unbearable. "Leave it, Madd," Kelley said. "I meant what I said when I told you this is none of your business."

Tyff took a small step forward. "Kelley, I think he has a right to—"

"*Shut* it, Tyff!" Kelley rounded on her roommate before she could say another word. Shocked by the reprimand, Tyff blinked and did as she was told. A tense, silent stand-off ensued, with Tyff staring grimly into some middle distance, Maddox staring unblinking at Kelley, and Harvicc the ogre shifting from one enormous foot to the other, his confused glower sweeping back and forth. Over near the far corner of the terrace stood the Fennrys Wolf—the Janus Guard so-named for his Viking origins—his lean-muscled arms knotted

10

over his chest, silently observing the whole thing.

High above, against a backdrop of ominous thunderheads, three vaporous figures twisted around one another, keening above the wind as though they were an extension of Kelley's agony. Which, in a way, they were. The Cailleach—Storm Hags—were her mother's minions. Her mother, the Queen of Air and Darkness. They were the representatives of Queen Mabh's power in the mortal realm, and so—by osmosis or inheritance or guilt by association—they were Kelley's as well.

She hated them.

She hated all of them. The Hags, her mother, her cold and cruel father, Auberon . . . the Faerie. They had done this to her. To Sonny.

They didn't do anything to Sonny. You did.

She had lied to him. Broken his heart. She'd done it to protect him. . . .

Liar. You did it because you were afraid of him.

A tumult of emotions surged in Kelley's chest, threatening to overwhelm her. She turned her back on her friends and gripped the stone balustrade, staring bleakly down at the park, so far below. A cold spring rain had begun to fall, but Kelley didn't notice its chill. Maybe it would help to put out the last of the fire, she thought, and a fresh wave of pain almost doubled her over the railing, making her feel as if she would retch.

The fire. The theater. Sonny. Gone.

Everything that mattered to her in life. *Gone* . . .

And Kelley had been the one to drive Sonny away. It was the right thing to do, she argued with the voice in her head that

11

called her "liar." Sonny was in possession of more magickal firepower than even the strongest of the Fair Folk, and he had no idea. But something had triggered his power—to devastating, horrific result—back in the theater. That something was Kelley. When Sonny had thought for a brief instant that she'd been killed, the resulting fury he'd unleashed had given them all a taste of what he was capable of.

Damn right I'm afraid of him.

She was also afraid *for* him. Maybe, hopefully, the leprechauns and their sisters were no longer a threat, but Kelley knew deep down that Sonny was still in real danger. Her nightmares of him lying dead on the ground—just like the Greenman—had told her as much. There were those in the Faerie realm who would kill for the Green Magick, and Sonny wouldn't be safe until Kelley could figure out a way to *make* him safe. In the meantime, she couldn't risk being near him—the weak link in his armor, the fuse to his dynamite—and she definitely couldn't risk revealing his secret. What made it infinitely worse was that she couldn't tell him any of this, because she knew he wouldn't understand. So she'd done the only thing she knew would make him leave her. At least until she could figure out what to do . . .

The small hairs on the back of her neck lifted. She turned slightly and realized Maddox was standing very close behind her.

"Where *is* he?" he asked.

"I don't know. He's gone."

"Just like that?" His voice was quiet. Hard.

"Yes."

"He was in no fit state to go *any*where when I left him. When I left him here with *you*." Maddox had never sounded like that before. His anger was colder than the rain. "Now you tell me he's gone off who knows where? And I take it you're not about to go looking for him."

"I can't."

"I see." He nodded once. She could feel his gaze boring into her even though she couldn't meet his eyes. "Well, let me tell *you* something. That boyo is like a brother to me. And I swear to all the gods, if something bad happens to him—there will be a reckoning." He turned to go. "This is on *your* head, Princess."

I already know that.

If something bad happens to Sonny . . .

Suddenly all of the pain and doubt was overwhelming— too much to keep knotted up inside. Kelley felt like she was suffocating. She didn't want to think. She didn't want to feel. She wished with all her might that she was someone—some*thing*—other than what she was. Something not defined by the words *Kelley* and *Faerie princess*.

She wished that she were *free.* . . .

Clawing at her four-leaf clover charm—the only thing that kept her magick in check—Kelley tore the necklace off, and a sudden, violent barrage of lightning flared magnesium-bright in the darkness of the storm. Kelley's eyelids squeezed shut, and another kind of fire—her own dark fire—flashed behind her eyes. Everything blurred and twisted in her mind. Thought, emotion, pain . . . all of it was suddenly gone.

Kelley was gone.

In her place, a kestrel falcon soared upward into the sky above the terrace of Sonny's penthouse apartment. She spread her wings—her *feathered* wings—wide against the wild, buffeting winds. Startled, she opened her mouth, and a shrill keening cry skirled above the sounds of the storm.

"Whoa!" shouted Tyff from far below. "Kelley! Get down here before you hurt yourself!"

Hurt . . . Fear! Panic!

The kestrel's thoughts swam with confusion. The frantic beating of her wings sent her sideways into a sheeting wall of rain.

"Kelley!"

Air currents buffeted her from all sides.

Helpless! Help me!

Mind fogged with terror and the effects of her drastic transformation, she flapped wildly and tumbled end over end, plummeting toward Sonny's terrace far below in an out-of-control dive.

"Kelley!" Tyff screeched.

Harvicc caught her before she hit the ground and wrapped his immense hands around her with a surprising gentleness.

She was trembling violently—her instincts suddenly those of the wild creature she had become, only barely colored by her rational mind. She could feel her own tiny heart fluttering madly in her feathered breast.

Fly! Escape!

Harvicc lumbered over to one of the ornamental potted trees with exaggerated care and deposited the kestrel gently on a branch, holding his fingers in a loose cage around her feathered, quivering body. Her wings ruffled, and Harvicc closed up the gaps between his fingers so that she would not attempt panicked flight again.

Caged! Trapped! Escape! Fly . . .

"Wait!"

The Fennrys Wolf stepped out from beneath the dripping eaves on the far side of the terrace and stalked toward them. Putting his hands on Harvicc's thick wrists, Fennrys slowly began to open the cage of the ogre's fingers wider.

Escape!

"What do you think you're doing?" Tyff grabbed at his arm.

"Wait." Fennrys shook the Summer Fae off.

The kestrel's wings shivered and furled. Harvicc closed his hands tighter.

Fear!

"Stop," Fennrys said to Harvicc in a firm, quiet voice. "You're frightening her. If she feels trapped, she'll try to fly."

"As opposed to what she was just doing before he caught her?" Tyff snapped. "You know—*flying*?"

"Trust me," the Janus said, glancing over his shoulder.

Tyff uttered a squawk of protest. "Trust *you*?"

"Kelley does."

Kelley . . . I'm Kelley. I trust . . .

Tyff's mouth snapped shut on whatever it was she was going to say, but her eyes still blazed, fiercely protective.

"Don't worry." Fennrys turned back to the potted tree and the bird perched there. "I know what I'm doing." His knuckles went white with the effort of peeling back the reluctant ogre's meaty digits. All the while he was crooning to the terrified creature that shifted and shivered on the too-slender branch that swayed in the gathering storm winds, threatening to dislodge her. "You're all right. *Shh* . . . you're all right. I'm here. I've got you. . . ." Fennrys reached out to gently stroke the chest feathers of the reddish-hued bird with the back of his fingers, shushing her gently.

Trust . . .

"That's my roommate you're pawing, Fido," Tyff growled.

He ignored her and, resting his other arm in front of the branch, slowly coaxed the nervous kestrel onto his wrist. "I've hunted with falcons since I was a boy in Gwynn's court. I *know* what I'm doing." He reached up and smoothed the feathers on top of the bird's—on top of Kelley's—head, continuing to croon to her under his breath.

The kestrel's talons scrabbled for a moment, and then she steadied on the perch of his forearm, tilting her head from side to side, trying to make sense of vision that was suddenly more acute—although less binocular than she was used to. Over Fenn's shoulder, Tyff's face came into focus as the beautiful Faerie peered down at her.

"You're just full of surprises, aren't you, little roomie?" Tyff murmured.

The falcon shifted and made a high-pitched, mewling sound.

"Okay. Okay . . . I know you're in there." Tyff took a step forward, trying to cajole Kelley back to personhood. "Kelley? Think 'people' thoughts. Legs and arms and stuff. No more of this pretty-birdie act, all right? You're freaking me out."

The kestrel ruffled her feathers in agitation.

"Not nearly as much as you're freaking *her* out," Fenn growled.

The strong pulse of his blood thrummed through Fennrys's wrist—she could feel it beneath the grip of her kestrel feet. The steady rhythm began to sooth her jangled nerves.

"Now all of you step back so I can try and get her inside the apartment. . . ."

Suddenly, lightning flashed. Thunder roared like a cannon discharged directly overhead. The kestrel shrieked in fear and rage. Her wings beat the air, clawing at an updraft. Maddox made a desperate grab for her; Tyff screamed and Harvicc lunged; and Fennrys howled in pain as razor-sharp talons sliced through the flesh of his forearm.

She felt the blood, wet and warm, as she launched herself skyward.

Up into the heart of the pummeling tempest.

Far below, the voices of her friends shouting for her to return grew small and then silent as she flew upward into the lashing rain and the storm clouds swallowed her up.

III

Sonny didn't know how long he'd been riding the subway. Long enough for it to have made its way north, all the way up to 168th Street, to the end of the C line in Washington Heights, where it stopped and headed south again. No one seemed to notice Sonny or care that he sat there, slumped in his seat, as the train headed back down toward Midtown. People got on and off—mortals hurrying from one place to another, going about their lives. Most of them made a point of actively avoiding glancing in his direction. He must have looked either dangerous or crazy. Or both. Sonny certainly couldn't have cared less. He had nowhere to go, and so the aimless journey suited him—just dim light, anonymous faces, and a rumble of sound to block out his thoughts.

He had no idea where he was when the train suddenly lurched, stuttering and grinding to a stop in the tunnel somewhere between two stations. The lights in the car flickered and dimmed to almost nothing, buzzing like lazy insects as they ran on emergency power. Sonny let his head fall back against the window and closed his eyes. Waiting for the subway to start moving once again. Taking him away from everything. From nothing. From Kelley.

"You look lost," said a voice in his ear.

"What?" Sonny opened his eyes again to see a small, thin slip of a girl sitting next to him, a brown paper bag clutched tightly on her lap. Her feet were bare and she swung them back and forth without touching the floor of the train car.

"Lost," she repeated. "Like me." She cocked her head and getured with her chin. "Like them."

Sonny looked around at the other occupants of the subway car. He'd been vaguely aware that it had been uncharacteristically empty for the last several stops, but he'd been grateful for the solitude. Now there were a handful of other occupants, scattered on seats up and down the length of the car. But not one of them was human. They may have worn human shapes, like Halloween costumes masking their true natures, but Sonny could see through the glamours to the creatures beneath: a trio of dryads with leafy hair huddled over a hand mirror, a nervous-looking banshee with haunted eyes drinking from a Starbucks cup, a shining Faerie girl clothed in a coat of silver chain mail, and one of the urisk—dwarfish solitary Fae noted for their shyness—disguised as a wizened old man. They were the Lost Fae. Marooned in a world away from their homes. Shipwrecked . . . like him. Lost.

The girl who had spoken to Sonny held out a slender hand to him. "This is my stop," she said. Sonny glanced out of the window but saw only the darkened walls of the tunnel. "You can come with me, if you want." Her fingers, he saw, were slightly webbed with diaphanous membranes. Her skin shimmered, and her long, fine hair was a shade of indigo so deep it was almost black. She was Water Folk . A naiad. She should have repelled him or made him want to fight. But her dark, luminous eyes, huge in such a tiny, delicate face, held his gaze, and all he felt was weariness.

She was right. He was lost.

With nowhere else to go, Sonny stood and looked down at the Faerie girl. The top of her silky head barely reached to his shoulder, but she smiled up at him serenely and held out her hand again. Sonny wrapped his fingers around hers and followed as she stepped toward the subway doors on the opposite side of the car from the ones that would open at the next station stop—the next *human* station stop. When the doors shimmered and vanished, several of the Lost Fae that had been sitting stood and stepped out into the darkness of the tunnel.

The girl leaped gracefully down, moving toward what seemed to be a service alcove recessed into the tunnel wall. Sonny followed. Behind him the doors of the car reappeared and the whole thing shuddered, its interior lights flickering back to normal brightness. Then the train jerked, rumbling and clanking into forward motion, and was gone.

The shadowed shapes of the other Fae who'd left the car melted into the darkness that followed in the wake of the train. Sonny blinked, waiting for his eyes to adjust to the murk. Then he saw, directly in front of him where the blank, sooty black wall of the alcove had been, a faint phosphorescent shimmering. He reached out a hand and felt nothing. Air. The wall had disappeared.

The Faerie girl at his side stepped through into another tunnel. This one wasn't man-made, Sonny knew that instantly. But it also wasn't natural. *A Faerie construct.* Sourceless light reflected off the gleaming facets of what looked like black cut glass. Sonny glanced around to see his own visage shattered and mirrored back at him in a thousand fragments. It was, he thought humorlessly, an apt metaphor for his present state of mind.

He trailed behind the naiad—both of them sure-footed, used to traveling in the dark—for what seemed like quite a while. Five minutes? Maybe ten? Sonny lost track of the time, but it wasn't as if he had to be somewhere. Eventually, the obsidian tunnel opened onto another tunnel. This one *was* man-made; brick and stone arched overhead, and a trickling stream of water flowed down the middle. Faerie-wrought sconces hung at intervals on the curved wall, set with smokeless torches that cast pale, flickering illumination. The tunnel veered at a slight angle and sloped gently upward in the direction they walked. After another ten minutes or so, Sonny saw the faint glimmer of brighter light far up ahead.

He supposed he should be wary—or, at the very least, curious—but his emotional responses were detached, distant . . . as though they belonged to someone else. It seemed almost like he followed behind the naiad more out of professional habit than anything else. The Lost Fae—Faerie that managed to get past the Janus Guard once a year when the Samhain Gate, the passageway between the mortal and Faerie realms, opened—were generally very good at losing themselves in the city. Some, like Kelley's roommate, Tyff, had managed to blend into human society with ease. Others found their way to scattered pockets of fae—like secret, underground communities—who would take them in. It looked as though Sonny was about to be introduced to one of those. And it was, quite literally, underground.

The circle of light in front of them grew as they approached the exit, and Sonny was dully astonished as he reached the tunnel mouth and looked out. In front of him stretched a vast cavern, the ceiling of which vaulted up and away into blue shadows and darkness. Shifting patterns of light danced upon rough-hewn stone walls—reflections of a series of pools, interconnected with streams and waterfalls—and Sonny heard the sounds of several voices raised in delicate, echoing song. A shiver ran down his spine. *Sirens.*

He stepped out into the grotto, and the singing stopped abruptly. He heard the sounds of startled splashing and then silence. *Fine*, he thought. *Good.* If they feared him, if they shrank from him, so much the better.

"Silly things." The Faerie girl at his side giggled. "They spook so easily. You're nothing to be scared of."

Aren't I? Sonny gazed down at her. *I hunt your kind. I've killed your kind.*

But the things that Sonny had come to define himself by had begun to fray and fall apart all around him. Ever since the moment, probably less than three hours earlier, when Kelley had said . . . the thing she'd said. Sonny shied from the memory, concentrating on the present moment. He backed a step away from the naiad.

What are you doing here in such a place? he chastised himself silently.

There had been no reason in the world for him to follow the Faerie girl. But then again, had there really been any reason *not* to? Sonny felt himself adrift without purpose. Nothing mattered anymore.

"Well, aren't you a sorry-looking thing," said a familiar voice from somewhere off to his left. He turned to see a slender young woman with long, dark hair and a bow and quiver strapped to her back descending down a narrow path carved into the bedrock wall. "Hard to believe that all it takes to wilt such a formidable creature as a Janus Guard is a little rain."

"Hello, Carys." Sonny recognized her from the time he'd taken Kelley to Herne's Tavern on the Green. The beautiful huntress Fae was not exactly friendly to members of Sonny's particular profession. "Lovely to see you again, too."

"What are you doing here, slave of Auberon?"

Sonny didn't have the will to put up a fight. Wordlessly, he turned to go.

She stepped in front of him, blocking his path. "How did you find this place?"

"I brought him," said the girl at his side, not loosening her grip on Sonny's hand. "He looked lost."

Carys took in Sonny's appearance with a scalding glance, head to toe. "He looks half-killed, is what he looks." She sniffed in disdain.

Her gaze drifted to his face, and Sonny locked eyes with her, a distant spark of anger flaring somewhere deep inside him. Not quite enough to start a fire, but enough to make the Faerie look away first.

"Neerya has a soft spot for strays." Carys glared at the slip of a girl. "Mongrels and hard-luck cases are her specialties."

Neerya just tilted her head and smiled, tugging Sonny back away from the tunnel mouth. "I like him. He's got pretty eyes. I wish they weren't so sad, though. . . ." Neerya wriggled past the huntress and led Sonny toward what looked to be a green meadow, stretching out for some way in the underground cavern. A soft light—blue and gold—filled the air, seeming to come from nowhere and everywhere at once.

"Come eat!" Neerya tugged him with surprising strength across the grass to a rocky outcropping where a cloth was spread upon the ground and set with silver platters heaped with a seemingly endless repast. "Food fixes everything."

Sonny knew better. And he also knew better than to partake of a Faerie feast in the company of unfamiliar Fae.

"It's not." Neerya giggled, seeming to read his thoughts— or perhaps just the wariness of his expression. She plucked an apple off a tray and held it out to him. "It's people food. For my 'strays.'"

It had a bruise on one side and the kind of waxy sheen to its skin that meant Neerya had probably pilfered it from a grocery store. Nothing magickal about it. A closer look at the silver platter pierced whatever weak glamour had produced the illusion of Otherworldly splendor. In fact, Neerya's "feast" was comprised mostly of produce past its prime. Scattered in among bruised apples, wrinkled tomatoes, and sparse bunches of red and green grapes, there were dented cans of soda and packages of Twinkies and potato chips. Neerya thrust the fruit out to him again, her eyes shining too brightly. It was somehow pathetic and endearing at the same time. Even though he wasn't hungry, he took the apple from her hand and bit into it, because it made the young naiad smile.

"I haven't been able to have any friends over for a long time now," she said wistfully. "Carys says I have to be careful who I talk to up there." Sonny assumed she meant up there in the city. "Hereside's not so safe for us these days."

"He knows that," Carys said from where she had taken up a perch on a crumbling support pillar that jutted from the ground like a broken tooth. "*He's* one of the reasons why."

Neerya turned and blinked at Sonny, a small frown creasing her brow.

"Hereside?" Sonny asked.

Carys shrugged. "Have to call this realm something. It's not home. It's just the side of the Gate we're stuck on. It's just . . . here."

Neerya looked like she was about to ask Sonny what Carys had meant before, but she didn't get the chance. Something roared angrily from the darkness of one of the tunnels, and the naiad squeaked in alarm. She shrank back, trying to hide behind Sonny while gathering the pitiful pile of food in to safety, as a hideous, leather-skinned nightmare came barreling out of the shadows. Driving boulder-sized fists down into the turf, hammering wild holes into the ground, the beastly creature knocked Neerya's carefully collected repast into disarray. Neerya cried out and scrambled to retrieve a rolling grapefruit—barely avoiding the ogre's massive fists. Sonny dodged beneath one of the descending blows and scooped Neerya up, tossing her toward the shelter of Carys's perch. Then he sprinted away from the naiad, trying to draw the ogre after him. It worked.

"I smell human!" roared the creature, thundering in his wake.

"You smell more than that," Carys called after the ogre, goading him on with grim amusement. "You smell changeling! Janus Guard changeling."

"*Janusss,*" the monster snarled, swinging its head back and forth, nostrils flaring, as if it tasted the air to capture Sonny's scent. Then it lurched with ponderous swiftness in Sonny's direction, launching roundhouse blows wildly as it came toward him. Thankfully, the monster had the worst aim Sonny had ever encountered. Still, there was nothing for him to do but retreat—and eventually, over near the tumbling falls and pools, Sonny found himself cornered, caught between a jutting stone buttress and a sharp drop to the dark water below.

The ogre was coming closer, and Sonny wondered if he should plunge into the water and swim for it. But then he heard a thrumming sound coming from beneath the surface of the pool and knew that there was no way in any hell he would take that option. It was not singing—not *quite*—but, rather, an eerie wail that set his teeth on edge. The Sirens, it seemed, had returned. He could not go that way. He *would* not.

Sonny recoiled from the edge, remembering the moment when he had let the Siren girl Chloe into his thoughts. She'd ripped a lullaby from his mind—the only memory he'd possessed of his mortal mother—and Sonny had let her do it, *let* her ravage his mind, because Chloe had possessed information about Kelley. He'd wanted to help Kelley. Be her knight in shining armor . . . and look where that had gotten him.

The ogre lunged for him again, a two-fisted hammer blow landing like an avalanche where Sonny had stood only a moment before. An eyeblink later and the ogre caught Sonny a glancing blow to the shoulder with an absurdly lucky slap at the air. It spun Sonny around and knocked him near-senseless against the stone wall. By the time he'd recovered, he was hanging upside down, dangling by one ankle as the ogre held him and shook him like a puppy with a chew toy.

All the blood was rushing to his head, which the monstrous creature repeatedly slammed into the rock. Sonny tried to protect himself with his arms, but the ogre continued to hurl him about. Sonny cursed himself, bouncing painfully off another rock. He was about to be mashed to a pulp by an ogre, and Kelley would probably never even know what fate had ultimately befallen him.

Not that she'd even care.

"Carys, please!" Sonny heard Neerya pleading from her hiding place. "Help him!"

He hoped the naiad could plead his case effectively before his skull cracked like an egg on the wall of the cavern, but it didn't seem likely. *This* was going to be a really stupid way to die.

IV

Wings spread wide, the kestrel drifted east with the wet, stinging rain. Far below her, the sparkle and sharp edges of the city gave way to a wide, winding ribbon of dusky blue-gray. The wind had carried her out over the East River, far from Sonny's penthouse. Far from the park and Tyff's Upper East Side apartment and everything familiar and comforting. Weary, chilled, barely held aloft by unfamiliar wings, the Faerie falcon peered sideways, looking downward, seeking a safe place to land. But all she saw was water. She was lost.

Just as she was about to falter, the kestrel spotted a tawny, swift-moving blur skimming the surface of the river below. Another bird. An owl. It glided on wide wings, silent as a ghost. Staying behind and above, trailing in the owl's flight path, she followed it toward the dark, humped shape of an island that suddenly loomed up in front of them. Her kestrel's eyes could make out human-built structures, but their angles were softened, the outlines blurred as though a charcoal drawing had been smudged by an enormous hand. And no lights. She could see the dark spaces where windows divided the brick walls, but her instincts told her that the place was long deserted. A huge old crane support, once used for offloading coal from barges but now reduced to its bare scaffolding, stood like a massive gate at the end of a rotted pier. The tawny owl flew between its uprights and on toward the buildings beyond.

Suddenly, every one of the kestrel's nerve endings was screaming at her to turn back.

A powerful air of foreboding hung about the entire place, but, exhausted and frightened, she had no choice and so followed reluctantly in the owl's wake. Once above the island, the kestrel wheeled through the air, seeking a place to rest and hide. She circled a crumbling smokestack, but her instincts told her that she would be better hidden by the foliage below. The owl had floated silently down toward the center of the tiny island, where the long-forgotten buildings squatted among overgrown trees.

The kestrel decided she would not venture so far inland,

to the places where the thick-stemmed vines crept inexorably up the crumbling walls and nightshade twisted elegantly around rusting window bars. . . . Instead, she banked and flew toward a clearing—the desolate remains of what had once been a tennis court. It was edged with a tangled thicket of spiky hawthorn that had thrust up through the asphalt. The dense branches promised refuge—she was just small enough to duck inside the brake, past the razor-sharp thorns. Once hunched safely in the crook of a branch, she tucked her head under her wing and drifted into uneasy, exhausted sleep as the late day darkened around her.

When she awoke, the rain had abated. The deep night held her firmly in its grasp.

The kestrel panicked briefly. *Dream! Not a dream!* But the feeling passed quickly, and she blinked and cocked her head from side to side, taking in her surroundings. Sights and smells and sounds washed over her; tangible things—things she could make sense of.

She was aware of the fact that this was not the way she usually felt—not the way she usually *was*. But she was also aware—and again, this was a vague, instinctual, animal awareness—that she felt better this way. Less angry. Less sorrowful. Less human.

You were never really human anyway. . . . The kestrel shook her head. The silent-sounds coming from inside her skull were distracting. They were not real. Not relevant.

Her falcon eyesight was keen in the darkness, as was her hearing. Keen enough to discern the clattering of horse's hooves on the rotted planking beneath the coal-dock arch and the sound, moments later, of wheels spinning on the gravel of the road beyond. A large black shape moved swiftly past her hiding place—she only caught a glimpse of it before it disappeared into the trees beyond—but it gave her an unaccountable shiver. In the distance, there was a sudden surge of light. And sound. Music. Then everything went eerily silent again. It was as if a door had opened somewhere and then abruptly shut.

Nervous, the kestrel ruffled her wings.

Time passed while she sat, hunched on the branch and shivering. The scent of the coming morning seasoned the air. Close by, she could hear the murmur of the river. All around her, bare branches and young leaves rattled and rustled in the breeze that followed the storm, whispering tree secrets to one another. . . .

When the air grew still, the trees continued to murmur and sigh. She turned her feathered head and listened. There was excitement among the trees. Their whispers were almost shouts now. At least, to her.

All around where the kestrel perched, leaves and shoots suddenly began to burst open and unfurl—eager . . . grasping . . . their growth rate accelerated, unnatural—spreading out under the moonlight as if it were a blazing noonday sun.

The kestrel shifted on the branch, clutching tightly with

her taloned feet. She could feel the sap, like blood flowing through veins, pulsing through the hawthorn stems. The leaves on her branch rustled, too, ignoring the creature that huddled in their midst. To them—to this tree—she was just a bird. But she was a bird who faintly remembered other trees. Angry trees. Green and growing things harnessed by a malevolent will that sought to harm her.

She remembered the Green Magick.

She listened fiercely now.

Elm and oak creaked and groaned at one another. Vines and creepers hissed in voices like snakes. *"Soon,"* they all seemed to say. And, *"Ours . . ."*

Other voices joined the rising cacophony, from every corner of the island, sibilant and thrumming; they filled the black air.

"He lives yet."

"There is need."

"Find the Green Magick. . . . Find its Bearer. . . ."

The rustling grew to a roaring.

"Take the Magick from the Bearer's veins. Water the ground with blood. . . ."

Every instinct screamed danger at her, and before she even knew what she was doing, she found herself tumbling through the air again, wings beating frantically, carrying her back across the river toward Manhattan.

Away from the strange island with its ghostly sights.

Away from its hungry, whispering trees.

Fennrys found her in the park, huddled in the predawn darkness beneath a yew tree in a grove in the Shakespeare Garden . . . in the place where she had seen Sonny for the very first time.

Kelley had shifted back into her human shape again after she had made her way to that familiar grove. Or, rather, her Fae shape.

Whatever, she thought.

She didn't know how she'd done it, but at least she was "Kelley" again. The wild magick that had transformed her so unexpectedly was tucked away once more, stashed somewhere deep down inside, where it would remain. At least . . . until the next time she lost control.

Thank goodness my clothes transformed along with me, she thought, grateful for small mercies.

When Fennrys stepped out of the shadows and headed straight toward her, Kelley was somehow unsurprised. Hunting, tracking—it was as natural as breathing to him.

Silently, Fennrys held out Kelley's clover charm, dangling from the fingers of one hand. His other arm he held protectively against his chest; the torn sleeve of his shirt was stained brown with dried blood, and his wrist was bandaged.

The bloodstains gave Kelley a sick feeling in the pit of her stomach. She could remember vividly the sensation of her hooked talons rending Fenn's clothing and flesh.

"I'm so sorry," she said.

"Not your fault."

Kelley shook her head. "It was. I did that."

"And you were thinking rationally at the time, I'm sure," Fennrys said, his mouth quirked in a mocking grin. "All those big, complicated Kelley thoughts suddenly crammed into that tiny wee bird brain."

"I . . . okay." Kelley smiled reluctantly as Fenn sank down beside her. He had a point. "You're right. I have no idea what I was thinking. I don't even know what happened. I don't know how I *did* that, Fenn."

"You're the heir to two thrones of Faerie, Kelley. There's very little you *can't* do." He gestured with the dangling necklace again. It glimmered in the moonlight and she reached for it this time, slipping the silver chain around her throat and fastening the catch. Instantly, she felt the surging tide of magicks in her blood quieting, receding into the equivalent of background noise. She hugged her knees to her chest and rested her forehead on her arms, breathing the wet air slowly.

Fennrys laid his good arm tentatively across her shoulders. Coming from Fenn, the unaccustomed comforting gesture made Kelley realize just how sorry a state she must appear to be in.

"You've had quite a little adventure," he said, almost as if he'd read her thoughts. "Haven't you?"

"I guess so. . . ."

"Where did you go?" he asked.

Kelley squeezed her eyes shut, sifting through the jumbled,

35

fragmented impressions left behind in her brain. "I'm not sure. I don't really remember specifics—not in any sort of way I can make sense of. It's all . . . like you said."

"How's that?"

"Bird-brainy. Kind of like a nightmare. I'm not even sure where I was or what I saw, really."

She shivered at the memory of fleeting, whispered voices and half-glimpsed sights. Half of what she "remembered" she was sure was just her own temporarily addled mind mashing up the last few days into a strange, incomprehensible dream/memory soup.

"How did *you* know where to find me?" she asked. "I don't even know how I wound up here."

"Birds are creatures of habit with strong homing instincts," he said matter-of-factly. As if he spoke of the migratory patterns of actual birds and not of a Faerie girl in a feathered guise tumbling around in the skies over Manhattan. "They'll always find their way back to somewhere safe. Familiar. This park calls to you. So I figured you'd wind up somewhere near here eventually—even if it was only because you were being true to your kestrel nature."

"Up until now, I didn't even know I had one."

"Yeah, well. Welcome to the life of a High Fae." Fennrys patted her shoulder. "Although I gotta say, even with your pedigree, shape-shifting is pretty elevated stuff, you know."

"Oh. Yay, me," Kelley cheered without enthusiasm. She imagined that, under other circumstances, she might've been tickled pink by her newfound talent.

Fennrys seemed to think it was impressive, at any rate. "You should be proud of your abilities," he said.

Kelley shrugged. "I guess. I remember my . . . I remember seeing Mabh turn herself into a raven once. And Auberon . . ." She thought about her father, his tall, regal shape blurring like smoke and a falcon taking flight in his place, soaring off through the Samhain night with Mabh's infernal bronze war horn clutched in his talons. That was the night when he'd stripped Kelley's Unseelie powers from her and called the Wild Hunt to action with the war horn. "My father can become a falcon, too. A big one . . ."

"I wouldn't know," Fennrys said. "We're not exactly pals."

Kelley turned her face so that she could look at him. "But you work for him."

"You know the deal, Kelley." Fennrys frowned down at her.

But—she noticed—he didn't move his arm from around her shoulders.

"Your dear old dad didn't give me much choice. I'm not saying he was wrong about making me a Janus Guard. Obviously, I have a talent for it. And a taste. It suits me and I have no regrets, but, in reality, I don't—well, I *didn't*—have a viable option."

"And do you now?"

"Uh, no . . . no." Then Fennrys *did* slide his arm away. His brow creased even more deeply and he adjusted the bandage around his other wrist. "That's not really what I meant.

37

Just that—it would have been nice to have been *asked*, you know? Instead of *told* what my destiny was. But that's not really the lot of changelings, is it? You folk don't really give much thought to the wishes and desires of us mere mortals."

"I'm not like that, Fenn. I'm not like *them*."

Fenn was silent for a moment. Then he said, "Really?"

Kelley stiffened in anger at the sudden shift in the tone of his voice. "What the hell is that supposed to mean?"

The Wolf sat toying with the edge of his bandage for a moment and then raised his eyes to meet hers. His voice was very quiet as he said, "I mean you and that Siren. Whatsername. Tinkering about in Sonny's mind. Because that's what you were doing, wasn't it?"

"No."

Fenn stared at her.

"Yes. But it's not like that. And as far as the whole 'mere mortal' thing goes, Sonny *isn't*. Not exactly."

"Yah." Fenn snorted. "I sorta noticed that when he blasted me through a hundred feet of thin air and a rather thick plate-glass window."

"He didn't mean to."

"Of course he did."

"Fenn—you're wrong. You said yourself once that it's not in Sonny's nature to be vicious. That he doesn't have the capacity to be cruel."

"And *you* said that you thought he might have changed," Fennrys countered. "*I* think, upon reflection, that you might have had a valid point. It doesn't matter. Whatever Irish was doing in that theater . . . from what I saw, he *was* being true to his nature, Kelley. Wasn't he?"

Kelley didn't answer.

Fenn's words held more than a grain of truth. Back in the theater—before the attack, before the Avalon burned—Kelley had stumbled upon a conversation that she was not meant to hear. A conversation between her mother and Herne the Hunter.

What Kelley had learned was that Sonny was no regular mortal taken by the Fae on a whim. Sonny was, in fact, possessed of a truly immense power. Within him resided the legacy of the Greenman: a pure, potent magick passed on to Herne as the Greenman lay dying. And then passed on from Herne to his child begotten of a mortal woman—to Sonny Flannery. By a cruel trick of Fate, Mabh's own dark power had also been transmitted through Herne to Sonny. It made Sonny incredibly powerful but also rendered him extremely susceptible to having that power corrupted. It made him vulnerable. It also made him hunted. The Greenman had been killed because someone had sought his power, and Kelley was desperately afraid that whoever was responsible for the old god's murder was still searching for the lost magick that was hidden in Sonny's blood—to steal it, or to use it for evil.

And so it had to *stay* hidden.

That was why Kelley had done what she had: she had made Chloe the Siren restore the charm that she'd stolen from Sonny's mind. It had been put there by Herne and Auberon, disguised as a lullaby, when Sonny was a baby, and it had shielded him. Protected him. The powerful magick of the veiling spell had hidden the knowledge of Sonny's true nature from the world, kept it secret even from Sonny himself. Replacing the lullaby had locked away Sonny's power—and his awareness of it—once more. It made him safe. Made him human.

Made him less than what he truly is, Kelley thought. *No . . . I . . .*

"Yes," she said finally.

You did that to him. Just as your father before you did it to him.

She had done it for Sonny's protection. Kelley had hidden away his secret and then she had made him leave her. That had been for his protection, too. In those few, panicked hours after the attack on the theater . . . after Sonny's horrific transformation into a vengeful almost-god . . .

What else was she supposed to have done?

Fenn's keen gaze sharpened. "He doesn't know what he is, does he? Whatever he became in the theater—it was as much of a surprise to him as to the rest of us."

Kelley nodded miserably.

"And now?" Fennrys tilted his head, and his eyes narrowed as he stared at her. "What did you do to poor old Irish, Kelley?"

I put the genie back in the bottle. "I hid him."

"Hid him. From who?"

"Everyone. Even himself. What he is . . . it's too dangerous."

"I see. And what about me?" Fenn asked quietly. "I seem to know something I'm not supposed to. You gonna try and erase my mind, too, Princess?"

"It's not like that." Kelley glanced at him sharply. "And I trust you, Fennrys."

"But you don't trust Sonny," he mused. "Well now. *There's* awkward for you."

Kelley thought about that. She *did* trust Sonny, didn't she? She loved him more than anything or anyone in the world. So why not tell him about his heritage? Again, the image of Sonny hovering in the air above the Avalon's burning stage— savagely tormenting that leprechaun like a cat playing with a wounded mouse before the kill—came unbidden to her mind. . . .

When Kelley remained silent, Fennrys laughed mirthlessly. She glared at him, not knowing what to say. In the far distance, they heard the sounds of thrashing and inhuman squeals. Fenn tensed, but the sounds died away to nothing and they didn't see what had made them. Kelley knew, though, that it was probably another denizen of Faerie, making mischief and wreaking a bit of havoc in the middle of her city.

When Kelley refused to say anything further, Fennrys rose and held out a hand. She took it, reluctantly, and he helped her to her feet. They stood there for a long moment, Fenn's hand wrapped around hers, until finally Kelley shifted uncomfortably and he let her go, turning away.

"Come on," he said over his shoulder. "I'll walk you home. And this time, we're *not* cutting across the park."

V

"Carys, *please!*" Neerya cried again.

The Faerie huntress seemed to be weighing her options. Then she sighed in resignation and, with the swiftness of a deer, leaped lightly up to the top of the crumbling brick outcropping. Pulling an arrow from her quiver, she nocked, drew, and loosed the missile in a single blur of motion. It parted the ogre's unruly hair with its razor-sharp edge and made him freeze in mid-pummel.

"That's enough, Dunn." Carys already had another arrow drawn.

"But—"

"I said *enough*, Dunnbolt." The wood of her longbow creaked as she drew back and sighted down the shaft.

"Carys . . ." Dunnbolt the ogre's ears twitched, and his misshapen head weaved from side to side. "Been *ages* since I killed something." The creature stuck out his bottom lip, murderously petulant. "Something *deserving* of it, that is . . ."

"Yes, well. I've told you to be more careful where you sit," Carys scolded.

The ogre muttered under his breath and rubbed the meaty palm of his free hand across his scalp—the arrow's kiss no doubt stung sharply. Sonny stared upward at him in disbelief; the monster was actually pouting.

"You can't kill him, Dunn," Carys explained patiently. "Neerya's the one who brought him down to the sanctuary."

"Neerya's back?"

"She is. You almost mashed her flat."

"Sorry, Bug," the ogre called out to the cavern at large.

"It's all right, Dunny. . . ." Neerya clambered out from where she'd been hiding. Long, thin wings, iridescent like the wings of a water beetle, shimmered into existence between the naiad's shoulder blades, and she flitted up to perch on the giant's shoulder. "I brought you pretzels." She held the paper bag she'd been carrying on the subway out in front of the ogre's nose. "With mustard."

"Dijon?" The ogre dropped Sonny unceremoniously to the ground and grabbed for the grease-darkened bag.

"Plain yellow."

Sonny could hardly see what difference the variety of mustard made. The ogre had barely paused to remove the things from the bag before stuffing them down his gullet, chewing maybe once. Sonny scrambled to his feet and backed away while Dunnbolt was otherwise occupied.

Carys lowered her bow and jumped down from her perch, landing soundlessly beside Sonny.

"Thank you," he said warily.

"Thank her." Carys nodded toward the tiny water Faerie, who stood balancing on the shoulders of the hulking ogre. "She likes you. We like *her*."

"I suppose I'm grateful, then, that Neerya's opinion holds such sway."

Carys spun the arrow in her hand and returned it to the quiver on her back. "The Lost take care of each other. We don't have much choice—not if we want to survive."

"New York's a tough town," Sonny said dryly.

"Tougher lately."

She was glaring at him flatly, as if he of all people should know what she was talking about. As if she expected him to defend himself.

"Carys . . . I've been away from this place for a good while. If you're spoiling for a fight, I'll be happy to oblige. But at least tell me what we're fighting about."

Her gaze drifted over Sonny's shoulder, and he turned to see what she was staring at. Now that Dunnbolt was standing still, it was easy to see the half dozen scars—only recently healed—crisscrossing the creature's broad, ugly face above the bridge of his nose. Underneath his browridge, the ogre's eye sockets were sunken and dark. And lacking eyes. Dunnbolt was completely blind.

Sonny looked closer and saw that it was highly unlikely the ogre's injuries had been the result of an accident. Rather, the blindness was a consequence of an attack with a bladed weapon. Whatever—or *whoever*—had done the job had been deliberate, surgical, and cruel.

Sonny turned back to see Carys observing him keenly. "He was one of the lucky ones," she said quietly.

"Who?" Sonny asked. Something told him he knew what her answer would be before she even said the word.

"Janus."

A surge of denial washed through Sonny. But, of course, the Fair Folk didn't lie.

"*Who?*" he asked again. "Which one?"

Carys stared at Sonny for a moment, as though deciding whether or not to answer. "The pale one," she said eventually. "I don't know his name. Only his handiwork."

Ghost, Sonny thought. *Why?*

Out of habit, he reached for the Janus medallion that normally hung from a braided leather cord around his neck before realizing that it wasn't there. He had lost it fighting one of the three remaining Wild Hunters in Mabh's Border-lands—and with it, any Faerie magick Auberon had gifted to him. That particular incident had only taken place a day or two earlier, but to Sonny it seemed like a lifetime had passed since then. So much had happened—most of which he didn't understand.

"This is . . ."

"Something new," Carys said. "Yes. Your king has changed his policies toward the Lost, it would seem."

"No, Carys. I don't think he has." Sonny frowned and turned away. He knew that Auberon in his present condition was not capable of much, though he would not tell Carys that. This, he was sure, had nothing to do with the king of the Unseelie Fae.

"Then what? The pups attack without their kennel master's say?"

Sonny's fist clenched at his side.

Carys put up a hand. "I only mean that a mad dog should always be put down. Before it ruins the whole pack."

"I am no dog, huntress. Have a care."

Carys's golden eyes glittered with amusement. "Well, now. It seems there is a spark in you after all. Here I thought you were content to let an ogre drop you on your head without so much as landing a blow in return."

"You must excuse me. I've had better days than this one. Perhaps I should go."

Kelley . . .

Whatever expression crossed his face in that moment, it made Carys suddenly relent. She walked over to a moss-covered boulder beside Neerya's scattered food and sank gracefully down, rolling a soda can toward Sonny with her sandaled foot.

"Go later. For now . . . sit," she said, an invitation that was half command. "Drink. You are welcome here as Neerya's guest. You are free to come and go as you wish. I grant it so in the name of this sanctuary and its maker."

Sonny hesitated. But, again, where would he go? He walked over and crouched on his haunches on the ground and picked up the soda, popping the tab. "I thank you for this hospitality," he said. If he'd been able to feel anything in that moment, it would probably have felt . . . nice.

In some respects, the cavern was much like some of the places that existed in the Otherworld. It had the same kind of wild, whimsical beauty to it—a melding of natural grace and stunning artifice. Sonny looked up and saw that the cavern was supported by an interlaced network of thousands of tree roots, large and small. The design in places emulated Gothic architecture, making the place seem like a kind of natural cathedral. He could hear the distant rumbling of the subway trains. It provided a counterpoint to the delicate, musical trickling of the underground streams.

As he and Carys sat in almost companionable silence, Sonny began to hear other things. Footsteps. Bits of speech. The Lost Ones were slowly returning to the sanctuary after his sudden initial appearance had spooked them away. All manner of Fair Folk began to gather at the periphery of the wide mossy sward, standing about in twos and threes as though waiting for something to happen. Carys turned to Sonny, a grin on her face that he wasn't sure was entirely benign.

"Tell me something, Sonny Flannery," she said. "Have you ever played at the game of hurling?"

"A little," he said, and was surprised to feel himself grinning back. "A long time ago . . ."

"Well. Seeing as how we have welcomed you here to our little world-away-from-the-Otherworld, perhaps you might be inclined to return the favor and provide us with some entertainment." She gestured to the gathering Fae. "It has been a long, long time since we had a mortal among us worthy to play at the game. I trust your skills aren't so rusty that you won't, at least, provide a bit of diversion?"

Sonny thought about that for a moment. He remembered telling Kelley stories about the hurling contests he had won in his youth, holding her close in the darkness of her theater as they'd waited for the coming morn. Then morning had come . . . and Kelley had said those words: *I don't love Sonny Flannery.* In light of that, a game he'd once reveled in seemed like a pointless waste of time. But, on the other hand, Sonny thought—in light of that—did he really have anything else to do with his time? Anywhere else to go?

He stood. "I will endeavor not to bore you, Lady Carys."

"Do better than that, changeling." She stood swiftly, and a murmur of excitement rippled through the air of the cavern. "Defeat me . . . if you can."

VI

Circling around the south end of Central Park may have taken them more than twice as long, but at least Kelley arrived at her building on the Upper East Side without incident.

"You might be going about this all the wrong way, you know," Fennrys said as Kelley fished around in her shoulder bag for her key ring. He had insisted on walking her all the way to her apartment door.

"What?" Kelley paused before putting the key in the lock. "What do you mean?"

"You," Fennrys said. "Sonny. Maybe you should take it as

an example to follow, you know. Sonny's busting out all crazy-powerful like that."

Fennrys was staring at her again, and Kelley was finding it increasingly difficult to hold his gaze for any length of time. She focused her eyes, instead, directly in front of her. Not that it really helped—because she then found herself staring at Fenn's chest, just above where his shirt buttoned.

"I'm not sure I know what you're talking about," Kelley said, blinking rapidly and trying to focus on the conversation.

"I mean," he explained, "that you might benefit from being true to *your* nature once in a while, Kelley." He was standing very close to her. He reached out a hand and tugged gently on the charm hanging around her neck. "Why do you still hide behind this? Now that you know what you really are, I mean. Why fight it?"

"Why do *you*?" she countered in a voice that was almost a whisper.

Kelley held very still as Fennrys leaned in closer and murmured, "I don't."

His breath was warm on her cheek and she closed her eyes, swallowing against the sudden tightness in her throat. When she opened them again, Fenn had backed off a step.

"I don't fight against my true nature," he said again, the hint of a smile curling one corner of his lips. "I just know how to use it to best advantage."

"Is that so?" Kelley struggled to keep a tremor from her voice. "I thought you didn't like being a Janus. But you still are one, aren't you?"

50

The grin faded from his face. "You pick your battles, Princess. The trick is in picking the ones you know you can win."

Behind Kelley, the front door to her apartment opened abruptly, and she turned to see her roommate. Tyff opened her mouth as if to speak, but then she saw Fennrys behind Kelley in the hall. Without a word, the Summer Fae turned on her heel and stalked back into the apartment, closing her bedroom door behind her with a loud bang.

"Think about what I said, Kelley," Fenn said quietly, and brushed a stray wisp of hair from her face. Then he nodded and walked down the hall—leaving Kelley standing there, one hand pressed to her cheek, where it felt as though his fingers had left a blazing trail.

As he disappeared down the stairs at the far end of the hall, something that had been needling Kelley on a subconscious level finally broke through the surface. Her fingers went to the necklace hanging about her throat, and she realized suddenly that the Fennrys Wolf's own charm—the iron medallion that marked him as a Janus Guard—had been notably absent.

"You *are* still a Janus Guard, aren't you, Fenn?" she asked the empty hallway.

Kelley heard a rumbling murmur of sound from behind Tyff's closed bedroom door and knew that Harvicc must still be there. Tyff had said that she would work up a veiling spell to hide the secret of Sonny's true nature from anyone who went looking for it in the minds of either Tyff herself or Harvicc.

Kelley felt a stab of guilt. She knew how much her roommate

hated using the magick she possessed and she knew that this procedure would wound Tyff and Harvicc at some deep level. Just as it had wounded Sonny. But she simply didn't know how else to keep Sonny's secret safe.

On the other hand, here she'd been standing in the hallway with Fennrys—who also knew Sonny's secret. He'd watched his fellow Janus sling magick around the Avalon Grande like water pouring from a fire hose. Even if he didn't know exactly what had happened to Sonny, he knew that it was something significant. And Kelley had left him alone.

That's different, she told herself. *You left Gentleman Jack alone, too.*

She couldn't bring herself to inflict that kind of enchantment on Jack, her actor friend, when he had nothing to do with the situation. As for Fenn, it wasn't as if he would ever *let* her alter his mind—he'd made that pretty clear when he chastised her for altering Sonny's. Also, neither Jack nor Fennrys had much if anything to do with the Fae. Fenn avoided them wherever possible—unless he was busily killing them defending the Gate, and that didn't leave much time for mind probing. Kelley would have to hope for the best.

But Tyff and Harvicc were a different matter. Both subjects of Titania, they were at her beck and call. If the queen summoned them, say, to attend upon her at her nightclub, the River, they *had* to go. If that happened, then Sonny's secret—left unveiled in Tyff's and Harvicc's minds—would be open to discovery.

It was getting very late, and Kelley was exhausted. She went to brush her teeth before heading to bed. She'd forgotten that Tyff had replaced the mirror she'd broken—otherwise, she might've been inclined to use the sink in the kitchen. Because, just as she was turning off the taps . . .

"Daughter."

Kelley looked up. "Oh. Hi."

"You are well?"

"No, Mom. I'm really not." Kelley tried to keep the startled expression off her face. She really hadn't meant to refer to Mabh in that fashion. She kind of hoped that it had sounded sarcastic. But judging from the look on her mother's face, it had sounded anything but—and Mabh was just as surprised as she was.

Kelley scrambled to find something to say. "Uh. How is . . . the king? Auberon, I mean."

"I know who you mean, child."

"Right. How is he?"

"He is also unwell," Mabh said. "Gravely so."

"What's wrong with him?"

"I do not know." Mabh shrugged. "There is a shadow growing inside of him—like a . . . like a poison, I suppose. Something works in his blood, sapping his strength. That much I know for certain. What I do not understand is that there is also a kind of light, cold and unforgiving, blindingly bright like his Unseelie power, that also claws at him from inside. Almost as if his own magic has turned against him.

I told the young Janus this—it is as if Auberon has poisoned himself."

"Why would he do that?"

"Dear child." Mabh's chuckle was low and lacking in real amusement. "He wouldn't. Auberon is many, *many* things but, above all, he is a self-preservationist of the highest order. You of all people should know that."

"Yeah. I know." *Do I ever.*

Kelley was painfully aware of that side of her father's personality—had been ever since he had forced her to bargain away her power in order to avert the catastrophe of the Wild Hunt wreaking havoc on New York. In return for his assistance, scant as it had been, Kelley'd had to agree to give up her own stake in the power of the Unseelie throne. She could still recall in minute detail how it had felt to have that silver, scintillating magick ripped from her soul. By her *father.* She could remember with startling clarity the taste of her own silent, bitter curses—sitting like burning embers on her tongue—as he had done so.

And now, it seemed, he was dying. *Do I care? Should I?*

Mabh was staring at her with the kind of expression that told Kelley she'd been silent for a long time. Kelley cleared her throat and turned away, straightening the hand towels that hung on the rack.

"This is all connected somehow, isn't it?" she said. "The Wild Hunt, Auberon's illness, that damned leprechaun suddenly appearing out of nowhere, looking for my charm . . ."

"I daresay it might be, yes," Mabh agreed. "Certainly, I think someone is trying to destabilize the Courts as a prelude to a power grab. And while I certainly didn't appreciate having all that suspicion thrown my way on the Nine Night, I have to give whoever's responsible credit. It was masterfully done."

"Whoever's responsible . . . ," Kelley echoed. "Tell me something . . . what happened to your war horn after the Wild Hunt was thrown down the first time?"

"It disappeared." Mabh shrugged. "I assumed that either Auberon or Titania had taken it or destroyed it. Obviously it wasn't destroyed."

"And if it wasn't Auberon . . . then could it have been Titania who reawakened them?"

Mabh laughed at the suggestion. "Don't be absurd," she said. "My birdbrained fellow queen doesn't have that kind of initiative. She's perfectly happy throwing her parties and canoodling with the Winter King—when he's in the mood. Anything else is just too much effort for her."

"But it makes sense," Kelley argued. "Titania tried to take the binding spell off my charm. Maybe she wanted it for herself—"

"Then why would she have allowed it to be bound to you in the first place?" Mabh countered.

"And I saw the leprechaun in the garage under her club."

"Which is a gathering place for many Fae in this realm," Mabh said. "His presence there means nothing. The fact of it is that you don't know who is behind this. Neither do I, and it is useless to go around pointing fingers. Believe me. *I'm* usually the one they get pointed at in such circumstances."

"But . . ." Kelley sighed in weary frustration.

Mabh was right. The threat *was* there—Kelley was sure of it—but it could be coming from anyone, from any Court. Until she knew who she was dealing with, she had to keep Sonny's secret safe.

"B— I mean . . . is the boucca still with you?" Kelley asked.

"He is. He has not left Auberon's side. He has questions."

And that, right there, was a big problem. "He knows everything," Kelley murmured to herself.

"He knows a great many things." Mabh cocked her head to one side. "But you know more than your fair share of 'things,' too, Daughter. Unless I miss my guess, you know his name."

"So what?"

"I told you that I would take care of him. And I will. But if you give me the secret of the boucca's name . . . it will make it that much easier." The queen's eyes glittered darkly. "Mostly for him."

"What's that supposed to mean?"

"You want to keep the young Janus's secret safe. I don't see how that is possible with the boucca walking around free, possessed of that knowledge. Even if he would not willingly give it up, the knowledge is still there in his head for some . . . unscrupulous party . . . to dig for and take." Mabh examined her long, sharp fingernails. "In order to prevent that happening, I can confine the boucca, I can kill him . . . or I can control him. Which would you rather?"

"I'd rather you left him in peace," Kelley said. She felt a cold knot of anxiety growing in the pit of her stomach. Giving up Bob's name would give Mabh absolute power over him. It could conceivably make him her slave.

Mabh smiled coldly. "That is a dangerous road and one I'm fairly certain you do not want to travel down. Not while you wish to keep Sonny Flannery's secret safe."

Kelley thought for a fleeting moment that perhaps she should cross over into the Otherworld and deal with the matter herself, but as she raised a hand to the charm at her throat—half forming the image of a rift in her mind—Mabh shook her head.

"I wouldn't if I were you."

"Wouldn't what?"

"Cross over and deal with matters yourself."

Kelley glared fiercely at the queen.

"Oh, don't be such a sourpuss. I'm not inside your head. I don't have to be. I only know that's what you were thinking because that's exactly what *I* would've been thinking. We are not so very different, you and I." Mabh laughed bitterly at the look on Kelley's face. "I know it pains you grievously to hear that, but it's true."

"So why can't I cross over and take care of things my own way then?"

"Because the space between the realms has become a very dangerous place of late."

Kelley eyed her mother skeptically.

"Oh, by all means—don't take *my* word for it!" Mabh snapped. "Go ahead! I think you'd look just as appealing to your Janus lover with deep scars and an absent limb or two."

Kelley reached out with her senses—*carefully*—and realized that her mother was telling the truth. She could feel a malevolent, crackling energy—like the magickal equivalent of razor-wire fences and booby traps—and she could sense the beings responsible for it. Shadowy shapes with teeth and claws. She put a tentative hand on the mirror glass and felt a sharp shock like a jolt of electricity. "Ow!" she yelped.

Mabh glared back at her with an "I told you so" expression.

"What on earth is causing that?"

"It's nothing the least bit earthly, I can assure you."

"That's just an expression." Kelley rubbed at the palm of her hand, where the skin was blistered an angry red. "Don't be a pain."

"They are wraiths—rogue spirits and unquiet dead caught between realms—and it seems that they have decided to wreak a little havoc. All those desperate to get either in or out of Faerie are easy pickings now, what with the rifts becoming so unstable. Still, there are those who would take their chances. Unwisely, I should say."

Kelley knew that there were Fair Folk who shared the Seelie queen Titania's near obsession with the mortal world— Fae who'd longed desperately to cross over ever since the days when Auberon had shut the Gates. She also knew that there were those who'd been trapped in this realm who longed just as desperately to go back to the Otherworld.

Now with all of the cracks that had appeared in the Samhain Gate . . . for the wraiths that lurked waiting to ambush unwary travelers, it must have been akin to bears standing in a river during a salmon run.

Mabh gazed unblinking at Kelley. "Decide then," she said. "If you want my help, you'll have to give me what I need to ensure the boucca's silence."

Kelley hesitated.

"You needn't worry so." Mabh smiled sweetly. "I will be kind."

"Kind of what?" Kelley muttered.

Mabh's smile dissolved and she crossed her arms, staring flatly at her daughter.

"All right, all right." Kelley acquiesced. She didn't have much choice. She bit her lower lip to keep it from trembling. What she was about to do . . . it felt like the lowest kind of disloyalty, even if she was doing it to keep Sonny safe. She knew that, left to his own devices, Bob would never willingly betray either her or Sonny. But she also knew how unlikely it was that he *would* be left to his own devices. She'd already seen the boucca tortured mercilessly and enspelled because he had tried to come to her aid. Surely, *this* was the better way. All she had to do was give Mabh his true name. Then all Mabh had to do was compel Bob to forget.

"Bob." Kelley scowled into the mirror, pinning her mother

with her fiercest gaze so that she would understand what it meant for Kelley to give her this thing. And what it would mean for Mabh to abuse it in any way. "His name is Bob."

"*Bob?*"

"Bob."

"You're joking."

"Of course I am," Kelley huffed sarcastically. "Because given the opportunity to mislead you about something like this, *Bob* was obviously the best I could come up with."

"All right." Mabh put up a hand. "All right. I believe you. Now you must believe *me*, Daughter. This is for the best."

"I doubt it. But I don't see much in the way of choices here—"

Mabh turned her head sharply to one side, as if listening to something.

"What?" Kelley asked. "What is it?"

A faint frown crossed her mother's face. "Nothing. Nothing . . . I should attend your father." The Faerie queen turned back to the mirror and raised one hand in farewell. "Be safe, Daughter. Be strong. Be wise."

Kelley would have settled for even one out of those three.

VII

The blood sang in Sonny's veins as he pounded down the outside margin of the pitch, running as if his life depended on it. In truth, it very well might. The Fair Folk took their game play *extremely* seriously. Fortunately, that was something Sonny had learned as a child.

Carys shouted encouragement to her team as Sonny swung his wide-bladed oak stave in a windmill arc, catching the silver ball a solid blow as it hurtled toward his head, and sending it back toward his Faerie teammates at the far end of the field. One of Carys's defenders was a second late getting into position, and the ball sailed past her cheek toward the goal—where it was snatched neatly out of the air by an enormous fist and sent back down in the other direction.

Sonny shook his head in wry frustration. Dunnbolt made a formidable goalkeeper, in spite of his blindness. He played the game with Neerya perched on his massive shoulders; she crouched there like a bug on a mountainside, tugging his ears and slapping the sides of his head, calling out player positions and the movement of the ball. And then, at her command, the hulking beast would react with swift, sure blocking moves, wielding his hurling stave like a weapon.

A shout went up from the watching Fae, and Sonny realized that Carys's forward was racing back up the pitch toward his goal, dekeing past Sonny's defenseman, who was too far downfield. Sonny cursed and spun on the balls of his feet, forcing his concentration back onto the game, and followed in the player's wake to see if he couldn't head off a scoring opportunity.

"Best three out of five?" Carys panted, leaning over, her hands on her knees. Her skin glistened, flushed with exertion, and her dark hair tumbled haphazardly around her face.

"Do you always play this hard?" Sonny collapsed onto the grass beside her. His team had barely held on to a one-goal lead to win, evening the score at two games each. He stripped off his shirt and mopped his brow with it. Tossing it aside, he rolled over onto his back, letting the stray eddies of breeze cool the sweat from his skin.

"Only when we've a worthy mortal in the ranks—and that hasn't been for a very long time!" She turned and called out to one of the nearby dryads for refreshments.

A tall, gaunt Fae with large eyes and a braided goatee—and bat-wing webbing between his abnormally long fingers and toes—paused as he passed by and handed Carys a small leather pouch. "Might need this," he said. Sonny noticed that the Faerie was one of the Ghillie Dhu, solitary Fae noted for their gentle nature and deep knowledge of healing. "You play well," he said to Sonny. "For a human."

"And you." Sonny nodded graciously and couldn't resist adding, "For a Fae."

Sonny rolled his shoulder, easing the deep muscle ache there—it had been a long time since he had driven his body this hard. The game play had been savage, the competition fierce. And it had served its purpose: it kept him from thinking. It kept him from feeling. His mind was blissfully numb; the steady thrum of blood and breath in his body were the only sensations registering.

He had no idea how long they'd been playing. It could have been hours or days. Sonny suspected, from the way he felt, that they might have been at it for close to a full day—maybe even two. It didn't matter. Having grown up in the Otherworld, he was used to the idea of time having no real, quantifiable meaning. He knew, somewhere deep in the back of his mind, that this—all of this: the games, the feasting, the Faerie companionship—was a dangerous indulgence. Sonny knew that he was allowing himself to tread perilously close to the edge of losing himself forever, of becoming little better than a thrall.

Thralls were all that remained of mortals when they allowed themselves to surrender completely to the lure of Faerie pleasures. In losing their individuality, their independence, their free will, they became little more than mindless slaves. Minions. It must be awful, Sonny had always thought. But, then again, thralls *didn't* think. They didn't feel, either.

And in the state Sonny was in, *that* was a fierce temptation.

One of the things that set changelings like Sonny and the rest of the Janus Guard apart from any other stolen mortals in the Otherworld was that they had all managed to maintain their independence—as much as they could, which was more than most. That strength of will was why the Winter King had chosen them in the first place. Auberon admired strength—especially if it could be used to his ends.

Lounging idly, Sonny followed his train of thought back to his friend, the blacksmith Gofannon. Like Sonny, Gofannon was a mortal in the Otherworld. Unlike Sonny, Gof hadn't had the same kind of resolve to resist temptation. Gof had been an artist in the mortal realm, a metalsmith with a love of his craft so profound that he had bargained his freedom away for the chance to spend eternity making beautiful things out of gold and silver and iron. It had been a hard lesson for him to learn, centuries later, that being a slave to one's passions was a lot more satisfying than simply being a slave. The price of an eternity spent in thrall to Auberon as the Winter King's black-smith had not been worth the reward. If only Gofannon'd had the strength to walk away. But some temptations, it seemed, were harder to resist than others.

Still, abhorrent as the idea of becoming a thrall was to Sonny, from the moment Kelley had denied any feelings of love for him, all he had wanted to do was to lose himself utterly. Being a thrall might not be so bad, he thought, if it meant an end to the pain that crashed down on him every time he thought of her name. Or her face. The way her green eyes had sparkled when they'd danced in Herne's Tavern, or the way her hair shone in the light of her Faerie wings . . . the way she had kissed him on the shores of the Lake of Avalon. How could she have kissed him like that if she didn't love him? He shook his head sharply to dispel the memory and dragged his attention back to the present.

The willowy fae who'd flitted off reappeared carrying a tray that bore none of the dents and scratches of Neerya's serving ware. On it were two blown-glass goblets and a dark-blue bottle that seemed to glow as if lit from within.

"Will you drink with me?" asked Carys as she tugged at the bottle's silver stopper.

Sonny eyed the bottle warily. *Faerie wine.*

Carys rolled her wide golden eyes. "I offer it freely for you to accept freely. No compulsion. No strings attached. On my honor."

Sonny relaxed a bit and nodded, holding out his hand.

"Then I accept it freely and with thanks."

She poured a measure of the precious liquid into his cup. Sonny took a sip and felt it sear a pleasant trail of sparkling fire down his throat all the way to his stomach. It reminded him of home. At least—it reminded him of the place he'd grown up in. Perhaps he should return there, he thought. It wasn't as if there was any welcome for him here in the mortal realm anymore. And yet, even as he thought that, his mind shied away from the possibility of leaving forever the world where Kelley Winslow walked and breathed and flew on wings of dark fire. . . .

He took another mouthful of wine. Carys was staring at him from under her delicately arched brows.

"What is this place, Carys?" Sonny asked, looking around at the strange landscape of the cavern. In some places, it seemed a natural phenomenon. In others, he could clearly see the remains of human architecture—stone archways and brick support pillars and walls, all overgrown with strange, night-blooming flowers and pale moss. Carys had called it a sanctuary. Like the Tavern on the Green. "Does Herne know it's here?"

"Know about it? Who do you think was responsible for its construction?" Carys waved a hand. "If you'd gone right instead of left when you hit the brick tunnel coming in, it would have led you south and up through a passageway to the Tavern."

Sonny looked at the brick buttressing while he dug his

fingers into his sore shoulder muscles. "Is that human-built?"

"That part, yes. All this used to be under water. When the city dwellers built an aqueduct to carry fresh water to this island from a place north of here called Croton, they originally built their reservoir here. It was a lovely haven for the Water Folk. Later, it was decommissioned and they covered it over. We appropriated the cavern for our own uses. Where you are sitting right now is directly under the Great Lawn in Central Park."

Sonny saw Dunnbolt cooling off from the match, dunking his massive head in one of the pools and ignoring the outraged squeals of the resident merfolk. Neerya threw him a ratty bath towel and he caught it without turning his head, using it to squeegee the water out of the insides of his tiny ears. Watching as Neerya playfully tugged on the great brute's ear—and seeing how gentle he was to the naiad in return—Sonny felt a pang of guilt for what had been done to the creature by one of his own fellow Janus Guards.

Sonny turned to see the Faerie huntress watching him patiently.

"You have been away," she said. "Things have changed since you've been gone. Since Samhain."

Sonny had suspected as much. He remembered—it was one of the only things he did remember about being in the fight at Kelley's theater—that Fennrys had alluded to the distinct possibility of all hell breaking loose in Central Park, the last remaining Gate in or out of the Faerie Realm.

"You and your princess may have averted catastrophe at Samhain, but there is fresh trouble brewing up there," she went on. "Cracks showing up all over the Gate. Dangerous rifts. Instability. Attacks on mortals—*they* call them 'muggings' and 'coyote attacks' and go about their business—but even they sense the change. Far fewer of them make their way to the park these days."

"Do you and your folk have any"—Sonny changed the wording of his question so as not to offend—"any knowledge of what's causing this?"

"Are you asking if we have anything to do with it?" Carys blandly retorted. "We do not. But that has not stopped your fellows from pointing fingers in our direction. And weapons."

"Do you mean what happened to Dunnbolt?" he asked.

"Aye. And he is not the only one. I'm getting a bit tired of my folk coming back from forays to the surface with missing limbs and arrow wounds. Or not at all."

"At the hands of the Janus."

Carys nodded.

Sonny chewed his lip, frustrated at his ignorance of the situation. He should know what was going on with the other Guards. He didn't. All he knew was that something felt wrong. Terribly wrong. "This is not—this *should* not be happening," he murmured.

"I agree with you," Carys said. "The peace between the Lost and the Janus has always been an uneasy one, I grant you. But it has always been *there*. This change is recent. And it has gone hard for my kind."

Sonny frowned deeply. He hoped she was exaggerating. Or wrong. Surely she was mistaken about the Janus Guard. "Why would they do this?"

"It feels to me like rebellion. Like warriors left defending an outpost too long, who take to trophy hunting to relieve the boredom. But it is the kind of thing that usually only happens when someone is there to stir things up."

"I'll do what I can to find out what's going on, Carys. And if I can help stop it, I will. You have my word on that."

"I'll take it," she said, opening up the pouch that the Ghillie had given her as he'd passed. It held a small jar of herb-scented unguent, and Carys knelt by Sonny and began massaging it into his aching shoulders. He tensed at the touch of her fingers, but the pain began to lessen almost immediately. If he closed his eyes, he thought, he might almost be able to imagine that those fingers belonged to Kelley. . . .

"Tell me, Carys," he said, "if there are rifts appearing everywhere in the Gate, why aren't the Lost Ones using them to escape back to the Otherworld? To avoid being hunted?"

"Some tried. But the Gate is unstable and the rifts are full of danger. Fair Folk *are* traveling between the worlds—in both directions—but only if they are desperate or mad. Even the Faerie monarchs are not immune to the predatory behavior of the things that lurk in the Between."

Sonny was silent.

"Speaking of Fae royalty," Carys asked, "where *is* your little princess, Janus? Last time I saw you, you had the look of one love-struck. Now you just look . . . stricken."

"What would you know of love, Carys? You or your kind." Sonny didn't necessarily mean to sound harsh as he asked the question. He was actually almost curious.

"You think the Fae incapable of love?"

"I know it."

He plucked a flower from the mossy ground and held it up before his eyes: it was purple and shining, just like Kelley's wings. His relationship with Kelley had, ultimately, turned out no better than the time when he had accompanied Auberon on a visit to Titania's court. In the woods, he had met a beautiful Summer Fae. Sparkling and scintillating, she had led him far from court, along a twisting path to a sunlit meadow. . . .

For some reason, he found himself telling Carys the story.

"And what happened next?" she asked, working the salve into his skin, as if the tale was no more than a fireside amusement told by a traveling bard.

"Days passed in the forest," Sonny continued. He could almost believe, as he sat there, that it *was* just a story. That it had happened to someone else or not at all. Not to him. "And then more days. And she led me to believe she was in love with me. More—that I was *worth* being loved." He crushed the flower between his fingers. "And then . . . when I told her that I loved her . . . she laughed."

Carys's hands paused on his neck.

Sonny shook his head, remembering. "'Silly thing!' she said. 'You're just a boy. A *mortal* boy. I could no more love you than I could an animal. . . .'" Sonny heard his voice saying those words and he felt for the boy in the tale. He'd been very young. "Her eyes flashed coldly, and it was like a thunderhead suddenly darkening the sky. All the light went out of the day. I fled the meadow. Her laughter followed me. Mocking, ringing in my ears, as I crashed through the grasping trees to fall, bleeding and ashamed, at Auberon's feet."

"And what did the king do?" Carys asked.

Sonny laughed a little. "He told me gently that, of course, the sylph had only been playing games with me. That was what the Fair Folk did."

"And you believed him."

"Was it a lie?" he asked, glancing back at her over his shoulder.

"We don't lie." Carys shrugged and looked away, the faint shadow of a frown on her lovely face. "But you thought it would be different with your princess."

"I did. It wasn't." Sonny cast around for some other topic to change the subject. He didn't want to think about just *how* different he'd thought it would be with Kelley. "Why are you here, Carys?" he asked to smooth his momentary lapse. "In the Hereside? Were you caught like some of the other Lost Ones when Auberon shut the Gates?"

"No." Carys grinned. "No, I fought my way past the Janus Guard and into this realm some years ago. I am here by choice because I like humans. I like . . . humanity. This is what Faerie like Auberon . . . and even Gwynn ap Nudd . . . do not understand. Once the Greenman found this world, we Fair Folk were doomed to want to be a part of it. You mortals are chaos incarnate. It's intoxicating."

Speaking of intoxicating . . . Sonny's head spun a little and he remembered belatedly the kind of kick that Faerie drink often delivered. Carys put away her jar of salve and refilled their glasses. She leaned back on one elbow, gazing at him. "You spoke before of the Summer Fae. The one who scorned you."

Sonny frowned. He had. It had been an unguarded moment, and he wished now that he could take the words back.

"She was a fool."

Sonny glanced at the lovely Fae. Her expression remained remote, polite, but Sonny thought that there was a spark in her golden eyes that hadn't been there earlier. He swallowed more wine.

"And your princess . . ."

"Carys—"

"She was twice the fool," the huntress said, her voice low.

Sonny looked away, back toward where the other Lost hurlers were drifting back toward the pitch, eager to continue the contest with another match. Thanks to Carys's ministrations, his shoulders no longer ached and there was every possibility that the competition would go on until he dropped from exhaustion. The Fae would play their games until the crack of doom if it pleased them.

Maybe it would please him.

"I . . . I should go," Sonny said, sitting up and reaching for his shirt. Even as he said the words, he felt the tug on his spirit that urged him to return to the pitch. To keep on playing. A whisper in the back of his mind told him that he need never leave this place. Or the gorgeous creature at his side . . . "Really. I should. Leave, that is . . ."

Carys schooled her expression, wiping the brief look of what might have been disappointment from her face, and nodded her head. "As you wish."

Part of Sonny truly wanted to stay, but he hadn't been home in . . . what? It might well have been days, at that point. The Faerie games had acted upon him like a drug. So had the wine. And, if he was honest, the company.

If only to hold on to his sense of self, he had to leave the reservoir. He pulled his shirt back on over his head and stood, holding out a hand to help Carys to her feet. She rose gracefully without his help, and then took his offered hand in a gesture of farewell.

"You are welcome here again, Janus," the huntress said, gazing at him in a way that made him feel as though she really meant it. She gave him a password that would let him return safely to the sanctuary in case he changed his mind. Her eyes lit with sly mirth as she said, "You are . . . what do the Heresiders say? You're 'all right.'"

VIII

Kelley woke with a start. She'd had the dream again—the one where she found Sonny lying on the sidewalk, his chest perforated by bullet wounds . . . the same kind of wounds that Herne had told her killed the Greenman back in 1903. The images of the dream were so clear to her, she could see the light fading from Sonny's beautiful silver-gray eyes, the blood bright at the corners of his lips. Lips that Kelley would give almost anything to be able to kiss again. Her arms ached to wrap around Sonny once more but, in order to do that, she had to keep him safe from the fate that she saw played out night after night in her dreams. Sonny's blood, seeping into the ground . . .

She didn't know how—yet. But she was going to find a way, and then they could be together again—for real and for*ever*. If she could only learn how to control her own magick, maybe she could find a way to protect him. Or help him use his power in a way that wouldn't result in disaster-movie carnage.

Sure, she thought. *Except that* you *can barely manage the occasional pair of Faerie wings as it is.*

If she'd been raised in the Otherworld, she wouldn't have this problem. Instead, she felt more a part of the mortal realm than anything. Her stomach growled with hunger as if to remind her of that. Kelley wondered if the Fair Folk felt hunger the way she did. Or if what she was feeling was all part of the illusion of "Kelley Winslow" and just another lie. She wondered what Sonny's favorite food was. She didn't even know.

Kelley sighed and got out of bed before she spiraled into a gloom deep enough to keep her under the covers for the rest of the day. She threw on a pair of jeans and a hoodie and went out into the living room. Tyff's bedroom door was shut and Kelley had to stop herself from knocking to see if her roomie was awake. She could really use someone to talk to, but she wasn't sure how open Tyff was to indulging in a heart-to-heart chat. Tyff had finished her spell on Harvicc and herself the night before, and the ogre was gone from their apartment, but Kelley had seen how much it had taken out of the Summer Fae, dimming her usual radiance to the point where Tyff had looked almost like a normal girl. *Better to let her get her beauty sleep*, Kelley thought ruefully. *Or suffer her wrath.*

She went to the kitchen to make herself some tea. Which, it seemed, they were out of. No tea, no coffee . . . barely any provisions at all. Kelley wistfully shook a half-full box of Lucky Charms and wished that the kelpie who had spent almost two weeks standing in her bathtub last autumn was still there. Lucky's calm, soothing presence had always managed to make her feel better. She wished she knew what had happened to the Faerie horse. She missed him. Not as much as she missed Sonny, but still . . .

Kelley put the cereal away—they were out of milk, too—and decided to head out to the corner café for a cruller and a bucket-sized cup of caffeine. She was surprised to see her fellow actor Alec Oakland sitting on the front steps of her walk-up, texting on his cell phone. He jumped to his feet when he heard the door open behind him. "Uh. Hey, Kelley. Hi . . . ," he stammered.

"Hi, Alec." Kelley tried to force a smile onto her face as she started down the stairs. Alec fell into step beside her. Which was exactly what she didn't need just then—more complications. "What are you doing here?"

"Well . . . it's just that . . . you're a tough girl to get hold of." His voice was quiet and he stared at his shoes as he walked, but there was determination in his words. He nodded his head back at the apartment. "I rang the buzzer."

"I was asleep. I didn't hear it," Kelley said. She really

hadn't—although it might have been the thing that had woken her from her nightmare. She supposed she should be grateful.

"And I've called your cell about a billion times," Alec said.

"Sorry."

"Please tell me you're not screening my number. The eternally deferred coffee date, I can handle—I live in hope. But rejection on *that* kinda scale, my fragile ego can't take." He was trying to be funny, but Kelley could hear an echo of hurt in his voice.

Great. Another name to add to my injured list. I'm getting good at this. . . .

"I lost my phone a little while ago," she said by way of explanation. She didn't bother to tell him that she'd lost it in a raging river in the Otherworld. By now, she figured, some Siren had probably found it and was scrolling through her ringtones, stealing the tunes for her own personal pleasure and the luring of doomed souls.

Yeah. Alec definitely doesn't need to know the details.

They walked the rest of the half block in uneasy silence until they reached the café. Alec hung back as Kelley ordered her pastry and a coffee, debating whether or not she should offer to buy Alec one. But she decided that to do so would just add insult to the "eternally deferred coffee date" injury.

"I guess you probably heard," Alec said finally, as they started the walk back to her building. "About the Avalon."

Kelley nodded, not trusting herself to say anything.

"Right. Well . . ." Alec stayed doggedly in step with her.

"Mindi's called everyone to let them know that Quentin is on his way back from London. She said that she hadn't been able to get a hold of you, so I told her I'd give it a try. The company is having a meeting. We're gonna get together to decide what to do about the theater."

"There is no theater, Alec," Kelley said. "There's not enough left of it to put on a puppet show."

A pained expression crossed Alec's handsome face. "Yeah. Well. 'The show must go on,' you know?"

That was what she'd always thought. And her heart quickened at the prospect of the company rising from the ashes of the ruined theater, but . . . "I can't," she said. "I have . . . other priorities right now. Responsibilities."

"Different ones than you had last week?" They were almost back at her apartment, and Alec stopped her with a hand on her arm before Kelley could bolt up the stairs and disappear into her building again. All of his levity had dropped away and he looked as though he was on the verge of being genuinely angry with her. "What the hell? Catastrophe strikes and you just walk away. Like the Avalon can't do anything more for you, so you'll just abandon it?"

"Alec—"

"Where'd you learn that from?" He let go of her, but he didn't back off. "I know you've only done one show with us, but we're not just a bunch of actors, Kelley. The Players are a family. Even Barbara deWinter is crawling out of her catacombs to offer any help she can. I thought you were one of us."

"That's not it. It's just . . ."

Her protestations faltered as Alec stared at her, waiting for some kind of reasonable answer. How was she supposed to make him understand that Sonny came first? That Sonny was in danger and she was the only one who could help him? She stood there, conflicted and miserable.

"There's been talk of maybe doing a benefit gala," Alec said. "After *Midsummer*, it was *your* name on the marquee that was gonna be the big draw. 'Rising star Kelley Winslow.' It still could be."

Whatever expression crossed her face in that moment, it was enough to make Alec relent slightly. He sighed and for a long moment looked away, off down the street.

"Look," he said. "I don't know what's going on with you. Obviously. I mean—it's not like you'll let me get close enough to find out." He took a deep breath and turned back to her. "We're meeting this afternoon at two, if you decide you're interested. At the Tastee Burger on Forty-third—you know, that place where the cast sometimes went for lunch during rehearsals. Together."

"Alec—" She was about to apologize, but he didn't give her the chance. Message delivered, Alec Oakland turned on his heel and walked away.

Kelley went back inside the apartment to find Tyff leaning on the frame of the open window in the living room. She still looked paler than normal, but some of the brightness had returned to her eyes. Her expression, in that moment, was a carefully composed blank.

"Hey," she said blandly by way of greeting.

"Hey." Kelley kicked off her shoes and headed toward her bedroom.

"Harv's gone back to the River, but my whammy worked. He won't be a problem," Tyff said. "Neither will I. You owe me big."

"Oh—okay." Kelley nodded. "Good. Thanks."

"Your aunt just called. She's back from Ireland."

"Okay." The conversation with Alec was swimming circles in Kelley's brain.

"There's a tree frog in your hair."

"Okay . . ."

"Kelley—*stop*."

Kelley turned her unfocused gaze on Tyff, who glared back at her in frustration.

"You didn't actually listen to a thing I said just now, did you?"

"Uh. No . . ." Kelley was yearning to go to the cast meeting. The Avalon Players *were* her family. But Sonny . . . Sonny was her life. And, besides, it was all her fault that the theater had burned to the ground in the first place. Maybe they'd be better off without her. "I'm sorry. I'm going to go take a nap, Tyff. I have a headache."

"That's a lie."

Kelley winced at the flat, disapproving tone of Tyff's voice.

"You don't have a headache. You're just trying to avoid me." Tyff nodded in the direction of the open window. "Like you're trying to avoid *them*."

"I don't know what you mean."

"Kelley . . . you can't push everyone in your life away."

"Tyff, I—"

"You *can't* protect people that way!" Tyff almost shouted. "I know! Believe me. In the end, you just wind up hurting them even more." She ran a hand through the messy cascade of her hair as she gazed at Kelley. Her blue eyes were full of compassion—and more than a few centuries of her own regrets.

Kelley looked away before she lost her own composure under the weight of that stare.

Tyff sighed and softened her tone. "There's one thing I've learned about mortals. They're a lot more resilient and a whole bunch more resourceful than they usually give themselves credit for. Why else do you think the Fae have always had such a fascination with them? Why d'you think Auberon uses changelings to guard the Gate? Trolls are stronger, cheaper, more plentiful, and nobody cares if they get exploded or ripped to pieces. But he uses mortals. Because they're full of hidden strengths."

"Tyff—what are you talking about?"

"Well—for starters—I'm talking about those actor people of yours. Don't turn away from them, Kell. They can probably help you as much as you can help them."

"I can't help them."

"Your little Romeo buddy seems to think you can." Tyff

jerked a thumb at the open casement window. Kelley's argument with Alec had obviously carried on the breeze.

"Alec's a nice guy." Kelley shook her head. "But he's wrong. He just doesn't know anything."

"And you're suddenly all worldly wise?" Tyff scoffed. "Since when? Give yourself a couple hundred years and *then* you can go around telling me about how naive guys like Alec are. Sounded to me like he pretty much had you pegged. You're giving up."

"I am not! Right now I just have to concentrate on figuring out how to keep Sonny safe."

"What?" Tyff looked at her sideways. "What on earth makes you think Sonny can't take care of himself?"

The image of Sonny bleeding his life out onto the thirsty ground assaulted Kelley's mind. Even if no one else believed her, Kelley knew. Sonny was in danger. "He needs my help," she said quietly.

"Really." Tyff stared at her, unblinking. "I'd say Sonny's not your concern anymore. I have a feeling he'd agree with me if you asked him. After all, you made it pretty clear back in his apartment—"

"You *know* why I said those things!"

"No! I *don't*, Kelley!" Tyff snapped. "Because whatever it is that has turned you into a raving lunatic, if it has anything to do with Sonny-boy, you made me make myself forget about it, remember?"

"I'm sorry—"

"Stop." Tyff's voice softened and she said, "You obviously

82

have your reasons. Look . . . whatever Sonny's deal is, it's *Sonny's* deal. You can't choose someone else's destiny for them, Kelley. And you shouldn't let anyone choose yours. Believe me, it's no fun."

"What am I supposed to do, Tyff? You tell me."

"Okay. For starters—if you want to be an actress? *Be* an actress."

"How'm I supposed to do that with everything else that's going on?" Kelley muttered miserably.

"Do what the humans do," Tyff said. "Do what you used to do when you *thought* you were human. Multitask."

"I wish it was that easy."

"It *is*." Tyff's blue gaze bored into her. "Save the theater. Save Sonny—if that's what he really needs. Save the world. Save yourself. It's all just variations on a theme."

"Tyff—"

"You gonna tell me to 'shut it' again, Kelley?"

"I . . . no. Of course not. I'm really sorry about that."

"Seriously." Tyff wasn't letting Kelley off the hook that easily. "'*Shut* it, Tyff'?"

"I only said that—"

"I turned a guy into a stoat once for a vastly lesser insult."

"Can we talk about that for a minute?"

"Stoats?" Tyff tilted her head and smiled, thoroughly enjoying raking Kelley over the coals. "They're like a kind of weasel—"

"No." Kelley needed Tyff to be serious for a moment. "No. I mean . . . I know it's kind of a taboo subject for you and all, but. Could we *please* talk about magick?"

"And the you-not-using-thereof?" Tyff shrugged. "Sure."

"How about, and the you-teaching-me-how-to-use-it-properly?" Kelley pressed.

"Oh sure. A variation on the old Sorcerer's Apprentice theme. That story *never* ends well, you know."

"Tyff . . . please. I'm going to need all the help I can get in the next little while, and that includes being able to use whatever Faerie tricks I can pull out of my hat. Just think about it?"

"I don't like thinking about things, Kelley. 'Thinking makes it so.'" Tyff frowned. "Who was it who said that?"

"Shakespeare."

"Ah. Right. The old rummy. Well, he certainly hung out with his share of Fae, so he should know. You want to learn how to use your magick, Kelley? Just listen to Shakespeare. Shakespeare knows best." Her lips bent upward in a sardonic grin.

"You mean . . . 'Thinking makes it so.' That's it."

"That's it. But I *wouldn't* if I were you."

"Tyff—"

"Unh!" Tyff held up a hand. "That's all you get out of me, kiddo. I'm sorry. Been there, done that. I've gotta go. I have a mani/pedi booked and if I'm late Tyrone takes it out on my cuticles." Tyff grabbed her purse from off the hall table and reached for the doorknob. She paused for a second, turning back to Kelley. "Think about what I said, okay?"

"You just said you were *anti*-thinking," Kelley grumbled.

Tyff shot her a look over her shoulder and then she was gone.

Kelley went into her bedroom and threw herself onto the bed. Staring up at the ceiling with unfocused eyes, she tried to concentrate on the wisdom of others. Fenn's words of the day before prowled around in her head: *You pick your battles, Princess. The trick is in picking the ones you know you can win.* Tyff's thoughts chased them at the heels, hectoring and contradictory: *Save the theater. Save Sonny. Save the world. Save yourself.*

Two pieces of advice. Pretty clearly irreconcilable. Or were they?

"Okay . . . okay." Mindi put up a hand, semi-silencing the debate raging around the tables at the back of the Tastee Burger diner. "Enough gab. *Love's Labour's Lost* and *The Tempest* seem to be the front-runners. So what's it gonna be, Q?"

A hush fell over the gathering of thespians. All eyes turned anxiously to the corner booth where Quentin St. John Smyth sat huddled in his black turtleneck. "'We are such stuff as dreams are made on,'" Quentin murmured finally, chewing thoughtfully over Prospero's most famous line. "It's perfect. *The Tempest* it shall be. Perfect."

The Mighty Q looked . . . fragile. His habitual black garb emphasized the sallowness of his complexion and the dark rings circling his eyes. But as he lifted his head, Kelley thought she might have seen a tiny flame kindle to life.

"What say you all?" Quentin cast his gaze from face to face. "*The Tempest*? Show of hands."

Kelley glanced surreptitiously around as the company responded unanimously. It made sense. *Romeo and Juliet* was a complete nonstarter since the fire. Apart from crispy-fried sets and costumes, Quentin was now convinced that the play itself held some kind of curse, and he wouldn't touch it with a ten-foot pole. He wasn't the only one.

Theater folk, Kelley thought. *As superstitious as they come.*

And every last one of them was precious to her. She and Gentleman Jack had shared a wordless moment when she arrived. He'd smiled and squeezed her shoulder to let her know that they were okay. But it was too soon and too public a place to talk about the things that had transpired at the theater, and about the fact that Gentleman Jack Savage was now one of the few mortals alive privy to the existence of the Otherworld and its inhabitants.

As everybody had finally settled down onto the cracked vinyl benches, there had been a great deal of back-and-forth trying to decide which play to do for the fund-raiser, and then more back-and-forth on where to do it.

Eventually Barbara deWinter had delicately cleared her throat and spoken up. "The managing company at the Delacorte Theater in Central Park has graciously—*oh*, so graciously—thrown a rope to the drowning man."

"What?" Quentin's head swiveled in her direction. "Why?"

"One of the company principals owes me a favor. A big

enough one that he'll open the place up for us, starting this very afternoon for a first-read rehearsal." Dame Babs beamed like the painted portrait of a benevolent saint. "If you want . . ."

Q eyed her with extreme suspicion. "'Owes you a favor,' hm? That translates roughly as 'you have naked blackmail photos,' doesn't it?"

"Only in *your* world, you demented miscreant," Babs said, sniffing. "No. *I* consort with civilized folk. Fair folk."

Fair folk. Kelley contemplated what Barbara's reaction would actually be if she were ever to have a run-in with one of the *real* Fair Folk—which was not beyond the realm of possibility if they were actually going to stage the play in the damn park.

A weighty silence at the table caused Kelley to snap out of her worried reverie, suddenly aware that all eyes were turned on her. Someone must have asked her a question.

"Pardon?" she asked, leaning forward.

Quentin was staring balefully at her. "I *said*, Miss Winslow, do you have anything meaningful to add to the discussion? What do *you* think of *The Tempest* as our savior show?"

"Well, uh, I know the play," Kelley stammered. "I mean . . . I wrote a term paper on the character of Ariel in school, but . . ."

"Done. Fine. You're cast." Quentin tapped Mindi's clipboard, indicating that she should record his imperious edict. "Ariel it is."

"I didn't mean—," Kelley tried to interrupt him.

"Under *other* circumstances," he continued, "I would have given that part to our former Robin Goodfellow. Pity he's quit the business or hit the rehab or *wherever* it is he's sodded off to. . . ."

Kelley thought of Bob and what her mother had likely done to him, and inwardly shuddered.

"At any rate," the Mighty Q continued, "Ariel is the secondary lead and an androgynous part that a woman can play just *fine*."

Kelley sat there, stunned.

"You're *welcome*," he sniffed.

"Q—"

"No need to thank me. Just *show* up for a rehearsal or two, will you?" The mercurial director turned to Mindi, muttering, "Give me a short list of which other girls can play Miranda. We'll pick the one *least* likely to embarrass the company on short notice, then divvy up the spirits and goddesses among the others. We'll make Barbara one of the goddesses—the one with the most lines; that should keep her ladyship happy."

"I *heard* that, you old windbag." Babs grinned wolfishly. "Your eternal gratitude is what will keep me happy. Nothing short of."

"But you *are* a goddess, darling!" Quentin turned on a dime and fussed over his new savior. "That's all I meant. Truly."

Kelley squeezed her eyes shut to keep from rolling them.

"Jack!" Quentin barked. The director was gaining momentum, slinging dictates around the table with something resembling his old spark. "You've lobbied me to play Prospero for years."

"I have."

"Knock thyself out."

"I live to serve, Q." Jack bent his head in a gracious nod.

"Mr. Oakland. I *suppose* you could manage to squeeze out a serviceable performance as Ferdinand, hm?"

"Golly, Quentin," Alec said dryly, "I'll see what I can do. . . ."

"Yes, well. It'll mean making goggle-eyes at someone *other* than Miss Winslow for the duration, but soldier on, old boy. Soldier on. . . ."

Alec blushed crimson to the roots of his hair.

Kelley found an interesting coffee stain on the Formica tabletop to study minutely.

The rest of the company laughed for a very long time.

IX

When Sonny opened the front door and walked into his apartment, he felt a wave of emptiness— inside and out. It was as if Kelley's brief presence there had made the place come alive, in exactly the same way she'd done for his heart. He could almost picture her curled up in the corner of the sofa, feet tucked under her, watching with a smile as he set the table and lit candles. . . . Sonny imagined what it would have been like to have invited Kelley over for an actual date. A real human date. It had been thoughts like that that had kept him going all those long months in the Otherworld. But now he was back, and the place echoed with hollowness.

Almost hollow . . .

The small hairs on the back of Sonny's neck raised as he realized that his apartment *wasn't* entirely unoccupied. He unslung his messenger bag and dug through its contents. He felt the familiar contours of his wood-sword but, without the Faerie magicks granted him by his missing Janus medallion, the bundle of twigs would stay just that. His crossbow wasn't loaded. He went instead for the dagger he carried in a sheath on his belt at the small of his back. It wasn't much, but it was sharp—and Sonny knew how to use it.

Moving silently in the direction of the terrace, Sonny could see, through the sheer curtains, a shadowed shape sitting motionless on a chaise, staring out at the skyline. He threw open the doors and had the sharp edge of the dagger at Maddox's throat before he realized who it was. Sonny's arm muscles snapped tight as he pulled the blow, stopping just short of severing the other Janus's carotid artery.

Maddox felt the cold blade-edge and sprang to his feet.

"Sonny! Thank the goddess. . . ." Maddox's face somehow managed to convey relief, anger, guilt, and reluctance all at the same time.

"What are you doing here, Maddox?" Sonny asked, lowering his arm.

"Waiting for you to come back."

"Why?" Sonny turned and walked into the apartment, returning the knife to its sheath on his belt.

"I wanted to make sure you were . . . you know. All right." The tall, lanky Janus followed him. "You've been gone days. . . ."

"Have I?"

"Erm . . . yeah."

"How many?"

"Couple. I mean—not that long, sure. But I was wondering. Not worried—I mean, you can take care of yourself, sure . . . just . . . wondering."

Sonny remained silent. Of course Maddox had been worried. He could hear it in his voice. Two days. It had only felt like hours down in the Lost cavern.

"So . . . uh . . . where've you been, old Sonn?" Maddox pressed.

"I've been around." Sonny gazed at his apartment. The opulent kennel that Auberon had furnished to keep his prize Janus pup happy—that was probably what Carys would have called this place. Why was he thinking of her? And what did it even matter? But she would be right. He didn't belong *here* any more than he belonged with the Lost. In fact, maybe less so.

"Where's 'around'?" Maddox asked.

"Just . . . around, Madd." Sonny shrugged, and noticed, for the first time, the bright green grass stains on his T-shirt and jeans from the hurling match. He headed toward the bathroom. "I'm going to take a shower. You can let yourself out, yeah?"

* * *

When Sonny reemerged—showered, shaved, dressed in a fresh shirt and jeans, and feeling almost human again—Maddox was, predictably, doggedly, still there. He sat on the leather settee, fidgeting nervously with something he held in his hands. Sonny saw that it was a single reddish-brown feather.

"What's that?"

Maddox raised his gaze to meet Sonny's. "Uh . . . it's Kelley's." He held the feather out hesitantly. "A bit of Kelley, I mean. She . . . uh . . . she turned herself into a falcon just after you disappeared."

A falcon!

Now *that* was something Sonny would have liked to have seen—

No. No, it wasn't. Because it meant that Kelley was becoming something else. Something . . . more. The Kelley Sonny knew had been hard-pressed to keep her fake, sparkly gauze-and-wire wings on straight during rehearsal. She barely knew *how* to fly. Before she'd met him, she hadn't even known that she could. She certainly didn't know how to transform herself into a *bird.* . . .

Sonny suddenly felt like he'd been asleep for a hundred years. Everything was different. Everything. Chest aching fiercely, he ground his teeth together and clenched his fists to keep from reaching out and taking the feather from Maddox's fingers. "That must have been impressive," he said flatly. The feather gleamed with the very same auburn tint as Kelley's hair. . . .

Before Maddox could reply, Sonny spun abruptly on his heel and went to the front-hall closet. He pulled a small duffel bag off the shelf and strode to the kitchen, filling the bag with an assortment of packaged food: granola bars and canned fruit and Oreos. Anything he thought Neerya might appreciate. He hadn't been sure, when he'd first gotten home, that he would ever go back to the reservoir. But he was sure now.

He couldn't stay in a place he'd once wanted to share with Kelley.

Maddox followed him into the kitchen and leaned against the island, watching, his arms crossed over his chest. "Yeah. Well," he said, continuing determinedly on with the thread of the awkward conversation. "Yeah—I mean, it's not the sort of thing you see every day. But, y'know, she *is* a Faerie princess and all that and, uh . . . aw, hell." He threw his hands in the air in frustration. "Look, Sonny. I don't know what's going on with you two. Kelley wouldn't tell me anything and . . . well . . . I just think maybe that's something you should keep in mind."

"What is?" Sonny asked, opening the fridge and adding a six-pack of soda to the bag.

"The whole 'Faerie princess' thing. I mean—she's nice and all, don't get me wrong, I like her—but . . . she's one of *them*, Sonny."

That did stop Sonny—briefly. He shot Maddox a pointed glance. "This, from someone who has, on more than one occasion, expressed a powerful yearning for a Siren."

94

"I'm not exactly holding myself up as a shining example." Maddox shrugged but held Sonny's stare with his own. "And there's a difference. Chloe's Fair Folk—but she's regular Fair Folk. She's not High-Bloody-Fae Royalty. She's not like Mabh or Titania. Mabh is Kelley's *mother,* for crying out loud, Sonn. How on earth is the girl supposed to fight something like that?"

"Why are you saying all this to me, Maddox?"

"Because . . ." Maddox ran a hand through his sandy hair, visibly ill at ease with the conversation. "Because I think it might be best for you—easiest, I mean—if you were to just . . . forget about her. Cut her out of your heart."

"I don't have to. She doesn't want anything to do with me."

"What?"

"Kelley doesn't love me."

"She said that? Actually *said* it?"

"Yes. She actually said that." Sonny was distantly surprised at the even tone of his voice.

"Because it really didn't seem—"

"It's over, Madd."

Maddox frowned. "But . . . when you disappeared . . . Kelley was really upset and—"

"Can we not talk about this?" Sonny zipped the duffel bag shut with sharp, jerky motions. He snatched up his leather messenger bag and was suddenly reminded, by the heft, of what it contained: Kelley's old script—the sheaf of rumpled pages of *A Midsummer Night's Dream* that Sonny had gotten used to thinking of as his good luck charm. He hesitated a moment and almost left the bag where it lay. But his weapons were in there, too. He slung the satchel across his torso, resisting the urge to open it, dig out the script, and leave it behind on the table—that would just give Maddox further heart-to-heart-chat fodder. Instead, he moved to the front door.

"Where are you going?" Maddox asked.

"Out."

"Yeah. I can see that."

Sonny paused with his hand on the doorknob. "That's all you get, Madd. Sorry."

Maddox's face flushed with frustration. "Seven hells!" he barked. "You'd think I'd become some kind of horrible gossipmonger with the way no one will tell me what's going on these days!"

"It's better for you if you don't know," Sonny said. "That's all. Safer."

As he closed the door behind him, Sonny thought he might have heard Maddox say, "Funny . . . that's exactly what Kelley said."

Sonny walked to the north end of the Columbus Circle station platform and waited until the next train pulled into the station. Passengers disembarked, hurrying up stairs and escalators, and everyone who'd been waiting trackside stepped onto the train. Everyone except Sonny. He wouldn't be using the train to reach his destination. In the brief moment that the platform was deserted, he swung himself around the safety gate barring access to a utility ladder and climbed down into the tunnel. Under normal circumstances, Sonny would have used the magicks gifted to him by Auberon to cast a concealing veil over himself. But with the loss of his iron Janus medallion, that wasn't an option available to him. He would have to rely on plain old human stealth.

With a glance over his shoulder to make sure that he had indeed remained unobserved, Sonny took off at a jog, trailing the fingers of one hand along the wall so that he would be able to tell when he got to the maintenance alcove that hid the tunnel entrance to the underground Lost sanctuary.

He was almost there when he heard voices. Human voices.

Sonny paused for a brief second, listening to be sure. He wondered if someone was following him—if maybe the security cameras had captured his forbidden entry into the tunnel and they had sent someone to investigate. Or perhaps it was just a transit worker. . . .

A tingling along his spine told him to beware, to be careful. He quickened his pace and concentrated on finding the hidden tunnel. He stopped just inside the mouth of the tunnel to the reservoir, masked from sight by the Faerie glamour that camouflaged the opening, and listened. Nothing. There was no sound now. Sonny turned back to the wall. He put up a hand and spoke the password Carys had given him. The rough-hewn wall went transparent, and Sonny stepped through into the obsidian tunnel. The glamour shifted back into place once he was through, and Sonny started down toward the reservoir.

"What's this place then?" Maddox's voice came from right beside him.

Sonny almost jumped out of his skin.

The air seemed to shiver slightly in the gloom, and Madd's big lanky frame appeared, leaning on the tunnel wall. "You never remember to veil yourself properly," he said, shaking his head.

"And you delight in trying to give me heart failure," Sonny snapped angrily. He was just as irritated with himself as he was with Maddox. It seemed that he had gotten used to relying on Auberon's gifted magicks too heavily—instead of depending on his own abilities and instincts.

"So?" Maddox waved a hand at their surroundings.

"I don't know why you followed me. You shouldn't be here, Madd."

Maddox pushed away from the wall he'd been leaning on and looked Sonny in the eye. "If *I* shouldn't be here, then I think it's a pretty safe bet to say that *you* shouldn't be either."

Sonny sighed in exasperation. Even having Maddox follow him through the veil and into the tunnel to the reservoir was a violation of the safe passage Carys had granted him. They both might be in a lot of trouble. Sonny felt the hint of a breeze coming from up ahead—like the breath of wind that preceded a subway train pulling into a station—and amended that thought. There was no *might* about it.

"Do you have a weapon on you?" he asked quietly.

Maddox blinked. "What? Yeah, of course I do. I don't go anywhere unequipped. And neither should y—"

"Whatever you do," Sonny said grimly, "*don't* draw it. And don't fight."

"Aw, seven hells, Sonn," Maddox muttered, but held his hands up and away from his sides.

Sonny did the same, bracing for the impact he knew was coming. The light from the torches danced wildly, then guttered and snuffed out as the wraiths came screaming down the tunnel. A gale-force wind slammed into the two Janus. In the confines of the tunnel, it felt like being caught in an avalanche. The wind spun viciously around like a tornado behind them, scooped them up, and hurled them forward in the direction whence it had come. Sonny and Maddox found themselves caught in a howling maelstrom that swept along the glittering black tunnel at breakneck speed.

Sonny had been warned by Carys of the "security system" in place to guard the reservoir against hostile intruders— and how not to get instantly maimed, should he accidentally activate it. But even armed with that foreknowledge, it took a great deal of effort *not* to struggle against the force of the wind wraiths. To do so would have meant being clawed at and pummeled against the jagged facets of the tunnel walls, and so Sonny just ducked his head and pulled his arms and legs in tight, hoping Maddox had done the same. He could hear nothing over the roaring.

Sonny could feel the grasping talons of the wraiths

skittering and brushing along his body, but they did him no injury. After a few brief, terrifying moments, the wraith wind spat the two Janus Guards out onto the rock shelf at the mouth of the reservoir's underground grotto . . . where they were surrounded by an unsmiling, heavily armed welcoming committee.

Sonny pushed himself to his hands and knees and glanced over at a sprawling Maddox, who was oozing blood from three long parallel gashes down one forearm.

"I told you *not* to go for a weapon."

"I didn't!" Maddox protested.

Sonny looked pointedly at Maddox's bloody arm.

"Well . . . I might have *thought* about it. Maybe twitched a bit in that direction . . ."

The creak of several yew-wood longbows made Sonny spring to his feet and take a step in front of his friend.

From where she stood halfway up the stone steps, behind the menacing circle of Faerie, he heard Carys laugh bitterly. "It's as if you think we'd have a problem shooting *you* to get to your friend."

"This is not what it seems, Carys."

"And what is that, Janus?" She was back to spitting out the title like it was a foul taste in her mouth. "A betrayal? For *that* is what it looks like. I—*we*," she corrected herself, "trusted you. And now you have violated our secret and put us in harm's way."

"Uh . . . he didn't, actually," Maddox said, getting very

slowly to his feet with his hands in the air, palms facing out. "Not on purpose. He was just a bit stupid, really, and—"

"*Thank* you, Madd." Sonny stopped him before he could dig either of them into a deeper pit. "Thanks. I don't think I need that kind of help."

"Well, it's true." Maddox looked over at him and shrugged. "I mean, if this lot is going to blame one of us for me being able to infiltrate their little play fort, they might as well blame the clever one."

Sonny sighed and gazed upward, expecting to be struck by a barrage of arrows any second.

"And as for 'harm'"—Maddox turned back to address the gathered Fae—"I don't mean any such thing! I was simply curious as to where my mate Sonny's been hiding out over the last few days. So I followed him. And I happen to cast a wicked good veil, so he never even knew it." Maddox must have figured that as long as he kept talking, the angry-looking huntress wouldn't be able to issue an order to have them killed. "Also—uh—nice place you got here. Very . . . grottoish and all—"

The arrow missed his earlobe by less than a hair's breadth. Maddox's jaw snapped shut and he fell silent.

"Lady . . ." Sonny put his hands down and took another step forward, ignoring the stares of the Fae who trained their weapons on him. "Carys. You should know by now that I would not willingly bring danger down upon you. Or your folk. Maddox is my friend and I will vouchsafe my life for his. I will also get him the hell out of here this very instant if you will allow it. But," he continued, his voice taking on a subtle but distinct edge, "I'm not going to stand here any longer under the threat of being made into a pincushion."

Carys seemed unmoved . . . until a swaying, willow-thin figure moved through the circle of warriors toward the two Janus.

"I stand as further surety for this one," Chloe the Siren said in a quiet voice, stopping in front of Maddox. "He has been kind to me." She put a hand on his chest and Maddox blushed crimson. Chloe seemed not to notice as her gaze slid away to fix on Sonny's face. Her golden eyes went dark for a moment. "And for this one." She turned to Carys. "He is . . . worthy of our respect, Carys. I think you already know that."

Carys slowly lowered her bow. Following her lead, so did the rest of her warriors, and the tension in the air of the cave began to dissipate. Carys came toward Sonny and held out her arm, which he grasped at the wrist in greeting.

"I . . . apologize for the harsh welcome." Carys turned to Maddox and said, in a tone sharp with sarcasm, "But you cannot entirely blame us for lacking in wide-eyed trust where you and your brethren are concerned. Especially lately."

"I don't know anything about that," Maddox said, shifting uncomfortably, his gaze following in Chloe's wake as she drifted back toward the spring pools at the far end of the cavern.

Carys didn't press the point, but her gaze remained steely.

"Have you come back to settle the tie, then?" she asked Sonny, her expression softening somewhat. She gestured the two Janus down toward the cavern floor, where another of Neerya's glamoured repasts was spread out and a half dozen or so dryads danced in a circle with intricate, weaving steps.

"What tie?" Maddox asked.

"Nothing." Sonny tried to dismiss the matter with a wave of his hand—he didn't want Maddox to think he'd been wasting his time playing at games—but Carys was staring right at him. He didn't want to insult her. "Only a bit of hurling," he said. "That's all."

"Ha!" Maddox barked a laugh, turning to the huntress Fae. "You haven't been going up against *him*, have you? He'll kick your lovely Faerie backsides all over the pitch, sweetheart! He's bloody legendary."

"Indeed, he has already earned a measure of respect here among us." Carys looked at Maddox sideways, her head tilted. "Not an easy task—for a Janus."

Maddox's grin grew slightly brittle under her scrutiny.

There was a gleam in the Faerie huntress's eyes as—with a delicate politeness, like the spider inviting the fly in for tea—she asked, "Would *you* care to try your skills against my folk, Guardsman?"

"Too right, I would," Maddox answered.

Sonny could only shake his head as Carys led them over to the greensward, calling all her folk to come play as she did.

* * *

"Right . . ." Maddox bent over, hands on knees, and sucked in great, gasping lungfuls of air. "Been a while . . . bit rusty . . . damn. . . ."

"Told you they were good." Sonny slapped his friend on the back, provoking a fit of coughing.

"The goal minder's cheating," Maddox wheezed. "There's two of 'em."

"C'mon, I'll introduce you to the little one. Her name's Neerya. She's the one who brought me down here when I . . . uh . . ." Sonny frowned. He'd rather not remember what had prompted him to go down into the subway on the day Neerya had found him. "She's the one who first showed me this place." He led Maddox over to where the naiad flitted among her spoils. She had been delighted with the goodies Sonny had brought her from his pantry. The tiny Faerie girl grinned widely at Sonny as they approached and tossed him a dented soda can. But when she saw Maddox ascending the stone steps behind him, she seemed to shrink back, hiding behind the curtain of her fine, dark hair.

Sonny thought she was just being shy and he handed the soda to Maddox, saying, "It's all right, Bug. This is a friend of mine. I know he's big and ugly, but he's harmless."

Maddox grinned and punched Sonny in the arm before slugging back the entire contents of the can in one long swallow. "You only wish you had my looks, laddie," he said, wiping his mouth. He crushed the aluminum can and tossed it casually through the air at the naiad. She caught it reflexively and her hair swung back over her shoulder. Maddox did a double take.

"Do I . . . know you?" Maddox tilted his head and stared down at Neerya, a shadow of a frown darkening his brow.

The naiad twisted her long fingers around the crushed aluminum, and the iridescent wings at her back rustled nervously. "You're one of mine," she murmured.

Sonny watched, astonished, as the blood drained from Maddox's face. He took a step back. "You. You were the girl in the reeds."

Neerya nodded.

"I followed you. Into the Otherworld. You led me there. You're the reason I'm a changeling." He turned away and clenched his big hands into fists, a look of almost murderous intensity on his face. "I should kill you where you stand."

Sonny looked back and forth between his friend and the Fae, tense and ready to step between them should Madd do something unwise. Large, luminous tears welled in Neerya's eyes, and she nodded again.

"It's not her fault," Carys said quietly from behind them.

Maddox rounded on her, his fists coming up instinctively, primed to let loose. Carys held her ground.

"She used to steal bairns for Titania until it all became too much for her," Carys said. "I think *you* were the one that finally did her in."

"What are you talking about?" Maddox snapped.

"I mean you're the reason she's here now, in exile." Carys

turned to Neerya, who stared at her feet, miserable. "Isn't that right, Bug?"

Neerya nodded once more.

Carys looked back at Maddox. "After the way Titania treated you, Neerya decided she couldn't take it anymore. She fled the Summer Lands rather than have to bring the queen one more pet to be tossed away when her ladyship grew bored."

"But why?" Maddox turned on the naiad, fists still tightly clenched. "Why did the queen send you to take me in the first place? She never even gave me a second glance once I arrived at the Summer Court. What did Titania want with *me*?"

"She didn't want you." Neerya's words bubbled out around a sob stuck in her throat. "*I* did. It's my fault she didn't like you. She wanted someone pretty, not plain. I was selfish. But I didn't think you were plain at all! When you saw me and you smiled at me . . . I just wanted you to come and play." Her voice dropped to a whisper as she said, "I'm sorry."

"So am I," Maddox said. When he turned back to Sonny, his expression was shuttered. Unreadable. "You people. You have no concept of consequences, do you? It's all a game to you. Everything is just a game."

"Life is a game, Janus," Carys said quietly.

"Yeah? Well, I'm taking my ball and going home." He turned to Sonny. "I'm getting out of this place."

"Madd—" Sonny put out a hand.

"You coming or not?"

He glanced at Carys, whose expression remained closed

to him in that moment. He tried to catch Neerya's eye, but the tiny Faerie wouldn't look at him. If he let Maddox leave without him, Sonny knew that he would be sacrificing a friendship. For the sake of Faerie. When all the Fae had ever done was to heap grief upon him.

"Yeah . . . ," he said, finally. "Yeah. I'll come with you, Maddox."

The two young men remained silent as they walked down the tunnel, an unspoken tension hanging in the air between them.

"Nice friends you've got," Maddox muttered eventually, as if the silence was just too much for him.

"Look, Madd—"

A noise echoed from down the tunnel, and both Janus turned sharply.

"Speaking of friends," Sonny said warily, "we've got company."

X

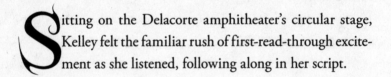itting on the Delacorte amphitheater's circular stage, Kelley felt the familiar rush of first-read-through excitement as she listened, following along in her script.

ACT I
SCENE I.

A tempestuous noise of thunder and lightning heard.
Enter [severally] a Shipmaster and a Boatswain

MASTER: Boatswain!
BOATSWAIN: Here, Master. What cheer?
MASTER: Good, speak to th' mariners. Fall to't yarely, or we run ourselves aground. Bestir, bestir!

Kelley didn't have any lines in the opening scene, but Q had already described how he would stage it: with storm sounds and lighting effects and the actors playing sailors throwing themselves violently around the stage as though on the deck of a tempest-tossed ship, and Kelley, as Ariel, dressed in full fantastical regalia, directing the storm. . . . As the actors read their lines, she could see the entire scene taking shape in her head and imagined herself perched up high in the rigging, lit dramatically. It would be *so* cool.

And then . . . a fat raindrop hit the middle of her script page with a juicy splat like a bug on a windshield.

Oh no, she thought, glancing at the water droplet that magnified the word *Fate* in one of Gonzalo's lines.

Within moments, the afternoon spring sky was blotted out by a bank of massive thunderheads. Rain sheeted down, lightning flashed, and thunder rolled on its heels without so much as a one-Mississippi pause. The center of the maelstrom gathered and seemed to settle right above their heads.

"An *omen*!" shouted Quentin, his face melting into an expression of wonder.

"Aw, crap!" the eternally put-upon Mindi yelled over the roar. "Everyone into the shelter! Go! Let's see if we can wait this one out!"

"It's *glorious*!" Quentin howled deliriously, spinning in a circle, arms outspread—his black turtleneck, heavy with rain, stretching away from him like Peter Pan's runaway shadow.

For a brief, panicked moment, Kelley thought they were in

danger of him stripping naked and running in ecstatic circles in the downpour.

"We are *destined* to do this play!" Quentin howled as Alec and Jack manhandled him out of the deluge.

A silver fork of lightning hit the stage deck in the middle of the theater, and everyone who was still standing around jumped and scrambled for cover.

Everyone except Kelley, who just snarled fiercely, glaring up into the sky.

She tugged the hood of her jacket further over her face and ducked down one of the theater's entrances. Once she was out of sight, Kelley unclasped her clover charm, shoved it into a pocket of her jeans, and rocketed into the sky, leaving nothing but a faint trace of purple light in her wake.

"Get over here!" Kelley shouted as she burst through the cloud ceiling into the midst of the storm and saw three shadowy figures. They were lounging on the bank of a thunderhead, desultorily hurling lightning bolts from long, skinny fingers. "Now!"

The glow from Kelley's Faerie wings cast eerie illumination over the faces of the Cailleach as they approached her, bobbing through the unsettled air like tattered gray kites.

"Mistressss . . . ," they murmured in chorus, voices hissing like rain on a tin roof. "Be thou pleased with thine ever-faithful servants? Is yon tempest to thy liking?"

Kelley rolled her eyes heavenward. "No! 'Yon tempest' is *not* to my liking! Yon tempest sucks!"

The three Hags exchanged confused glances and mutterings of "more lightning?" "louder thunder?" and "thou didst a shite job on wind duty. . . ."

"Stop it!" Kelley yelled above the gale. "Just . . . stop!"

The Storm Hags drifted over to surround her, hunched and weaving in a circle around where Kelley hovered, their robes and long gray hair crackling with tiny forks of fire.

"Look. Here's the deal." Kelley reined in her urge to blast the lot of them out of the air. "I'm in a *play*. It's not real. The thoughts I'm thinking when I'm acting the part of Ariel— thoughts about creating, *yes*, I know, a magical tempest—they are *not* for the purposes of literal translation. Okay? It's make-believe."

The expressions of disappointment on the faces of the Cailleach were so exaggerated they were almost comical. But then Kelley remembered that her director had come very close to getting a bolt of lightning to the head a few minutes earlier, and the humor of the situation lost its appeal.

"Here, in this place, there will be *no* storm-brewing. All right? None. Nothing but clear skies and gentle breezes until the play is done." She pegged each Hag in turn with a stern glare. "Dost. Thou. Understand?"

There was further muttering, but they seemed to take her meaning. Grudgingly.

"Look." She sighed. "Just . . . clear off this cloud cover and dry up the rain. And behave. Okay?"

Under the influence of a Storm Hag–conjured, unseasonably

warm breeze, the dampness from the sudden downpour cleared away almost completely within the half hour. The read-through carried on after the interruption, and excitement was restored throughout the general cast—and returned to its proper place behind Quentin's jaded demeanor. Kelley did her best to share in the joy, ignoring the constant, hissing whispers of Fae-based worries that sifted across her mind.

Multitask, kiddo, she thought. *But do it one thing at a time.*

After the reading, the company players began to depart out of the theater entrances in tight little groups. Some of the cast were scheduled to meet again that evening to do a first blocking rehearsal of some of the big scenes. Time was short, so the company had to make as much use of the Delacorte as possible, and that meant night sessions. Kelley gathered her stuff and went to join Jack and Alec. But then she caught sight of a silhouetted figure in the back row of the amphitheater. Kelley's steps faltered and she hung back. Jack turned and followed her gaze, frowning faintly.

"You coming along now, Kelley?" he asked.

"Uh . . . no. No, Jack—you guys go on ahead. I'll be okay."

Alec shot her a quizzical glance. He obviously hadn't seen the Faerie king sitting in the audience, cloaked and hooded in sable robes, like a deeper shadow in the shade of a pillar.

"D'you want us to wait for you?" Alec asked.

"No!" Kelley shook her head. "No . . . I just want to hang out for a bit. By myself. Get to know the new space. Y'know?"

She was grateful when Jack nudged Alec gently toward the

exit. *You be careful*, the expression in the older actor's eyes said, as clearly as if he'd spoken the words aloud. Kelley nodded and gave him a reassuring smile. There really wasn't anything for him to worry about. It wasn't as if it was her father—or her mother—who waited. It was Gwynn ap Nudd, the king of the Court of Spring—the only Faerie monarch out of the Four Courts who had ever helped Kelley without exacting a price.

"Highness," she greeted the king, jogging up the wide, shallow steps.

Gwynn pushed back the deep hood of his cloak and inclined his head, smiling placidly at her. He was exactly as she remembered him—pale and elegant, with piercing blue eyes and long midnight-black hair that fell down straight to the middle of his back. His gray robes fell in graceful folds beneath the dark mantle.

"Princess," he murmured in his gentle tones. "I hope you don't mind the intrusion." He waved a long-fingered hand at the stage before them. "I thought I'd sit in and watch. I am such a lover of the theater."

"You are?" Kelley was a little surprised by that. But then again, she was well aware that, for some of the Fae, humans were nothing but an endless source of amusement. At least they had been—up until her father had barred the Fair Folk from consorting with them in the mortal realm. Kelley didn't suppose that there were any theater troupes wandering among the Faerie courts in the Otherworld. "Well . . . how'd we do?" She grinned. "I mean, for a first read-through."

113

"I thought the performances, embryonic though they may be, impressive. The mortal playing Caliban is suitably earthy and raw, the lovers fresh and full of wonder. And you, of course, shall shine brightly as the airy spirit of the isle. And he who plays the sorcerer Prospero is powerfully gifted. He understands. He . . . *sees.* I should like to talk to him. . . ."

Kelley shivered. Much as she liked Gwynn, she didn't want him to suddenly start consorting with her mortal actor buddies. The thought of Gentleman Jack suddenly vanishing into the Faerie realm, never to be seen or heard from again because one of the Fae had taken a fancy to him, made her heart clench a little.

Gwynn glanced at her sideways beneath the dark wings of his brows and laughed. "Allay your fears, lady. I would not steal away your friends. I do not covet mortal companionship in the way that some of our kind do. I am merely, as I said, a . . . lover of theater. *The Tempest* is one of my favorite of Will's plays. I do so love the idea of that island, so rife with wild magicks, and the storms and shipwrecks . . . and I admire the character of his Duke Prospero—one man strong enough to control those elements and make them do his bidding."

The whole "exiled ruler" theme probably resonated pretty strongly with Gwynn, too, Kelley thought—although she certainly didn't say so out loud. She wasn't about to bring up the fact that Gwynn had been deposed from his throne as sole ruler of the Otherworld by her father.

But it seemed that the king's mind had drifted down that

avenue of thought without her help. "How is Auberon of late, lady?" Gwynn asked politely.

Oh . . . you know, Kelley thought, *he's dying. . . .*

"He's fine," she said out loud.

Gwynn gazed steadily at her, almost as if he sensed the lie. Of course, he wouldn't—because Faerie were incapable of telling untruths. Except Kelley . . .

"At least, he was when I saw him last." She shrugged. It wasn't that she actually cared about her father's failing health. Really. She didn't. But she also didn't see any reason to broadcast it. "I mean . . . it's not as if we're particularly close or anything. I'm sure he's perfectly fine."

"I see. You do not much care, is that it?" Gwynn asked.

Kelley glanced sharply at the king, but she got no sense that he was mocking her. Merely asking the question. "I suppose," she answered.

"That is a pity." Gwynn sighed. "For Auberon, I mean. He lacks in not knowing you, lady." The king stood and pulled the hood of his cloak back up around his face, bowing slightly to Kelley as he did so. "I thank you for the entertainment, Princess. Good fortune go with you and yours."

Kelley nodded silently as the Faerie king turned and descended the steps, inky cloak flowing in his wake like a shadow fleeing sunlight. Watching as he turned toward the park interior, she wondered where he was going. Under other circumstances, when the Gate wasn't throwing tantrums, she suspected he would have conjured up a rift and returned to his court in Faerie. Maybe he just fancied strolling through dangerous places. Maybe it wasn't that dangerous for him. After all, who was going to attack a Faerie king?

Well . . . who attacked Auberon? she thought.

She watched the King of Spring until he disappeared out of sight underneath a grove of pines. For *her* part, she was going to hightail it out of there by the fastest route possible. The park just wasn't a safe place anymore—not even for her.

"Hey there!" A voice hallooed her from up in a tree as she took the path veering sharply west. "Kelley!"

"Beni?" She peered up into the branches of a tall oak. "What are you doing up there?"

"Boggart. Big one."

"In broad daylight?" Kelley was surprised by that.

"Yup," Beni said. "If a news crew had caught sight of it, they'd probably call it just another rabid raccoon, but it was definitely a boggart."

"So say you," said another voice.

Kelley saw Bryan, the other half of that dynamic Janus duo, leaning against the bole of the tree, not helping Beni out of his precarious situation in any way whatsoever. In fact, the way he was leaning against the tree, it looked as though he'd probably been trying to shake Beni out of its branches. They probably had some kind of bet going.

"Personally, I didn't see the thing. But, seriously, Ben. If you say so." Bryan grinned over at Kelley. "Hello, Princess."

She smiled back at him. "Bryan, please just call me Kelley."

"It disappeared into a rift," Beni protested as he swung himself down out of the branches and dropped lightly to the ground. "A raccoon wouldn't have done that."

"Why didn't you follow it?" Bryan taunted him.

"No way! I think that rift had actual teeth. . . ."

The lads started to aim punches at each other, and Kelley shook her head, smiling at the good-natured roughhousing. For such a couple of goofs, they sure knew how to fight. "What's going on, guys?"

"Trouble," said Bryan.

"Fun," said Beni.

"Gate's coming apart at the seams."

"And we get to kill anything that comes through the holes!"

"Listen . . . ," Kelley said. "Seeing as you guys are hanging around anyway . . . could you do me a favor and keep a bit of an eye on any of the theater company who happen to be coming or going in the park for the next little while? We're rehearsing—sometimes at night—and I don't want anything to happen to them."

"Sure thing," Bryan agreed. "Not like there's anyone else to protect. I haven't even seen a power jogger all day. And you'd practically have to shoot those freaks in the knees to keep them from running around the park."

"Yeah. Well. News gets around," Beni said, rubbing his arm where Bryan had landed a blow. "Even the maintenance workers and groundskeepers are finding themselves conveniently fluish these days. Nobody wants to hang out around here just at the moment. It's worse than it was during the Nine Night!"

"Where are the rest of the Guard?" Kelley asked, looking around. Not like she expected to see them—the park was enormous, and the Janus tended to spread out to cover more territory.

"Dunno." Bryan shrugged. "We just got orders to stick mid-Gate and keep an eye out. I haven't seen any of the others for days." He didn't seem concerned. Kelley figured that, outside of work, the Guard didn't really socialize, en masse. It wasn't like they did potlucks or went bowling.

In the distance, they heard low, rumbling snarls. Beni's face lit with excitement, and the two Janus started moving in that direction. Bryan turned to Kelley before they went and said with a grin, "Y'know, Kelley—when Sonny gets back from the Otherworld, you should both come with us on a hunt some night. Sonny's actually fun when you're around."

Kelley felt her smile freeze on her face.

As the lads disappeared into the trees, she turned and headed for the nearest exit out of the park.

XI

Sonny held a finger to his lips—unnecessarily. Maddox had already gone dead silent and was listening intently. Voices. Two voices. Someone was in the subway tunnel, near the Faerie glamour that concealed the entrance to the obsidian passageway where they stood. Sonny thought he might have detected a familiarity in the tones of one of the two speakers.

The first was female. Sharp with anger: "Of course I'm sure. We've been searching around down here for days, and I haven't had so much as a twinge from anywhere else."

The hard stone of the subway tunnel distorted the words,

but Sonny suddenly knew who they belonged to.

"This is it—it has to be—but I still don't understand why we're doing this. I don't like it. . . ."

Maddox's eyes went wide, and Sonny knew that he had recognized the voice as well. With a tap on his shoulder, Sonny gestured Maddox to follow him closer to where the sound was coming from.

Standing just inside the tunnel mouth, they waited. After a few moments, they could see shapes moving, dim and shadowed, in the train tunnel beyond. From their side of things, the veil made it look as if they peered through a heavy gauze curtain. Sonny and Maddox edged as close as they could and listened.

"You're not afraid of the dark, are you, Cait?" said the second voice.

Cait. They'd heard right. She was a fellow Janus Guard—one of only a few other than Maddox who Sonny considered a friend as well as a comrade in arms.

"That's not what I meant and you know it," she snapped.

Sonny strained again to make out the male voice. It could have been . . . yes. Maddox knew it, too. He turned to Sonny and mouthed the man's name. *Godwyn.* Godwyn's low chuckle unaccountably raised the small hairs at the back of Sonny's neck. What were the Janus doing underground?

Cait seemed to be wondering the same thing. "I've heard nothing about any disturbances in the city's tunnels," she said. "Or on any of the trains or in the stations. Not from the Lost Ones. Only human misbehavior, and *that* is not in our mandate to . . . correct."

"We're not looking for Fae in these tunnels. We're looking for other tunnels that will lead us *to* the Fae. To their gathering places."

"To sanctuaries. I know that. What I don't know is *why*."

"Why do you think?" Godwyn's tone remained pleasant. Friendly.

But Sonny stiffened as he heard the rasp of a blade being partially drawn from a sheath, followed by the slap of the hilt as it was returned home with a flourish. A braggart's gesture, except for the fact that Godwyn was virtually unparalleled in the use of a sword.

"Where are the others?" Cait asked. "Where's Ghost?"

"Don't worry about Ghost. And don't worry about the others, either. We'll have support soon enough. In the meantime, what you need to do is concentrate on tracking down and neutralizing whatever Faerie trickery keeps their little Lost clubhouse hidden from prying eyes. You say the entrance is around here somewhere. Find it. Then we'll have some fun breaking up their nasty little party."

"We've never taken the fight to them before," Cait argued. "Not like this."

"About time then, wouldn't you say?"

Beside Sonny, Maddox frowned deeply, shaking his head.

Cait was silent for a moment. Then she said, in a carefully neutral voice, "When was the last time Aaneel spoke to the Winter King?"

Godwyn's own voice went flat and hard. "You think Aaneel

gave orders without sanction? I suppose you could always go and ask Auberon yourself—if you really want to question that. Do you, Cait?"

There was another long silence. "No. I guess I don't."

"Good. Then find the damned glamour and let's get on with it."

Sonny and Maddox watched silently through the veil as Cait unslung her leather tote from across her body and knelt beside it on the ground, fishing through her stores of magickal paraphernalia. "This could take a while, you know," she muttered in reluctant tones. "A long while."

"I'm not going anywhere," Godwyn grunted, and Sonny could see his shadow hunch against the wall as he settled himself to wait.

A distant rumbling sounded—like far-off thunder.

"Train," Godwyn called blandly, and Cait picked up her things and pressed herself against the opposite wall, a bare instant before a southbound train hurtled down the tracks, rattling and squealing, making a tremendous racket.

By the time the end car had passed the veiled archway, Sonny was already running back toward the reservoir grotto. He'd heard enough.

Thoughts in a tumult, Sonny pounded along the tunnel, Maddox running silently at his heels. As if the treacherous political machinations of the Fair Folk weren't enough, now it seemed that he had Janus double-dealing to add to his list of bewares. Whether or not Godwyn was acting under orders from Aaneel, Sonny would have staked his reputation that Godwyn was *not* following the wishes of *Auberon*. Even Sonny's own lingering mistrust of the Unseelie lord wasn't enough to convince him that Auberon had issued some sort of Lost Fae extermination edict. But that was exactly what he suspected Godwyn was up to. There was no other reason to seek out a hidden community of the Lost who were responsible for no greater transgressions in the mortal realm than the theft of day-old baked goods.

Sonny had to warn Carys. He had to get Neerya somewhere safe. He had to—

"Sonny!" Maddox hissed—for what was probably the second or third time by the sound of things. He reached out and grabbed Sonny by the arm, pulling him to a stop. "What in seven hells is going *on*?"

"You tell me. Just what exactly happened while I was in the Otherworld?" Sonny whispered fiercely. "Was Carys right? Have the Janus gone rogue, Maddox?"

Maddox shifted his shoulders nervously and looked as though he would laugh off the question—until Sonny turned abruptly and, grabbing him roughly by his jacket, slammed Maddox up against the wall of the tunnel, beside another archway that branched off into darkness.

"Tell me!" Sonny demanded. "Are we hunting for sport now? Is that our noble purpose?"

Maddox went very still. Sonny knew there was a decent chance that—if he'd really wanted to—the other Janus could flatten him where he stood. He didn't. Instead, he lowered his hands to his sides and looked Sonny square in the eyes.

"I think maybe, yeah," he said quietly. "For some of us."

Sonny took his hands off Maddox and stepped back. "Why?" he asked, wounded that he would even need to ask such a question.

"I dunno, Sonn." Maddox ran a hand through his sandy hair. "Boredom? Rebellion? But . . . yeah. It's gotten bad. The real hard-arses—Godwyn and that little psychopath, Ghost . . . even Camina, I think—they've been tracking down Lost on a full-time basis. Tracking them and . . . well, you know. I suspect Aaneel's been egging 'em on."

"Then we have to warn Carys and her folk."

"No, Sonny!" Maddox made a grab for his arm as Sonny turned to continue on to the reservoir.

"You want them to get caught unawares? Only Carys and a few of the others are warriors of any sort. The rest are just misfits. Maddox—it'll be a bloodbath in there."

"I—" Maddox snorted in frustration. "Gods! Am I the only one who hasn't lost my crackerjacks lately? Look." Maddox pointed back toward where, at that very moment, Cait was working to breach the enchanted veil far down at the mouth of the tunnel. "Those guys—they're the ones we're supposed to be siding with. *That's* our team. Not some half-wit water beetle like your little playfellow."

"She's just a child, Madd."

"She bloody well is *not*—"

"And what about Chloe?" Sonny interrupted.

Maddox's anger wavered. "What about her?"

"I thought you cared about her."

"Yeah. Well." Maddox's chin jutted out stubbornly. "You said it yourself, Sonny. She's just a Siren. A monster." The sarcasm sounded particularly bitter coming from someone with such a big, open heart as Maddox. "I'm probably just another pathetic human plaything to her. Why should I give a damn? About any of them?"

"I don't know," Sonny said quietly. "Do you stop caring about someone you love—just because they don't feel the same way?"

In that moment Sonny realized that he still loved Kelley. In spite of everything. Maybe when this was over he would try to find her. Talk to her and find out what the hell had happened between them. When there was time. At the moment, there were other pressing matters.

Maddox kicked at the ground, miserable, and then his gaze drifted back down the tunnel. Back toward the reservoir. He *did* care. Still, Maddox was a good soldier—a good Janus Guard—and he said, "I dunno. You heard Godwyn back there—he seems to be under the impression that all this stuff that's happening . . . that it's under Auberon's orders."

"It isn't. He's not issuing any orders. He's barely—" Sonny stopped himself before he said anything further.

"He's barely what?" When Sonny didn't answer, Maddox pressed him on it. "Auberon's barely *what*, Sonny?"

125

"He's dying, Madd."

"Oh. Oh . . . hell."

Maddox looked as though he was at an utter loss for words. Sonny understood the reaction. To even think of the Unseelie lord as anything other than invincible and eternal was to question everything they had grown up learning. It also meant that things were seriously awry in the Otherworld. And it meant that wherever this new Janus agenda was coming from, it *wasn't* from Auberon. Sonny gazed at Maddox, waiting for him to make up his mind.

But there wasn't going to be time for that. A rumbling vibration of sound and a flash of weird light washed over them from the direction they'd just come.

"Damn it!" Sonny hissed.

Maddox nodded grimly. "Cait's no slouch."

When Sonny turned to keep running toward the reservoir, Maddox grabbed and pointed toward the archway next to them. "Where does that lead?" he asked.

"Up to the Tavern on the Green, I think," Sonny answered impatiently. "Why?"

"I've got an idea," Maddox said. "Will Herne help the reservoir Folk?"

Sonny nodded. "He's the one who built the place."

"We'll never make it with enough time to warn the Lost properly," Maddox said. "You go topside, find Herne, and get reinforcements. Let me take care of this."

"I'll stay," Sonny said. "You go."

"No." Maddox shook his head. "The other Janus don't know you're back, Sonny. I can—"

There was a noise from down the tunnel. Maddox shoved Sonny over the threshold of the Tavern archway and threw a quick-and-dirty veil up in front of the opening, hiding Sonny from sight. Then Maddox moved swiftly in a loping run, stopping a dozen yards back down the tunnel where it bent at a sharp angle, still close enough that Sonny could clearly hear his friend's voice as Maddox said, "About bloody time!"

"Maddox?" Cait's voice floated back.

"What the hell are you doing here?" asked Godwyn—and Sonny could hear the edge in his voice.

"Waiting for you lot," Maddox answered, as if it should be perfectly obvious what he was doing there. "Hullo, Ghost. Camina. Where's Bellamy?"

"Don't be cute, Maddox," Camina said sourly. "You know Bell's no part of this."

Sonny held his breath at the misstep, but Maddox recovered quickly.

"Yeah—of course. It was a joke. Don't be so touchy." Maddox laughed derisively. "This is it then. . . ." He left the statement hanging.

Sonny knew what Maddox was doing. He was trying to give him a head count—to let Sonny know how many of the rogue Janus were there in the tunnel.

"This is it," Godwyn answered.

"Except for the redcaps you told us abou—"

"Shut up, Mina." Godwyn silenced Camina, coldly.

Redcaps, thought Sonny. This was going to get ugly fast. He could hardly believe that Godwyn would stoop to using the likes of those mercenary trolls to fight his battles.

"Who sent you, Maddox?" Godwyn asked.

Maddox snorted. "Same person who sent you, Wynnie-boy. No reason to get pissy just because I found the Faerie freaks' hidey-hole before you did. Now listen up, you lot." He turned his voice on its edge, and began speaking as though issuing commands. "I've already done recon, and there's a sanctuary up ahead about three hundred yards. Didn't see anyone in the passageway, but that doesn't mean they aren't there. Cait, you should go back out into the subway tunnel. Reinstall the veil and keep watch so's we don't tip off the mortal authorities and get some poor transit worker killed—or get ambushed from behind. Send up a flare if anything's on the move."

So, Sonny thought, Maddox trusted Cait. Or, at the very least, didn't think she was exactly culpable in this madness. Sonny was glad of it. He'd heard the uncertainty in her voice before she'd breached the tunnel veil.

"The rest of you," Maddox was saying, "sanctuary's that way, if you please. Get a move on."

Sonny sensed the Janus starting to head in his direction.

"Hey!" Sonny heard Maddox call out from where he now brought up the rear of the group. "If any of you darlings brought party favors, I'd get 'em out and ready. Arm yourselves, kiddies. You never know what might be coming for you."

Sonny shook his head, grinning viciously at his friend's perfidy; Maddox, of course, knew *exactly* what would be coming for them. And he knew the consequences of fighting back. Sonny retreated farther back from the opening as he heard the sounds of blades being unsheathed, a crossbow ratcheted and loaded, the rasp of a mace chain. . . .

Within seconds, there was the roaring in the distance that signaled the onrushing approach of the tunnel wraiths that came screaming out of the darkness. Sonny felt a momentary surge of conflicting emotions as he heard one or two of the Janus Guards scream in alarm—and pain. Then he shut the lid on his feelings and, turning, ran, climbing upward toward where the tunnel he was in would come out inside Herne's Tavern on the Green.

XII

"Transformation isn't like casting a glamour, Kelley," Tyff said.

Kelley ignored her and frowned fiercely, staring at the corkscrew lock of fiery auburn hair she held up in front of her face.

"It isn't easy. Seriously. It's almost impossible."

"Tyff—*shh* . . ." Almost impossible, maybe. But she'd *done* it. And she was determined to do it again. . . .

"You are *so* messing with stuff you shouldn't be."

"I'm Faerie, aren't I? Shouldn't I know how to do this?"

"It's high magick, Kell. Most Fae don't."

"Do you?"

"I'm not most Fae."

"Neither am I," Kelley said obstinately.

"Oh gods!" Tyff tossed her nail file onto the coffee table and stood in a huff. "I give up on you! Haven't I told you that magick taints things? Just look at whatsisname. . . ."

"What's *whose* name, Tyff?" Kelley asked. She knew Tyff meant Sonny—she just wanted to know if *Tyff* knew who she meant.

Faint confusion clouded Tyff's eyes. "Um . . . I forget. What the hell are we talking about?"

The enchantment held. Kelley felt relief and guilt all at the same time.

"Magick," she said. "You were going to teach me how to use mine, remember?"

"You really are the world's worst liar," Tyff muttered, and wandered off to her own room, taking one of her glossy magazines with her as she went.

Kelley turned back to the task at hand. Transformation. At least she tried to, but her mind kept drifting off onto tangents that always, eventually, circled back to thoughts of Sonny. If *he'd* been there, he would have thought what she was trying to do was worthy of the effort. She remembered the look on Sonny's face the first time he'd ever seen her Faerie wings— how he'd reached up to catch her and keep her from flying away. And when her wings had flickered and dimmed, he'd told her she'd "have to work on that" with a smile playing on his lips and a proud gleam in his beautiful eyes.

Kelley stared at an auburn curl and redoubled her efforts. One feather. Just one . . .

Eventually, instead of being able to transform a lock of her hair into even a single feather, all Kelley's intense concentration managed to conjure was a headache. A pounding one. For a moment, she thought she could actually *hear* the pounding.

No . . . that's the door.

"Are you gonna get that?" Tyff hollered from her bedroom. "I'm trying to relax here!"

Pulling her hair back into a ponytail and securing it with an elastic band from around her wrist, Kelley went to get the door, which was shuddering under the blows from whoever was knocking so insistently. She stood on tiptoe and peered through the peephole—straight into one of Fennrys's ice-blue eyes.

"Hey," Kelley said, opening up. "Did my door do something to really piss you off, Fenn?"

The Wolf stood in the hallway, fist raised. "There's trouble," he said without preamble. "In the park."

"Trouble . . . in the park," Kelley said. "And this is different from every other day *how*, exactly?"

"Because it's more trouble than I think I can handle alone."

That was a worrying thought. Still, Kelley was a little wary of Fennrys and his whole pick-your-battles demotivational speech. "Well," she said, "I guess it's good you've got the other Janus Guards to help you out, then."

But Fennrys shook his head, his expression grim. "The other Janus Guards *are* the trouble."

"Aren't the Janus supposed to be the good guys?" Kelley was appalled. "Code of honor and all that?"

She paced back and forth in front of the couch, where Fenn-rys sat impatiently, elbows on his knees, lacing and unlacing his fingers.

"Where, exactly, in this code of honor does it say that it's okay to plan a surprise attack on a bunch of Folk who are, as far as you know, living in peaceful accord with the mortal realm?" Cold anger made it hard for Kelley to speak without raising her voice. "I thought you and your buddies were only supposed to fight against dangerous lunatics like the Wild Hunt," she said. "Or that leprechaun jerk."

"That's what *I* always thought," Fenn said. "I mean, don't get me wrong—hell, I'm just as happy to go on a rampage as the next changeling—but I don't go in for sneak attacks on non-aggressors."

"Non-aggressors?" Kelley stopped and crossed her arms.

Fenn smiled wanly. "You know what I mean. Most of the Lost who live in this realm are just a bunch of sparkly misfits, and I'm really not into ripping the wings off butterflies."

Kelley felt a sharp, phantom ache where her own silvery wings had once briefly fluttered. "How on earth am *I* supposed to help you?"

Fenn shot her a look. "I've seen you in a fight, remember? I've fought by your side. *And*, more importantly, you're Auberon's daughter. I'm hoping that your words might hold a bit more sway than my fists with some of the Guard who think they're doing this thing on Old Man Winter's orders. Failing that, your power packs a wallop that might do some convincing."

Kelley frowned and thought about what he was saying. She didn't want to see innocents get hurt—Lost Fae like Tyff who were just victims of circumstance.

She was startled by Fennrys reaching a hand toward her face. Kelley jerked backward away from his touch before she could stop herself, and he smiled grimly. Then he reached for her again . . . and pulled something from her hair.

It was a single small, fluffy reddish feather.

Kelley snatched the thing from Fenn's fingers, blushing furiously.

He shrugged and stood. "I just figured you might want a piece of this action," he said. "But, y'know, just tell me if I'm wrong and I'll go."

"No . . . no, you're not wrong, Fenn," she agreed reluctantly.

He wasn't. But Kelley also wondered, in the back of her mind, if this shift in attitude among the Janus might have something to do with the gathering unrest in the Faerie Courts. Still, even if it *was* just the Guard going rogue for no other reason than because they were bored, she wasn't about to stand idly by and let it happen. "I'll come with you."

She went to get her shoes but stopped dead in her tracks.

"Except I can't. Crap."

"Why not?"

"Because I have rehearsal later tonight."

Fennrys glared at her. "And?"

Kelley glared back. "*And* it's important for me not to let the company down. The only reason the Avalon burned to the ground in the first place was because of *me*, remember?"

Sure. And she'd made herself a promise to help save the theater company—just like Tyff had told her she could. But what if *this* situation was the "save the world" thing her roommate had referred to? The lightbulb went off in Kelley's head. Without another word to Fenn, she went and knocked on Tyff's door.

"Sucks to be you, sometimes," Tyff commiserated blandly from behind the creamy-pink frosting of a honeysuckle-scented facial treatment. "No lie."

"But you could," Kelley said, excited by the prospect. "Be *me*."

Tyff's eyes narrowed. "I just said it *sucks* to be you."

"You wouldn't actually be me. I mean, you could just cast a glamour that would make you look like me and then you could go to rehearsal in my place and I can go with Fenn and—"

"Whoa there, tiger!" Tyff cut her off. "I'm a model—*not* an actress."

"It wouldn't be for long. Just so you could learn the blocking and give me notes. Just for a rehearsal or two."

"Not just no, Winslow." Tyff crossed her arms over her chest, her facial mask creasing into a clownish frown. "*Hell* no."

"Tyff . . . hear me out," Kelley pleaded. "I can't be in two places at once. At least, I don't think I can. Tell me right now if that is something I can do, and I'll totally forget this whole idea."

Tyff glared at her. "It's *not* something you can do," she admitted reluctantly. "Damn it all."

"Okay." Kelley took a deep breath and plunged on. "Weren't you the one who told me that I should do what mortals do? Weren't you the one who told me to multitask? What better way to do that than this!"

"I said that?"

"You said that." Kelley nodded emphatically. "'Save the theater. Save Sonny. Save the world. Save yourself.'"

"Me and my big, perfectly shaped mouth," Tyff muttered darkly. She stalked to her dressing table, plucked a handful of Kleenex from a box, and began to tissue off the cream with waspish little swipes. "I was *ob*viously waxing poetic."

"But you were *right*. I can do this. At least, I can try to do this—all of it—but only with your help. Will you help me?"

"The last time I agreed to help someone—i.e., you and Sonny-boy—out of a bad situation, it ended even badder, Kelley," Tyff said bleakly, wadding the now-greasy tissue into a ball and lobbing it a foot wide of the wastebasket. "I'm pretty sure I don't need to remind you of that."

She didn't. Tyff had been the one Sonny had asked to help disenchant Lucky the kelpie before he turned into the Roan Horse of the Wild Hunt. She'd agreed, but had missed three of the charms tied into Lucky's forelock because they had been hidden under a sophisticated glamour. It hadn't been Tyff's fault. She had been duped—they all had. And it had almost cost them everything.

"That wasn't your fault," Kelley said.

"Yes, it was." Tyff's voice turned harsh. "And the time before that, and the time before that. Any time I try to help people, Kelley, I leave a swath of catastrophe in my wake. Why do you think I was exiled to this crummy realm in the first place?"

"I just thought—"

"I'm a screw-up, little roomie." Tyff threw her hands in the air. "I'm a blindingly beautiful screw-up, true, but I'm still a screw-up."

"Tyff . . ." Kelley grabbed for one of Tyff's flailing wrists and held on to it. "You're not a screw-up. You're my best friend."

"Don't." Tyff's eyes glittered with the sheen of unshed tears.

"I have faith in you. And I need you."

"Kelley . . ."

"Fenn says he can't do this alone," Kelley said quietly. "And I can't help him without you."

Tyff sighed and went silent for a long moment. Then she blinked rapidly and said, "I'm not wearing your clothes."

XIII

S onny ran swiftly upward, following the twisting path of the tunnel as it angled sharply toward the surface. Carys had told him that it came out somewhere inside the confines of Herne's Tavern on the Green, where Herne entertained the Lost Fae, who delighted in the sumptuous, Otherworldly atmosphere of his halls and gardens—as close as most of them would ever get to going back home.

At the end of the tunnel, bathed in a growing luminescence from somewhere up ahead, the hewn rock floor turned to smooth, polished steps of gleaming marble that spiraled upward. Strains of haunting Faerie melodies trickled toward him.

The Tavern was usually a nonstop party, but Sonny noticed the dance floor was almost empty. The High Fae, it seemed, were avoiding the Samhain Gate while lesser fae—the nastier denizens of the Otherworld—roamed free.

Sonny stepped into the chandeliered hall and wound his way among the few Faerie revelers. When he spotted a green-coated satyr in a top hat—Herne's doorman and seneschal—hurrying past on woolly, backward-bending legs, he grabbed him by the elbow.

"Master Flannery!" The creature nodded his little curving horns in Sonny's direction, without actually stopping—forcing Sonny to walk beside him. "Welcome back. I thought we would not see you again until after the last of the Wild Hunters had been dealt with."

"There have been other pressing matters of late, Master Seneschal," Sonny said, lengthening his stride so that he could keep pace with the swiftly trotting satyr.

"Might I inquire, Sir Janus," the doorman asked politely, "how it is that you come to be here by way of the back door, for want of a better term?"

"The lady Carys granted me safe passage to and from the sanctuaries," Sonny said. "And I have urgent business with Herne the Hunter."

The doorman grunted, pawing one delicate hoof on the marble floor. "As do I. Let us find him together."

Sonny followed in the creature's loping wake out to the central courtyard, where Herne was engaged in conversation with what appeared to be an enormous animated shrub. In fact, it was a manifestation of the ancient soul of the natural world, the Greenman. Herne had created the simulacrum in honor of his murdered friend, when the Greenman had bequeathed all of his awesome power to the once human Hunter.

When Herne noticed his doorman hurrying over, accompanied by the unexpected presence of a Janus Guard, he rose and met them halfway.

"Sonny!" His warm, full tones filled the space between them. The Hunter's gladness at seeing Sonny was genuine and generous, surprising Sonny a little. Not that he didn't consider the Hunter a friend—he did. He admired Herne greatly and thought of him as an ally but, at the same time, Sonny really didn't know if the man-god knew *him* well enough to consider him a friend.

Herne seemed to think otherwise. He took Sonny's hand in a fervent, bone-crushing grip. "I am so pleased to see you hale after hearing of that bad business with the princess and her theater."

Sonny felt a momentary, familiar pain in his heart. "Thank you, lord," he said. "Forgive my intrusion, but there is trouble brewing in the tunnels below your house."

"And trouble already well-fermented at the front door," said the doorman at Sonny's side, his black, inhuman eyes sparking coldly.

Herne looked back and forth between them, his brow furrowing under the garland of oak leaves he wore that night instead of his usual shining horned helmet. After a moment's thought, he gestured the satyr to lead them to the main entrance of the Tavern. "Both of you—tell me of these troubles. You first, Sonny."

Sonny told him of the Janus who were on the hunt for the reservoir and felt the heat of shame creeping up his cheeks as he described what his brethren were about. Herne's brown eyes darkened, but his expression remained impassive. He nodded curtly as Sonny finished his brief report. Herne stopped at the entrance to a mirrored corridor before a tall Faerie wearing a long, silvery shirt of chain mail, who stood in a relaxed but guarded pose. The Hunter spoke in low tones to the Fae, but Sonny was close enough to hear him order all but a handful of the Tavern Fae down into the tunnels to help those in the reservoir defend the sanctuary. Without a word, the Faerie guard turned on his heel and disappeared back the way they had come, already drawing a slender-bladed sword from the sheath at his belt. Then Herne gestured for his seneschal to lead them on, saying, "Speak. What trouble else?"

They had navigated the corridors of the Tavern with speed, and the main doors were in sight. The satyr just nodded toward the entrance with a sour glare. He spat one word: "That."

The sight of a familiar figure who stood fidgeting nervously in the vestibule of the Tavern brought Sonny up short.

Clothed in a flowing green gown, face half hidden by her pale hair, Jenii Greenteeth stood just outside on the curved stone steps, framed by the graceful arch of the Tavern's open doors.

Sonny felt his fists clench involuntarily at his sides.

"Glaistig bitch," he snarled. "What is *she* doing here?"

The seneschal tugged a wrinkle out of his green velvet top-coat, smoothing the fabric down over his woolly legs, and said in tones of rich sarcasm aimed in the glaistig's direction, "She is Fair Folk, honored Janus. All of whom are welcome here." Then his voice went flinty. "So be they keep the peace of this place. *And* I decide to let them pass, in the name of the lord of the Tavern."

In the air before Jenii there was a faint, crackling shimmer—like a curtain of tiny sparks—a magickal barrier preventing her entry into the Tavern proper. Without looking, Sonny could sense that Herne had gone very still.

Sonny reined in his anger and ducked his head in a polite nod. It would be unwise of him to offend Herne's own second-in-command. "Forgive my rudeness, Master Door-keeper. Your judgment is, doubtless, without flaw."

"I take no offense. You know something of guarding door-ways yourself, Master Janus. I took your query in the manner in which, I am certain, it was intended—simply an inquiry into matters of professional interest."

"How long has that creature been here?" Herne asked his seneschal, his voice tinged with the rumble of low, far-off thunder.

"She only just arrived, lord. Craves admittance and sanctuary. *Actual* sanctuary. Says she's being hunted."

Herne grunted. "And so she comes to the Hunter."

142

"So she says."

"Hunted by whom, I wonder?" Herne murmured to Sonny, turning away from the door so that the glaistig could not hear him. "Perhaps it is no coincidence that there is a party of several heavily armed Janus down in the aqueduct tunnels seeking for the entrance to Lost Fae safe havens, Sonny Flannery."

Sonny considered that. "I cannot say that I would find it entirely surprising if we were to learn that she is part of the reason." Regarding the creature with distaste, he raised his voice enough so that she could hear him. "As dark Fae go, she is darker than most."

"You're only saying that because I ate your predecessor," Jenii said, with an expression that was almost a pout.

Sonny stared at her flatly, careful to keep a tight rein on his emotions. "You," he said. "It was *you* who ripped out his throat."

"He was sweet. . . ." The glaistig hissed wetly, lips peeled back in a grotesque parody of a smile as she licked the points of her bright green teeth. "Like nectar."

"Do not let her provoke you, Sonny." Herne's voice rumbled through the air and he put a cautionary hand on Sonny's chest, even though the young Janus had not twitched so much as a muscle. "You know the rules of this place," he said, making sure the glaistig heard him clearly, too. "Kill her, and my seneschal will be forced to kill you just on principle, for having violated the accords of the Tavern."

The satyr looked up at Sonny and shrugged apologetically.

"You could *try*, Master Seneschal," Sonny said politely.

"And if he failed, that would then put *me* in a very awkward position," Herne continued. "In all the years this Tavern has stood, Mabh is the only one who has caused blood to be spilled on these floors. I will not suffer such a thing to happen again, no matter who instigates and what the point of contention. This is my house."

Jenii cackled delightedly at the look of frustration that must have flashed across Sonny's face.

"Have a care, weed," Herne said as he turned a frown on the glaistig. "I might not let the Janus kill you, but I also won't let you disrupt the peace of this sanctuary. As it is, I tolerate your presence at my door only for the sake of your father's memory."

"You mean that mockery of him that lives on in your house now?" the glaistig scoffed. "How could you suffer that insult to exist?"

"It is all that I have to remember my friend by," Herne answered stiffly. "I honor him."

"My brothers would have killed you for the insult of that 'honor' if they could have gotten past your infernal wards."

"A shame they will not ever have the chance now, insomuch as they are both dead," Herne said flatly.

Sonny held very still so as not to show his surprise on his face. Both dead? Both leprechaun brothers had been at the theater. Sonny remembered fighting them. Sweet goddess— he remembered one of them attacking Kelley and . . .

"*One* of my brothers is dead, true," she sneered. "The other yet lives."

Beside him, Sonny felt the air around Herne crackle with silent tension. Sonny had the distinct feeling that Herne would have stepped protectively in front of him in another moment.

The glaistig tilted her head on her long neck and regarded Herne. "This disturbs you, noble lord?" she said, her voice a mocking simper. "I wouldn't worry just yet. He was sorely wounded in the fight at the upstart princess's playhouse. He clings to life but by a thread."

"While you, who were also there," Sonny observed dryly, "appear remarkably healthy."

"I was smart enough to quit the fray when the other Janus arrived on the scene. I do not like even odds."

"What a well-developed sense of self-preservation you must have," Herne said.

"Pity my poor sisters who did not share that trait," Jenii answered bitterly. "For my part, I'd rather like to maintain my appearance of remarkable health."

"Good luck with that," the Hunter said, and turned to go without lifting the barrier.

"Wait!" Jenii called after him, a sudden note of desperation creeping into her voice. "They will kill me if you do not let me in. I have always heard that the Horned One did not judge. That he was fair and kind and welcoming to all—especially those in need. I *am* being hunted. Truly."

"By whom?" Herne asked.

"By those who seek to tap me like a sugar maple and use the sap in my veins to feed another's blooming. I speak the truth—my brother lies close to death. Only Green Magick will restore him. And that, I'm sure you know, is in gravely short supply these days. They would take it from me, to give it to my brother."

She shook the hair out of her eyes and, for an instant, all Sonny could see was what looked like a terrified young girl standing out in the cold needing help. He knew that she was anything but, yet in that moment it was a powerful impression.

"It will be my death," she said in a whisper.

"Why sacrifice your life for his?" Herne wondered. "Who would do such a thing?"

Jenii swallowed nervously, the muscles of her throat constricting, and her eyes flitted back and forth from Sonny to the seneschal to Herne. "Just before my brother fell insensible, he claimed he'd found where the lost Greenman's power had been hidden away. I rather think that's valuable information to quite a few people. I can see why there are those who would seek to revive him, no matter the cost."

Sonny watched as the Hunter's posture went stiff, rigid with tension. Then the Hunter turned to him and beckoned him away from the door, out of earshot of Jenii Greenteeth.

"You say she was also at Kelley's theater?"

"Aye. Part of the attack party, in the moments before it burned. I thought she and her kin might have all been disposed of in the battle but . . . I cannot be sure."

"Sonny," Herne murmured ruefully. "One of the harsher rules of warfare is to never leave your enemy alive on the field at the end of an engagement. How could you not be certain?"

Sonny frowned. How, indeed? "I don't exactly remember what happened, Herne," he admitted. "I think I must have hit my head. The end of things is a blank to me. I remember flashes—light and . . . blinding color. Heat like the hottest sunshine . . . burning in my brain . . . and then nothing. Like I said, I must have hit my head."

Herne gazed deeply into Sonny's eyes for a long, searching moment.

"Excuse me. . . ." Jenii's sibilant tones drifted toward them. "I really don't mean to interrupt but, if you could make a decision on whether or not to extend me sanctuary with some haste, I would appreciate it. Otherwise, I'd best hightail it somewhere else."

The Hunter turned to his doorman and gave him a single terse nod. "Let her in. See that she is given refreshment and kept safe."

The little satyr bowed to his lord and stepped up before the barrier that shimmered between him and the glaistig. As he began to mutter his way through a complex incantation, wiry fingers twitching, Herne beckoned Sonny to follow him back into the tavern.

They had gone only a few steps down the hall when there was a sharp snapping sound, like someone breaking kindling over their knee. Herne and Sonny turned and saw the body of the seneschal slump to the ground in front of the Green Maiden, his head hanging limply at an odd angle. In one swift motion Jenii bent over him and, when she raised her face a moment later, her sharp green teeth were stained with blood. "Thank you, lord Hunter," she said. "That *was* refreshing."

The glaistig spun on her heel, turning back to the doors the seneschal hadn't had the chance to lock. She raised her arms above her head and, with a sweeping gesture, brought them down around in a circle. The ancient oak doors of the Tavern blew off their hinges, and cold, city-gray light flooded into the Faerie sanctuary. Sonny threw up an arm, shielding his face from the storm of three-inch splinters that flew through the air.

Beside him, Herne swore viciously and bellowed a call to arms.

There were few to answer it. Most of the Folk who were capable of fighting had already gone, on Herne's orders, in the direction of the reservoir tunnels. Surely though, Sonny thought, they were enough of a match for a lone Green Maiden.

She wasn't alone.

Sonny flinched and dived as half a dozen arrows flew out of the darkness beyond the tavern doors.

Sonny went for his crossbow, but Herne shouldered him aside, shoving Sonny back toward the hallway whence he'd come.

"Go!" shouted the forest lord. "That way!"

He gave Sonny another shove, which almost sent him sprawling, and Sonny had no choice but to head in that direction. He raced down the twisting marble corridor, the Hunter close behind him. But once they had gotten well away from the front doors of the Tavern, Sonny screeched to a halt and turned on Herne. "Why are we running?" he demanded.

Herne paused briefly. "Because we cannot afford to fight."

"Herne—"

"The Tavern's wards are breached. I cannot ensure your safety here."

"My—? I can take care of myself!" Sonny protested.

Herne glanced back at the empty corridor behind them. In the distance, they heard a cry of defiance—and then one of pain. Herne spun back around, grasping Sonny by the shoulders, and stared deep into his eyes. The Hunter's features shifted through a litany of expressions before coming to rest on something that was halfway between fear and regret.

"I don't understand what's happening, Herne," Sonny said quietly. There was something in the man-god's behavior that struck a chord deep inside Sonny. "I need to know what's going on here."

"No," the forest lord said. "You don't. Not now, Sonny. You just have to trust me."

Sonny felt his own heart rate increasing as he saw the rapid pulse beating in the vein on the Hunter's neck. Herne was genuinely afraid. *That* was truly worrying.

"Just *go*, Sonny," he urged. "Please. Find Carys—tell her

what has happened here—and then get away. Get to safety."

Sonny shook his head. "I'm not leaving you to fight on your own, Herne. That is madness—"

"It is my wish!" Herne's words came out in a frustrated snarl. "And if you have any respect at all for me and my house, you will do as I ask, Sonny Flannery."

If it had been anyone else urging him to flight, Sonny would have ignored them and stood and fought. Anything else would have been cowardice and dishonor. But so great was his respect for the forest lord, and so insistent was Herne that he follow his demands, that Sonny could do nothing but reluctantly agree.

"Auberon," Herne said rapidly. "Find Auberon. I cannot explain it all to you—perhaps he can. But you must trust me, Sonny. And you *must* do as I say."

Sonny nodded, not trusting himself to speak. Herne gripped his shoulder tightly once more. Then the Hunter brushed his hand against a mirrored wall that shimmered and disappeared at his murmured word, opening a hidden passageway that would lead back down to the aqueduct and the reservoir. Sonny stepped over the threshold and was several yards down the passageway when he heard the telltale thrum and whine of a bow shot.

He spun back around in time to see that Herne had heard it, too. It had been enough warning that the Hunter was able to twist out of the way. The arrow did not pierce his heart, but it slammed into his shoulder, spinning Herne around in a grotesque parody of a dance.

"No!" Sonny cried out, and bolted back toward the archway. He only got halfway before Herne reached back with a flailing hand and reinstated the barrier, cutting Sonny off from the Tavern. The hiss and whine of more arrows reached Sonny's ears where he stood, balled fists hammering against the magickal wall. He heard a stifled grunt of pain from Herne that told him another of the missiles must have found its mark. But he could not see the Hunter.

Fortunately, it seemed, neither could Jenii Greenteeth.

"Come out, come out, wherever you are . . . ," the glaistig murmured in a singsong voice from somewhere very close by.

Herne must have called up a veil to hide himself, Sonny thought. He desperately hoped the Hunter was not so grievously wounded that he wouldn't have the strength to maintain it.

"You should have made me promise to keep the peace, first, before letting me through your doors, Horned One," Jenii called out merrily, her taunts echoing down the marble-and-mirror passageway. "But I'm glad you didn't. I hate playing by the rules. Don't worry—this won't take long." Jenii's voice grew indistinct and wavering, as if she were moving away from the hidden archway where Sonny stood unseen, but her words were still loud enough to hear as she said, "Find him if you can. Although I doubt you will—the Hunter is as wily as an old fox. Don't waste too much time. As soon as I get what we came here for, you lot can head down to help the others.

As for me, I'm off to find a princess!"

Sonny stiffened.

"She'll prove a charming playfellow for my brother once he regains his strength, no doubt." The Green Maiden laughed, and it was a bone-chilling sound. "Maybe he'll let me watch when he strangles her with that pretty, pretty necklace."

XIV

"Cait?" Fennrys asked for what Kelley sensed would be the last time. "*Where* are the others?"

"She's not going to tell you anything." Kelley sighed.

"Why would you think that?" Fennrys didn't take his eyes off the other Janus, who stood with her back to the subway tunnel wall. The satchel containing her weapons and spell-casting paraphernalia lay off to one side, just out of Cait's reach.

"Because *I* wouldn't."

Fennrys smiled. It wasn't a pleasant expression. "Why not? I asked nicely."

"Still." Kelley shook her head. "Tone of voice is one thing. Holding a knife to someone's throat is another." She gently but firmly put a hand on Fennrys's wrist and forced him to lower the blade. "I'm really sorry about that, Cait," she said over her shoulder. "I like you. You've always been a friend to me and, as far as I can tell, an outstanding Janus Guard. I think my father would agree with that. I don't want to see you hurt."

Cait put a hand to her throat where Fenn's knife blade had drawn a thin line of blood. "Thank you, Kell—"

"But if you don't tell us what we want to know"—Kelley reached up under her hair and undid the clasp on her necklace; the sudden blinding flare from her wings lit up the tunnel like a supernova, and Cait shrank back from the crackling eldritch energy—"I'm going to make you wish you'd never heard of the Otherworld or my father. Or me."

It was hard for Kelley in that moment to ignore Fennrys and the mile-wide grin that split his face. Even though she had invoked her father's name, Kelley was perfectly well aware that she very closely resembled her *mother* in that moment, and she used it to her best advantage. She tucked her clover-charm necklace away in the pocket of her jeans.

"Are you listening to me, Cait?" she asked politely.

Cait nodded, squinting against the fierce, dark light of Kelley's wings.

"Good. Now open the door, and then get out of my way."

* * *

Cait had warned them that they were in for a fight if they went down into the Faerie sanctuary, and she'd been right. Fenn insisted that she accompany them—a good call on his part. Cait's spell-casting skills were the only thing that kept the three of them from being horribly mangled by the screaming wraiths that guarded the tunnel, since she'd overheard what happened to the others after Maddox told her to stand guard outside. As Cait relayed the story, Kelley suspected that gratitude for Maddox's act was one of the reasons she had agreed to help them—that, and the fact that she seemed genuinely appalled by Godwyn's little "mission."

Chaos was in full swing when they emerged from the old Croton Aqueduct tunnel into the vaulting underground hideaway. The shadowy air of the upper reaches of the cavern was made darker by screeching clouds of smoke-winged birds. Below, Lost Fae of all shapes and sizes battled fiercely with a battalion of redcaps. And more—strange, horrid Fae darted here and there, wielding claws and fangs and weapons. There was blood. And bodies.

Sonny. Where is he? Kelley thought, scanning.

She didn't see him—but she did see Godwyn, hacking the head off a tall, gray-skinned goatish Fae with a savagery that turned her stomach. She couldn't hear him over the din, but she knew from past experience that he was singing.

Distracted by the sight, Kelley stepped away from the mouth of the tunnel entrance, out onto the wide ledge and into the open. She'd furled her Faerie wings as she'd run

155

through the tunnels with Cait and Fennrys. She probably looked just like any other human changeling, and she was in the company of two Janus. It was only natural that the Lost would take her for one of them and act accordingly. As far as they were concerned, the Janus were the enemy—and so Kelley couldn't really blame the huge, hideous creature that came thundering up the path toward them, roaring and swinging mallet-like fists.

Jeez! she thought, scrambling desperately out of the way. *Harvicc must have been the* runt *of his ogre litter!*

The creature paused for an instant, sniffing the air, and swung his massive head in Fenn's direction. Suddenly Fennrys was scrambling, too. If the ogre managed to connect with one of his wild blows, there would be nothing left of the Wolf but a fine red mist. Kelley gathered herself, but an explosion right beside her head sent her diving for cover.

The Faerie girl attacking her was tiny, almost doll-like, but she had a wicked throwing arm. With the speed of an automatic tennis-ball cannon, the creature fished can after can of Dr Pepper and cream soda from the burlap sack slung over her shoulder, lobbing them at Kelley's head wrapped in some kind of incendiary magick spell. Kelley frantically dodged the glowing aluminum missiles—which exploded when they hit the cave wall behind her, spewing hissing liquid that ate holes in the rock like sulfuric acid.

The tiny creature threw her last can. Sprouting a pair of iridescent wings, she took to the air, zipping toward Kelley. Her slender wings flicked out from her shoulders, glittering like switchblades and—Kelley discovered—just as sharp.

Bleeding from a long shallow cut on her forearm, Kelley spun away from the girl's frenzied attack. As her assailant swept past, Kelley lashed out with an angry indigo firebolt that stunned the naiad and sent her careening into a shallow pond. She hit the water hard with a pained shriek.

The ogre, fighting both Fennrys and Cait, swung his massive head around when he heard the cry. He snorted like a bull in an arena, focusing all of his murderous attention suddenly, acutely, on Kelley.

Tired of being intimidated—especially by people she was there to *help*—Kelley unfurled her wings, and the dazzling brilliance made even her own vision dance with spots for a moment. But she swallowed nervously and backed up half a dozen steps when she saw it didn't exactly have the flash-blinding effect she'd intended.

"He's got no eyes, Princess," said a voice from over her shoulder. "But nice try."

Kelley spun around and saw Maddox standing there, glowering down at her.

"Madd! Thank God!" she gasped, almost weak with relief. Behind her, Fennrys charged the ogre again. "Where's Sonny?"

"What do you care?"

Oh, right. Maddox was pretty pissed at her . . . and she didn't have time for it.

"Shove the righteous indignation, Maddox," she snapped. "Fenn told me about the rogue Janus—we're here to help!"

"She's telling the truth," Cait said over her shoulder. She

157

looked as though she was struggling to weave some kind of binding spell that would hopefully subdue the monster without hurting him, but even she didn't seem to be having much success.

Maddox looked back and forth between them for a moment. Then he seemed to make up his mind. He sprinted past Kelley and leaped for one of the troll's hammer-fisted arms—holding him back while Fennrys attacked from the other side, punching the creature in the head repeatedly to no avail.

"Oy! Careful!" Maddox called to his Janus compatriot. "He's one of the good guys!"

"Tell that to him!" Fennrys grunted in pain as the ogre heaved himself backward, slamming the Wolf hard into the cavern wall. Cait cast another bunch of binding strands—to barely discernible effect—and Kelley stood by feeling utterly useless. She had so much power roiling around inside her, but neither the skill nor the experience to wield it effectively. One panicked turn as a kestrel hardly counted for much—especially when she couldn't seem to replicate the feat.

"Thinking makes it so," my ass, *Tyff,* she thought.

The hulking thing swatted Cait into the air with a flailing backhand and she hit the ground heavily, all the air leaving her lungs in a whoosh.

C'mon, Kelley told herself angrily. *It's just like performing. It's just like that moment before the curtains slide open: you take a breath, you reach inside yourself, and you make something out of nothing.*

Magick, theater . . . was it really so different?

She looked up at the ogre and thought of Caliban, the monster in *The Tempest*, and how the spirits of the island had subdued him—lulling him into sleep with sound. *This* monster might not have eyes, she thought, but she was pretty sure there was nothing wrong with his ears.

In her mind, Kelley could see the lines on the page of her latest play script, and she concentrated on shaping those words with her magick, just as Shakespeare's spirits had:

> *Sometimes a thousand twangling instruments*
> *Will hum about mine ears, and sometime voices*

Kelley imagined Caliban's rough voice, full of wonder and longing. . . .

> *That if I then had waked after long sleep*
> *Will make me sleep again . . .*

She let the words flow silently through her mind like an incantation.

> *. . . and then in dreaming*
> *The clouds methought would open and show riches*
> *Ready to drop upon me, that when I waked*
> *I cried to dream again.*

And then she gathered the sensation, almost like packing together a big fluffy snowball, and cast it out toward the ogre, imagining the ball bursting just above him. The sweet sounds of far-off music drifted around the great beast, and he shook his huge, lumpy head in sudden confusion.

Dream, Kelley urged silently. Sleep and dream. . . .

For a long, breathless moment, she didn't think it would work. The creature had shrugged off even Cait's most expert spells.

But then she saw his great head nod. His tiny, tufted ears twitched drowsily, and then the ogre pitched forward onto his front and began, almost instantly, to snore.

Cait struggled to her feet, looking back and forth from Kelley to the rumbling mountain of unconscious ogre. "Nice."

Kelley furled her wings. "Thanks."

Fennrys and Maddox were staring at her.

"Satisfied?" she asked Maddox.

He nodded.

"Good. Where's Sonny?"

He was, of course, right where she expected him to be.

Smack in the dead center of the chaos. And he wasn't alone.

Even from where she stood, on a ledge midway between the high tunnel entrance and the floor of the cavern below, Kelley instantly recognized the beautiful huntress at his side. Her name, Kelley remembered, was Carys, and she'd confronted Kelley in Herne's Tavern all those months ago about the unsavory company she kept. Kelley didn't exactly know what to think when she saw the Faerie woman fighting back-to-back with that very same unsavory company—Sonny Flannery.

Working in effortless tandem, Sonny and Carys dispatched a trio of attacking redcaps. She saw Carys laughing breathlessly with excitement—and couldn't help but notice Sonny's answering grin.

Camaraderie isn't supposed to look that much like flirting . . . is it?

At her side Kelley heard Cait draw breath in a hiss. She followed Cait's gaze. Selene, another Janus, was hiding far up in the shadows, picking off Lost Fae one at a time with her deadly accurate arrows.

"Traitorous bitch," Cait snarled. "She's mine."

Cait glanced over her shoulder at Kelley, almost as if waiting for her permission.

Kelley nodded curtly. "Go," she said.

Cait pulled a pair of short, wicked-looking swords out of her bag. The blades gleamed with a subtle orange light when she whirled them through the air in a brief salute. And then Cait was gone—running along the narrow path that led up toward the alcove where Selene perched.

Kelley watched her go. She knew that Cait and Selene had been good friends before that moment—but the look on Cait's face made her glad she wasn't Selene just then.

Suddenly, Kelley found herself yanked backward through the air by the grasping talons of one of the screeching black demon birds. Fennrys and Maddox both made a desperate grab for her and missed as the bird released its grip. Kelley plummeted through the air. Her wings flared brightly—but not fast enough—just before she hit the surface of the dark pool below with a loud, painful splash. She sank beneath the surface, and something sinewy and scaly wrapped around Kelley's waist and began to pull her down. The light from her wings flickered and died, and she was drawn into darkness.

She was getting *so* damned tired of almost drowning—and she wondered if this would be the time that wasn't "almost." Her vision began to tunnel, a reddish-gray haze creeping in at the edges. But before the light disappeared completely, Kelley looked up and saw the silhouette of a head and shoulders appear, and then the silvery surface of the water was shattered as a strong hand reached down and grasped her by one wrist.

With a heave, and the slash of a blade, Sonny had her out of the deadly pool and up onto the mossy bank, his body falling heavily onto hers as he interposed himself between her and the flailing water wight. Coughing and kicking, Kelley pushed herself back from the edge of the pool. Sonny kicked one last time at the creature with the heel of his boot and then scrambled back himself, half dragging Kelley with him. She was shaking hard enough for her teeth to rattle, and he wrapped her in a fierce embrace.

Without thinking, Kelley lifted her face to his. Sonny's lips felt as though they would devour her as his hands tangled fiercely in her hair. Kelley wrapped her arms around his neck and returned his passion in equal measure. He was there. He was real. He was kissing her, stealing her breath away.

XV

Sonny had thought for an instant that he'd been imag-ining things—that the flaring purple light he'd seen plummeting through the cavern like a falling star was just his mind playing tricks on him. But he'd run for the water anyway, diving in without a second thought, to find it wasn't his imagination. She was here and she was in his arms. Kelley's mouth opened hungrily beneath Sonny's lips, and his arms tightened around her, crushing her to his chest. Water poured off them, pooling on the ground where they lay wrapped around each other, arms and legs entwined. Sonny kissed her lips, her eyes, the side of her throat. . . .

And then he remembered.

He pushed Kelley to arm's length as the memory of her words came crashing down on him again like a tidal wave.

"How can you kiss me like that?" he said, his voice husky, thick with choking emotion. "How can you kiss me like that when you don't love me?"

Kelley opened her mouth, but no words came out. Her shoulders heaved with each breath and she dropped her gaze, shaking her head from side to side.

"Sonny, I . . ."

She looked up at him, her green eyes shining too brightly, as if brimming with unshed tears, and he had to look away. He couldn't bear to look into her eyes. If she really didn't love him—and she'd already said that plain as day behind his back—then it would kill him to have her say it to his face. Sonny stared over his shoulder at the ruffled surface of the dark water he'd just dragged her out of.

When Kelley remained silent and shivering, he said, "Are you hurt?"

She just shook her head.

Sonny rocked back on his haunches and pushed the dripping hair from his face, peering at her closely. She seemed almost as if she was in shock. "*Are* you?" he asked again.

"No," she said, her voice barely above a whisper.

"Good." His own voice was cold and hard in his ears. "Then tell me what you're doing here." He stood and backed away from Kelley where she knelt upon the ground. "Are you with *them*? The ones killing the Lost—"

"No!" Kelley protested, climbing to her feet. "How could you even think such a thing! I came here with Fenn to help stop them!"

Fennrys. Sonny felt as though he'd been sucker punched. Kelley was with Fennrys. "I see," he said.

The blood drained from Kelley's cheeks. "I don't think you do," she said.

Sonny uttered a brief, humorless laugh and turned to walk away.

"I lied, Sonny," Kelley said abruptly.

Sonny's glance snapped back to her face. "What?"

"I *lied*," she said emphatically. "I almost can't believe that you haven't figured that out yet."

"You . . ."

"Lied. To you. *About* you. About the way I feel."

"So you never—"

"*Stopped* loving you."

It was Sonny's turn for shock. He shook his head slowly in disbelief, uncertain whether he'd really heard what he thought. "But . . . Faerie can't lie," he said.

"Of *course* they can!" Kelley said. "They do it all the time. They just do it while telling the truth."

He stared at her. A single word clawed up his throat and tore from his lips: *"Why?"*

"I . . ." Kelley hesitated. "I can't tell you."

"I see." *Faerie games*, Sonny thought bleakly. "May I ask,

then," he said with brittle politeness, "exactly how you managed such a thing?"

His gaze followed Kelley's hand as she dug into her pocket and pulled out the clover charm on its silver chain. Sonny stared at the green amber pendant for a long moment as it swung before his eyes, gleaming softly. Then he shook his head.

"I don't understand."

"The charm *lets* me lie," Kelley said, her cheeks turning red. "It reins in my . . . my Faerieness so well that I can lie just like a normal person."

"No," Sonny said. "I understand how you did it. I do *not* understand why."

"I know. Just . . . let me explain," Kelley pleaded. "I *promise* this will all make sense and then you and I can be together and things can get back to normal—"

"No. Kelley." Sonny stopped her before she could say anything else. His mind was reeling. "No. I don't think they can."

"What?" Kelley's voice cracked on the word. "What do you mean?"

Sonny turned and looked at her. "I mean that—whatever's really going on here—when this is all over, I'm going back to the Otherworld, Kelley. Alone."

"You can't be serious. Do you really think I would have done what I did without a really good damned reason, Sonny? Is that what you think of me?"

166

"No, Kelley. I—"

"Then what? Is your going back to the Otherworld supposed to be some kind of punishment for me hurting you?" Kelley asked. "Is that it?"

"No. I'm not punishing you." His heart ached. "I wouldn't do that. I just don't know if I can ever actually trust you again."

"Because I lied to you."

"Because you *can* lie to me!" Sonny rounded on her, finally. Angry. Hurt. More hurt than he'd ever been and more angry than he'd ever thought possible. "How in hell will I ever know when you're telling the truth?"

"That's called being human, Sonny!" Kelley almost shouted back at him. "No one *ever* knows! Some things you just have to take on faith and believe in at the risk of getting hurt. It's one of the things that the Fair Folk will never understand, and it's something that sets us apart from them. The fact that each and every time we believe in each other we take a risk. Because we know that it might *not* be truth. But we also know that it *might* be."

Sonny didn't know what to say. Kelley was standing right in front of him, telling him she still loved him . . . and he stood there *arguing* with her. What in the name of the goddess was wrong with him? He didn't know.

Of course you do. You're afraid.

Sonny had never been afraid of anything in his life. Not like this. He'd faced down nightmares—Black Shuck and Wild Hunters, all manner of Faerie abominations—without so much as breaking a sweat. But this girl he'd once thought of as nothing more that a "silly little actress" could reduce him to a quivering boy. The thought of losing Kelley again sent panic tremors cascading down his limbs, and Sonny realized that the only thing he was afraid of was her absence. And as much as he'd tried to shield her all those times, tried to be her hero, Kelley wasn't the one who needed protecting.

What she'd done . . . he didn't even remotely understand why she'd done it, but at least now he knew that it wasn't because she'd stopped caring. Sonny wondered—if the tables had been turned—if *he* would have had the strength to drive *her* away.

He doubted it. She was stronger than he was. He was proud of her.

And it was killing Sonny to have her standing there in front of him, close enough to touch and so achingly beautiful. Her damp hair cascaded in dark auburn ringlets around her pale cheeks, and her eyes glittered fiercely, lashes spangled with water droplets. His Firecracker . . .

"Don't leave me, Sonny," she said softly.

It was too much.

He was across the space between them in two strides, and she was in his arms again. Sonny shoved aside his uncertainty for the moment and lost himself in her kiss.

"I cannot lose you again, Kelley," he said urgently. "I will not. Not again. You have to tell me the truth. If this is not . . . *real* . . . if it's not . . ."

She kissed him, silencing his doubts as he gave in to the elation of having her in his arms once more.

"Did that feel like a lie?" she whispered against his lips.

Sonny pulled her close in a fierce embrace. Kelley's hands splayed across his chest as he held her. He could feel the coolness of her fingertips dancing lightly in the hollow at the base of his throat.

"Sonny," she asked, after she'd been silent for a long moment, her head resting in the hollow of his shoulder, "where's your Janus medallion?"

"I lost it in the Otherworld," he murmured, brushing his lip across the top of her hair. "Fighting alongside your other boyfriend, the Fennrys Wolf."

Kelley sputtered hotly. "He is *not*—"

But Sonny silenced her with another kiss. He took her face in his hands so that he could look into her eyes. "I know," he said. "It was a joke."

"It was a lousy one."

"Will you *please* tell me now why you lied to me, Kelley?" he asked.

She hesitated for another moment, looking up at him. She opened her mouth to speak.

Overhead, another cloud of demon birds swept past, cawing harshly, and Carys vaulted suddenly over the stone parapet, breathing heavily and bleeding from a cut over her eye. She nodded curtly to Kelley, then spoke directly to Sonny. "We could use you back in the fray. We are outnumbered."

Sonny reluctantly broke away from Kelley and looked back toward the main cavern, where the sounds of fighting had intensified. Suddenly, a terrible thought occurred to him. "Outnumbered and outwitted," he said grimly, and swore under his breath, stooping to pick up the sword he'd borrowed from the huntress earlier.

"What's that supposed to mean?" Kelley asked.

"He means this is no joyride, Princess," Carys explained, wiping her forehead with the back of her arm. "No whim of an excursion. There is muscle and a *lot* of magick behind this attack."

"Thanks. Yeah. I got that." Kelley bristled at the huntress. "Why are they doing this, Sonny? Why attack the Lost?"

"Because they were defenseless," he answered. "And because the attack here drew off all of Herne's warriors that were topside. The two attacks were coordinated, yes—but the objective, I think now, was *not* the sanctuary."

Carys's eyes went wide. "It was the *Tavern*. . . ."

In the distance, the sounds of violence erupted again, and the entire structure of the reservoir seemed to be in danger of collapsing. A rain of dirt and small stones rattled down the far rock face of the cavern, where a huddle of dryads shrieked and scrambled for cover.

Carys's expression became anguished.

"Go," Sonny said. He turned to Kelley and she nodded. He swung back to Carys and said, "Go—I'm right behind you."

The huntress nodded and disappeared swiftly back over the earthen wall.

"Kelley . . ." Sonny turned to her. "I need you to do something."

"Anything," she answered without hesitation.

"I need you to go."

Anything except that, it seemed. "What?" She looked stricken. "*Why?* Sonny—"

"It's not that." Sonny gripped her shoulders and looked her in the eyes. "I cannot go back up to the Tavern. But I need to find out what's going on up there. Can *you* do that for me?"

"Why can't you come with me?"

"Herne made me promise him I would not go back that way. I don't know why."

"Oh . . ." Kelley went suddenly very still.

Sonny looked at her, wondering.

"You're right," she said abruptly. "You should stay here. I can handle this by myself."

She gazed up at him, unblinking, with those perfect green eyes, and Sonny felt a surge of longing. He'd only just gotten her back. How could he send her away again? "You know how to cast a veil now, right?" he said.

Kelley nodded. "Yeah. Pretty good one." She flickered out of sight and then reappeared right before his eyes.

"That's my girl," he said, grinning. "Cast a veil and hold it fast. Don't drop it for anyone. Not even Herne. Just find out what's going on up there and come back and tell me. Can you do that?"

"Of course I can." She lifted her chin and returned his stare.

"All right," he said, wanting to hold her fast and not let her go. . . . "Go then."

"I'll be back as soon as I can."

He felt his heart clench but struggled to smile encouragement.

"Sonny . . ."

He held a finger to her lips. "We'll talk later," he said. "For now, just . . . go."

"Okay." Kelley nodded and headed toward the archway.

"Kelley . . ."

She stopped and looked back.

"Be careful" was all Sonny could say. Then he turned his face away so that Kelley would not see what it cost him to let her leave him. Again.

"You, too," she said.

When he looked back, the only thing left of her was the sound of her already invisible feet pounding up the dark passageway toward the tunnel.

XVI

Kelley slowed her pace as she approached the end of the corridor. She stepped up to the wall blocking her way and placed her hand on its smooth surface. It almost felt like water under her palm. A veil. A strong, magickal barrier between the passageway and Herne's Tavern, which would have been impossible for almost anyone to break through. Kelley simply ran her fingertip down the center of the veil, and it parted as surely as if she'd just undone a zipper.

She stepped into the hallway, staring at her finger. It tingled a bit.

The polished marble floor branched off to the left and the

right. Kelley mentally flipped a coin and followed the left passageway. It led through a series of galleries, curving toward the courtyard at the center of the Tavern. By the time she reached the yard, Kelley had been forced to step over no fewer than five bodies of dead Faerie warriors and she was nearly hyperventilating. The air in the garden was filled with the perfume of night-blooming flowers and Kelley gulped at it, trying to clear the horrid images of the dead Fae from her mind and maintain her focus and concentration enough so that her veil would not fall. Not, she thought, that it would do her any good if her heart kept beating so loudly.

The garden courtyard lay silent, relatively undisturbed. At least, it certainly wasn't the shambles it had been in the aftermath of Mabh's attack on Halloween, when she'd come to claim her daughter. Rather, it was eerily still. Kelley noticed that all of the fire sprites—the tiny incandescent fae that had lit up the garden like strings of Christmas lights the last time she was there—were gone. Fled, most likely.

The whole place had a stark, forlorn feeling to it. Moving between the delicate garden furniture and the splashing fountains, Kelley realized something was different. Wrong . . .

Missing.

The Greenman.

The great old gnarled shrubby creature was gone. Kelley ran over to a hole in the earth that gaped like a jagged wound. It was the spot where Kelley had once seen the Greenman— all that was left of the Greenman—rooted and settled, a giant living lump of tangled forest greenery, drinking whiskey from a barrel-sized mug. It looked as though someone had dug him up by the roots and carted him away.

Now there was only the scent of wet clay and the sharp, piney tang of broken branches. Bright green sap oozed from the splintered ends of roots still stuck in the ground. The hole went down so far that Kelley could barely see the bottom in the dim light.

A splash of color in the corner of her eye caught her attention. Trampled in the dirt at the far edge of the hole was an orange floppy hat. Not far from it lay the crumpled form of a small, gnomelike creature. A dagger lay on the ground next to him and there was an arrow in his back. Kelley swallowed and turned away. There was nothing to be done for the poor thing—that much was certain.

Over near where the fountain stood in the middle of the flagstone terrace, Kelley saw a dark shape spread out upon the ground. She approached it warily and saw that it was a large, dead bird. Kelley nudged it with her foot, turning it over. It was just like the ones that had attacked in the underground sanctuary, with midnight feathers on its back and long, tapered wings. Splashes of silver-gray and white ran down its front. Its beak was long and sharp—Kelley thought it looked like some kind of heron, maybe—and its eyes, frozen open in death, were blood-red. There was something familiar about the dead bird. It reminded her of . . . something. A powerful sense of recognition swept over her, and she could not tear

175

herself free from the gaze of that unblinking crimson eye staring reproachfully up at her.

Finally she turned away from the courtyard and went running through the Tavern halls, from room to sparkling room, checking to see if she could find anyone else. Here and there, another dead Fae warrior in glittering armor lay crumpled on the floor, but she found no one who could tell her what had happened. She investigated the ballrooms, the chandelier-festooned dining hall, the hidden oak-paneled hallway that led to the shores of the lake surrounding the Isle of Avalon.

Kelley stepped through the archway and saw with relief that the Isle still slumbered peacefully far out in the middle of the lake. Whatever strife had occurred in Herne's sanctuary, it had not reached this far. She gazed out upon the scene of timeless tranquility and felt a sharp pang, remembering the time when Sonny had brought her here. He had first kissed her on that shore.

You don't have time for this, she told herself sternly, and turned back toward the Tavern. Invisible, sneakered feet carried her swiftly, silently, as she backtracked all the way around to where she'd come up from the reservoir. Only this time, she started down the hallway that angled off to the right—and stumbled over a patch of empty space. At least, it looked empty. Kelley reached out a hand, feeling tentatively for whatever it was that had tripped her. A barefooted leg shimmered into view, followed by the rest of the tanned, heavily muscled form of Herne the Hunter, sprawled on the ground, his fingers curled senselessly around the hilt of a sword.

"Herne!" Kelley gasped in horror, dropping her own veil of invisibility as she fell to her knees next to the Hunter's inert form. She pushed the chestnut-brown hair from his face and saw blood at the corner of his mouth. A consequence, no doubt, of at least one of the two arrows that protruded from his chest. Kelley went weak with relief when she saw that the feathered fletchings still quivered slightly with his breathing.

She tried to lift him into a sitting position but he was deadweight. She heaved with all of her might, and he moaned in semiconscious agony. He slumped back down in a heap. Kelley was struck in that instant by how much Sonny resembled him. It was in the small details—the line of the Hunter's jaw and the set of his eyes—but it was unmistakable. She felt a sharp stab of fear at the thought, her mind replacing the father with the son. What if it had been Sonny lying there?

It was an eerie echo of her recurring nightmare, and Kelley felt a momentary sense of rising panic. But then Herne twitched and coughed raggedly, spilling more blood from his wounds onto the Tavern floor. Kelley knew she had to do something quick.

She moved around behind him and tried to help him sit up, gasping when she felt a searing pain along her forearm. She glanced down and saw that Herne carried a small, elegant dagger tucked into his belt at the small of his back. The blade must have been pure iron because the barest brush of her skin along its surface had left an angry red welt. Kelley figured that

177

the Hunter must have carried it as insurance against Faerie violence. He hadn't drawn it, though. Hadn't had a chance to use it, because he'd been attacked from afar—by an archer. Kelley thought of Selene, and a hot, violent wash of rage flooded through her.

She heard a noise coming around the corner, and the anger was replaced by cold fear. Jenii Greenteeth stepped into view, the goat hooves hidden under her long green skirts making a delicate clicking sound on the polished marble floor.

"*There* you are, you naughty Hunter." The glaistig's eyes flashed with red fire as she regarded Herne with venomous hatred. Her gaze flicked to Kelley. "And if it isn't the little princess. Thank you so much for saving me the trouble of having to track you down in the city. My brother craves his property back."

Her brother? Kelley thought with rising terror. *Her brother is supposed to be dead!*

"What have you done with the charm, little princess?" Jenii sauntered up close to her—*click click click*—and touched the hollow at the base of Kelley's throat. Kelley shuddered in revulsion and batted the glaistig's hand away. She could feel her magick flaring deep within her and she had an overwhelming urge to blast the Green Maiden into a pile of mulch.

The arrogant, smiling goat-girl seemed to know her thoughts—she tsked at Kelley through her horrible teeth and wagged a long, talon-nailed finger. "Now, now. I am of the Autumn Court. Like your mother, you cannot raise a hand against me in violence."

That, Kelley thought with a sudden flash of insight, *is a half-truth*. It was true if the glaistig didn't raise a hand against her first. When they'd fought the glaistigs in the Avalon Grande Theatre, Kelley had been able to shove them around some with her magick. But that had been it—because the Green Maidens had been careful not to attack her directly. So that part was true. But it was also, Kelley thought—if she was to go by twisty Faerie logic—only true insofar as her inheritance of her *mother's* power was concerned. She was only half descended from the Autumn Throne. The other half of her came from the Court of Winter. Of course, her father had inconveniently stripped her of her Unseelie powers, and so her Winter half was, in theory, useless. At least, as far as magick went.

But . . .

Kelley mentally crossed her fingers, hoping her desperate idea would work, and imagined, as hard as she could, that it was her "Winter" hand that she was curling up into an *un*magicked fist. A fist she drove straight into Jenii Greenteeth's nose.

Kelley heard a crumpling sound, and the glaistig howled and threw her arms up instinctively. The long claws of one of her hands raked parallel gashes along Kelley's shoulder, drawing blood, and Kelley grinned triumphantly.

"I'd say *that's* raising a hand against me, Jenii," she snapped, and flared out her wings, blinding the glaistig, who

179

stumbled back a teetering step.

But the Green Maiden recovered almost instantly—much faster than Kelley had expected. She launched herself at Kelley, screeching terribly and baring her mouthful of sharp, emerald teeth. She lunged for Kelley's throat, and Kelley barely managed to scramble back away from the murderous Faerie. She tripped over Herne's prone form and went sprawling herself, badly shaken.

Jenii was on her in a flash, fingers closing around Kelley's windpipe.

Kelley gasped for air, groping behind her to where the Hunter lay still. Her fingertips burned as they brushed the blade of the dagger in his belt. Kelley gritted her teeth and grasped the weapon. Before she could give herself time to think about what she was doing, she thrust it forward, plunging Herne's knife up under the glaistig's rib cage, burying the blade to the hilt. The Green Maiden jerked spasmodically, releasing her grip on Kelley, and her eyes went wide. Her mouth opened in a tiny gasp and she fell backward, dead before she hit the ground.

Slowly, Kelley got to her feet. She looked down at the dead Faerie. The edges of Jenii's skirts were folded back, and Kelley could see that the dainty goat hooves were stained black with the blood of uncounted victims. Viscous green liquid seeped out in a widening pool around her, and weedy-looking seedlings sprouted up and shriveled in the blink of an eye where the spreading edge of Jenii Greenteeth's lifeblood reached.

Kelley stepped away and resolutely turned her back on the creature. She looked down at Herne.

He was barely breathing.

Kelley raised her hand, ignoring the painful welts raised by the iron, and formed the image of a rift in her mind. But the mental picture darkened and twisted of its own accord, and she heard a high-pitched screeching whine. She drew back from the conjuring, startled, before the passageway manifested itself in reality and remembered, suddenly, what her mother had told her about the spaces between the worlds. How they had become dangerous and unnavigable.

Great, she thought. *No mystical highway.*

She might have been willing to risk the passage on her own; not with Herne in such grave condition. But Herne would die if she didn't get him help. Soon.

Kelley didn't know what to do. She certainly didn't have any medical training, and she didn't think dragging an arrow-riddled man-god dressed in buckskin trousers and an oak-leaf wreath through the emergency-entrance doors at Roosevelt Hospital would get her very far. She ran back to the main entrance. Bursting through the shattered archway that used to house the Tavern's front doors, Kelley hailed a Faerie cab.

"Well, hello, missy." The tall blond carriage driver stared down at her through arctic-blue eyes. "Fancy meeting you here."

"Oh thank God!" Kelley gasped.

"Thank Belrix." The driver nodded at the great white horse

who stood looking at Kelley, his ears pricked in her direction. "He was adamant we come round this way again tonight. I didn't know why, but he seemed to sense there was someone who needed a ride."

"I do. Badly. Thank you, Belrix!" Kelley gave the horse a brief, heartfelt hug and turned back to the driver. "Please, ma'am . . ."

"You may call me Olrun."

"Olrun. Okay. Thank you. I'm Kelley."

The driver inclined her head politely, even though it was fairly obvious that she knew perfectly well who Kelley was. Most of Faeriekind did.

"Listen, Olrun." Kelley glanced at the carriage. "Can you drive this thing *out* of the park? Into the real world—I mean the *mortal* world?"

Belrix tossed his head, but his driver just gave Kelley a long look. "For what cause would I do such a thing, Princess?"

"I need to get Herne to safety."

"The Horned One?" Olrun's eyes flashed with concern. "But he is—"

"Injured. Badly." Kelley gestured behind her at the ruins of the Tavern's front doors. "I can explain as we go, but time's wasting and he needs medical attention."

Olrun nodded and wrapped the reins around the front rail of the carriage. "If it is for the sake of the Hunter, then yes. I will help you."

"I can't pay you. Not now. But I will—"

"Say nothing of this." The driver held up a hand, very kindly saving Kelley from committing herself to an unspecified indebtedness. "The Horned One long ago earned my friendship." She leaped down from her perch on the driver's bench with a surprising lightness for one so tall and stalked alongside Kelley as she ran back into the Tavern and led the way to where Herne still sprawled beside the body of the dead glaistig.

"Boy. It's a good thing you've got clout, pal," Kelley ground out between clenched teeth as she struggled to raise Herne up off the ground so that she could help Olrun get him out to the carriage. It was wasted effort. The Hunter was far too heavily muscled. But Olrun shouldered her gently out of the way. Kelley stood back as, without even a grunt of effort, the big blond woman knelt down and lifted Herne in her arms, carrying him as effortlessly as if he were a baby, out to the waiting carriage, where she settled him on the plush upholstered seat. Kelley climbed up and sat on the bench opposite, staring worriedly at Herne's chest, where the rise and fall was barely discernible. His breathing was so shallow. . . .

Olrun leaned him gently forward and eyed the two arrows. One of them had gone all the way through Herne's chest and protruded out his back, making it impossible for him to lie down flat. "Can't leave it sticking out like that . . . ," she muttered grimly.

Kelley fought down the surge of bile in her throat as Olrun snapped off the barbed arrowhead and pulled the shaft free, fresh blood following in its wake. She stripped off the jacket she wore and wrapped it around Herne's shoulder, stanching the flow a bit. Not enough, Kelley thought as she held the garment pressed to the Hunter's wound while Olrun tucked the fluffy purple carriage blanket around him, unmindful of the blood.

Then Olrun vaulted into the driver's seat and snatched up the reins. Kelley told her where they were headed and, without so much as a raised eyebrow, the woman turned and slapped the reins, shouting encouragement to her massive white horse. The carriage lurched forward, and the spoked wheels began to turn faster and faster.

Kelley held on to the side rail of the carriage and watched as the world around her began to blur.

XVII

Sonny tightened his grip on his sword and started to run.

He had spotted Fennrys in a far corner, busily engaged in hand-to-hand combat. Hand-to-hoof, more like— the thing he fought was bestial; the deer-hoofed creature reared and kicked with a viciousness that was as surprising as its mouthful of knifelike teeth. A sianach, it was one of a particularly scarce breed of solitary Fae—even among the Fair Folk, the creature was regarded as almost a nightmarish myth.

But that wasn't the only reason Sonny was running. Ghost was climbing behind where Fennrys fought the sianach, light glinting off the dagger clutched in his bloodless fist. He would ambush Fennrys from above and drive that knife between the Wolf's shoulder blades before Fenn even knew what was happening.

Sonny leaped as the pale renegade Janus sprang at Fennrys from above. Sonny's shoulder caught Ghost high on the side of his rib cage and knocked him from his trajectory. He hit the ground heavily and rolled down an incline. Sonny scrambled after him, struggling to keep his footing on the loose shale of the uneven cavern floor. Ghost twisted in his tumbling and, with the kind of startling agility that had been trained into all the Janus, sprang back to his feet.

He flew at Sonny, eyes rolling white in his head and his mouth open wide, teeth bared in an animal grimace. Sonny shuddered to think of all the Fae that had met their ends at his hands, whether they deserved it or not. He'd never seen anyone so far gone in battle madness—not even Fennrys, with his legendary berserker Viking rages—and the sight of it was horrifying. The corners of Ghost's screaming mouth were webbed with foam, almost as if he were a rabid dog. He went for Sonny's eyes, knife in one hand, fingers of the other splayed wide and hooked like talons. Sonny knocked those lethal hands aside with a sweeping block of his forearm and pivoted away as Ghost lunged off-balance to one side. But the other Janus used his sinewy strength to his advantage. Propelled by his own momentum, he snaked back around in front of Sonny to deliver a head-butt to Sonny's temple that momentarily blinded him and sent him reeling backward.

The next thing Sonny knew, Ghost was on him. His dagger looked as if its black blade had been hewn from obsidian, and it glittered wickedly as it descended toward Sonny's heart. Sonny fell, his spine slamming into the stone floor, and rolled frantically to the side, taking Ghost with him.

In the scramble, he felt a sudden, sharp jolt.

Sonny gasped as the wetness spread outward from the center of his T-shirt and, heaving Ghost's tangled limbs away from him, he frantically felt for the wound. There wasn't one. The knife had not pierced his chest. Instead, the blade had twisted in Ghost's sweat-slick palm and slid effortlessly between the young man's ribs. It quivered with the beating of his heart—once, twice . . . and then was still.

Sonny sensed Fennrys coming up to stand with him as he looked down at the face of the tortured young man he'd only ever known by a mocking nickname.

"Ghost . . . ," he murmured.

"Étienne," Fennrys said, as if sensing what Sonny was thinking. "His real name was Étienne."

"I didn't know."

"I don't think many of us did." Fennrys shrugged. "He wasn't really the type to tell you unless you asked."

Sonny turned and looked at Fennrys. "You asked?"

"We got on."

"Did he ever say anything about . . . this?"

"No, Sonny." Fennrys stared at him flatly. "We got on, but

I'm not one of the renegades. They didn't include me in their devious little games. I knew nothing about any of this until I overheard Bryan and Beni talking. And *they* didn't really seem to have the whole picture either. Neither did Cait, although she still led Godwyn and his minions down here, in spite of any misgivings she might have had."

"I didn't think you were involved," Sonny said quietly. *Not with this . . .*

"I'm not."

It *had* been a joke when Sonny called Fennrys Kelley's "new boyfriend." Still . . . he couldn't help feeling a hot rush of blood behind his eyes as he stood there beside the other Janus—at the thought of all the time that he had spent with Kelley while Sonny had been chasing the Wild Hunt. Time that should have been *his.*

Trust her, he said to himself. *Believe in her.*

He had to. But *why* had she lied to him?

Fennrys crouched and slid Ghost's eyelids closed, shuttering his sightless, staring gaze. He stood quietly and said, "Anyway. Thanks for the save."

"No problem," Sonny said, and made himself unclench his hand, which had balled into a fist at the thought of Fennrys and Kelley together.

They gazed down at the lifeless body at Sonny's feet. With his eyes closed like that, Sonny thought, Ghost looked almost peaceful. There was the hint of a smile on his lips. Sonny felt a wave of sadness wash over him. It was followed closely by a surge of anger. He thought of Dunnbolt, Neerya's ogre companion, viciously blinded, and he remembered that he had made a silent promise to exact an answer for that cruelty. That answer had come. All Sonny knew was that *this* was not what he had wanted. This was not supposed to have happened.

Cait appeared beside them suddenly, panting for breath. She gazed down at the lifeless form of their once-brother. Then she turned and spat to one side, as if to clear a bad taste from her mouth, and glanced at Sonny's face. "I wouldn't shed too many tears over that homicidal little rodent if I were you," she said. "He got what he deserved."

Sonny saw that Cait held a broken bow in her small, capable hands. The Janus sorceress threw the weapon to the ground in disgust, anger dark in her eyes.

"Selene got away from me," she said. "But she won't be shooting any more arrows anytime soon. Not with that dislocated shoulder . . ."

"Remind me never to make an enemy of you, Cait," Sonny said quietly.

She blinked in surprise and glanced at Fennrys, who smiled thinly and nodded at Sonny. "What he said."

The tide of the fighting had finally turned in their favor. Carys had marshaled her forces, and the redcaps were in danger of being surrounded. But just before that could happen, the lead redcap pulled a shimmering glass orb out of a leather pouch at his belt. He held it high and then smashed it on the stony ground, instantly opening a rift between the worlds that crackled with eldritch energy.

Shrieking redcaps, demon birds, and all of the mercenary fae they'd brought with them abandoned their adversaries and scrambled for the rift, clawing at and climbing over one another in their haste to get away.

In seconds it was over.

The silence left behind in the wake of the departed foe was weighty, blanketing the cavern. After a moment, sound returned—the drip of water and spilled blood trickling from the stones, the soft moan of someone in pain, the shuffling of ogre feet as Dunnbolt lumbered over, finally awakened from his slumber.

Sonny stared at where the rift still hung in the air, the ragged edges puckering slowly closed around the dark passageway. Fennrys moved to stand beside him.

"What, exactly, just happened here?" the Wolf asked quietly.

"I'm not entirely sure."

Maddox appeared at Sonny's other side. He was limping slightly, but otherwise seemed unhurt. "Looks like a tactical retreat," he said. "Whatever their purpose in coming here . . . I'd say they accomplished it and it was time to cut their losses and run."

"Should we follow them?" Fennrys suggested halfheartedly.

Sonny turned to say something pointed about the relative wisdom of that idea when a frenzied movement from deep within the narrowing rift caught his eye.

"Little help here!" Bob the boucca shouted frantically as he struggled to heave himself out of the rapidly closing rift. Sonny lunged forward and pulled him out just as the thing closed.

Fennrys circled the spot where the portal had appeared. "Okay . . . I know the Gate's unstable these days, but I didn't think rifts were just showing up on command."

"They're not." Bob stooped painfully and picked up a shard of glass from the globe the redcap had shattered on the ground. The boucca was covered in scratches from the grasping things that had attacked him in the Between. "*That* one your redcap leader brought with him. In this."

"Now I know what to ask for, for Christmas," Fennrys said dryly.

"That would be a rare and prized gift indeed," the boucca snorted.

"Right." Maddox gestured to the broken glass. "So who gave it to that bloody redcap then?"

"I really have no idea," Bob said. "But one thing's for sure, whoever it is that's equipping thugs with high-level magickal implements, it is not what I'd call a positive development. Except for me, that is. The timing of the redcaps opening their escape hatch was fortuitous. Another few moments stuck in the Between would have been . . . unpleasant."

The denizens of the reservoir had begun to sort things out in the aftermath of the battle, and Carys was directing her folk to gather and care for the wounded—and sweep the cavern's many nooks and alcoves to see if any of the enemy wounded remained alive.

Bob gestured Sonny out of earshot of the others and, settling himself on a rock, regarded Sonny for a moment. The ancient Fae sighed heavily.

"Right," he said finally. "Telling you any of this goes against my absolute better judgment. But I don't fancy being used. And I don't fancy my friends being used either."

"I'm your friend?" Sonny asked, incredulous. That was not something that he had ever expected to hear Bob say.

Bob turned and glared under a raised eyebrow. "Did I say that?"

Sonny blinked. "Er—no."

"Then just let it alone, why don't you."

"Yes. Yes, I think I will." Sonny wasn't at all certain that friendship with a boucca wasn't substantially fraught with peril.

"At any rate . . ." Bob cleared his throat and continued. "Some time ago, I think I bragged to you in some fashion that I'd never been Auberon's fool."

"You did."

"That statement may not have been entirely accurate."

Sonny glanced up sharply at the boucca. "You . . . *lied* to me?"

"I was misinformed. There's a difference." Bob snorted. "You know perfectly well that I'm not capable—"

"Of lying," Sonny said impatiently. "Yes. Yes, I know. All right, so you were misinformed then. About what? Tell me."

"In a moment. Perhaps."

Seven hells, Sonny cursed silently. Faerie prevarications could be so tedious. He could have made a simple amendment to his demand. He could have said, "Tell me, *Bob*," and the boucca would have had no choice. Instead he waited.

"A question, first," Bob said. "So please you."

Sonny waved a hand for him to get on with it.

"How stands it between you and the princess?"

Sonny frowned and stared at the wall as if the answer to that question might be written there. "I . . . don't know," he said.

"Shouldn't you?" the boucca asked.

Sonny lifted a shoulder. "A few days ago, she said she wanted nothing to do with me."

"She *said* that?" Bob's eyes grew wide.

"Plain as day."

"Are you sure *you* weren't misinformed?"

"I don't know," Sonny snapped. "How does the phrase *I don't love Sonny Flannery* strike you?"

"Oh."

"Yeah."

"And now?"

"And now . . . I'm not really certain what's going on." That much was true—he could still feel Kelley's kiss burning on his lips—but Sonny wasn't sure he felt like telling Bob about what

193

had passed between him and Kelley only a short while earlier.

"So . . ." Bob tugged on his earlobe. "If something were to happen to her . . . something bad . . . that wouldn't bother you?"

"Is she all right? If Kelley is in trouble—"

"That's not answering questions. That's asking them." Bob was gazing at him so intently it almost made Sonny's skin start to crawl. "What if the princess was in dire peril, right at this very moment. Would you care?"

"Of *course* I care." Sonny felt a surge of dread at the thought of Kelley in danger. He could hear the blood begin to pound in his ears as his heart rate accelerated. Bob was still staring, and the air between the two of them began to feel charged, as if a microstorm were brewing in the cavern. Very suddenly, Sonny could not look away from the boucca as Bob took a step toward him. He found himself locked in the circle of that ancient, wily gaze as surely as if it were a prison. The edges of his vision began to tunnel, but the boucca Fae continued to stare deep into Sonny's gray eyes. Fire flashed at the periphery of his sight. Green witch fire. Red mist. Smoke and shadows. Sharp agony lanced though Sonny's head, and he heard a murmur of song from far off. . . .

The music grew louder, and Sonny struggled to remember where in the world he'd heard that tune before. It was *maddeningly* familiar. Then he heard Bob grunt in pain as though he'd been struck by something. The music stopped abruptly, and Sonny staggered back a step or two as though a rope connecting him to the boucca had snapped.

Silence passed between the two of them.

What in the name of the goddess was that all about? Sonny wondered. "If Kelley is in some kind of danger," he said quietly, "I think you'd better tell me."

Bob laughed nervously. His voice, Sonny noticed, was tremulous, and his gnarled hands shook violently as he clasped them together. "Resourceful young thing like that?" Bob muttered. "I think she can take care of herself."

"Are you going to tell me what's going on or not?"

Bob looked up at him, his expression inscrutable. The boucca was, of course, painfully aware that Sonny could compel him with a single word. Sonny didn't. Even if it meant he was sacrificing any chance of learning *why* Kelley had done what she'd done—even if it meant losing her because of that—he could do nothing else. It wouldn't be right. The ancient boucca waited, watching closely as Sonny came to that decision.

Sonny would let Bob keep his secrets.

So Bob told him everything.

"Where is Kelley now?" Bob asked Sonny once his silence had stretched out for a very long time. "Do you know?"

Sonny only half heard the question. His mind was still reeling with the implications of all that Bob had told him.

"She was here," he murmured. "Only a little while ago. I sent her up to the Tavern to try to find Herne."

Herne the Hunter. Herne, his father. *I have a father....*

Sonny dragged his attention back to Bob, who sat waiting patiently for Sonny to digest the bombshell revelations he'd just dropped on him. Not just that he had a father—although that, in itself, was enough. But the idea that his father had apparently passed on the Green Magick to him . . . Sonny was having a hard time assimilating that notion. It was a lot to take in.

The boucca brushed idly at bits of grit that had stuck to the pale green blood seeping from the scratches on his legs.

"What exactly did that to you, Bob?" Sonny asked. "Was it the redcaps?"

"No . . . but good luck to them. Whoever gave them that bottled rift may have wanted them dead rather than just gone, you know. The Between is full of wraiths. Mean ones." The boucca grimaced, gesturing to his leg. "Once I hightailed it out of the Autumn Lands, I hunted around for a rift—they're popping up all over the place now—and tried to make my way here. But the rifts are unstable. I got stuck halfway, and it's not an experience I would recommend. The space between the realms is full of peril. Restless, angry shades. Unquiet dead. A lot of them."

"Where did they all come from?"

"I don't know. There's always a few wanderers—ones that never seem to find their way to their chosen afterlife, be it Heaven, Hell, Elysium, Valhalla, Annwn. . . . But it's never enough to even notice during a passage through the Gate. Now, though, it's like a hornet's nest. And something—or someone—is throwing rocks at it. Mind you"—he looked around at the strewn bodies of fallen Lost Fae—"it seems things are perilous everywhere. Almost makes you want to crawl into a hole and pull it in after you until the storm blows over."

"Except you didn't. You could have lain low in the Otherworld, but you came here instead. Why?" Sonny asked. "What are *you* really doing back in the Hereside, Bob?"

"*Hereside?*" Bob snorted. "Aren't we sounding ever so hip and underground? You've been spending too much time with these Lost Ones, boyo."

Sonny gave him a look and waited.

"Oh, all right." The boucca relented when he realized that Sonny was in no mood for games. "In truth, I was trying to find *you.*"

"Me? Why?"

"You have unique qualifications that I figured might come in handy in my attempts to keep one step ahead of Mabh so she doesn't manage to track me down and wipe clean the tables of my poor memory." He shrugged nonchalantly, but his weird stare intensified. "I also figured I owed you the chance to discover who and what you really are before Mabh compels me to forget."

Sonny stared at him blankly. "How could she? Unless . . ."

Bob's mouth twisted in a grimace. "Aye. Your girlfriend, sweet and lovely, sold me down the river. Handed over my name to the Queen of Air and Darkness without much in the

197

way of a moment's pause."

"Are you sure?"

"In my long years, I've developed certain helpful skill sets. Listening at keyholes is one of them, and it's saved me from having my bacon smoked on more than one occasion."

Sonny shook his head. "I can't believe she'd do a thing like that. Not willingly. Mabh must have coerced her."

"Nudged, yes. Coerced, no." Bob lifted a shoulder. "She didn't have to. All Mabh had to do was remind Kelley what grave danger *you* would be in if anyone found out about your little secret. Insofar as I was at the theater when you went all 'Green Power' scary, I was obviously something of a liability in that respect. Mabh told Kelley she'd take care of things and all she needed was my name. Wasn't long before the dear girl sang like a bird."

"Falcons don't sing," Sonny murmured absently.

"Beg pardon?"

"Oh . . . nothing." When Bob raised an eyebrow at him, he explained. "Apparently Kelley's recently got something of a handle on transformation—glamoured herself into the shape of a fine kestrel, Maddox told me."

"Talented wee thing, she is. So much potential. More's the pity."

"I'm sorry, Bob. I truly am. I still don't understand the way Kelley's been acting. The lies, the betrayal . . . I cannot fathom it."

"You can't?"

"No. Why didn't she come to me? Why didn't she just tell me what was going on? All this deception . . ." Sonny raked a hand through his hair in frustration. "Perhaps her mother's influence is too strong for her to fight against."

Bob snorted in grim amusement. "Oh, Mabh's not blameless, certainly. She rarely is. But if you ask me, I'd say it's really mostly *your* fault."

Sonny opened and closed his mouth. How could this possibly be his fault?

"Don't look at me like that," Bob said. "Weren't *you* the one who conjured a vision for Kelley of the night Mabh went bonkers and transformed Herne and his followers into the Wild Hunt?"

"Yes, but—"

"But what?" Bob pegged Sonny with his keen stare. "But you didn't think that sort of image might make an impression on the girl? Might make her think twice about the consequences of too much power mixed with too much love? What? Never occurred?"

"Not at the time. No." Sonny ground his teeth together. At the time, he hadn't even known that he was in love with Kelley. It had certainly never occurred to him that she felt that way about him.

Bob sniffed in faint disgust. "Mortals have absolutely no sense of prescience."

"No, Bob," Sonny snapped. "We don't. We're *mortal*. We can't see into the future."

The boucca waved a hand dismissively. "It's not so much that you can't as that you choose not to. Everyone can extrapolate possibilities, you know. Ach—never mind. Done's done and, at the end of the long day, none of this is Kelley's fault. Not really."

Sonny looked at him, waiting for an explanation of that statement.

Bob gave him one, but it didn't make him feel any better. "For one thing, she thinks she's your weakness. That if you were able to access the Green Magick, and someone wanted to turn you into a weapon, all they would have to do to get to you would be to go through her. And while she may have overreacted, she also has a point. You were a sight to behold, back at the theater, Sonny Flannery," the boucca said gravely. "You must have scared the hell out of that poor girl. You certainly scared the hell out of me."

XVIII

When Kelley's parents—when the Winslows, that is—had been alive, Emmaline Flannery had trained under Dr. Winslow to work as his assistant in his medical practice. She'd learned enough that, after the Winslows had died in a car accident, she'd gone to work part-time for the local veterinarian.

It wasn't Faerie medicine, Kelley thought, but it was something at least. She hoped she was doing the right thing. The Catskill Mountains seemed awfully far away . . . but that, she soon realized, was only because she was used to taking the bus.

In front of the carriage, Belrix had turned to smoke and mist in front of Kelley's eyes.

As the carriage slowed and Kelley could make out familiar landmarks, she began to have grave misgivings. Especially about how Em would react.

You shouldn't be doing this, she told herself. *This is cruel. You should have called first.*

Of course, she'd lost her cell phone in a river in the Otherworld, and it wasn't like there were any phone booths along the kinds of roads they were traveling.

The sun had disappeared behind the hills by the time they reached their destination. The yard in front of the house where Kelley had grown up was neatly manicured and illuminated by a thin wash of light that spilled down from the screened porch. Kelley was somehow unsurprised to see her aunt standing silhouetted in the doorway, almost as if she was expecting someone. The forgotten tea cup in her hand spilled chamomile dregs onto her slippers as she watched the gleaming white coach pull up in front of the little house, shooing a rolling cloud of ground mist before it.

Kelley leaped from the carriage before it had come to a full stop and ran to hug her astonished aunt, trying to explain in a rush of words that were vastly unqualified for the task. When, really, all Emma needed to understand things was to see the unconscious form of Herne carried up her front steps in the arms of the carriage driver.

Emma looked the same as when Kelley had seen her last—sweater; skirt; her beautiful black hair, just starting to silver in streaks, piled high at the back of her head—except the blue-gray eyes that, of course, reminded Kelley so strongly of Sonny were star-bright with sudden, unshed tears.

"*Acushla*," she said softly, her voice breaking a little on the Irish endearment—"oh, my heart . . ."

Olrun nodded to Kelley's aunt and then brushed past, moving into the house and looking for somewhere to lay the wounded man-god down.

"The guest bedroom," Emma said, recovering her wits more quickly than Kelley would have thought possible. "The second door on the right. Kelley, fetch water into the big pot to boil and bring clean cloths from the linen cupboard and a few of the old sheets to tear for bandages. And the first aid kit—the big one from your father's study."

Emma raised her head high and followed briskly in Olrun's wake, already pushing up the sleeves on her sweater, her expression closed—like a window shuttered tight against a storm. The lone arrow left still protruding from Herne's chest quivered with every pulse and breath.

Questions could wait.

Kelley woke with a start, her head snapping up from the cushion of her forearms on the oak table. Panic crowded her throat for a brief instant before she recognized her surroundings. Home. Emma had sent her out of the room as she and Olrun

203

went about the work of tending to Herne's wounds. Exhausted, Kelley had fallen into a doze sitting in the kitchen—and straight into the same wrenching nightmare as always, or, at least, a variation of it . . . the city, overgrown with rampant vegetation, the black carriage, the white stag.

Sonny dying on the sidewalk.

Only this time, it wasn't bullet holes in his chest that leaked his precious blood onto the sidewalk. This time it was scores and scores of thin, deep cuts, crisscrossing his bare arms and the naked flesh of his torso. As though he'd run at speed through a barbed-wire fence. Blood trickled out onto the ground all around him, and roses of the same brilliantly crimson hue sprouted up in a circle around his body, blooming on twisted canes thick with wicked-sharp thorns. A heavy, sick-sweet floral scent assaulted Kelley's nostrils in the dream. Not the smell of roses, but of something else. Something familiar, but she couldn't quite put her finger on it.

It had turned her stomach in the dream, and she'd awoken with the urge to retch. Kelley grimaced and swallowed a few times, trying to clear the vague queasiness that crept up the back of her throat. In the darkness, she gazed around at the familiar silhouetted shapes of the furniture. Light from the risen moon filtered through lace curtains that hung over the sink, just below the bunched sheaves of dried herbs and wildflowers pinned to the upper sill with rusty iron horse-shoe nails. Kelley knew the names and properties of some of them: sage for clarity of thought and vision, Saint-John's-wort for restfulness and peace, marigold and primrose—those two were for protection, and they hung from every windowsill and door lintel in the place. Protection from the Fae, Kelley knew, and she wondered again what it must have been like for Emma.

All those years, sheltering a Faerie princess under her roof. Wondering what had happened to her own child. It had been a wondrous thing for Emma, the night she and Sonny met. In the theater, on the opening night of Kelley's play. He'd held Emma's hand throughout the entire performance and, before he left to return to the Otherworld, he'd promised Emma that he'd be back. For her, and for Kelley.

He'd come as promised, and Kelley had driven him away.

Kelley went to get a glass of water. Glancing out the kitchen window, she saw that Belrix and the carriage still stood in the little gravel drive. The immense horse had one leg bent, and his head was down, nodding in sleep. Kelley noticed a thin drift of fog clinging to horse and carriage and figured that there was probably a concealing veil cast around them to keep passing motorists from noticing the oddity.

Kelley saw that Emma had cut down some of the herbs from over the window and crushed them with the marble pestle and mortar that she had always used to make homemade poultices and tisanes when Kelley was a little girl. A whiff of odor from a sheaf of dried purple blooms assaulted Kelley's nostrils. It brought back a wave of nausea—that was the same pungent smell from her dream. She suddenly remembered the *last* time she had smelled such a thing and, frowning, she turned on her heel and went to the study.

She sat down at Dr. Winslow's old mahogany desk. It took what felt like forever for the dusty PC to boot up, and then all Kelley could do was glare violently at it as she waited for the painfully slow dial-up connection to pull up a search engine. She had made Emma buy the thing when she decided that she was moving to New York to pursue her acting dreams— so that they could keep in touch. Kelley should have known better. The fact that her "aunt" had been born in rural Ireland well before the turn of the last century and was only now living in modern-day North America because she'd stolen a Faerie king's child—after he'd stolen hers—and had tumbled through time and space was not something Kelley'd had knowledge of when she made the equipment purchase. At the time she'd just thought her aunt was being typically quaint. Her insight into Em's character had grown by leaps and bounds since then. As had her respect and admiration for her strength of will.

"Do you really need to check your email now, dear?" Emma asked, wiping her hands on a towel as she softly closed the bedroom door across the hall and came to stand behind Kelley. Her face was lit only by the blue glow of the electronic screen. She hadn't wept upon seeing Herne—hadn't shed a single tear as she'd worked to save his life—but it looked as though a hundred years of sadness had flowed through her in the last few hours. "Are you expecting messages?"

"No, Em." Kelley reached up to take the hand that Emma laid upon her shoulder and squeezed gently. "I was just trying to Google something that was bugging me."

"I'm not even going to pretend that I know what you're talking about," Emma said, laughing a little wearily as she sat down.

Kelley smiled back. "Google. It's like research."

"Ridiculous piece of machinery. What's wrong with books?" Emma gestured to the walls of books.

"I'm interested in some pretty specific info, Em."

"About?"

Kelley shrugged, uncertain how to explain the niggling thing that had been intruding on her thoughts like a bit of song stuck in her brain that she couldn't shake loose. "A . . . plant."

"Which one?"

"It's stupid."

"A stupid plant?"

"No, no." Kelley shook her head, frowning. "It's stupid that it's bothering me. I just wanted to find out something about vervain."

"It helps to stanch bleeding," Emma said. "I just used some in a poultice dressing. For . . . him."

"I know," Kelley said softly. "How is he?"

"Resting," Emma said. "Your friend the Valkyrie is keeping watch."

"She's a . . . what?" Kelley blinked in surprise. Olrun was a

Valkyrie. Why Kelley should be surprised by that, she didn't know. Not with everything else that she'd experienced lately.

The computer made a wheezing sound, and Emma glanced at it in disdain. She went over to the wall of books and ran a fingertip along the spines. "So. Vervain . . . let me see. What do you want to know about it, dear?"

"Um. Well. Yeah. I sort of wound up in the Otherworld kind of by accident a little while ago—"

Emma turned around, a look of alarm on her face.

"No, no," Kelley assured her quickly. "It's okay. *I'm* okay. I mean . . . except for Sonny and the theater burning down and everything, I'm okay. But that's a whole other story and . . . and . . ."

Suddenly, Kelley found that she could no more stop the tears spilling down her face than she could the words pouring out of her. The events of the last few days came crashing down all around her as she told Emma the whole sorry tale. Emma, who put an arm around her and shushed her as her shoulders shook and her voice cracked. When Kelley was finished, when the tears had finally subsided, Emma pushed the tangled auburn curls away from her face, tucking them behind Kelley's ever-so-slightly pointed ears. Then she dried Kelley's cheeks with a corner of the towel, like she used to do when Kelley was a small child.

"You poor thing." Emma smiled sadly at Kelley. "You should have known you could no more leave behind Sonny than you could leave behind your own arm. He's a part of you.

As much as you're a part of him. I knew it the minute I first saw him. He loves you so, Kelley."

"But he was going to *leave* me, Em." Kelley swallowed painfully, trying not to break down again at the thought. "I don't know if he can ever forgive me for lying. I'm so scared that, when this is all over, he's still going to leave me."

"Nonsense." Emma scoffed as if the idea was too ridiculous to even consider. "I did not give birth to an imbecile. Never you mind. It'll sort itself out. Now." She got up and smoothed down the apron covering her skirt as if that was that, and all Sonny needed was a good talking-to and it would straighten everything out once and for all. It made Kelley feel better knowing Emma thought that. She was his mother, after all. Even if she'd only ever met him once.

"Now. Vervain," Emma said, hauling down an old, leather-bound book from a shelf devoted mostly to gardening texts—both practical and arcane.

"Right. When I was in the Court of Spring, Gwynn ap Nudd—the king—had a container full of the stuff in the palace."

"Vervain in the Spring Lord's house?" Emma asked, a faint frown on her face. It was no small help to Kelley that her aunt didn't even bat an eye at the subject of their discussion. "But 'tis a summer bloomer—in fact it only flowers in mid-to-*late* summer."

"Exactly," Kelley agreed. That much knowledge, at least, she had gleaned from spending summers weeding Em's garden. "And all the other flowers I saw there were spring bloomers, which, y'know, made sense. It just kind of struck me at the time as odd."

"There's not only medicine but very potent magick in that herb, if I recall." Emma frowned down at the book in her hands. She turned on the desk lamp, and Kelley saw that the spine read *A Miscellanie of Mystikal Herbs and their Magikal Properties*. Emma muttered softly to herself as she thumbed to the last of the yellowed pages. Kelley sat fidgeting, staring at the dim band of light that flickered under the closed bedroom door across the hall. Emma must have lit candles to give Herne light in case he regained consciousness. *When* he regained consciousness . . .

"Is Herne going to be okay, Em?"

"Of course he is. Hush now. Don't even talk elsewise." Her aunt's features stiffened, but she didn't look up as she ran a hand down the index at the back of the book. "Don't even *think* it."

Kelley nodded, silent.

Thinking makes it so, she thought, and tried very hard to imagine Herne well and whole again.

Kelley shuddered a little at the remembered sight of the arrow that hadn't gone all the way through. . . . Her aunt had actually had to cut it from the Hunter's flesh. There had been so much blood. Kelley didn't know it was possible for someone to survive that kind of blood loss. Never mind that Herne was centuries old and something of a deity—he bled like every other plain-vanilla mortal Kelley had ever seen hurt.

"Here we are now. Vervain. Latin name *Verbena officinalis,*" Emma read from the entry. "Although not an uncommonly found plant, it has historically been held in sacred regard. It was once as highly revered as mistletoe by the druids and was frequently employed in mystic rites and spells—both harmful and helpful. Used in a medicinal capacity to stanch the flow of blood . . ." Her aunt's eyes flicked toward the guest bedroom door and then back down to the page. "It is also known as iron wort. Vervain is often associated with this metal in ancient cultures, and infusions of vervain were used by blacksmiths in the water baths they used to cool swords, because of the belief that the magical properties of the herb would strengthen the iron. . . ." Emma raised her eyes from the page and scanned the books in front of her, not really seeing them. "Iron is anathema to the Fair Folk. Poison."

Kelley thought about that. She'd always been protected by her clover charm, and so iron had never been an issue for her—not until the fight at the Avalon Grande, of course. She felt a twinge from the wound to her side that was, by now, mostly healed. And the tips of her fingers still throbbed dully from the touch of Herne's knife. *Iron wort.* Why would Gwynn have something like that in his court? *Why do the Fair Folk do anything?* She had been able to make so little sense of most of them that this one mystery added to the bunch didn't really tip the scales.

"What was he like, the Lord of Dreams?" Emma asked.

"Who—Gwynn?"

"Aye. There are a lot of stories about him in the old folk-tales. Mostly contradictory, of course. He's the Lord of Light one moment, the Lord of Darkness the next. Sometimes the Lord of Dreams, sometimes Nightmares. . . . He sounds very mysterious."

Kelley smiled. "I dunno. I like him. In fact, Gwynn is one of the only High Fae that I really almost feel comfortable with. I sort of feel sorry for him, too. For the way Auberon and Titania stole his kingdom from him." Still, she did wonder what on earth Gwynn was doing with a bunch of iron wort, and she said as much.

"Perhaps he uses it for its healing properties, love. You don't know. And there's no sense drawing sinister conclusions out of the thin air. Sometimes what looks like a weed is really just a wildflower. Still . . . it strikes me that something so powerful as *that* particular wildflower should be considered with a great deal of respect. Especially when it finds its way into the hands of beings like the Fair Folk. They wield power like rich men spend money."

"Emma," Kelley said suddenly, thinking of the Hunter, "how did you . . . I mean Herne was—he *is* . . . and you . . ."

"How did a simple country girl ever wind up with a for-est god as a lover, do you mean?" Emma laughed quietly and swept a stray tendril of hair back from her face.

Kelley felt herself blushing. She wasn't sure she was ready to have this kind of conversation with her aunt. "Um. I suppose.

You really don't have to tell me if you don't want to. . . ."

"When I first met Herne," Emma said, "he was mourning the loss of a friend."

"The Greenman," Kelley said.

"Aye. There was something about his sadness that was so deep and so filled with pain—not just for this one friend but for all the ones in his long life that he had lost. He touched my heart." Her voice, the way she said it, made it sound like a song. Like the lullaby she used to sing. "I always suspected that one day he would break it."

"You knew he'd wind up hurting you," Kelley said. "And still you went to him."

"The future's not set in stone, Kelley. And some things are worth risking hurt. A great deal of hurt." Emma's gaze drifted back to the closed door of the guest bedroom, where one of those things now lay, and the hurting in her eyes was all for him.

For Sonny's father.

Kelley thought of Sonny and of how she'd promised to return from Herne's Tavern to tell him what she'd seen. She'd been gone a long time and she wondered if he missed her. Wondered if he was worried about her. If he was looking for her. She hoped he wasn't. She hoped, in fact, that he was far, far away from that place.

"I should check on him," Emma said.

Kelley nodded and followed her aunt across the hall.

Herne lay still and pale in the bed. Olrun was sitting in

the old rocking chair by the window, and she inclined her head silently as Emma crossed to sit on the edge of the bed. Emma put her hands on either side of the Hunter's face, and a small sound escaped his lips. His eyes fluttered open and then closed again. Kelley watched as his lips twitched in the ghost of a smile and he sighed.

"I'm dreaming," he murmured thickly. "It is a good dream. . . ."

"*Acushla,*" Emma whispered. "It is no dream."

Kelley felt her heart swell as Herne's eyes opened again and his face, ravaged with pain, softened into a smile of pure, radiant happiness. Silently, Olrun crossed the floor to where Kelley stood at the threshold and, together, they left the two long-ago lovers to have their reunion in private.

XIX

Carys's folk had set up a kind of Faerie triage and were dealing with the wounded as best they could. Those Lost who possessed healing magick of any kind were moving among those with the most dire injuries. Sonny spotted Neerya flitting among knots of Faerie, distributing food and drink from her precious hoarded stores.

"It seems as though they have things under control here," Bob noted. "Perhaps we'd best go find our girl. I don't like the fact that she hasn't come back yet."

Sonny stood up. He didn't like it either. And he didn't think the Horned One—he didn't think *his father*—would fault him for going topside again on that account. Not when it seemed that all danger had passed . . . and he had so many questions he needed to ask both Herne and Kelley.

He told Maddox and Cait and Fennrys to stay and help. There were an awful lot of hurt Lost. Then he went to find Carys and tell her that he was going up to the Tavern to find Kelley. Carys just embraced him briefly and turned away. She made a fussy show of pouring a mug of water for a wounded gnome, almost as if she didn't want Sonny to be able to read her reaction to his departure. She must have known, Sonny thought, that there was nothing that could have kept him from going. Not if Kelley might be in trouble.

"Powerful trouble," Bob surmised, as he and Sonny headed topside. "It's that damned charm. When I stole it from Gofannon before he could deliver it to the leprechaun, I—what?" He blinked at Sonny's disapproving look. "Oh please! He'd confided in me that he was making a powerful charm that could find and harness enormous magicks—his finest work, he said. He never should have done that. It's not as if he didn't know who he was speaking to."

"He hasn't exactly forgiven you for the theft, you know," Sonny said, keeping his sword at the ready as they strode upward through the long passageway. Everything up ahead seemed quiet, but he wasn't taking any chances.

"Nonsense," Bob scoffed. "I doubt he even knew who he was making the talisman for in the first place or why. And it was *ages* ago. Literally. I'm quite sure all is forgiven." He waved the matter away. "That's the thing about you mortals. You don't know how to properly hold a grudge. I've held grudges for millennia."

"That and we're not prescient."

"Exactly. I mean really," Bob went on, warming to the subject of the failings of mortals as they hurried, "Gofannon's problem was his pride in his work. That and he's just a touch weak-willed. Not his fault. It happens with the artistic types. Sensitive and all that. It's how Auberon talked him into that wee bout of eternal servitude in the first place: 'All the shiny metal you can forge forever, and the only thing you have to give up is your freedom.' . . . Lord, what fools these mortals be, indeed."

"Aye. If only we were all so levelheaded and pragmatic as the Fair Folk." Sonny increased his pace. They were close to the Tavern now.

Bob let the sarcasm pass. "At any rate, whoever wants the Green Magick, they'll need that shiny trinket to get it. That is, if they want to have any hope of *harnessing* all that power instead of being *consumed* by it. Of course . . . they'll also need to find out where the Green Magick is hidden."

"Right. Inside of me."

Bob nodded.

Sonny slowed and stopped before the illusory dead end that led to the Tavern proper. He frowned. "You shouldn't have told me. Kelley was right. No one should ever know—not even me. It's too dangerous."

"Nonsense. I mean—yes, of course, it's too dangerous. If they—whoever 'they' may be—find you, then that's it. This game is up. And only bad things will follow." He looked at Sonny with a vast, unwavering sympathy. "It is a harsh, heavy burden for you to carry, Sonny Flannery. That's why Kelley did what she did. But it is a part of you, and you have the right to know. That's why I did what I did."

The stillness in the Tavern was eerie. The Fae who'd stayed behind to help Herne defend the place were all dead, a lot of them pierced through with arrows. Sonny didn't need magick to tell him they had come from Selene's quiver. Suddenly, as they rounded a corner of one of the Tavern's twisting hallways, Bob stuttered to a halt.

"Careful," he said, putting out a cautionary hand.

There was a red pool of blood on the floor. And beside it . . . a dead glaistig. Sonny stepped over to where the body of Jenii Greenteeth lay in a twisted heap, surrounded by a pool of her own blood—green and thick and smelling sickly sweet like rot. Like mildew. Like flowers that had been left too long in a vase.

Bob nudged the glaistig delicately with his toe. "Very dead."

A dead Green Maiden and no sign of Kelley. Or Herne. It was all very worrying. None of it, however, affected Bob quite so much as the sight that greeted them in the Tavern's main courtyard. When Bob saw the gaping pit in the earth in the corner of the garden, a black hole in the pale moonlight, the expression on his face was exceedingly grim.

He turned to Sonny. "Are you sure Jenii said her brother was still alive?"

"She said barely. That he was insensible. At death's door."

"Not anymore, I'll wager. We have to get out of here," he said suddenly, shouldering past Sonny and edging his way along the ragged lip of the gaping pit. "Now. Damn. *Now* . . ."

"What's the rush?" Sonny asked. Bob had an uncanny nose for smelling trouble approaching and an unusually canny way of dealing with it. But then they both froze. There was a noise coming from the hallway. Bob hissed for Sonny to hide himself.

When Sonny didn't react instantly—hiding was fundamentally against his nature, after all—Bob spun around and delivered a sharp kick to the back of one of Sonny's knees. His leg went out from under him and Sonny tumbled forward into the deep hole in the ground.

"Keep your head down if you want us to get through this, boyo," Bob whispered, and then disappeared.

Sonny heard him running across the flagstones toward the long, mahogany bar that curved around one side of the courtyard. From his position lying at the muddy bottom of the earthen pit, Sonny could see nothing but a patch of darkening sky above his head. But he could hear everything.

"Jenii?" a deep, rumbling voice called from the hall beyond the courtyard. "Jenii, where are you?"

Sonny froze. He knew that voice. He heard Bob hiss under his breath—a raw swear word in a very old tongue—and knew that he recognized it, too.

"Hello, Gofannon," Bob called out casually. "Looking for someone?"

"Hello, Puck, old friend," the blacksmith said, his voice lacking any warmth.

"Told you he wasn't over it," Sonny muttered. "So much for Faerie prescience . . ."

Don't be smug, Flannery, Bob's voice hissed inside his head. *It's unbecoming.*

"Pour you a drink?" Bob said out loud, and Sonny heard the clinking of glassware. "The service in this place appears to have gone downhill rather badly."

And whatever you do, boyo—whatever happens to me—you stay hidden.

Every instinct in Sonny cried out against that imperative. But he knew Bob was right. He did as he was asked—for the moment.

"What are you doing here, you miserable pook?" Gofannon asked angrily. There was a clanging sound, as if he'd thrown something heavy and metal to the ground.

"The Tavern used to serve a lovely brisket," Bob said blandly. "I had a hankering. But from the look of things around here, I suspect the kitchen's closed. And so, I'll be on my way. Nice shovel. Lovely to see you again."

"No. Puck."

"Beg pardon?"

"We've a score to settle with you, the Wee Green Man and me," Gofannon growled.

Sonny felt his jaw clench involuntarily at the mention. The leprechaun. Gofannon was in league with him and his sister. Or had been, at least, before Jenii Greenteeth was killed. Sonny thought of the glaistig's lifeless body lying out in the Tavern hall and wondered fleetingly who had managed that feat.

"I won't have you pulling another one of your disappearing acts," the blacksmith said to Bob.

"And how will you stop me, mortal man?"

There was an echo of power that thrummed through the ancient Fae's voice. Sonny could hear it from where he hid. But he also heard the sound of something else—a slithering, metallic sound. The sound of an iron chain uncoiling.

Bob shouted something in an arcane language and there was a flash of light and a shock wave that boomed out over Sonny's earthen pit. But the chain was already singing through the air, and Bob's imprecation turned to screaming as—Sonny feared—the cold metal bit into his Faerie flesh.

That's it, Sonny thought. He couldn't stay hidden any longer.

Yes. You. Can. Bob's voice in his head was thick with pain, but insistent. *You must.*

Sonny clenched his fists in frustration. *Bob—*

Trust me, Sonny Flannery.

221

Sonny felt a surge of anguish rush through him, accompanied by a distracting noise inside his head. A thrumming sound pulsed in his mind, but it was wrapped in a kind of crackling static made up of broken bits of music. All around him, torn roots protruded from the dark earth—all that was left behind of the Old Shrub—oozing bright green sap onto Sonny's arms and legs. Wherever it fell, Sonny felt a charge like an electric current dance across his skin, invigorating, vitalizing. But with each spark, the music in his head swelled, distracting him and dampening the growing fire in his blood.

It was maddening. Familiar.

A lullaby.

A lullaby that he hadn't heard and hadn't been able to even *remember* . . . not since Chloe the Siren had kissed him and stolen it from deep within his mind. Sonny concentrated on *that,* and—suddenly—the melody became crystal clear. The Irish lyrics, sung to him when he was a tiny baby, echoed through his mind in a clear and lovely voice. His mother's voice. Sonny didn't know the meaning of the words, but he knew intimately the sound of every syllable . . . and now he knew exactly what the song *itself* meant. It was meant to keep him safe. It was meant to keep him hidden.

And it was there because Kelley had made Chloe put it back.

Oh my dear, sweet Firecracker, Sonny thought, staring up at the circle of sky above him, *when all this is said and done, you and I are going to have to have a little talk.*

That all depended, of course, on Sonny staying hidden. He winced as he heard another wail of pain. Bob was suffering greatly.

It's not the first time, boyo, said Bob's voice in his head. The words were weak now, but they were still clear. *With any luck it won't be the last. Make it count.*

The chain rattled. Gofannon laughed. One final cry tore from Bob's throat. Sonny heard a thud and the sound of something being dragged across the floor and away down the hall. . . . Then all was silence.

"I know what she did."

After Gofannon had taken Bob away, Sonny had climbed out of the hole and headed back to the reservoir cavern at a dead run. Now he stood, panting for breath, in front of Maddox—who stared at him, openmouthed. Sonny knew he must have presented something of a sight, all muddied and covered in bits of leaf. And alone.

"I know what Kelley did," he gasped. "What she made Chloe do."

"Where's the boucca?" Maddox asked. "What the hell happened to you?"

"In a minute. First—tell me something." Sonny brushed aside Madd's astonishment. "Kelley made Chloe give me back the song she stole, didn't she?"

Maddox glanced back and forth between Sonny and Fennrys, who'd come to find out what was going on.

"Didn't she, Maddox?" Sonny pressed.

"Tell him," the Wolf said.

Maddox frowned. "Well, yeah. Uh—at least I think so. . . . I wasn't really clear on the whole thing—"

"I need her to steal it back."

"Are you out of your mind?" Maddox spluttered.

"No—but *it* has to be. It's a charm, Madd. There's a charm stuck in my head." Sonny knew, now, that this was what had been done to him. This . . . this lullaby. This was the thing that had hidden him—even from himself—for all those years. "I can't explain it right now. But I need to get this thing out of my brain if I'm going to be of any use at all. Chloe's the only one who can help me. Where is she?"

Maddox nodded at the chain of pools in the corner of the cavern. "Some of the Water Folk escaped through those during the fight. Who knows where they come out. She's probably somewhere out in the East River by now."

"We've got to find her, Madd."

"I'll go," said a small voice at Sonny's elbow.

"Neerya." He knelt down and looked her in the face. "Can you find her? Do you think so?"

The little naiad shrugged. "I know all the tunnels where the Sirens swim. Some of them come up in the storm sewers where I shop for my feast food. I like to play hide-and-seek there sometimes."

"Can you find Chloe and bring her back to me?"

Neerya glanced around the cavern. "She won't come back

224

here. Not after what happened. Sirens are silly scaredy things, I told you."

"She's right." Maddox frowned. "She's not the hardiest of souls—wait. . . ."

Sonny turned and looked at him.

"I know where Chloe will feel safe," he said. "She felt safe in your apartment."

"All right. Then that's where we'll go." Sonny turned back to Neerya. "Bug? Can you bring Chloe somewhere if I give you directions?"

She gave him a look and said, "I don't *need* directions. All I need's an address."

Sonny flashed her a brief, grateful smile, remembering how she'd found him on the subway. She probably knew the city better than he did. He gave Neerya the address and watched as she flitted off through the air and dived sharply into the pool, leaving barely a ripple behind on the surface of the water. Then he rose and turned to face the others.

"What exactly are we doing?" Fennrys asked.

"I've got a plan."

"You do?" Maddox raised an eyebrow.

Sonny shrugged. "No. But I will. Get Cait. Let's go."

XX

"So. Valkyrie, huh?" Kelley said to Olrun. The silence between them had begun to make her uncomfortable, although Olrun didn't seemed to mind. They'd gone outside—ostensibly to check on Belrix, but mostly to give Emma and Herne a moment alone. The great white horse turned and nuzzled Kelley's shoulder. "That a good gig?"

"Used to be." Olrun ran a hand over Belrix's flank. "Until I bent one too many of the All-Father's rules and he exiled me to the mortal realm." She laughed a little and patted the horse. "We used to convey the souls of heroes across the Rainbow Bridge to the golden halls of Valhalla. Now we ferry tourists in a circle around a park. Take my advice, missy. Don't ever try to bend the rules too far."

Kelley smiled in sympathy. Sage advice . . . she wished Olrun had been there to give it to her before she'd bent certain Faerie rules past their breaking point. Maybe she wouldn't be in this mess now.

"Kelley?"

She turned to see her aunt beckoning her from the doorway.

"He wants to see you," Emma said. "But only briefly, dear. He's very weak."

Kelley went back inside the house and down the hall with Emma to the guest room. Olrun had stayed out in the yard, but through the window Kelley could see her where she stood by the carriage, her glacier-blue gaze fixed unblinking on the house.

Kelley looked at the man in the bed. Even groggy and as full of as many homemade pain concoctions as Emma had managed to pour down the Hunter's throat, his eyes still lit up at the sight of Kelley's aunt. *That* was what would heal him, if anything could.

Emma left the two of them alone, saying she was going to make more tea.

"Hey," Kelley said in a quiet voice as she crossed the room. "How are you doing?"

"Better than if you had not found me, lady." Herne's voice, normally so rich and warm, was barely above a whisper. "Thank you," he said. "For my life . . . for bringing me here. . . ."

"Please call me Kelley."

Herne nodded his head, and even that small exertion seemed to drain strength from him. Kelley moved to sit on the edge of the bed.

"Tell me," Herne said.

Kelley had to strain to hear the request.

"Tell me what happened in my Tavern."

Kelley told him about what she had seen, about the dead Fae and the hole in the ground where the Greenman tree had been. She watched as a hazy alarm grew in the Hunter's pain-clouded gaze. Then she told him about Jenii. By then, Emma was back in the room, and her hand was on Kelley's shoulder, squeezing gently in reassurance. Emma, who Kelley had thought would be horrified and disappointed in her at her act of violence.

"You did the right thing, my girl," Em said, her voice quiet but firm as she went to raise Herne's head up so that he could sip from the herbal tea she had made for him. "Don't go tearing yourself up inside over it. If it had been me, I would have done the exact same thing, wiped the knife, and called it a task well done. That was plain evil you killed and none other. Used to drown children, she did, that one. Back in the day, around near where I grew up. Plain evil."

"Maddox once told me a glaistig killed Sonny's predecessor in the Janus Guard. Might have even been Jenii. . . ."

"And she'd have killed Sonny and you and whoever else she pleased, given the chance," Emma said, her blue-gray eyes gone hard as stone, the set of her mouth unforgiving. She made the Hunter drink again and set the cup on the nightstand. "She'd have killed Herne if it hadn't been for you," Emma said, smoothing an imaginary crease from the comforter he lay beneath.

The Hunter had been silent for some time, and Kelley thought that maybe he had slipped into unconsciousness again. But then she saw the shadow of a frown on his brow and she knew that he was still listening.

Herne beckoned her closer and asked Emma to fetch him a small embroidered pouch that hung from his broad leather belt. She and Olrun had taken the belt from around his waist and laid it on a chair along with his bloodstained clothing when they'd gone to work on his wounds. Herne opened the pouch and withdrew a black silk cord, tied to a glittering onyx jewel—a talisman in the shape of a stag's head. Kelley held out her hand and took the charm. It was cold in her hand.

"In case," Herne said, quietly. "In case I do not . . ."

"Herne—"

"Give it to Sonny when you see him again. To remember me by." Herne closed his long, elegant fingers around hers and squeezed with what was probably most of his remaining strength. It wasn't much. He was very pale. "Tell him I'm sorry."

"Tell him yourself," Kelley said gently. "When I bring him back home."

She stuffed the jewel into the pocket of her jeans, unwilling to think of any alternative to that scenario. Herne's eyes

229

slid half-open again, and his gaze went to Kelley's throat.

"Where is *your* charm, Kelley?" he asked. "The clover charm you wear?"

Kelley put a hand to her neck. "Oh . . ." She fished in the other pocket of her jeans. "Here it is. In all the excitement, I forgot to put it back on." It seemed that she had been far too tired and preoccupied to notice that her Faerie power had been unfettered for the last few hours. Or maybe she was just getting better at controlling it. Whatever the case, she slid the chain around her neck and fastened the catch, just to be sure.

"Keep it safe, Princess," the Hunter murmured. "Keep yourself safe. Whosoever seeks to steal the Green Magick from Sonny will need that charm to do it. They will not rest until they find it. Until they find you."

At that, Emma looked up at Kelley, her expression deeply worried. "Can't you hide it somewhere, Kelley? Get rid of it?"

Kelley gave Em's shoulder a reassuring squeeze. "I'm not getting rid of it," she said emphatically. "And I'm not giving it up either. Don't fret, Em. Nobody knows where I am, and so long as I actually wear the charm, none of the Fair Folk can find me."

It was true. Kelley recalled her desperate attempts to attract the attention of her mother's Storm Hags when the charm had been magickally bound around her throat. She'd been all but invisible to them.

"Still . . . ," the Hunter murmured thickly. Emma's pain concoction must have been taking effect. "Better to be safe.

230

Stay away from the Gate. Stay away from the park. That's where they will be looking. The charm ties you to the Green Magick. The Green Magick is tied to the Gate. It will always pull you back."

"I'm not going back, Herne. Not until this is over. I'm not about to take that risk." Even though it hurt Kelley to say it, she knew it had to be that way. She thought about the theater company with a sharp pang of regret. The Avalon Players would just have to find a new Ariel—

Oh no . . . Kelley felt her heart flutter in sudden panic. She glanced at the clock on the bedside table. It was just past ten o'clock. Rehearsal that night had been scheduled to go to eleven. *Tyff* . . .

Tyff who, at that very moment, was wandering around in exactly the one place Kelley shouldn't be . . . looking exactly like Kelley! She had to warn her. In spite of what she'd just told Emma, she *had* to go back. . . . She kept the thought to herself. If Emma had the slightest inkling of what she was about to do, she'd never let her out of the house again. So instead, Kelley turned a small smile on her aunt and told the Hunter to get some rest. The last thing either of them needed to do was worry about her.

Kelley went into her old room and closed the door behind her, locking it tight. She called the cell number of every company member that she could remember. Which wasn't a great many—she'd had them all programmed into her long-lost phone. She called Tyff. No one answered. Of course they weren't answering. They were in the middle of a rehearsal—and anyone who left their cell phone on during one of Quentin's rehearsals faced notoriously dire consequences.

Although maybe not so dire as having a vengeful leprechaun hunting you down so he can kill you with one of his damned possessed trees . . .

Kelley had to get back to the city. She had to warn Tyff.

Before she left, Kelley made another attempt to get hold of Queen Mabh. She was disturbed by the fact that her meddlesome mother had seemingly dropped out of existence. She'd vaguely expected that Mabh would appear in a plume of smoke to gloat over Herne's injuries . . . but the queen had stayed conspicuous by her absence.

Kelley sat in front of the mirror of her antique vanity table and dropped her clover pendant into the little porcelain dish where she used to keep her regular old non-magickal jewelry. She raised her hand and put it against the cold, reflective glass. And waited.

"Well now," Mabh said from the shadows, her voice a pale-sounding imitation of its usual mocking musicality. "I *am* impressed, Daughter."

Kelley frowned and tried to peer through the hazy gloom that shrouded the vision in the mirror. She couldn't quite see her mother clearly. The flickering fog was like bad reception on a television, and Kelley wondered if she was doing something wrong.

"You're learning," Mabh said. "You wouldn't have been able to cast a half-decent scrying spell even so little as a month ago."

"And it really burns your cheese to see that I can now, doesn't it?" Kelley snapped. Even when Kelley wanted to be civil, Mabh just had a way of needling her. Kelley'd always heard of those kinds of stereotypical mother-daughter relationships, but she had never thought she'd find herself in one. She didn't know what to think of it. On the one hand, she had a *mother*. On the other hand . . .

"Where have you been?" Kelley asked, straining silently to clear up the Otherworldly interference in her scrying. "You haven't bugged me in days."

Mabh clicked her tongue impatiently against her teeth.

"Like this," the queen said brusquely, and put her hand on her side of the mirror. Kelley let the pull of Mabh's magicks sweep her own fingers across the surface of the glass, drawing after them sparkling trails that cleared away the obscuring, misty veil.

The view cleared, Kelley was shocked by her mother's appearance. Mabh's shoulders sagged, and she staggered back a step or two as if she would collapse. The Queen of Air and Darkness was so pale she was almost translucent. Her hair was pulled back from her face and hidden beneath a dark mantle, but the stray locks that had escaped hung in wisps about the queen's hollowed cheeks. Her eyes were ringed with shadow, and her lips were bloodless and pressed together in a tight line.

Still, the Autumn Queen was staggeringly lovely—perhaps even more so because she looked . . . vulnerable. Mabh hugged her elbows tightly, drawing her cloak closely around her body, and stared at her daughter with a defiant gleam in her eyes, as if daring Kelley to make a comment on her appearance. Kelley bit her lip and said nothing.

"My power wanes," the queen said finally, lifting her chin as if to belie that statement.

"I . . . um . . . why?" Kelley asked. First Auberon, now Mabh. . . . It was as if someone was taking down the monarchs of Faerie one at a time. She wondered how Titania and Gwynn fared. "How? Who could do such a thing?"

"It's not that difficult to topple a monarch, Daughter," Mabh said. "Just ask Gwynn ap Nudd, after what happened to him. All you need to do is find a weakness. Or make one."

"Is that what's happened to you?"

"I daresay it is. Someone has found a conduit to siphon power from the Autumn Court's throne."

"A conduit?"

"Something already touched by my magicks. I thought they might be using *you*." She raised an arched brow. "I'm pleased to see that is not the case."

"Wow." Kelley blinked. "Thanks for giving me a heads-up that there was a possibility that might happen. . . ."

"I never really considered it a likely scenario. You're not exactly what I would call a pushover. I daresay you'd fight back rather vigorously, and that, in itself, would draw far too much power to make you an effective channel." Her expression went dark. "But don't worry, darling. When I find out who is behind all this, I will teach them the error of their ways."

Sure, Kelley thought. *Plot that vengeance all you want. You look like you can barely stand upright.* First Auberon, then Mabh . . . that left two Faerie monarchs in full power. Which one was responsible? Or were *they* targets, too? She remembered when Gwynn told her that he had once been the only king in the Otherworld, in the time before the Greenman created the Four Gates of Faerie. Gwynn had told her of the war, and how Auberon and Titania, upstarts both, had banded together to usurp his power. And how Mabh had gathered enough of her own power while they did so to become a force to be reckoned with in her own right.

Was that what was happening now?

Maybe the Wee Green Clan themselves had simply decided the time was ripe for a New Otherworld Order. The thought of the Greenman's offspring getting control of their old man's power made Kelley shudder inwardly, but it still didn't quite add up. They might have been acting independently, but from the way Mabh was talking, there was more muscle behind the unrest than just a few disgruntled weeds. She remembered that she had found the leprechaun in the garage of Titania's club, but . . .

Kelley shook her head. She didn't have any kind of proof, beyond the uneasy feeling she got around the Summer Queen and, as the daughter of the crazy-dangerous Queen of

Autumn, she really wasn't one to point fingers. Instead Kelley cast about for a change in subject.

"How's Auberon?" was the only thing she could think of.

"Still dying," Mabh said blandly. "I'm sure that pleases you no end."

"You're wrong," Kelley said.

"Am I?" The queen stared at her flatly. "It would please me, were I you."

"You're not me. And I don't even think *you* mean that."

"It is true that Auberon has been the only thing that has kept the Four Courts from tearing apart. Your father may not be the most benevolent ruler at times, but he at least had the strength to keep the realm from dissolving into chaos."

"I thought you were a big fan of chaos."

"I am a 'big fan,' as you say, of *my* chaos. It's not quite the same thing."

"Whoever's doing this to Auberon . . . it has to be the same person that's after the Green Magick." Kelley sighed, wishing she had more to go on. "At least Sonny's secret is safe for the time being," she said, half to herself.

When Mabh grew uncomfortably silent, Kelley glanced up sharply.

"*Isn't* it?"

"Well . . ."

Kelley went cold. "Where's Bob?"

Mabh chewed on her lip and avoided Kelley's stare.

"What did you do to him? Is he all right?"

236

The expression on the queen's face turned to one of sour annoyance. "I'm sure he's just fine. His kind always manage to survive nicely."

"What happened?" Kelley asked anxiously. "I thought you said you'd take care of things with him."

"And I *would* have, if the little snake hadn't developed such a talent for eavesdropping all those years ago."

"He over*heard* us?" Kelley's mouth dropped open.

"I daresay he did. And didn't stick around much afterward. He's gone. I don't know where."

This was not good. This was, in fact, potentially disastrous. Bob on the loose, possessed of the knowledge of Sonny's power, put Sonny in grave danger. The fact that he knew Kelley had given Mabh his name put Kelley at risk. The boucca had always been friendly to her, but this . . . *this* was the kind of thing that just might turn him against her. Or Sonny. Kelley felt a knot of apprehension tighten her stomach. "That's great," she muttered through clenched teeth. "That's just super, Mabh—"

"Oh honestly!" the queen snapped at her peevishly. "Would it kill you to call me *Mother*? Just once, and not in irony, or mockery, or by accident?"

Kelley blinked in surprise at the outburst.

"This whole situation is none of my fault. And yet you make me suffer."

"Uh . . ." Kelley raised one hand defensively. "This whole . . . 'situation' has an awful lot to do with what you did

237

to Herne back in the day."

"One mistake."

"It was a pretty big mistake."

"I was in love."

"And that's your excuse?"

"Yes." The queen raised her eyes and glared flatly at her daughter. "What's yours?"

That stung.

"He's hurt, you know. Herne. Badly." Kelley wasn't sure if she said it to sting Mabh back. But the second the words were out of her mouth, she regretted them. Pain, like a livid scar, flashed across Mabh's face.

"Tell me," the queen whispered in a voice gone raw.

Kelley told her mother everything she knew. It still didn't add up to who was behind it all.

"This scheme is not something your average Fae could engineer," Mabh murmured, regaining her composure.

"Average Fae or no, whoever is behind this better tread carefully. Because if they harm one single hair on Sonny's head," Kelley said matter-of-factly, "then *I* will kill them. Just like I killed Jenii Greenteeth."

It was Mabh's turn, then, to look startled.

"Like mother, like daughter." Kelley shrugged, ignoring the fact that her stomach had clenched at what she'd just said. "I have to go. Take care of Auberon for me." Then she wiped her hand over the glass and watched as Mabh's visage disappeared from view.

XXI

hey emerged from the subway tunnels at Columbus Circle, largely unnoticed—thanks to Cait's glamour. As they headed north up Central Park West, Sonny was almost amused to see people instinctively cross over the street to avoid sharing the sidewalk with a handful of changelings, a Faerie huntress, and a very tall man with decidedly odd features. The Ghillie Dhu—the web-fingered Fae who had befriended Sonny between bouts of hurling—had approached Sonny quietly as he was preparing to leave and had offered his services.

"Call me Webber," he'd said, and spread his fingers to illustrate the pun. His Fae name was probably unpronounceable by a human tongue. "I have some small skill as a healer." Sonny had thanked him and told him that he'd probably be best utilized by helping tend to the injured Lost in the reservoir. The tall Fae shook his head solemnly, staring down at Sonny with large, fathomless eyes. "I also have some smaller skill at catching glimpses of the future," he said. "Nothing clear. Nothing definite. But I can tell you this: wherever it is you are going, Janus . . . you will have need of a healer."

It hadn't been the most encouraging conversation. But it had made Sonny take Webber along with them. For the moment, he put the ominous prediction out of his mind and called Cait to him as they walked.

"Who in the Guard do you know for certain avoided this . . . this taint of rebellion?"

Cait winced but thought about it carefully before answering. "Bellamy is clean. He'd never have agreed to that attack on the sanctuary. How Camina has managed to keep the whole thing from him, I don't know."

"Do you know where he is now?"

Cait frowned. "No. . . . As a matter of fact, I haven't even seen Bell in days."

"That might go a ways toward explaining how she was able to keep him out of it," Sonny said grimly.

Cait's eyes went wide. "You don't think . . ."

"I don't know anything for certain, Cait. All I know is that the Janus Guard has been severely compromised."

"They're twins. . . ."

"I know. But they didn't always see eye to eye. Let's face it . . . there are those of us who've never been happy living like this. In servitude to the Winter King." Sonny was probably the most loyal of all the Guard to the Unseelie king, and even *he'd* had cause to chafe under Auberon's dictates.

"But we've always been loyal to the Guard itself, and to each other." He glanced over his shoulder at where Maddox and Fennrys brought up the rear of the group, and gestured them forward. "Even the Wolf," he said before they reached them. "Now something has broken that bond. Something strong enough to make thralls of the Janus."

"Power," Cait said quietly. "The promise of it, at least . . ."

"Aye. Do you remember the stories about the demise of the Greenman? Back in the days before the Gate was shut?"

"Of course I do. You don't grow up in the Otherworld without hearing the tale."

"The Greenman was killed because he was too trusting. He took on the guise of a mortal man, and when someone shot him to death with iron bullets it was a blow to the very fabric of Faerie existence." It pained Sonny to think of the old god lying there bleeding out his life as he gifted his phenomenal power to Sonny's father. "There was always intrigue and plotting among the High Fae. But to murder the creator of the Four Gates, the architect of the Four Courts, was to give notice to all of the Otherworld that no one among the Fair Folk should consider themselves safe."

"But it was never discovered who was responsible, and the

Green Magick was never recovered," Cait mused. "Its hiding place was never found, and so the threat was never made good on."

Until now, maybe, Sonny thought.

Of course Cait would know all about the subject of the Greenman's power. Magick was her special love. She had studied it all her life.

"At any rate," Sonny said, "whoever we're up against, whatever their goal, we can count *out* Camina, Godwyn, and Selene. Ghost is no longer . . . a variable, and Bell is missing in action."

Maddox and Fennrys had come up beside them and caught the tail end of the conversation. "What about the others?" Maddox asked. "What about Percival?"

Cait shook her head. "Don't know. I couldn't say for certain . . . but Perry idolizes Aaneel."

Fennrys raised an eyebrow. "And Aaneel is . . . ?"

"Again, I do not know. I was . . . I would say 'recruited,' but I think now a more appropriate term is *coerced*, into this whole mess by Godwyn. He tells everyone that this has all come down from Aaneel, but that could just be because he wants everyone to believe it comes directly from Auberon."

"Believe me," said Sonny quietly, "it does not."

Cait shrugged one shoulder. "Then it is either Godwyn acting on his own, or Aaneel is the one behind it all. But if that is the case, then we can count out any help from Perry. Like I said—he idolizes Aaneel."

"And what about the lads?" Maddox asked, meaning Bryan and Beni.

Cait laughed. "Godwyn can't stand them. He wouldn't invite them along if he could help it. I think he's sent them into perpetual Gate patrol—again, supposedly at Auberon's behest."

"We could probably use them," Sonny said, glancing off to his left as he walked. The sidewalk ran parallel to the stone wall that surrounded Central Park.

"I'll go," Fenn offered. "With the mess those two usually leave in their wake, it shouldn't take much to track them."

Sonny wondered fleetingly why the Wolf hadn't been included in the recruitment, but he suspected he already knew the answer. Fennrys may not have had any love for Auberon, but his rebelliousness would cut both ways. He wasn't about to be swayed to any particular cause. Fennrys was in it for himself. He was undependable in any other capacity.

But Sonny thought he could trust him to at least run and collect Bryan and Beni from the park. Whatever the storm they were about to head into . . . he had to admit, he was going to need all hands on deck.

Once Sonny and his companions got past security and up the elevator, he dismantled the protective wards guarding his front door and let them inside. After he'd reinstated his wards and told everyone to make themselves comfortable, all they could do was wait and hope that Neerya found the Siren and could convince her to take the lullaby charm once more from his mind. And then? Sonny had no idea what should come next.

What he *did* know was that he wasn't going to hide anymore. That was what had got them all into this mess in the first place. It seemed to Sonny that everyone had been trying so hard to keep him safe that they'd left him blind and in the dark and unable to defend himself. If the Old Shrub had been taken for the purpose of reviving the leprechaun, then whoever was responsible probably knew by now who—and what—Sonny was. Sonny might as well do his companions the courtesy of letting them know, too. Then they could decide for themselves if they wanted to stick with him.

Webber took the news in stride, but it seemed he wasn't one for emotional extremes at the best of times. Both Cait and Carys were staring at him, and Sonny thought Maddox's jaw would hit the carpet.

Madd shook his head in utter disbelief. "You're yanking my leg," he scoffed. "You can't be serious. You . . . the Greenman . . ."

"Fennrys probably didn't think I was joking when I blasted him through a window, decimated the Wee Green Clan single-handedly, and burned down Kelley's theater," Sonny said dryly. "But you can ask him his opinion when he gets back, if you want."

"And you don't remember doing any of it?"

"Not a single damned second. Nothing past the moment

when I thought Kelley was dead. I only know what Puck told me. I guess it was pretty bad, though."

Maddox whistled low. "And you want to let this . . . this *thing* inside you off its leash again. Is that really such a good idea?"

"I don't know." Sonny turned to Cait where she still stood, stunned. "Is it?"

"I . . ." She shook her head. "I don't know. I certainly understand now why Kelley did what she did. Sonny . . . that is a tremendous amount of power. More power than anyone other than the Greenman himself should ever possess."

"I know. But he isn't here. Because someone killed him and tried to take his power. If someone comes to take it from me, I'd like to avoid a similar outcome."

"You say the Green Magick can only be taken from you with the help of Kelley's charm?" Carys asked, having found her voice—an unsteady version of it.

Sonny nodded. "As I understand it. That's what Puck told me."

"Then she is in grave danger," said the huntress.

"Yet another reason I'd like to be able to access this convenient arsenal within me."

There was a quiet knock on the apartment door. Sonny muttered the words that dismantled the wards and opened it. Chloe stood at the threshold, her eyes wide and darting. Neerya held her firmly by the hand, and Sonny had the feeling that, if she hadn't had such a grip on her, the Siren might have bolted. Sonny could hardly blame her—things hadn't been easy for Chloe lately. She wore a thin, filmy scarf around her neck to cover the scars inflicted by Mabh when she'd tortured the poor creature to get information about Kelley. As Neerya dragged Chloe inside, Maddox motioned Sonny over into the kitchen.

"It . . . uh . . . you probably don't remember but, the last time, it didn't go so well for her, Sonny," Maddox said to him quietly. "That green voodoo attached to the song in your head . . ."

"It's immensely powerful." Sonny nodded. "I know."

"It's bloody toxic, is what it is. It near drove her out of her mind."

"I need her help, Madd."

Maddox shook his sandy head and said, "If she agrees, then so do I."

Chloe turned and went into the bedroom. The two Janus followed, and Maddox took up a position standing in front of Chloe, arms crossed over his chest, glowering a bit at Sonny like some kind of self-appointed security detail. In truth, Sonny was glad he was there. Sonny still didn't trust the Siren and, if he was honest with himself, the very idea of letting her back into his head was nothing short of terrifying.

"Chloe?" Maddox turned to the Siren where she had perched on the edge of the bed. "This is up to you. You don't have to do this if you don't want to and, much as Sonny here's my best mate, I'll break his arm before I let him force you into

246

it." He glanced over his shoulder at Sonny. "Sorry."

Sonny shrugged. "Don't be." He would have done exactly the same thing if it were Kelley.

Chloe reached up a hand and slid a shining strand of her pale gold hair behind her ear. She looked up at Maddox for a long moment. Her dark golden gaze traveled over his face, and the barest hint of a shy smile ticked at the corner of her mouth. The Siren turned to Sonny and nodded her head.

"I'll try very hard not to hurt you this time," she said.

He and Maddox both breathed a deep sigh of relief.

In spite of her assurances, Sonny still flinched violently as Chloe's lips touched his and the familiar sensation of paralyzing cold—like ice damming behind his eyes—lanced through his skull.

Sonny heard Chloe begin to whimper as if from a great distance. The sound of singing in his mind shifted subtly—the voice changing from his mother's rich lilt to the airier, more ethereal sound of what Chloe's haunting Siren voice had once been. But she seemed to shy away from the song and, for an instant, the pain intensified. Then Sonny heard Maddox's voice in the room.

"Chloe," he urged gently. "Hang on, sweetheart. . . . You can do this."

Sonny felt his limbs start to shudder as he reacted physically to the psychic agony, but he tried not to move. Tried not to pull away from the icy kiss the Siren bestowed upon him. He could feel her hands on the sides of his face, fingers

247

knotted in his hair to keep him there, and he struggled to stay focused beyond the pain. He concentrated fiercely on the tune—a simple, heartbreakingly lovely Irish lullaby, and tried to add the strength of his own inner voice to the melody. As he did so, Chloe seemed to rally. Sonny felt the tearing away of the charmed memory deep within his mind but—this time—he was content to let it go.

Suddenly Chloe gasped in wonder, breaking the kiss, and fell away from him. She staggered back a step and collapsed into Maddox's arms, weeping soundlessly. But in spite of the tears, there was a smile on her face as she looked up at Sonny.

"No one has ever given me a song freely before," she said, wonderingly. "I didn't know what a difference it could make. Thank you."

Chloe turned back to Maddox, a wan but playful gleam in her eyes, and touched his temple lightly, brushing at his sandy hair. Sonny saw him shiver.

Then Madd grinned and said, "Nah—you don't want what's in there, luv. I've got a mighty tin ear."

Carys was waiting for Sonny out on the terrace. "What now?" she asked as he came and leaned on the balustrade beside her, staring out at the city.

"Now . . . I go find Kelley."

She nodded. "Where do we look?"

"I'm not asking you to come with me."

"I wasn't waiting for an invitation." She turned her head

and gazed at him, unblinking. "It wasn't *your* home they invaded."

Sonny couldn't argue with that. He stood silently, gazing out over the darkened expanse of the park's trees and fields, and imagined, for a moment, that he could feel Kelley's presence there . . . her firecracker spark. It was, of course, only his imagination. Without his iron medallion, Sonny's Janus senses were nonfunctioning. Still . . . for a moment he thought . . . no.

He turned and went back into the apartment, Carys behind him.

Kelley, he was sure, was nowhere near the park. She was far too smart. Wherever she had gone after she'd left Herne's Tavern, Sonny was certain that it would have been somewhere far away—if she'd left under her own power, that is. She'd promised him that she would come back. And if she hadn't, it was because she'd been taken or had been forced to flee. Either way . . . he was going to find her.

He just didn't know how, exactly.

"Use the Force," Maddox suggested, grinning as though vastly pleased with himself over some private joke.

"Force of what?" Sonny asked.

Maddox rolled his eyes and said, airily, "You should get cable, Sonn. You can learn all sorts of things from the movies."

Cait pressed her lips together in order, it looked like, to keep from laughing. "He has a point, Sonny," she said after a moment. "Sort of."

249

"What's that, Cait?" Sonny asked.

"The Green Magick." She said the words with a degree of reverence. "Use it. You say that the charm was originally created to find the power that lies within you. Well . . . you should, in that case, be able to reverse engineer it, so to speak. Follow that same connection in the other direction to find the charm. And, if she still wears it, Kelley."

That made sense, Sonny thought. And, from somewhere deep within, he felt a kind of stirring excitement at the thought of tapping into the magicks that had lain dormant inside of him for so long. He mentally shook himself.

"All right," he said. "But you're going to have to give me the guided tour, Cait. Magick this big is a foreign country to me."

Before they began, Sonny opened up his leather satchel and checked to make sure the small, compact crossbow and quiver were still there. His wood-sword was there, too, in its guise of three bundled branches. Sonny lightly ran a fingertip over the familiar surface of each; oak, ash, and thorn. Even though he couldn't transform it into a blade without his Janus magick, its presence comforted him. As did the sheaf of paper his fingers brushed next. Kelley's *Midsummer* script. He'd carried it with him since the day he'd first met her. It was his talisman. His good luck charm. He ran his thumb over the brass page fasteners and slung the bag over his head. Then he added a pair of easily concealed short swords from a trunk in his front hall closet and went back to face the others.

"All right, Cait," he said. "Tell me how to do this thing, and let's go find our princess."

XXII

"Ye elves of hills, brooks, standing lakes and groves . . ." Kelley heard the words ring out as she stepped from the rift just on the other side of the Delacorte's fence wall. The "Between," as Mabh had called it, had indeed been populated with wraiths. But Kelley had fastened her charm around her throat after she'd created the rift—and before she'd stepped through—so she'd managed the passage without even really being noticed.

Well . . . without being noticed by anything in the Between.

The bundled shape of a homeless guy lying on a park bench was another matter. He shifted at her approach, and Kelley saw that his eyes were wide open and staring right at her.

"Oh," she said. "Hi . . ."

"You just . . . appeared," he mumbled. "Right outta thin air."

Kelley hesitated. "Uh . . . yeah. Yeah, I did."

"What . . . *are* you?"

She wondered what she should say. He had just seen her step through a rip in the fabric of reality accompanied by a crackling blaze of magick. Really, what *else* was she going to tell him? She told him the truth.

"I'm a Faerie princess," Kelley said. "Look . . . Central Park really isn't the best place to be these days. There are all sorts of nasty creatures popping out of rifts like the one I just came through. I'm trying to help fix that but, in the meantime, if any of them find you here, they'll probably try to eat your face. Would you mind if I asked you to relocate for a little while? For your own safety?"

The guy blinked at her. Then, much to Kelley's astonishment, he nodded. She stood there as he clambered up to his feet, picked up a bottle that had lain underneath him, and a teddy bear. Peering at her, the man said, "Thanks."

"For what?"

"Well . . . I seen a lotta weird stuff in this park over the years. Everybody else always tells me I'm either stone-cold crazy or stupid-drunk. But I know what I seen. I appreciate you tellin' me the truth. Maybe I'll try Bryant Park down by the library for a change. Is that one okay?"

"Oh! Yeah!" Kelley nodded. "Bryant Park's really nice."

He nodded again and shambled down the path, calling, "Good luck, Princess . . ." over his shoulder as he went.

Kelley suddenly understood the Fair Folk compulsion for telling the truth. When it worked, it felt pretty good.

She turned back to the Delacorte, where the sound of Gentleman Jack's voice echoed through the still night air.

"I have bedimmed the noontide sun, called forth the mutinous winds," he intoned, "and 'twixt the green sea and the azured vault set roaring war. . . ."

Kelley waited, veiled, in the shadows outside the amphitheater. Rehearsal was almost over. When that scene ended, Quentin called a halt and told everyone to pack up and head home. *Notes* on the morrow, look over your *scripts*, write down your *bloody* blocking, or heads *will* roll . . . all of that good stuff. Kelley felt a pang of longing.

Someday soon, she thought, *I will be back onstage.*

All the actors started to drift away, and Kelley moved closer to the stage door, invisible and silent, waiting for the moment to catch Tyff's attention.

"Psst!" she hissed at the spitting image of herself—if she'd ever been inclined to carry a Prada bag, that is. "Tyff!"

"Whoa!" Tyff jumped half a foot. "Winslow? Where are you?"

Kelley glanced around and, not seeing anyone else nearby, dropped her veil and shimmered into view.

"You're getting good," Tyff said in a voice that was somewhere between her own sharp tones and Kelley's softer ones.

"And you're taking the massive risk of sneaking around here . . . so I figure you're about to warn me that something fairly dire is riding over the horizon. Right?"

Kelley nodded. "You're—*we're* in danger."

"Do I get a prize for guessing correctly?"

"How much danger?" Gentleman Jack asked, stepping out from the shadows beneath the backstage house eaves.

Tyff jumped again. "Jeez! Would everybody please stop sneaking up on me like that?"

"Sorry, ah . . . it's Tyff, isn't it? I don't think we were formally introduced last time we met." Jack nodded politely at the glamoured Faerie, unfazed by the fact that there appeared to be *two* Kelley Winslows standing in front of him at that moment. And one of them had appeared out of thin air. He turned to that one and said, "Welcome back, kiddo. How've you been?"

Kelley gave the older actor a hug. "How did you know? How *long* have you known?"

"From the start of rehearsal." He tapped his temple. "Keen powers of observation, remember?"

Tyff glanced down at her chest and muttered, "I *knew* I made them too big. . . ."

Jack cleared his throat. "Actually . . . I just knew it wasn't Kelley on*stage*. No offense but . . . you could use an acting lesson or two. Purely for the mechanics. You know—diction, phrasing . . . Kelley here's an old pro."

Tyff rolled her eyes, and Kelley blushed and looked away.

As she did so, she saw a familiar figure standing under the shadow of the trees, just beyond the path that circled north of the Delacorte.

"Jack?" Kelley turned back. "I have something I have to take care of, but I need to make sure Tyff gets out of the park safely. Can you walk her home?"

The beautiful Summer Fae snorted. "I'm several thousand years old, you know. I think I can manage to look out for myself."

Jack inclined his head gracefully toward her. "But you would do me a great honor if you would allow me the *privilege* of escorting you."

"I . . ." If there was one thing Tyff was susceptible to, it was gallantry. "Oh . . . fine. I'll just go grab the rest of my stuff." She swung her temporarily fiery auburn hair over her shoulder. "I'll even let you buy me a latte on the way, Mr. Savage."

"I'd be delighted, Miss Tyffanwy."

Tyff sashayed off to collect her gear, and Jack turned to Kelley.

"How's your dad doing?" he asked quietly.

Kelley shrugged and looked away. "Not good. I guess. I dunno."

"I'm sorry to hear that. I rather got on with the man."

"Yeah. Well. He's real charming. Right until he rips your wings off." Kelley stared hard at the ground between her feet. "Some people get what they deserve, you know?"

"Kelley Winslow." Jack put a finger under her chin and

tipped her face up so that she was looking him in the eyes. "You don't really mean that."

Kelley blinked rapidly, the sting of gathering tears pricking behind her eyes.

"I think I got a pretty good read on your old man in the time I spent with him," Jack continued, his deep voice quiet in the night air. "Somewhere, buried deep inside of him, beneath all of that frost, there is a part of that man that sees you as his daughter. That *loves* you. And the pity of it is, he's just way too damned proud to let that part show."

Love? Kelley thought. *Impossible.* Jack was wrong. Auberon didn't see her like that. As a daughter . . . no. An inconvenience, maybe. A potential rival, definitely. A threat even, one day. Only . . . he *had* gone to an awful lot of trouble to hide her in the mortal realm. And instead of eliminating a potential threat to his reign, he had constructed an elaborate ruse, tricked Bob into helping Emma steal her away from the Unseelie Court, all just to keep her safe. . . .

Jack smiled at her as she stood there silently, frowning, lost in deeply conflicted thought. "There are always two sides to every story, Kelley. Something I learned playing Richard the Third and Macbeth: if you're playing the 'bad guy,' you never really think of yourself as bad. It's just that your motives are often . . . misunderstood by everyone else."

Kelley breathed a sigh of relief as Jack and Tyff disappeared down the bridle path. It was only a brief stroll to the park perimeter, but Kelley had made Tyff transform back into her own non-Kelley shape so that there would be no mistaking if someone came looking.

Now to get *herself* the hell out of there. But first . . .

"Fennrys?" she called as she approached the spot where she'd seen him standing.

The tall, blond figure stiffened and pushed away from the tree he'd been leaning on. After a moment of what seemed like hesitation, he turned and smiled at Kelley. She wished he wouldn't do that. Fennrys's smile was a strange, disconcerting thing. It wasn't his fault—he just didn't seem used to the expression. He rarely employed it, after all.

"Hello, Princess," he said, walking toward her. "Fancy meeting you here."

"What are you doing here, Fenn?" Kelley asked, as she walked toward him.

"Ah, jeezus," he muttered, dropping all pretense of casually running into her. "What am *I* doing here? What are *you* doing here? Won't you bloody learn? This park is bad news for you."

"It's bad news for everybody these days. Or hadn't you noticed?" she said, startled at his snappish response. In the distance, Kelley could only just hear faint howling sounds. She ignored them—just like every other New Yorker was trying to do. *Coyotes. Yeah, right.*

"It's worse for you, and you know it." Fennrys took a step toward her. "Why in hell do you insist on coming here?"

"Why do you?" she asked again.

The Wolf glared at her. Then he shook his head sharply and answered her question. "I'm here because I am a glutton for punishment. Apparently. Now c'mon. I'll walk you to the street."

He took a step past her, and Kelley realized she'd had enough of his evasions. He obviously wasn't going to tell her why he was there, so she blurted out another question.

"Where's your Janus medallion, Fenn?" she asked.

Fennrys stopped, an expression of surprise on his face, and was silent so long that Kelley thought maybe he wasn't going to answer that question either. Then, finally, he said, "I lost it."

Funny . . . she thought. *That's exactly what Sonny said.*

"How? Don't lie to me, Fennrys. Please." Kelley waited as he turned and walked back the few steps he'd taken, stopping directly in front of her. Close enough so that she had to tilt her head and look up at him.

"I gave it to Gwynn," he said finally.

Kelley's mouth dropped open in surprise. And dismay. That was the last thing she'd expected him to say.

"*Why?*" she asked.

"Because he wanted it. I didn't ask why. I don't care why."

"Fenn—"

"I did it for you," he said. So quietly Kelley wasn't sure she'd heard him right.

"What?" she asked. "What are you talking about?"

Fennrys took a slow breath, and his gaze locked with hers.

"In exchange for your safe passage back to the mortal realm when we were in the Otherworld—"

"Fennrys, no!" Kelley was aghast. "What on earth did you do that for?"

"I wanted to keep you safe." The shadow of a frown creased his forehead. "Kelley . . . I don't want anything bad to happen to you. That's all."

That's all? she thought. *That is* so *not all!*

Alarm bells were clanging in her head—if Gwynn had wanted that medallion after all that time, it wasn't just so he could have some trinket, some way of flouting Auberon's authority and his ownership of the Janus Guard's loyalty. There had to be more to it than that. Even if it *was* just that . . .

"That medallion is part of who you *are*, Fennrys," Kelley said.

"You mean who Auberon *made* me," he snapped, the corners of his mouth turning down in disdain. "Bloody Faerie meddling. I had a *destiny* in this realm, you know. I was a prince. I was a warrior. I would have lived and died and gone to my reward in Valhalla along with my brothers and forefathers if it hadn't been for the Fair Folk."

"*Gwynn* was the one who stole you from this world—not Auberon. Auberon was the one who made you a Janus. I thought you were loyal to him. Even if you didn't always agree with his methods, I thought . . ."

"Yeah, well. I've come to realize something, you know? I realized that, in order to be loyal to someone, *they* have to be loyal to *you*. I don't owe loyalty to anyone in the Otherworld. Now I'm all about saving my own skin. And maybe, every now and then, yours. No offense, Princess, but your old man's a bit of a bastard." The Wolf took another step toward her, close enough so that she had to fight the urge to take a step back. "And Sonny's his man, through and through."

"Why are you saying this to me, Fennrys?"

"I don't want to see you hurt."

"I'm not—"

"Auberon hurt you." He was so close now that she could see herself reflected in his eyes. "He took your wings. And Sonny? He took your theater. That place was your home. I can't see how that proves he really cares so very much for you, you know? You should give it some thought, Kelley."

"You don't know what you're talking about." She turned her face away from him.

"Yeah?" Fenn's hands were on her shoulders now, making her look back at him. "Why did Sonny leave you?"

"You know already," she said angrily. "You know I *made* him leave. *I* did that."

"If it had been me, I *never* would have left you," Fennrys said. "No matter what you said or did. But then, I never would have left you in the first place. If I'd been Sonny, I would have told Auberon to take that business with the Wild Hunt and stuff it sideways."

"Fenn . . . stop."

"You barely know him, Kelley." His voice was low, urgent;

his expression so intense it frightened her. "You said you thought Sonny had changed—I think he's always been *exactly* that. He was raised by a man with a shard of ice where his heart should be. I'm not saying it's Sonny's fault, but you should wonder, maybe, if he's even capable of loving you."

"You don't know what you're talking about. . . ."

But by then, Fennrys had *stopped* talking.

And his kiss effectively stopped Kelley from saying anything else, either.

When, finally, Fennrys let her go and she could breathe again, he said, "I'm not going to apologize for that."

Even though she hadn't asked him to.

She hadn't done anything, in fact. She hadn't pulled away. She hadn't punched him. She hadn't even moved back. She stood there, gasping, stunned. Fennrys relented and took a small step away, allowing Kelley to catch her breath. The Wolf dropped his hands to his sides, and Kelley found some remnant of her voice hiding at the back of her throat. "Where is Sonny?"

The Wolf laughed mirthlessly and shook his head. "I don't know. Back at his apartment by now with that huntress and her traveling circus of Lost Fae losers, I suppose."

Kelley's gaze automatically went to where she could just see the lights of the apartments on Central Park West shining through the screen of trees. Not that she could see Sonny's penthouse from where she stood. And what would she have expected to see, anyway? Sonny standing on the terrace with his arms wrapped around Carys? Would that have made her feel any less guilty in that moment than she did? She should have punched Fenn. He shouldn't have presumed. . . .

"You sure that's what you really want, Kelley?" Fennrys said quietly, following her gaze. "You sure that's *who* you want?"

She turned back to him and said coldly, "I can't believe you'd even ask me that."

"And I can't believe that you'd mess with the guy's mind." Fennrys shrugged. "Lie to him—however you managed *that* little trick, Faerie Princess—abandon him, and think that somehow things will work out in the end. You sure you're not intentionally trying to sabotage this thing you have with Sonny? Maybe when he was gone, you figured out that, in some ways, Irish just doesn't measure up—"

The invisible blow that came out of nowhere snapped Fenn's head viciously to the side, and he grunted in pain. Kelley looked down at where she held her hand cocked in a tight fist—as if she'd actually, physically delivered the blow herself. Her knuckles actually stung.

Fennrys looked back at her, rubbing the side of his jaw. His eyes glittered dangerously, but his mouth quirked upward in that maddeningly inscrutable half grin.

"Right," he said, turning aside to spit blood. "Ain't love grand."

Kelley reined in her rage. "Tell me something. Was I one of those battles you told me about, Fenn? When you said 'pick your battles'—did you pick me? Is that it?"

"What if I did?"

"Then I'd say you made a tactical error." She lifted her chin and stared him in the eyes. "You said the trick in knowing which ones to pick is knowing which ones you can win."

"And?"

"You lose." Kelley turned and walked away from him, anger lengthening her stride.

If only Fennrys hadn't delayed her departure from the park . . . she would have been long gone well before trouble stepped out from beneath the Winterdale Arch bridge: six large black shapes, red eyes burning like embers, long white fangs gleaming in the darkness. Black Shuck.

"Oh goody," Kelley muttered, swallowing painfully against the sudden lump of fear in her throat. "Demon dogs."

Perhaps she'd been hasty to leave Fennrys and try to make it through the park on her own. Foolish. No. Not foolish. *More like really, really monumentally stupid*, she cursed silently. Her palms went slick with nervous sweat and her muscles tightened. The Shuck paced around her like well-trained pets to form a tight, menacing circle. Slowly, Kelley tried to reach up and unfasten the charm around her neck—if she could manifest her wings and take to the sky, she'd be fine—but the lead dog's lips curled back in a snarl the moment she moved her arm.

When she lowered her hand, Kelley noticed the gleaming black carriage parked in the shadows beneath the bridge. The door stood open and a large tawny owl perched on the roof of the cab, staring at her with cold golden eyes. Kelley realized that she didn't have much choice as to what would happen next. She was going to have to get into the carriage. Or the Black Shuck would tear her to pieces.

She turned back to the biggest of the dogs and said, "Okay, Scooby. Let's go. Take me to your leader."

The head Shuck jumped up into the cabin after Kelley climbed in and sat staring balefully at her. The air inside the carriage was heavy with the scent of narcissus and tiger lilies. And mildew. There were dark green stains on the bench seat. As the carriage began to move, Kelley hazarded a glance out of one of the curtained windows. The lights of the city flowed past in a ghostly haze as the antique coach sped unseen through the streets. Another peek, a few minutes later, showed Kelley nothing but darkness, and the glimmering of stars reflected on the black surface of a wide stretch of water that flowed beneath the carriage wheels.

The trip, though brief, didn't give her much time to ponder the circumstances of her present situation. *Not good* was the least terrifying way she could think of to classify it. She listened to the other hellhounds baying as they ran beside the carriage, eagle-taloned feet skimming the dark waves. Then she heard the crunch of gravel beneath the carriage wheels and Kelley felt cold dread clutch at her heart.

The carriage rolled to a stop. After a long moment, the handle on the inside of the door twisted. The door swung open. Kelley heard the ghostly hooting of the owl as it flew off into the darkness.

A hand reached into the carriage to help her alight.

"Hello, Princess," Bob the boucca said. "Welcome to North Brother Island. Or, as I like to call it . . . Hell on Earth."

XXIII

"What happened to you?" Sonny heard Maddox ask.

He looked up from where he sat with Cait to see that Maddox had opened the door for Fennrys to walk in, followed by Bryan and Beni. There was the shadow of a fresh bruise on the Wolf's face.

"Nothing," Fenn said. "I just ran into something with a bit of a temper in the park, that's all."

Cait snorted. "I hope you gave as good as you got."

"Yeah." Fennrys touched the back of his hand to the corner of his mouth. "I hope so, too. . . ."

From Bryan's and Beni's expressions, Sonny knew that

Fennrys must have already filled them in on what was going on with the Janus Guard. Beni looked extremely dismayed, and Bryan's brow was creased in a deep frown.

"Lads," Sonny said. "Thanks for coming."

They nodded.

"Maddox . . . could you fill these three in on everything that's just happened while Cait and I get to work on this locator spell?"

"Sure." Maddox gestured them out onto the terrace. "C'mon, boys. Story time."

"Locator spell, huh?" Fennrys asked, not moving. "Tell me something . . . what if someone else has already found Kelley? What are you gonna do then?"

Something in his tone made Sonny stand and grip the other Janus by his arm. "What do you know, Fennrys?"

"Get your hand off me, Irish," Fenn said in a low, dangerous tone.

Sonny felt a rising bloom of heat in his chest, and his fingertips began to tingle. Fenn must have felt it, too. He glanced down at where Sonny held him, and anger sparked in his gaze as he looked back up.

"You gonna blast me through another window?" he said, grinning dangerously. "Because I just can't get enough of that kinda thing, let me tell you."

Sonny didn't move, but he didn't let go either. The two men stood there, toe to toe. Then Fennrys grinned his lopsided grin.

"I thought we were on the same side here, Sonny-boy."

"Are we?"

Cait looked as though she shared Sonny's skepticism. Fennrys laughed. "Can't you people ever have a little faith?"

A little faith, Sonny thought. Hadn't he said almost the same thing to Kelley not so long ago? He let go of Fenn's arm.

"I'd be careful with that, if I were you." The Wolf's gaze flicked toward Sonny's hand, where the Green Magick still pulsed and thrummed under his skin. Then he stalked out into the night air to join Maddox and the lads, ignoring the assortment of Lost Fae scattered about the apartment.

What's wrong with you? Sonny chastised himself silently. *Is it just because you are jealous of him?*

It made him angry with himself to think that he could be so petty-minded. He'd never felt that way before. He looked down at his hand, where the tips of his fingers still tingled with power. Power that he really didn't have any kind of handle on. Power that he itched to use . . .

Now that he knew it was there, he could feel it, coursing through his veins like the strongest Faerie wine. Dangerous. Intoxicating.

Maybe Kelley *had* been smart to keep this from him.

Under Cait's guidance, Sonny concentrated on following the thready tendrils of power—the ones that connected him to Kelley's charm—through the darkness behind his closed eyelids. Images cascaded through his mind: dense forest and ruined buildings overgrown with masses of tangled vines, shadows beneath trees and scores of birds soaring through the dark sky above—birds with dark wings and pale faces . . . and bright red devil's eyes. Birds like the ones that had attacked them in the reservoir.

In their midst, he sensed a bright green flame, flaring with Kelley's signature firecracker energy. Sonny's eyes snapped open.

"What is it, Sonny?" Cait asked urgently. "What did you see?"

He told her everything he'd seen, the words pouring out of him in a rush before the images could flee. "That's all I can tell you," he said finally, running a hand through his hair in frustration. "But it's useless. Trees, birds . . . she could be anywhere."

Cait thought for a moment and then called Maddox in from the terrace. "Give me your phone," she said, holding out her hand.

Sonny had never seen the need for a computer or a cell phone. But Maddox had recently decided that he would master his wariness of technology once and for all. The shiny little trinket made Sonny seriously rethink his own position. Cait's delicate fingers danced over the glowing screen, calling up a page devoted to the identification of different species of birds. She entered the search terms "red eyes" and "black, white, gray plumage." One of the very first entries that came up on the tiny screen had an accompanying picture.

"That's it!" Sonny pointed triumphantly.

Cait batted away his hand so that he wouldn't alter the screen. "The 'black-crowned night heron,'" she read from the description.

"Sounds ominous enough," Maddox noted dryly.

After his initial rush of excitement, Sonny deflated somewhat. "That's all well and good, Cait," he said, "but I don't see how knowing the species—"

Cait shushed him and tabbed to another screen. She entered the species name of the bird, and requested information on nesting grounds in and around the vicinity of New York City. One mention stood out. Cait did a further search on that entry . . . and suddenly, just like magic, they knew exactly where they had to go.

Less than an hour later, they were on a boat.

Sonny stood, feet braced, on the deck of the rusty old tug as it plowed through the dark water of the East River. Chloe's former profession had left her with an affinity for sailors. Over the years, after her mortal lover died, she'd spent a lot of time down at the docks on the lower East River. She'd gotten to know one old salt who'd actually been a minor river deity in Greece a few centuries back but who, through a series of wanderings, had come to own a fleet of barge tugs. The aging boat they stood on now was one that was due to be decommissioned, and he'd let them have it for free.

"If you don't return it, or sink the damned thing," he said, "I'll turn a profit on the insurance money anyway."

From the way he'd said it, Sonny figured he expected to be collecting a check the next day.

With Maddox at the wheel, the little craft chugged upriver in the darkness, riding low in the water. Sonny took watch from the prow as they headed toward an ominous hump of land that lay dark and seemingly uninhabited, just northwest of the sweep of the Rikers Island prison searchlights. Their destination.

They were close enough now that Sonny could make out the dark shapes of buildings hidden under an untamed canopy of thick forest growth. The remains of a crumbling dock made for treacherous landing, but Maddox managed to get them close enough to the shore so that they only had to wade knee-deep through the water.

The second Sonny's boots hit the ground, he felt a thrumming, disturbed energy. The very island seemed angered by their presence. The trees at the edge of the shingle creaked and moaned as they splashed ashore, swaying in the absence of any wind. Sonny was also reasonably certain that, in the distance, he heard the baying of one or more Black Shuck.

He exchanged a glance with Maddox as they stepped ashore along with Fennrys and Carys and the others. The plan was simply to split up and cover as much ground as possible, find Kelley, and—if someone did—send up a signal for the others to hightail it back to the boat.

But their adversaries had other ideas.

A barrage of arrows came zipping out from the trees, shot

by an unseen archer. Sonny and Carys were forced to run for cover behind a stack of rotting timbers.

It seemed that the island's first line of defense was the rogue Janus Guard.

"I thought you said you dislocated Selene's shoulder!" Sonny called to Cait, who'd tumbled for safety into the black water behind the stern of the boat.

"I did! I guess someone else *re*located it!" she shouted back.

Slender spears arced out toward the boat along with the arrows, forcing Fennrys and the lads to retreat and take cover on the deck of the boat behind the gunwales. *Camina*, Sonny thought grimly. The throwing spear was a favorite weapon of hers—and she'd obviously stocked up.

Crouched beside Sonny, Carys pulled her own bow from her shoulder and nocked an arrow, but there was nothing visible to shoot at. The forest cover was too thick.

"Bug!" the huntress called to Neerya, who still crouched behind the wheelhouse on the tug. "Can you get airborne and see if you can spot anything? I need to know where to shoot!"

Neerya nodded bravely and soared upward through the air like a tiny blue meteor. She hovered there, zipping back and forth to avoid getting hit, so focused on finding the shooter that she didn't see the demon-eyed heron plummet silently toward her out of the darkness until it was too late. She shrieked and tumbled through the air to avoid it. The bird slashed the air with knifelike talons, catching an edge of one of Neerya's iridescent wings—tearing it away from her shoulder blade with a bright flash of light. Neerya screamed in pain and dropped through the air toward the water's edge, witch-fire trailing behind her from her torn wing.

"No!" Sonny screamed as she fell.

"I've got her!" Maddox shouted, and leaped from the bow rail of the tug. He caught the naiad in midair, pulling her in tight to his broad chest before she could hit the ground. They landed in the shallow water a stone's throw away from the safety of the boat. Sonny saw a flash of movement darting out from under the trees. He shouted a warning at Maddox, who ducked as Godwyn came charging like an enraged boar down the narrow strip of beach toward him, swiping at Maddox's head with a long-bladed rapier.

The rogue Janus was laughing wildly. Maddox had dropped his own weapon so that he could catch Neerya, and that had left him vulnerable. The naiad stumbled back toward the boat as Maddox turned to defend himself. But Godwyn was faster. Maddox howled in excruciating pain as the sword pierced straight through his shoulder. Godwyn pulled the rapier out, smiled viciously, and—as was his custom—began to sing.

A mistake, that.

Blood cascaded down the right side of Maddox's chest, soaking his shirt. And then the left side as well, as Godwyn cruelly ran his sword through the Janus's other shoulder joint. Maddox fell forward onto his knees, his arms hanging uselessly at his sides as Godwyn reared back for the killing blow that would have taken Maddox in the heart.

If only he hadn't been singing. . . .

Chloe had stayed safely hidden in the tugboat's hold up to that point. But the music drew her up onto the deck. Even from a distance, Sonny saw the rage ignite in the Siren's golden eyes as she realized what was happening to Maddox.

She ran and leaped from the bow of the boat, flinging herself at Godwyn, clawing wildly at his head and shoulders, knocking him to the ground. Godwyn flailed desperately in an attempt to dislodge her, but the Siren clung to him like a barnacle on a ship.

Chloe fastened her mouth on Godwyn's. Her Siren's kiss stopped the singing in his throat, even as she stole every bit of music mercilessly from his mind. Godwyn was dead almost before the echoes of his song had faded into silence.

A moment of stillness blanketed the beach, and Carys took the opportunity to fire blindly into the trees so that she and Sonny could make a run for it. They got to Maddox and heaved him back up over the low starboard side of the tug to safety. Cait threw up a shielding spell around the boat as they did.

"That doesn't happen *every* time you kiss someone, does it?" Maddox said to Chloe, gasping through the pain of his double injuries. The Siren knelt before him and pressed the palms of her hands to the spreading bloodstains. She leaned forward and kissed Maddox softly on the lips . . . to no harm whatsoever.

"Webber!" Sonny called the Fae. "Over here. You were right. We do need you."

Webber bent close to Maddox, a deep crease forming

between his brows. "I . . ." He shook his long head, as if trying to make sense of something only he could see. "I do not think this is why I'm here. This isn't what I saw. . . ."

Sonny glanced at Carys, who frowned faintly. He looked back down at Maddox, whose face had gone ashen with pain. He was losing a lot of blood. "I don't care what you think you saw, Webber," he said urgently. "You're a healer. Please. *Heal* him."

The tall Fae turned to Carys, and she nodded. "Do what he asks, Webb. They've earned it from us."

"Hey!" Bryan's head suddenly popped up from the deck hatch. "Look what I found!" He held up a pair of emergency flare guns and a box of flares.

"Good man," Sonny said, and called them all together to tell them his plan.

"Have fun storming the castle," Maddox said through a tight, pained grin, as Sonny and Fennrys got ready to bolt.

"Won't be nearly as much fun without you." Sonny smiled grimly and pulled the short swords from his satchel. "Cait, get ready to lower the shield. Carys, protect them as best you can. Especially Webber—while he works on Madd and Neerya, he'll be the most vulnerable."

"I'd rather be coming with you," she said.

"I know. But I need you to stay here. They need you more than I do right now."

Carys nodded and gave him one of her fierce, brief hugs. "Luck."

"Thanks. Lads . . . on my mark."

Bryan and Beni nodded in tandem.

"Fenn . . . let's go."

Fennrys nodded as Bryan and Beni started laying down covering fire, shooting flares into the forest. Sonny and the Wolf snaked over the sides of the boat and sprinted away in opposite directions. It would be up to the two of them to find Kelley—if they could.

Sonny pounded down the strip of gravelly beach until he could no longer see where they'd moored the boat. As he stepped onto the leaf-littered ground under the trees, he heard a familiar, chilling voice whisper through his mind, the words colored with a rasping lilt: *You're on my playground, now, boyo. . . .*

All around him the trees shivered, as if in response to the leprechaun's threat.

Let's have some fun. . . .

Sonny felt a surge of magick. He took off at a dead run as the ground suddenly rippled and bucked under his feet. Weedy grasses whipped at his ankles, trying to trip him as he sprinted across what had once been a manicured lawn. Sonny ran for all he was worth. In among the trees and wild unchecked saplings, he saw flickering lights and wispy, flitting shadows. His feet pounded over the uneven ground as he leaped to avoid fallen logs and gnarled, grasping roots that would trip him if he were not careful.

The surging wave of moss and mud was at Sonny's heels,

almost overrunning him. He saw an opening through the trees, a bare patch of what appeared to be asphalt, only a dozen yards distant. He headed for it, finding himself on what used to be an old tennis court. The paved surface was covered with fallen leaves, but it provided a minimal barrier between Sonny and the Wee Green Man's twisted magicks. Trees that had sprung up from cracks around the edges of the old court reached gnarled and twisted fingers, but they could not reach far enough. Out in the middle of the paved surface, he was safe enough. For the moment.

Then Aaneel stepped out from under those same trees, Percival at his side, and the moment was gone.

The trees surrounding the tennis court on all sides grew still, as if they were spectators in the stands of an arena.

Or a coliseum.

XXIV

Stunned, Kelley followed Bob up a crumbling staircase and into a looming Gothic building that had obviously been left to rot for decades. The whole structure was draped in a thick tangle of creeping viny growth. Once inside, Bob led her through wide, institutional hallways piled with drifts of trash. Sickly greenish light filtered through broken windows. The scent of decay clung to peeling paint and crumbling plaster on the walls.

"What is this place?" she asked quietly, uncertain whether Bob would deign to answer her. *I gave Mabh his name*, Kelley thought. He wasn't going to forgive her for that. She wondered just how much trouble she was in. "You called it North Brother Island?"

"I also called it hell. And for a lot of poor doomed souls, it is."

As they walked, the half dozen Black Shuck that had accompanied Kelley on her journey stalked along on either side of them, like an escort. Kelley hugged her elbows against the chill spring breeze. Almost every pane of window glass had been shattered, but she still couldn't see much. The view was mostly obscured by thick, woody vines. "Are we in the Otherworld?"

Bob snorted. "This place is nowhere near the Otherworld. But it is rife with magick. Rotten with it, I should say. North Brother Island—a fairly innocuous name for a place that has seen more than its share of horrors down through the years— lies in the East River. Just above that mortal penal colony."

"Rikers Island?"

"That's the one." Bob nodded. "This place here is off-limits to the general mortal populace. Has been for years. Ever since they shut down the rehabilitation programs."

Kelley felt an uncomfortable shiver run up her spine as she gazed around at her bleak surroundings. "Creepy . . ."

"Oh . . . I'm sure it didn't always look like this. Before the mortals decided to build this facility to quarantine their smallpox victims, it was probably lovely and pastoral."

"Smallpox!" Kelley gaped at the boucca. "I thought you said it was a rehab facility."

"That was later. First it was a hospital for infectious diseases. Smallpox, tuberculosis . . . typhus." Bob grinned wickedly at the look on Kelley's face. "Yes, indeedy. North Brother Island—before it was forgotten—was somewhat infamous. The name Typhoid Mary ring any bells? She was a 'guest' here for a few decades."

Kelley felt her throat tightening. She couldn't catch typhus. Could she? No. Of course she couldn't. She hadn't really ever been sick a day in her life. She was Faerie. She didn't get sick.

In the same way that Auberon doesn't get sick?

"And then, of course, they turned the hospital into a treatment center in the fifties for poor unfortunate heroin addicts." Bob turned a corner, where he gestured Kelley up a staircase to the second floor. "Treatment. Huh. If you can call locking a bunch of strung-out young people in rooms and forcing them to quit cold turkey 'treatment.' Some went mad. Some died. Place is full of the unquiet shades of those who passed here. The sick, the addicts, the victims of the *General Slocum* disaster back in 1904 . . ."

"The what?"

"A steamboat ran aground here. Over a thousand dead . . ."

"You're serious."

"It's a storied little thirteen-acre lump of dirt, this island."

Kelley's skin was virtually crawling. She stopped halfway up the stairs, paralyzed by the thought of all the horrors the place had played host to.

"Come on, now," Bob said grimly. "We mustn't keep the queen waiting."

* * *

Kelley felt a cold finger of fear trace up her spine as she stepped into the main hall and saw the regal figure of Titania, Queen of Summer, standing framed by tall, shattered windows. The Shuck surged forward, padding across the floor to sit in a circle at the queen's feet. Over in the corner, on a broken settee piled with cushions, lay the twisted figure of Hooligan-boy. The Wee Green Man. On the cracked marble floor in front of him lay an enormous, jumbled mass of withered leaves and branches—all that was left of the Old Shrub from Herne's Tavern.

It looked as though they had drained the gentle old creature of every ounce of his Green Magick in order to revive the leprechaun. Kelley looked back at the leprechaun on the settee and saw that it had worked. Hooligan-boy's eyes were open and fixed upon her. They were full of hate . . . and triumph.

That can only mean one thing, Kelley thought.

"I knew there must have been something extraordinary about that little Irish boy for Auberon to have taken such an interest in him," Titania said with a knowing smile as Kelley approached the windows.

It meant that Kelley's desperate lie had all been in vain. The pain she'd put herself and Sonny through, meaningless. It meant, in spite of everything, Titania knew that it was Sonny Flannery who carried the Greenman's power.

And she knew how to tap it.

Gesturing, the Queen spoke an ancient word, and Kelley found herself frozen. Spell-stopped. Unable to move a muscle as the beautiful Faerie monarch drifted toward her and, with sunbeam-warm fingers, reached up and unclasped the clover charm from around Kelley's neck.

Over in the corner, the leprechaun laughed—a harsh, rasping sound like gravel sliding down a mountainside.

The charm dangled from Titania's fingers, swinging hypnotically on its silver chain. "Come," said the queen. "Let me show you what I can do with *this*. Here. In this realm."

With a deceptively simple waft of her hand, the Queen of the Seelie Fae transformed "here" into "there."

And "there" was . . . spectacular.

Kelley knew instantly, instinctively, that she was looking at a vision of the Summer Kingdom. In the same way that Sonny had once shown her the world of Herne the Hunter, Titania wove a glamour of her Court, only more so.

All around Kelley a world burst into bloom in such exact, minute detail that she could breathe in the scent of the rich earth beneath her feet, and hear the distant call of a plover, tumbling through the sky over the far hills. Kelley and the queen stood, high on a gentle swell of wildflower-carpeted hill, surrounded by a ring of willow and white-skinned birch, ash and alder and thorn, magnolia and cherry and apple trees.

Before them, the land rolled away in hills and dales. Silk tents dotted the landscape, each one surrounded by gatherings of Fair Folk so beautiful that they almost hurt to look at. There were feasts laid out on silver service, wine—sparkling star-bright—filling crystal glasses. Everywhere, the hint of glistening water caught at Kelley's gaze—hidden pools, rushing brooks, tumbling falls. In the distance a broad, winding river beckoned. There was not a bare branch or a fruitless shrub or a brown patch of grass anywhere to be seen. The busiest of bees could occupy themselves for an eternity in this place.

Kelley felt the thrumming presence of great power behind her and, at Titania's prompting, turned to see that she stood before the throne of the Summer Lands—formed by a living oak tree that had grown into the shape of a magnificent royal chair. Sheer, shining lengths of Faerie-spun cloth hung in panels from the oak's branches, providing shade and decoration. Tiny, sparkling fire sprites filled the spaces between the leaves overhead.

"This is my home," Titania murmured softly. "*This* is what I would wish to bring to humanity. They used to have it, you know—I remember when their realm was a green and lovely place. Somewhere, deep in their hearts, they remember it, too."

It was paradise. It was perfect.

And, to Kelley, it was absolutely terrifying.

She understood something in that moment. As pristine as Titania's kingdom was, it was stagnant. Stale. Without the unpredictability of mortals, without their foibles and strangeness and odd, surprising strengths, the Fair Folk grew bored with their unending perfection. Tyff had been right. From the minute that the Greenman crossed over into the mortal realm, he had doomed the Fae to need mortal-kind. Kelley had a vivid mental picture of what Titania's "wish for humanity" would result in—she'd had the dream of it for months now. Manhattan reclaimed by nature. Human innovation and error and all the crazy imperfections that made New York so wonderful, wiped out—buried forever beneath a thick pall of unbroken beauty. New Yorkers made thralls.

The Summer Queen's grand vision.

Titania's expression radiated benevolence and goodness. But Kelley also saw hints of something like intoxication lurking in her gaze. Kelley clamped down hard on the fear building inside her. For a moment, she almost thought she could hear Sonny calling out to her.

"Magnificent, isn't it?" Titania sighed.

"Sure," Kelley muttered. "Fabulous." She wished she could cross her arms over her chest in a show of defiance, but her muscles still wouldn't obey her commands. "Enjoy your little gardening hobby, Highness. Can I go now?"

"Oh no, sweeting!" The queen's merry laugh trickled away to a tipsy giggle.

"Why? You've got your necklace. *My* necklace," Kelley said mutinously. "What do you need me for?"

"I don't need you, my darling. I need *him.*"

Kelley understood now why she was there on North Brother Island—why they hadn't just taken the charm from her in the park. *Bait.* How do you get to Superman? Kidnap Lois Lane.

Way to go, Lois, Kelley thought bitterly.

284

"A pity . . . ," the queen murmured, raising a languid hand to tuck a stray lock of Kelley's hair behind her ever-so-slightly pointed ear. Kelley had her father's ears. . . . "Such a pity that your father will not be the one to rule this earthly kingdom by my side." Although her expression remained unchanged—dreamy and unfocused—large, luminous tears welled in the queen's lovely eyes. They spilled over and ran down her cheeks. "I did so love him, you know. . . ."

Titania's use of the past tense made Kelley's heart thud painfully in her chest. Was Auberon dead? Had her father succumbed to his illness without her even knowing it?

The glamour faded, and once more they stood in the dilapidated old hospital pavilion. Kelley's motor-function control was restored.

"Do as I told you," the queen said to Bob. "Take her away for now." She gazed out the broken windows, as if she still saw her verdant kingdom rolling away to the horizon in front of her.

Bob led Kelley down the rubbish-strewn corridor and into a tiny, cell-like room where he said she was to wait. Graffiti from the room's previous inhabitants decorated the walls: a weeping eye, a twisted tree shaped like a woman with her arms held out like branches. Shards of filthy glass held suspended in a rusted frame that had once served as a wall mirror reflected Kelley's dismayed expression.

Bob perched on a backless chair and watched her silently.

Slowly, it dawned on Kelley that she and Bob were not alone in the room. She could feel . . . others, as though she was being watched by dozens of unseen eyes.

She brushed a hand over her forehead—*a cobweb*, she thought fleetingly, but there was nothing there. Just ghost kisses—like mist swirling around her. Like the presence of restless shades. Like when she'd come through the rift and had felt herself surrounded by wraiths. There were more of them here.

"You get used to them," Bob said. "The unquiet ones."

"Why are there so many of them?"

Bob shrugged. "There shouldn't be. Even considering the history of this place. You see . . . there are realms beyond the mortal world. Beyond the Otherworld, even. Places that those departed—mortal and Fae—cross over to when they depart. But something about this place keeps these poor shades tied to this realm. This island's like a nexus of negative energy, feeding on the shadows of all the lost souls that have come to inhabit these shores. Stirring them up. Setting them loose in the Between. Using all that anger and confusion to open rifts in the Samhain Gate. Capturing even more wraiths—shades of Fae killed by the Janus—using those to thin and break down the walls between the worlds . . ." Bob subsided into silence.

Unspoken tension stretched out between the two of them. Kelley glanced at Bob. He was staring at her, his fierce glare piercing the dusky air. Kelley began to fidget uncomfortably.

"So," he said finally. "You sold me out."

She'd been wondering when the boucca would get around to broaching the subject. There wasn't much point in denying it, so Kelley returned his gaze as steadily as she could, and said, "Yeah. I did."

The bitter disappointment in Bob's eyes wounded Kelley to the core—much more than his anger would have. Was there *anyone* she cared for that she hadn't hurt?

"I'm sorry," she said quietly. What else could she say? "I know that you'll probably never forgive me and I have no right to expect that you would. What I did was all kinds of wrong. To you. To Sonny . . . I've really made a mess of things, haven't I?"

"No argument there."

Kelley felt her cheeks burning with shame. "I'm so sorry," she said again.

Bob sighed gustily. "Fair enough," he said.

Kelley blinked at him. "That's it?"

"You gave Mabh my secret name. And you're right. Under other circumstances, I'd probably muster up a revenge scheme that would curl your toenails, Princess. But I understand why you did what you did. And, anyway, it so happens that it doesn't really matter all that much anymore."

"Why do you say that?"

"Because *I* turned around and gave my secret name to *Titania*."

Kelley was shocked to see him grinning.

He explained. "I once told Sonny that no one can compel me by the name Puck or Robin Goodfellow anymore. You see . . . once a boucca's secret name becomes common knowledge, it loses its punch. Having two Faerie monarchs know my name considerably lessens the power they each have over me."

Kelley felt her jaw drift open in astonishment.

"Titania thinks she's got an exclusive, but she's wrong." Bob chuckled wanly. "Add Auberon into the mix—*he's* known it for ages—and you and Sonny and Fennrys and whoever else might have been listening at keyholes over the years, and I'm almost free of the compulsion entirely. Once the name loses all its power, I'll be free to choose another. If I live so long . . ."

"That's still pretty risky, isn't it?"

Bob shrugged one shoulder—which told Kelley it was.

What in the world made him give Titania his name? she wondered.

As if in answer to her thoughts, Bob looked at her, his green eyes glittering, and said, "She promised not to kill you if I did."

XXV

Aaneel left Perry standing at the edge of the asphalt and walked toward Sonny with a relaxed, easy gait. The man who was once the leader of the Janus Guards was dressed not for battle but in the flowing, brightly colored silk trousers and tunic of an Indian prince. His thick black hair, only just silvering at the temples after all his long years of living in the Otherworld, was tied back off his face, and his dark eyes glittered coldly as he stepped toward Sonny. In his hands, he held twin khukuri knives.

"Why?" Sonny asked.

Aaneel seemed to consider the question for a moment,

stopping in the middle of the tennis court. Then he said, "I was never meant to be what I am. My mother was a princess in this world of long-ago. She was a pure-hearted woman and a treasured confidante of the Seelie queen. Before my mother died giving birth to my own sad self, Titania told her she would take care of me." He smiled indolently. "It is past time I honor that pledge and let the queen do just that."

Titania, Sonny though grimly. So it seemed it was the Summer Queen who was behind all the recent chaos after all. He shook his head in disgust.

"In other words, you grow tired of having to earn your keep."

Aaneel's smile grew a touch brittle. "In other words, I am no longer willing to be the Winter King's lackey."

"But you're more than happy to be the Summer Queen's lapdog." Sonny knew that Aaneel had always had a taste for the finer things in life. Gourmet food, fine clothing, beautiful women. Luxury. Titania must have offered him all that. And more. Over Aaneel's shoulder, Sonny saw Perry stiffen, a frown crossing his brow.

"What about you, Percival?" Sonny nodded to the young man. "What's your excuse?"

"She saved my village!" Perry said defiantly. Sonny knew the story of his taking by the Fair Folk—Titania had promised gentle weather and bountiful harvests for Percival's drought-plagued hamlet in exchange for him. "I owe her."

Sonny gazed at him a little sadly. "Do you, now? Do you

not think a Faerie queen might have had something to do with all those bad harvests in the first place, lad?"

Aaneel laughed. "Don't listen to him, Perry. He clings to his loyalties like a drowning man to driftwood. There is a new order coming, Sonny. A glorious time approaches like a majestic ship sailing over the horizon. You would be wise to get on board or get out of the way."

"I'm not always wise, Aaneel," Sonny said. "But I've been treading these same waters a long time and I've grown accustomed to them just the way they are."

The rogue Janus sighed. "More's the pity. Stay how you are then. Sink or swim, I will not throw you a lifeline."

"I wouldn't take it if you did."

Sonny tightened his grip on the two short swords in his hands and braced for the coming attack.

Aaneel was across the breadth of the tennis court before Sonny had time to even draw breath. So swift were his actions that the blades in his hands were nothing more than a blur. But Sonny had studied Aaneel—he had studied all the Janus guards, eager to learn all he could about the arts of war—and he knew that the khukuris were hacking weapons, most useful when employed with an overhand, downward swinging motion—like a machete. So long as he kept his blows high up on Aaneel, he had a chance.

Sonny sidestepped Aaneel's first vicious attacks and launched a series of head-cuts in retaliation. Sonny had to draw on all his speed to evade Aaneel's flashing knives. Aaneel was the best of the Janus. The oldest, the most experienced . . . the most treacherous. Sonny fought with a grim determination.

He pictured Auberon in his mind, lying weak and dying because of the betrayals of those like Aaneel—a man the king had trusted above all others. He thought of Ghost, who would not now be dead if only Aaneel had remained true. He thought of Percival, who stood watching, teetering on the edge of corruption because of Aaneel and the Summer Queen's taint.

Sonny tried to reach for the Green Magick, but the power lay dormant and unresponsive deep within him. Because Chloe had removed the shielding charm, he could sense its presence now, but—contrary to his hopes—he could not shape it to his will. It was his training, he realized suddenly, slashing upward with the blade in his right hand. Aaneel swore and came at him again. Sonny had been taught to fight from the time he could walk and he had been taught to fight cold—trained to ignore the emotions that were a liability in a battle. He was not a berserker like Fennrys or Ghost. As a warrior, his cool-headed detachment, the ability to divorce himself from the blinding effects of intense feelings, was the strongest weapon in his arsenal.

Except in this particular instance, when he really could have used a violent emotional response to ignite all that dormant power. Now that Chloe had taken away the charm from his mind, he remembered the rush of rage and fear that had filled him when he thought Kelley was dead—and he knew that that was what had triggered his magick. He'd felt stirrings of that same kind of rush back in the apartment when

Fennrys had goaded him about Kelley. But that reaction wasn't something he could just manufacture.

Aaneel came at him again, windmill slashes cutting the air side to side in front of him. Sonny retreated, shifting his weight onto his back foot, ducking low as the blades whistled past his cheek. He leaped back, taking quick stock of his surroundings; the fight had taken them past the edge of the tennis court and onto a cracked walkway that led directly to a large brick building.

In the briefest of moments, as Sonny glanced up, he was startled to see Kelley standing framed in the arched windows of the second story. At her side stood Titania.

"Kelley!" Sonny shouted, parrying another of Aaneel's strikes with the crossed blades of his swords as he did. Sparks flew from the screeching metal, and he had to dodge out of the way of another of Aaneel's furious slashing blows. He glanced back over his shoulder for a brief second. "Down here!"

Kelley stared out over the courtyard as if she couldn't hear him.

On Aaneel's next attack, Sonny dived low and took the other man out at the knees. Aaneel tumbled away, but Sonny didn't follow. Instead, he sprinted in the opposite direction—toward the window where Kelley stood. Directly underneath, he saw what looked like a raised stone dais, covered in a thick layer of foliage. It was high enough so that he could use it to leap to the stone overhang just under the window. All he had to do was reach that ledge and then he would climb to her—just like Romeo had to Juliet.

It was a good plan.

Only it was thwarted by a better one.

Sonny realized an instant too late why the leprechaun had yet to show himself. He'd had no need. The instant Sonny's foot touched the top of what he'd thought was a solid stone platform, he was done. It wasn't solid, or stone.

It was an uncovered well.

The deep cistern—a stone-walled hole in the earth—had been cleverly camouflaged, not with a glamour, but with greenery. It was the same technique Aaneel had once told him they'd used in India to trap tigers. The second Sonny put any weight on the top, the thatch of vines and leaves gave way under him, and he plummeted into blackness. His head struck the stone as he fell, and he landed heavily, unable to rise.

Sonny reached up a hand to the warm wetness on his forehead, and his fingertips came away dark with blood. The nausea and dizziness he felt as he struggled to his knees told him that he had most likely suffered a concussion—a bad one. The stone sides of the well wavered and tipped as he fell over heavily onto his back, staring up at the circle of sky far above him.

As Sonny's consciousness began to fade, he saw the tall, elegant figure of Gwynn ap Nudd, his features silvered by the moon's watery light.

Titania and *Gwynn?*

It was worse than Sonny had imagined. Much worse.

The pain in his head flashed blindingly behind his eyes, and Sonny slid away into nothingness.

XXVI

"When Auberon drifted from Titania's side into a dalliance with your mother, he surely did not know what poisoned fruit the Summer Queen's hurt would produce," Bob mused.

"Yeah, well . . ." Kelley thought about that—and about what she knew of Titania. "I don't know if I blame her entirely. *I'd* still be a little miffed about the whole love-potion/ass-head thing if I was her."

"Oh, pish. That was just good fun."

Kelley raised an eyebrow at the boucca. "Auberon manipulated and humiliated Titania all for the sake of bragging rights over who got to parade around with that pompous jerk Aaneel."

"Who, by the way, has defected to Titania's side," Bob informed her.

"Color me shocked," Kelley said sarcastically. She hadn't exactly had warm fuzzy feelings toward the erstwhile leader of the Janus Guard lately. "And anyway, you know my mother's track record with love affairs. Do they *ever* end well?"

"Oh, no. I shouldn't think so. Perhaps that's one reason she's so meddlesome in your, well, your affairs."

"Right," Kelley said. "She doesn't want me to succeed where she failed."

Bob shook his head sadly. "You're awfully young to be so jaded, Princess. Did it ever occur to you that she doesn't want you to fail as she did?"

Kelley opened her mouth to retort. But then she stopped and thought about it. Had Mabh—for all her scariness—ever really done anything to hurt Kelley? Really? In a way, all she'd ever done was try, in her own signature pathological way, to protect her.

Kelley couldn't say the same for her father.

Only . . . what was it Jack had said? The bad guy never thinks of what he's doing as bad. Could it be that her parents, in their own bizarre, nonsensical, inscrutable ways, actually . . . *loved* her? That was stretching things maybe. Maybe they just didn't *hate* her. She wondered if, after everything that had happened, it might just be possible for her to return the sentiment. To Mabh . . . and maybe to Auberon as well.

Auberon, who'd stolen her wings when he'd taken back the power of his throne from her veins. Power that, at the time, she'd fervently wished he'd choke on and die—

"Oh no . . . ," Kelley whispered.

A terrible realization came crashing down upon her.

Bob was gazing at her curiously. Kelley glanced wildly around the room until . . . *there!* The flash of reflection that had caught her eye earlier—a shard of glass, all that was left of a shattered mirror, hanging askew on the other wall. She carefully worked the triangle of broken glass free from the old bent frame and, with the sleeve of her jacket, rubbed the grime from the surface until she could see her own face reflected clearly back at her.

She concentrated.

Long minutes passed as she sent out the silent call to her mother. Perspiration beaded on her forehead with the effort to navigate through the veils that separated the Otherworld from the mortal realm, trying to avoid contact with the drifting restless shades that haunted the Between.

"Think small," Bob murmured from where he hunched, watching her keenly. "Think small and slippery, light and little. A gnat, a newt, a hummingbird on flitting wings, a leaf on a breeze, a puff of dandelion fluff . . ." His voice hummed in her ears like a singsong nursery rhyme, nonsense and instruction wrapped up together. She tried to think of it as an acting exercise and let herself be guided by the boucca's murmured wisdom. She felt herself slip between the layers of enchantment, from world to world, to drift into the circle of the Autumn Queen's court.

Kelley brought her gaze back down to the mirror she held before her and stared into her own eyes. They flickered, sparked, and then grew unfocused for a moment. And then her gaze sharpened, and the Queen of Air and Darkness stared back at her, a look of surprise on her face, quickly stifled when she realized what had been done.

"Daughter," Mabh said with carefully affected blandness. "You are getting rather good at things. You called?"

Kelley exhaled the breath she'd been holding and rolled the exertion from her shoulders. She'd done it.

"Master Goodfellow." Mabh bowed politely to the boucca, who stood warily a few feet behind Kelley. "We've missed your presence here."

"My lady." Bob bowed, without taking his eyes off the queen. "You're looking . . . rather lovely."

"Only rather?"

"Wow. You guys really don't lie, do you?" Kelley was starting to get the hang of the games the Fair Folk played with one another, but that didn't mean she was necessarily going to play by exactly the same rules. "Mom—you look terrible. For a Faerie queen, that is. For a normal person, you look like a rock star. How are you?"

"Heavens. Is that a note of concern I hear in your voice?"

"Knock it off, Mom. How's Dad?"

If Mabh was shocked by Kelley's mode of address—and she obviously *was* by the look on her face—she had the good sense not to push the matter by drawing any more attention to it. "Worse and worse, I hate to say. And it seems that I am unable to do anything to help him. In fact, I'm feeling rather unwell myself these days. Not near as bad as Auberon, but—"

"It's going to be okay," Kelley said. "Put him on the phone."

Mabh did so. It took all Kelley's self-control not to flinch in revulsion at the sight of her father. His eyes were sunken pits, and the arteries along the sides of his neck pulsed with dark blood. The Winter King's cheekbones and the angles of his forehead stood out in sharp relief.

There was a desperate fear in his bloodshot gaze that squeezed Kelley's heart to see. She put her hand on the dirty shard of glass and pressed her fingertips hard against the surface. At Mabh's urging, Auberon did the same, reaching out with one claw-like, emaciated hand to touch the circle of mirror she'd brought to his bedside.

"Give me back the power you took from me that night at Samhain," Kelley said as gently as she could.

She still remembered how it had felt when Auberon had ripped away her Unseelie gift, and how she had wished him nothing but ill as he'd done so. Her hatred and her fear had been so great in that moment. And she had sent all of that toxic emotion along with her power.

"Please. Give it back to me."

There was a flicker of uncertainty in Auberon's gaze, and

then he closed his eyes. Kelley felt as if she was suddenly falling forward into a dark and formless place. Her vision grew dim, and the shabby prison cell all around her disappeared. Shadows and silence enveloped her, and she breathed slowly and deeply, trying to still the pounding of her heart. The blackness thickened and became absolute and Kelley continued to fall, without even knowing which way was up.

Just when it became almost too much to bear and a cry began to bubble up in her throat, she saw a tiny, pale flicker of light in the darkness. She arrowed her consciousness toward it, and it grew larger and brighter. Soon the gleaming silver light was all around her, surrounding her.

Her power. Her birthright. Her Unseelie gift.

It burned like a star, and suddenly she was at its heart. But, looking outward, she saw that the edges of the flaring brightness were knitted to the shadowy umbra through which she'd just passed. The bleak blackness was tied into her power, and she knew that *this* was what she had sent along to the Lord of the Unseelie Fae when she wished her hurt upon him.

Head and heart, mind and soul, she thought. *Thinking makes it so.*

She had done this with her magick. Now she would undo it.

Slowly, carefully, she drew the brightness back into herself, and with it the darkness with which it was entwined. . . . Her anger. Her fear and hatred. She revoked the unspoken curses she had unwittingly sent against Auberon the king

300

and, in their stead, sent out an apology to Auberon her father. Understanding. Not . . . love—she was not there. Not yet. But understanding. It was a start, she hoped.

From far away, she heard Auberon gasp. It was a sound as if someone had suddenly loosened a tight band from around his chest, allowing him to draw a clear breath again. The last of Kelley's power flowed back into her, and she was no longer falling.

She was flying . . . on star-bright, silver wings.

Kelley looked about and saw that the darkness, the shadows, had receded and a pristine, wintry landscape stretched out below her right to the horizon in every direction. It was pure and beautiful . . . only . . .

Here and there stands of trees, branches black and bare, reached grasping fingers into the pearl-white sky. Kelley flew closer and saw that they looked . . . *wrong* somehow. She reached out a hand and touched one of those thorny twigs and screamed in pain as the cold fire of pure iron lanced through her fingers and down her arm.

Kelley threw herself backward and suddenly found that she was back in the cell on North Brother Island. She lay on the floor, clutching her hand and writhing in pain. Bob crouched before her, concern twisting his pale green features. Kelley could hear her mother's voice calling out to her. She groped senselessly for the shard of mirror and held it up, looking into Mabh's anxious face.

"What happened?" the queen asked. "Are you all right?"

"Ow." Kelley clambered up onto her knees. The fingers of her hand that had touched the phantom iron looked scalded an angry red. "Yeah. Ow . . ."

"Daughter . . ." Auberon was calling her, his voice weak, but clear.

"Dad?" She tried to see around Mabh, who was peering anxiously through the mirror at her. "Mom—give him the mirror."

Mabh handed the scrying glass to the king, the scene of the room in the Autumn palace bobbing wildly as she did. The change in the Winter King's appearance was subtle. But it was substantial. Auberon's eyes seemed less sunken and their black depths glittered fiercely. The drawn tightness of his features had loosened; it almost seemed as if some of the flesh had returned to his bones. He still looked terribly weak, and flashes of pain shot across his face when he moved.

"How are you?" Kelley asked, leaning close to the mirror.

Her father nodded. "Better. But you know it will not last. You saw. You felt it—the curse."

"Yeah. I did." Kelley swallowed thickly. "I'm sorry."

"There is nothing for you to be sorry for."

"We both know that's not true. It was my fault you were even vulnerable to this thing in the first place. My anger—"

"*My* fault," the king interrupted her. "I have not done right by you, Daughter. I am sorry." He held his hand up to the mirror again, and Kelley touched her fingertips to the glass. The icy chill of Winter cooled her skin, soothing away the sting of the iron's burns.

She looked into her father's dark eyes. "Call me Kelley, okay?"

Auberon hesitated for a moment and then smiled. "Kelley," he said.

"Mom, Dad . . . I gotta go. And don't worry. I'm going to find a way to fix this. I promise." As the image faded from the stained surface of the glass, Kelley stood and turned toward the empty middle of the room. "We're getting out of here," she said to Bob.

Concentrating, she formed an image of a rift in her mind, poured all of her heightened emotion into creating it, and slashed her hand through the air like the blade of a sword. The air in the middle of the room tore open with a sound like screaming and Kelley flew back, wide-eyed and horrified. Within the dark, swirling space beyond the opening, Kelley saw a horde of nightmares crowding to pour through the rift, all tearing claws and foaming, screaming mouths full of teeth.

"Close it!" howled Bob. "Close it! Close it up again!"

Frantically, Kelley struggled against the thrashing and, imagining the rift was a giant zipper, yanked it shut. She collapsed forward onto her hands and knees, exhausted by the effort.

"Oh yeah . . . ," she panted. "Right . . . rifts bad. . . ."

"Especially here!" Bob agreed emphatically. "Why else d'you think they use that bloody carriage to get to and fro? There are more wraiths surrounding this island than almost anywhere else I've ever seen."

Fine, Kelley thought, staring at the broken windows. *I've got wings. I've got* all *my wings! I can* fly *out of this place.*

She raised her arms in the air and called the dark, fiery wings of her Autumn Court heritage into being.

Nothing.

She tried the silvery ones that sprang from her Unseelie power.

More of the same.

She imagined herself a kestrel falcon.

Less than nothing.

Well, now I just feel kind of stupid, she thought. She dropped her outstretched arms to her sides and turned back to Bob, who was smiling kindly, politely not pointing out the uselessness of her efforts.

"It takes a lot of magic to even just conjure a scrying," he consoled her. "And what you just did *there*? With the king? That was . . . something. You're probably just a little tapped out. You're new at this, remember. And there are all sorts of inhibitor enchantments on this island, I'm sure."

Kelley knew Bob was just being nice. But she had to admit, she did feel like she'd just been hit by a truck.

"What about you, Bob?" Kelley asked, swaying a bit on her feet. "You have more power than most. Can't you get out of here? Do that sparkly disappearing thing you do?"

"If I was operating at full capacity, perhaps. Sadly, I am not."

"What do you mean?"

Bob grimaced and said, "They used an iron chain to bind and bring me here. Forged by your father's own blacksmith—just another disgruntled defector, it seems." The boucca lifted the edge of his leaf-green tunic, and Kelley gasped at the sight of the livid blisters that had risen in the shape of links in strips around his rib cage.

"Oh, Bob . . ." Kelley reached out a hand but did not touch the marks. Bob lowered the tunic edge gingerly, wincing. The ancient Fae must have been in pure agony.

"All of my power is otherwise occupied in healing this. I simply don't have enough spare magick left in me even to perform card tricks, Princess. Sorry." The boucca sighed. "The only ones using magick in this place, it seems, are the masters of the island."

Who at that very moment, apparently, required Kelley to attend on them. She knew that because Bob's eyes suddenly rolled in his head and he clutched at his temples.

"All right!" he muttered, when the pain appeared to have subsided. "No need to yell. . . . Showtime, Princess. I'm sorry," he said, struggling to make the words come out of his mouth. The compulsion might be fading, but Bob wasn't free from the Faerie queen's will yet—not by a long shot. "I really am sorry, Kelley . . . but you must come with me now."

Kelley didn't like the sound of that. As the door to the cell swung open, she put a hand on the boucca's arm. "Bob— tell me something, quick. Mabh told me that if you are in possession of something that is magickally connected to another person, you can use that—whatever it is; person, object—as a conduit. Right?"

"Yes."

"That smith guy you said used to work for my dad—did he make the Janus medallions?"

"He did."

"Would he have incorporated my father's magick into them?"

"Yes. That's where the Janus get their power from. Blood magick. It's very powerfully tied to the king."

Kelley thought of Fennrys and the iron charm that all of the Janus wore around their necks. His had been conspicuous in its absence, as had Sonny's. Sonny had told her he'd lost his while fighting alongside the Wolf.

"Why do you ask?"

"I think I know what's *really* wrong with my father," she said. Her anger might have made Auberon vulnerable in the first place, but somebody else went and cast a real-live curse on him. Kelley was pretty sure she knew how—if not who.

Oh, Fenn . . . , she thought, as Bob led her out of the cell and through the hospital pavilion's back doors, out into the night.

XXVII

It was the smell that woke Sonny. Sharp and acrid in his nostrils—like a bouquet of lilies left too long in a vase and gone to rot.

"And here I was worried you were gonna sleep through all the fun. . . ."

At the sound of that voice, Sonny struggled instinctively to raise his hands into a defensive posture but found that he couldn't move. It took him a moment to realize he was lashed to the trunk of a hawthorn tree by thick, woody vines wrapped so tightly around his arms and chest that he could barely breathe. His head was swimming badly—he could barely hold it up—and his eye wouldn't open all the way. Probably because it was crusted shut with blood.

He must be a ghastly sight to behold, Sonny thought.

The moon came out from behind a cloud and shone down, illuminating the Wee Green Man, who crouched on the stump of a tree in front of him.

"Oh . . . ," Sonny mumbled a bit deliriously, "I guess I don't feel so bad then."

"What's that?" the creature asked in his ravaged voice.

"I was just thinking how rotten I must look right now. But it's probably nothing compared to you." Sonny shook his head to try and clear his vision. "I mean . . . you *really* look like hell." He hissed in pain as the vines tightened sharply around him, cutting into the flesh of his bare arms and torso. Sonny looked down in detached, concussed bemusement. "Where's my shirt?" he asked.

"Shut up," the Wee Green Man snarled.

"I liked that shirt. . . ."

His short swords and his weapons satchel were, of course, also gone. His boots were gone, too. Sonny could feel the thick cushion of moss and decaying leaves beneath his feet. He thought he could sense an almost seismic vibration traveling up through his soles, as if the island quivered with anticipation.

Sonny glanced up again. Hooligan-boy didn't look the same as he had the last time Sonny had seen him. It wasn't just that he seemed the worse for wear; rather that his appearance was . . . transformed. Revived now by the life-force of the Old Shrub, he could have almost doubled for a swamp creature in one of those old horror movies Maddox was fond of watching.

The leprechaun's long, shaggy hair had darkened and taken on a greenish tinge, as if mosses and leaves grew there. In places along his browridge and the sharp angles of his cheekbones, there was a roughening to his skin—a patchiness—that made it seem almost as if he were growing an outer casing of bark. Sonny could see the arteries on either side of his neck pulsing with dark greenish blood. The soles of his silver-buckled boots were caked with swampy mud.

In the hollow at the base of his throat, there was a dark, angry-looking scorch mark in the shape of a four-leaf clover.

The leprechaun's venomous gaze raked over Sonny.

"You think I'm a sight to behold, pretty boy? I can tell you, when I'm done with you, there won't be anything left of you to look at that won't send your girlie screaming. Maybe she'll run screaming straight to me, and I'll have a bit of fun with her."

Fire burned in Sonny's head, behind his eyes, at the thought of that. He felt the Green Magick ignite. The ground beneath the hawthorn tree began to tremble.

The leprechaun grinned his terrible grin. Sonny felt poison ivy tendrils snaking over the bare skin of his ankles and around his wrists. Like manacles made of acid, they burned his skin on contact. His hands knotted into fists—how he wished he had his sword. His satchel lay on the ground in front of the leprechaun's tree stump. Hooligan-boy bent down and picked the satchel up when he saw Sonny glance at it, lazily flipping open the top.

"What do we have in here, now?" he said as he started to dig through the contents. He plucked out the spell-disguised bundle of three branches. "Sticks," the leprechaun sneered. "How quaint." He tossed them over his shoulder. Then he drew forth the compact crossbow pistol, holding it daintily by the carved oak grip, and glared at Sonny. "Cold iron. Naughty boy." He threw that over his shoulder, too, along with the leather quiver full of short iron bolts.

Next, he pulled out a crumpled sheaf of paper held together with two brass fasteners. He turned it over in his hands, looking at it. Then he stood and walked toward Sonny, fanning the pages.

"'Kelley's Script'?" he said in a simpering tone. "'Please return'?"

Sonny tensed as the leprechaun held the pages up in front of his face.

"A memento, is it?" the leprechaun asked. "A love token?"

Sonny ground his teeth together and strained against his bonds. "Put that down, you piece of filth," he snarled.

"Now, now. What are you worried about? You're not going to be returning to that lass anytime soon. And certainly not intact. I'm gonna rip you apart, boyo. Just . . . like . . . this . . ."

Hooligan-boy smiled and tore the script to pieces.

Sonny roared in protest and thrashed against his bonds.

Blood from his wounds spattered the torn white pages as the leprechaun laughed and threw the ragged bits of paper into the air like confetti.

A raging wind sprang up and whirled them up into the darkness.

The fire in Sonny's heart kindled to a blaze, and tree roots, like sharpened staves, suddenly thrust out of the ground all around Hooligan-boy's feet—but he leaped nimbly into the air, screaming, "That's it! Pour it on, little fleshling!"

The tree to which Sonny was lashed groaned and shifted. Blackberry canes studded with brambles snaked out of the undergrowth, whipping through the air, chasing the leprechaun as he bounded toward an oak and swung himself up into its branches.

"Is that all you've got?" he taunted Sonny. "No wonder she ran straight into the arms of the Wolf the minute you left! Girl needs a real man!"

White-green light burst in Sonny's brain like an exploding star. The ground beneath his feet was shaking now, responding to Sonny's fury, feeding on it. But not controlled by it. Not controlled by *him*. North Brother Island had too long been under the sway of Gwynn ap Nudd. And even though he possessed the Greenman's magick, Sonny Flannery was not himself the Greenman.

The magick poured out of him nonetheless, rousing the spirit of the forest all around, awakening it. The Wee Green Man howled with wild laughter and leaped from the tree. He charged at Sonny, sprinting across the bucking ground. He reached for Sonny's throat and, in one swift motion, fastened the silver chain with Kelley's clover charm around Sonny's neck.

Sonny screamed in agony as the Green Magick boiling out of him was suddenly, violently forced back under his skin.

"Now . . . ," murmured the leprechaun in the sudden stillness. He was so close that Sonny could feel the creature's too-hot breath on his cheek. "We can't have all that power blowing hell outta the place, can we? That would be counterproductive. So you just take it easy. One drop at a time, boyo. Just like brewing fine whiskey. One drop at a time."

The leprechaun stepped back. Clawing at the air with his fingers, he wove a spell of twisted, knotted magick. The branches of Sonny's tree bent and folded down around him, braiding together into the tangled bars of a cage made of thorns. The thorns grew unnaturally long. They bit into Sonny's flesh, and his blood began to flow, dripping down onto the thirsty earth below.

The charm pulsed icy-hot on his skin.

Sonny closed his eyes and pictured it back where it belonged—fastened around Kelley's graceful neck, the green-amber clover nestled in the hollow at the base of her throat. In the picture in his mind, she was smiling at him, her green gaze sparkling.

When Sonny opened his eyes again, he saw that a rose had unfurled in a froth of peach-colored petals on the thorn branch beside his face. And another below that one, and another . . .

Then the ground beneath him shivered and heaved again. The roses grew larger, overblown, their petals changing color from peach to blood-red. Then dark purple. Then black. The island knew its masters, and Sonny was not one of them. His head fell forward in despair. The flow of magick was leashed in, confined to a trickle.

But inside Sonny, the dam had burst and there was no way to stop what was happening to him. The Greenman's power gathered and roiled like an electrical storm. Sonny would bleed out every ounce of it, along with his life, into the soil of this forsaken island. Then Gwynn and Titania would take it and shape it to their own twisted ends.

Sonny had only just discovered who he and Kelley had been up against all along.

And their enemies had already won.

XXVIII

Above the door of one of the clustered outbuildings, a rusting sign declared that this was the facility's recreation center . . . and theater. Bob led her around to the stage door, and Kelley got a cold, uneasy feeling in her guts.

She stepped through the door into what had once been the backstage area of the little playhouse. *This whole place is like one big nightmare.* As if in answer to those unspoken words, she heard the voice of Gwynn ap Nudd echo from the back of the darkened auditorium.

"And what are nightmares but dreams, Princess?" he said. "Just bad ones."

The Faerie Lord of Dreams. King of the Court of Spring. The one monarch who had seemed to Kelley as if she could relate to him. Like him, even. He'd been kind to her. Generous.

Deceitful beyond measure.

Suddenly, the houselights in the auditorium blazed up to full. The "houselights" were chandeliers dangling in rows from the ceiling, illuminated not by candles or electric bulbs, but by dozens of tiny fire sprites. Of course, the fixtures themselves were a Fae illusion—just like everything else beautiful in that room. It seemed as if Kelley stood in a grand circa-1900 theater palace, complete with ornate decoration and velvet seating banks and brocade curtains over high windows. But if she looked hard enough, Kelley could still see the night sky through the gaping hole in the roof and the torn curtain that hung over half of the collapsing proscenium arch at the front of the dinky stage.

Only four of the original chairs remained upright and intact in the very back row, where Gwynn ap Nudd sat with Titania. The other two seats were empty, of course—Auberon and Mabh had been left off the guest list.

Kelley's heart couldn't sink any lower. "You," she said. "All this time, it was you."

Gwynn spread his hands and nodded graciously, as if accepting a generous compliment. "Me," he said. "With the help of my dear Queen Titania, of course."

Of course. How else would he have come into possession of Mabh's war horn in the first place? How ironic that it was the one Faerie monarch Kelley had actually come close to trusting who had put her life and Sonny's and the fate of New York City on the line.

The two faerie monarchs were surrounded by a few dozen "courtiers"—painted and pretty young things, girls and boys. They laughed and lounged all over one another in a revelry of bacchic abandon. Kelley realized with a shock that some of the partygoers were human—patrons of the River, Titania's midtown nightclub, judging by how they were dressed.

She saw Gwynn stroke Titania's temple. Then he reached for a crystal decanter to refill the glass in her hand. The Summer Queen, Kelley saw, still smiled dreamily. Whatever it was—enchantment or intoxication, or both—that afflicted her, Titania was as much in thrall as the mortals that sprawled at her feet. Kelley wondered if most of them even realized that they weren't in Manhattan anymore.

At her side, Bob made an apologetic noise as he stepped forward with a flourish to introduce Kelley. She recoiled in sudden horror when she realized what was happening. She was going to be made to perform like a trained animal. She tried to resist but, pulled along by Gwynn's magick—like a puppet on strings—Kelley's feet moved her downstage center against her will. What was it she had so recently thought, back at the Delacorte Theater? That she would find a way to get back onstage soon . . . that it was where she belonged . . .

Be careful what you wish for.

The houselights dimmed to black, and a bright white shaft

316

of light lit up a circle on the broken little stage where Kelley stood. An unseen orchestra broke into an overture. A gaggle of dryads, tittering and tipsy, tumbled out of the wings with a length of shimmering gossamer that they draped over Kelley's street clothes. They wove garish flowers in her hair and threw handfuls of sparkling Faerie dust over her. In the darkness, a human girl laughed, crass and rude, but Kelley's gaze remained locked on Gwynn's face where he sat, smiling back at her.

"I told you, I think, my dear, how much I adore the theater," he said. "While we wait for the evening's main event to get started elsewhere on this island, you will indulge us with scenes from your latest show, won't you?"

Not if it was up to her, she wouldn't. But, apparently, it wasn't up to her.

"Speak!" Gwynn commanded.

"Woof!" the girl with the awful laugh heckled from the audience. The king, to his credit, turned a withering glare on that corner of the house, and the girl uttered a choking gasp that rattled away to nothing.

"Probably the type to leave one of those ridiculous pocket phones on at the picture shows," he sneered. "Cretin." Then he turned back to Kelley where she stood on the stage, and graciously gestured for her to continue.

Lines of Shakespeare came tumbling suddenly from her mouth, against her will. This was worse than the most humiliating audition Kelley had ever had—and there had been a few. She felt naked under the lights—manipulated like a puppet on strings for the cruel enjoyment of others. She tried to close her eyes, but she couldn't. She tried to shut her ears, but she couldn't block out the sound of Ariel's lines from *The Tempest*. Kelley listened to her own voice speaking words she hadn't even fully memorized yet, from a role she might now never get to play. She thought of her last three roles and realized that she was getting a little sick of life imitating art so closely.

The fairy . . .

The doomed young lover . . .

The enslaved spirit on the island . . .

On this island where man doth not inhabit, you 'mongst men being most unfit to live, said Ariel, disguised as a frightful harpy. *I have made you mad.*

Life imitating art, all right.

Gwynn had fed on the madness of the island.

If Shakespeare had been alive, Kelley thought desperately, she might have counseled him against writing any more parts that she could conceivably play. As it was, she realized that the only way she was going to get through this was to let herself sink into the role. Kelley made herself relax and stretch to inhabit the skin of Prospero's airy familiar and, as she did so, she felt herself gathering strength. She thought about the tormented souls who had sat in this place, watching their fellow patients and inmates perform for them. As a diversion, as a way of combating boredom or despair, as escapism . . .

As escape.

What else was theater but that?

Kelley clutched the idea of escape to her heart. She thought of Ariel and of Prospero at the very end of *The Tempest*. She imagined Gentleman Jack standing on the stage beside her in that moment, with his magician's staff and cloak . . . granting her liberty. Freeing her.

Kelley drew on Ariel's fierce elation and joy.

She was the child of not one but *two* Faerie monarchs. And she would not be a slave to anyone.

The ice-crystal singing of her father's magick surged in her veins, a chiming counterpoint to the stinging, fiery whisper-hiss of her mother's. She felt the two of them melding, merging, building to a crescendo in time to the beating of her own heart.

Kelley heard Prospero's voice in her head, sounding just like Gentleman Jack. She remembered all the things he said to Ariel about freedom in that final scene. Lines tumbled through her head like incantations. *The charm dissolves apace. . . .*

Thou shalt be free. . . .

Untie the spell. . . .

To the elements be free, and fare thou well.

The voice in her head grew to a roaring, and a winter-white sunburst exploded all around her, like the brightest spotlight she'd ever stood in. Kelley's wings burst forth, and she could see them at the edges of her vision—furling outward like silver lace, edged with purple flame. She leaped and they swept her up through the crumbling rafters of the derelict theater and out into the night sky. Behind her, below her, she heard

Gwynn shouting furiously as Titania cried out in surprise.

I guess they might want a refund, Kelley thought triumphantly, *seeing as how the rest of tonight's performance has been canceled!*

For all her momentary elation, Kelley knew she wasn't safe. She soared through the air, then dived low, skimming the ground under the thick canopy of trees. Free for the time being, but her freedom would prove worse than useless—unless she could find Sonny. Before she could do that, there was something she had to take care of. She flew toward the main hospital pavilion.

Once back inside the pavilion's dank halls, Kelley furled her wings and made her way carefully, quietly. Since the theater hadn't been set up as anything other than a theater, she knew there must be somewhere else on North Brother Island where Gwynn held court. She headed for a set of wide double doors that opened into a large gallery.

Bingo. The room had been decorated with Faerie glamour, but there were also corporeal luxuries strewn about—plush couches and cushions, rugs piled thick on the floor, and glass lanterns hanging by delicate chains from the sagging ceiling grid.

Planters full of flowers stood everywhere. Underneath the froth of scents, Kelley could smell the air-churning odor of vervain. She looked and saw the tall purple stalks, standing in the same silver planter that she had seen in Gwynn's hall in the Otherworld.

Even as her stomach clenched at the smell, her heart leaped with excitement. Kelley knew what she'd found. She took another step into the room—and a flash of movement and a sound caught her eye. Kelley gasped.

In the corner, wrapped in a constricting net of thick vines, stood Lucky—the gentle kelpie she had rescued from drowning in Central Park Lake, the same night she'd met Sonny. The poor creature's head was down and his legs were splayed wide in an effort to keep himself upright against the pull of the foliage. His red mane was woven with the trailing, grasping fingers of creeping green tendrils. The vines were strangling him, and the poor creature's flanks heaved with the effort to draw breath.

Kelley had found more than she'd bargained for. Not only the source of her father's affliction . . . but her mother's as well.

Lucky had once been the Roan Horse, ridden by the leader of the Wild Hunt. Created by Mabh as a gift to Herne, her lover in centuries past, the Roan Horse had been corrupted along with the rest of the Hunt and called into being once more last autumn during the bad business on the Nine Night. Lucky would, of course, be saturated still with the residual magicks from that experience, Kelley reasoned. It made him a perfect conduit to tap into Mabh's strength.

Lucky whickered softly at the sight of her. Kelley took a few steps toward him. "How did you get here?" she asked under her breath. The kelpie had been with Sonny when he disappeared, she knew. And Sonny had been with Fennrys—hunting the last three remaining Wild Hunters. That was when Sonny had been hit from behind. When he'd awoken, Fennrys and Lucky and Sonny's Janus medallion had all been gone.

Fennrys . . .

"You didn't think they'd go off to the party and leave the place completely unguarded, did you, Princess?" the Wolf asked as he stepped out from behind a pillar, a sword held loosely in his hand, and his eyes full of regret.

"*Why*, Fennrys?" was all Kelley could say.

"It was a long time before I'd even met you that I set my feet on this path, Kelley," he said. "This is nothing personal."

"Nothing personal," Kelley scoffed. "You're a bigger liar than I am, Fenn."

His gaze darkened. "Gwynn promised me my freedom. Said I could return to the mortal realm once it was all over. For good. Do you have any idea what that means? A chance to live like a real man. A chance to grow old and die like one. I should have died with my brother warriors hundreds of years ago."

"Well, I hope you get your wish," Kelley spat angrily. "Try and stop me and you just might."

She turned her back on him before Fennrys could make a move. Heaving with her shoulder, she knocked the silver planter full of vervain to the ground. It made a sound like an alarm bell clanging, but Kelley didn't stop. Rich dark earth spilled everywhere and the scent of the herb was overwhelming. Ignoring the surge of nausea that clawed up her throat, Kelley tore through the stalks of vervain, yanking them free by the roots, which had grown into tangled, twisted masses of ropy fibers around three soil-encrusted iron disks.

Wrapping her hands with the gossamer Gwynn's nymphs had draped around her, Kelley ripped the roots away from the Janus medallions. The metal felt blazing hot through the filmy fabric. She tore the last strand of vervain away, and there was a bloom of blood-colored light, momentarily blinding her as Gwynn's vile enchantment broke. And then the metal went icy cold.

Auberon, Kelley thought desperately, hoping she hadn't been too late. *Father . . .* She closed her eyes and waited in suffocating silence for what felt like an eternity. Then Kelley felt a brush of thought against her mind, feather-light. A sound like the keening cry of a falcon—angry, vibrant. A rush of winter air. Her father was *alive*.

She slumped forward, weak with relief and utterly exhausted. She might have actually collapsed were it not for the strong arms suddenly circling her shoulders. Senseless in the moment, she sank back into that embrace and heard a voice whispering her name into her hair.

Fenn's voice.

Kelley's eyes snapped open and she scrambled away from him, shaking with emotion. She still clutched the medallions in her fabric-wrapped hands—but she only realized it when Fennrys reached out and gently pried them from her fingers. The metal had left angry welts on her palms, even through the cloth.

Fennrys looked down at the Janus medallions in his hands. They didn't burn his skin. Because he was mortal—and all he'd wanted, all the long years, was to be able to live like one. Kelley felt her anger begin to melt.

"It might not have been the destiny you would have asked for, Fennrys," she said quietly. "But I'm starting to think that the only destiny there is . . . is the one we make for ourselves."

She looked down at the three medallions in his hand. One was Sonny's. One must have been his predecessor's—the Janus Guard killed by a glaistig and the first conduit through which Gwynn had begun to weave the poison into her father's magick, once Kelley's own power had weakened him in the first place. And one was the Fennrys Wolf's.

Kelley reached out a hand and took up the braided cord of the one she'd always seen Fenn wear. Her father had bestowed it upon him when he'd made the Viking prince a Janus Guard all those long years ago. The Wolf swallowed convulsively and almost flinched away from it.

"Embrace it or walk away from it, Fennrys," she told him. "Make a *choice*. But don't make an excuse out of it."

She dropped it back down into his palm.

"Pick your battles?" he murmured.

"Something like that."

There was a rumbling sound from somewhere outside, and the floor beneath their feet shivered as if from an earthquake.

Fennrys said quietly, "I don't know if we can win this one, Princess."

"None of us does, Fenn." She smiled at him gently. "You Vikings are a bunch of fatalists . . . isn't that part of the fun?"

Fennrys was silent. His glance returned to the little iron disks in his palm. Kelley picked up the one that had belonged to Sonny and stuffed it into the pocket of her jeans. As she did so, she felt the contours of the other talisman she already carried. The stag-head charm from Herne . . . Kelley bent down and picked up the sword Fennrys had dropped on the floor when he had caught her, and walked to Lucky.

"Wait," Fennrys said.

Kelley turned back and saw him fastening his medallion back around his neck. He stepped toward her and held out his hand. "Let me do it."

Kelley hesitated, but Fennrys stood firm.

"Go find your man, Kelley," he said. "I'll free the kelpie. I promise. I won't hurt him. You need to find Irish and stop what's happening."

Lucky nudged her a little with his nose, as if in agreement.

"Please don't make me regret trusting you, Fenn," she said, and handed him the blade.

"I won't, Princess," he said. "Not this time, anyway."

Kelley nodded once. Then she turned and ran. She hoped Fenn had been telling the truth. Because if the desperate plan that had just blossomed in her mind was going to work, it was going to depend on him.

XXIX

The kestrel was small and sleek, her burnished feathers a deep, blushing shade of auburn. She was dainty enough that she could slip inside his cage between the points of the spiky thorns. Sonny stared blankly at the bird for a moment, but his head was far too heavy to keep lifted, and he let it fall forward again. His long dark hair curtained his face, blocking out the sight of the bird perched on the branch in front of him.

All around him, leaves and stalks and swirling masses of vines heaped up in overgrown drifts. He stood—barely, only kept upright by his imprisonment—at the heart of a green nightmare.

The falcon mewled impatiently. Sonny forced himself to lift his head again and he looked into the kestrel's bright eyes—its bright *green* eyes.

"Kelley?" Sonny murmured.

The kestrel tilted her head, her gaze fixed upon him, unblinking.

"Firecracker . . ." Sonny leaned forward, heedless of the thorns biting deeper into his flesh. He felt himself smiling, the gesture cracking the mask of blood that had already dried on his face. "Maddox told me how you'd transformed . . . I wish I'd been there to see it. . . ."

The bird hopped forward onto a closer branch, careful to avoid the needle-sharp thorns. She bobbed her head up and down, and there was a kind of urgency to the gesture.

"I know now why you lied, you know . . . ," he said, the words rasping through his parched throat. "I know I was a monster. But it wasn't your fault. You think you're my weakness. You can't ever think that, Kelley. . . ." He was babbling now, definitely delirious. "Ever since I met you . . . you've been my greatest strength."

It was only then that he noticed the silken black cord dangling in a loop from the kestrel's sharp beak. The moon had set but, by the pale gleam of starlight, Sonny could make out the familiar shape of the charm that hung from the cord—a glittering black jewel in the shape of a stag's head. At first, Sonny didn't understand. But then it dawned on him what it meant. . . .

He was the son of the Hunter. He was all that Herne had been.

Sonny carried the Green Magick that had been bestowed upon his father—the power that was even now being siphoned out of him with every drop of blood. It was not, however, the *only* magick that Sonny Flannery possessed. He also possessed the magick that had been thrust upon his father by Queen Mabh when she made him the leader of the Wild Hunt all those centuries ago. But there was only one way to tap into that. The thought of doing so made what was left of Sonny's blood run cold.

The falcon mewled again, impatiently, as if expecting an answer to a silent question.

"Oh, my heart." Sonny shook his head minutely. "No. That way madness lies."

But the kestrel just stared intently at him and bobbed her beak up and down, making the talisman dance. The look of impatience on her face was so very "Kelley" in that moment, it was almost comical. Sonny would have laughed if he'd had the strength.

"Haven't you had enough of me turning into monsters lately?" he murmured.

The kestrel gave him a look that seemed to say, *Do you have any better ideas?* He really didn't. His head began to fall forward again, and Sonny knew that, if they didn't do something soon, he wouldn't be able to argue the point further. His fingertips and toes had gone from cold to ice to numb. His limbs were starting to feel hollow, his head and heart empty. . . .

He dragged his head upright again. The kestrel was moving, hopping from branch to thorny branch, deftly maneuvering herself above Sonny. He felt the circle of the silk cord lowering over his head.

"Are you really sure you've thought this through?" he asked. "It might not exactly prove the *lesser* of two evils. . . ."

The falcon rustled her wings and, opening her mouth, let the black cord slip from her beak. The onyx jewel dropped into place over Sonny's breastbone.

Instantly, he felt the electrifying current of the magick of the Wild Hunt surge through his body. The burning sensation of his wounds lessened. He closed his eyes, breathing deeply, and felt some of his lost strength flowing back into his limbs. And with it . . . a kind of hunger.

Darkness flashed behind Sonny's eyes.

He heard a fearsome scream coming from above. He lifted his head to see a huge, tawny-winged owl come plummeting out of the sky. Perched on a branch in front of him, the kestrel turned her head and shrieked in alarm at the sight. She launched herself through the thorns of the cage and into the sky, beating her wings as fast as she could. Above her, the owl stretched out its talons, gleaming like knives. The blur of the kestrel shot through the air, spinning in an out-of-control barrel roll and narrowly evading the predator.

As Sonny watched the aerial battle, he felt his heart begin to beat faster. With each evasion, he could *feel* the owl's rage at being denied its quarry. The Hunter within him snarled in shared frustration. His blood sang with the thrill of the chase, the anticipation of the kill. . . .

You fool, he thought, shaking his head to clear the sudden red mist that had descended upon him. *That's Kelley up there fighting for her life. Not prey.*

The kestrel banked sharply, suddenly—surprising the heavier, less maneuverable owl, who hurtled into a stand of saplings. The kestrel shot toward the cover of the deeper woods. Safe for the moment.

"Go, Firecracker!" Sonny shouted hoarsely in her wake, the effort sending a fresh wash of blood spilling from his wounds to seep into the ground.

Suddenly, the clover charm at his throat burned like a magnesium flare, sending liquid fire coursing through his veins. Sonny couldn't stifle the cry of agony that tore from his mouth. At the sound, the forest floor all around him surged like a tidal wave. Trees groaned, reaching black branches into the skies. Sonny stared up and squinted, wondering for a moment if his vision was ebbing along with his strength. The sky directly above him began to waver like a desert mirage—a product of thirst and madness—and Sonny assumed that his mind had finally broken.

But then he saw the faint edges of a roughly circular, crackling band of light appear, spreading outward, growing, clawing downward through the night.

A rift. A *huge* rift descended on the island. Big enough to swallow it whole. The circle drifted down, and North Brother Island vanished from the middle of the East River, as if it had never existed there at all.

XXX

The kestrel emerged from the other side of the forest, where only a narrow strip of rocky beach separated the trees from the East River. Shifting back from her kestrel form, Kelley wobbled and almost fell to her knees. But she'd *done* it. She'd actually—willfully—transformed into a falcon . . . and then back again.

In her hand, she still clutched the torn, blood-spattered scrap of paper she'd found on the ground outside the hospital pavilion after she left Fennrys to free Lucky. She glanced down at it and felt the same rush of emotion that had finally, once and for all, allowed her to successfully harness her magick.

HIPPOLYTA: How chance Moonshine is gone before Thisbe comes back and finds her lover?

Reenter Thisbe

THESEUS: She will find him by starlight. Here she comes; and her passion ends the play.

The page was torn away after that line. Kelley's fingers trembled, and the remnant of her play script shivered like a leaf in autumn. The script had been the one thing she had given Sonny.

As she gathered herself, preparing for the thing she had to do next, a wash of shifting light suddenly illuminated the beach, and Kelley glanced up, her mouth falling open at the sight of the Otherworldly rift appearing in the sky, slowly growing out, an expanding circle of light that sank downward over the whole of North Brother Island. All around her, the trees and rocks and buildings of the island began to wink out of existence.

Kelley felt herself shimmering along with the island. She closed her eyes and waited for the gut-churning ride to end.

The Jacqueline Kennedy Onassis Reservoir was the largest body of water in Central Park, a serene lake covering over a hundred acres, surrounded by a one-and-a-half-mile path that was a favorite of New York joggers. It was also, Kelley now realized, ideally situated within the magick-ridden park to provide a new home for Gwynn's relocated island. The wavering effects of the rift travel dissipated, and the shores of the

Reservoir shimmered into view, ringed by the distant silhouettes of office buildings and apartment towers.

Kelley looked around. The island had been transported completely intact . . . but it was different than it had been. The hulking scaffold of the coal-dock gate, thirty yards down the beach from where she stood, now appeared to be constructed of the woven branches of white birch trees. It was a majestic entrance to the new seat of the Faerie world here on Earth.

The Samhain Gate wasn't just full of cracks anymore. It'd had its doors blown clean off.

Fair Folk of every description were coming through the shimmering portal—running and bounding and fluttering through—and even from a distance, Kelley could hear their joyous singing. She could hear other sounds, too—howls and snarls and mad cackling. There were a lot of Faerie who had long awaited such a day—the day when the Gate to the mortal realm stood wide and unprotected—and they were taking advantage of it.

The roads leading up from the shore were no longer covered with decaying mulch and overgrowth, but paved with gleaming cobbles and moss, lined with lushly flowering hedgerows of roses and bougainvillea. The hospital pavilion stood opulent as a palace—with facades of carved marble and shining pink granite, and windows of sparkling colored glass. Kelley saw the outline of what had once been the broken finger of a smokestack, now a shimmering bronze spire, topped with a gleaming, pulsing light, like a beacon in the darkness.

Looking at the water, Kelley saw that the surface of the reservoir had grown ruffled with weedy, creeping growth. Ropy tendrils of reeds and lily pads and thick scummy blooms of algae turned the dark water swampy.

The island was stretching out greedy green fingers toward the park.

Frantic, Kelley looked up into the night sky and sent out a silent summons. Within moments, three familiar cloud-shapes descended to hover before her, resolving themselves into her Storm Hags.

"I think we could really use a bout of unseasonable weather, ladies," Kelley said, holding out her hand. The space above her upturned palm flared with cold silver light. Drawing at last on her Winter power, she created the image of a bitter ice storm in miniature.

The Storm Hags squealed and hissed in glee as Kelley told them what she wanted them to do. They each thrust a gnarled hand into the icy spell, augmenting their own powers with hers, and then tore off in three separate directions to spread a killing frost over Gwynn's unnatural flora—to try to keep it in check until their mistress could finish what she had started.

Kelley knelt on the beach, now thickly carpeted with foliage. She cleared her mind and opened herself to the flow of her emotions, channeling them . . . molding them like clay with her will. She concentrated on the torn half-page, spattered with drops of Sonny's blood, gently rolling it into a tube—a long, spiraled trumpet shape. In her mind, Kelley stretched that shape out, etching detail and function, calling into being the tall, bronze horn that her mother had used to summon the Hunter.

Kelley had held the instrument in her hands only once before, but she remembered how it felt, how it sounded—the earth-shattering notes it had produced on the night when Sonny had first transformed into the terrifying Rider on the Roan Horse. She remembered how it had felt when she'd snapped the instrument in two over her knee, destroying it so that no one could ever again call upon the awful power of Mabh's horn.

Kelley's horn, she whispered silently in her mind. *This time it's my horn, Sonny. Please hear that. Please understand. . . .*

The magick flowed out of her, and she felt the sudden weight of cold metal in her hands. Kelley stood and put the horn to her lips. The triple-note clarion call rang through the air, leaving deathly silence in its wake.

Too exhausted to transform back into a falcon, Kelley ran, stumbling, through the island's forest back toward the clearing where she had been forced to leave Sonny in his prison of thorns.

When she got there, she saw that the cage had been blown apart.

As she stood before the shattered remains, a tawny owl glided out of the shadows. Kelley stiffened in alarm as the bird shape blurred, transformed, and Titania stepped into the clearing opposite her. She stared, aghast, at the horn in Kelley's hands. Looking at the shredded cage, Titania said, "You stupid girl! What have you done?"

Kelley let the war horn fall from her fingertips into the weeds at her feet. Staring up into the sky, she felt the stirrings of dread. She'd thought that, this time, it would be different. *Her* horn. *Her* Hunter. But Kelley feared that maybe she really was just too much her mother's daughter.

What have *I done?*

In the sky above, Lucky—no, *not* Lucky—the Roan Horse of the Wild Hunt hovered in the air like a crimson fireball, Sonny Flannery astride his back, clothed in a shimmering coat of chain mail and a horned helmet.

The last three remaining Wild Hunters rode by his side.

Kelley felt her heart constrict painfully as Sonny hauled on the mane of the Roan Horse and sent the fiery charger plunging over the treetops, toward Gwynn's newly created Faerie palace, drawing a flaming sword as he went.

"You would doom us all," Titania cried to Kelley.

Kelley snorted indignantly. "Only because you would first, Your Highness."

"Insolent wretch!" the queen spat furiously, unfurling wings that were more glorious than anything Kelley had ever seen. Anger blazed in Titania's lovely face, and her wings flamed with all the colors of a sunrise.

Kelley unfurled her own wings in a flash of diamond-and-amethyst brilliance. Together, Faerie queen and Faerie princess

336

lit up the grove, bright as day. Kelley thoroughly expected that they would square off and fight—and that she would stand about as much chance as a snowball in a microwave. But Titania did not hurl sun-fire at her as Kelley expected. Instead, she hesitated, her gaze locked, not on Kelley's face, but on her wings.

"Your wings . . . ," the Summer Queen said, her voice tangled with emotion. "I thought . . . in the theater . . . I thought I was imagining things. How . . . ?"

"Gwynn failed," Kelley said defiantly, "in his bid to kill my father. He failed, and Auberon gave me my Unseelie wings back—which he never would have taken in the first place if it hadn't been for your stupid, stupid evil-villain plans, I might add. *Your Highness.*"

"Gwynn . . ." Titania seemed to have gotten hung up on that initial detail. "He told me only that Auberon was ill . . . a tragedy for the Courts and all the more reason for us to push forward with our designs before someone else could usurp his power. I wanted to go to him, but the Winter Court is so guarded—and Gwynn told me there was nothing I could do to save him. That he would be dead by now . . ." Tears spilled down her cheeks.

"I'm sure Gwynn thought he would be. And I guess he just neglected to mention that *he* was the reason Auberon was sick." Kelley shook her head, almost pitying the queen. She seemed like a lost little girl all of a sudden. "Did it never occur to you to *call* him on that?"

Titania's mouth opened in vague astonishment. "Of course not," she said. "We Fair Folk do not—"

"Don't!" Kelley cut her off before she could say the words. "Just . . . don't."

If one more person told her that Faerie didn't lie, she was going to lose it. And what did it matter anyway? Titania was a lost cause. Gwynn had been manipulating her for so long that the queen's wits and will were virtual strangers to her. It reminded Kelley of how Shakespeare had portrayed her—enspelled, manipulated, and not, ultimately, all that unforgiving of the fact.

A roaring sound came from the direction the Wild Hunt had gone. Glancing at each other, Kelley and the queen both took to their wings to see what terrible thing had made that noise.

In the sky above the palace's courtyard, the Wild Hunters tore through the air, fiery swords blazing. Down below, the denizens of Faerie—called by Gwynn to attend his new court in the mortal realm—ran screaming, fleeing for their lives, as the war band chased them down. The tops of the trees surrounding the yard burned furiously, set alight by the hunters to drive their prey out into the open.

In the shadow of the palace, Kelley saw a gaggle of Titania's mortal thralls—the party girls and boys—terrified and hunched together, trying to escape from the mayhem. She saw Bob standing before them, his hands twisting through the air as he struggled to draw on his depleted magick to weave a veil

338

to hide the unfortunate creatures.

Kelley also saw Carys, charging out from beneath the canopy of burning trees, along with a tall gangly Fae, and Bryan and Beni from the Janus Guard. They split up and began herding straggling thralls and some of the newly arrived Fae to safety.

One of the hunters spotted them and plunged toward the two Lost Fae. Kelley dived, shouting Carys's name. Carys glanced over her shoulder and hit the dirt, leaving the hunter free to snatch one of the shrieking thralls into the air, tossing him like a rag doll into the burning forest before joining his companions as they raced toward Gwynn's palace. Kelley dived beneath the flames and pulled the singed, shaken boy out of the trees by his wrists, turning him over to Carys for safekeeping.

The Wild Hunt was above the palace now. They clattered over the rooftop, shattering the glass skylights and marble statues, sending them crashing into the courtyard.

Finally, that drew the Lord of Dreams forth.

Fury darkening his brow, Gwynn strode out the front doors of his palace and into the open, Hooligan-boy following close behind like a leashed hound. The King of Spring threw his arms wide, black cloak billowing out behind him as he knelt, laying his palms flat to the earth.

Kelley had once seen the leprechaun send an enchantment down into the ground in Central Park. This was the opposite.

Gwynn drew the Green Magick out of North Brother

Island like he was sucking it up a straw. The veins of his hands and arms pulsed dark green under his pale skin—skin that began to darken with swirling patterns, like knotted, writhing tattoos. The air filled with sound and fury as Gwynn's red-eyed birds gathered and descended toward their master in a cloud of inky feathers.

From where she hovered just above the burning trees, Kelley watched, horrified, as dozens of birds converged on the spot where Gwynn knelt, melting together like shadows in the air, coalescing in two giant, winglike shapes behind him.

"No!" Hooligan-boy howled. "It must stay in the earth—you can't control it!"

But the Lord of Dreams ignored him, siphoning the Green Magick up out of the enchanted soil. Gwynn himself began to grow and change, his outline shifting, blurring, melding with his demon birds . . . unfurling, stretching, re-forming into the shape of a fearsome, black-winged dragon.

A freaking dragon.

With a hundred-foot wingspan.

In the middle of Central Park.

XXXI

The Rider on the Roan Horse pulled his mount into a rearing turn as the dragon in the courtyard beat its wings, sending out buffeting gales. Its dark hide glowed with green iridescence. Its eyes blazed with emerald fire.

Worthy prey, the Rider thought.

Certainly something you don't see every day, said a voice in the back of his head.

"No!" The leprechaun in the courtyard pulled an iron knife from a sheath at his belt, holding it tightly by its ebony handle. He looked like a child's doll standing next to the great beast. "It is not for you alone . . . you promised we would share the magick!" he howled, and charged at the enormous creature. "You promised me Green Fire!"

Gwynn the Dragon King kept that promise. He turned. Opening his massive jaws, he spat forth a roaring column of acid-green flame that consumed the leprechaun, killing him instantly.

Tremendous sport! the Rider thought. He sent his steed plunging toward the scaly monster, his blade flashing fire.

Kelley turned to Titania, who hovered in the air beside her. The queen's honeyed complexion had gone ashen at the sight of the transformed Faerie king. "You really want to sit on a throne beside a giant lizard, Highness? Seriously?"

The Summer Queen shook her head, mute.

Suddenly, Kelley heard her mother's voice in her head. *Daughter* . . .

And then her father's. *Kelley* . . .

Twin streaks of light, comet tails of silver and violet, streaked toward Kelley and Titania from the island's Gateway, and Auberon and Mabh joined them in the sky. Her mother looked as though she was back to her vibrant, wild-eyed, fabulous self. Auberon was still pale . . . but then, he was always pale. The planes of his face may have stood out more sharply, but Kelley was surprisingly relieved to see him looking as well as he did. The king gave her a small smile as he held out his hand for the Summer Queen to take.

"Lady," he said, with a hint of warmth in his voice, "we have dealt with great threats to the realm before. Shall we do so again?"

Over Auberon's shoulder, Kelley saw Mabh roll her eyes.

"My lord." Titania took Auberon's offered hand, her eyes shining as she gazed at him. "We shall."

"Oh, get a room," Kelley muttered as they soared away together.

Mabh heard the comment and threw back her head in a burst of laughter. Then she, too, streaked toward where the Dragon King beat the air with enormous wings that sent forth great gusts of wind, flattening trees and extinguishing the Wild Hunt's flames.

But despite Auberon's bravado, it swiftly became apparent that Gwynn could not be cast down from the sky with their combined efforts. Driven back, maybe. Nowhere near defeated.

He was also not the only threat facing them.

From out of nowhere, one of the Wild Hunters came tearing through the night to knock Kelley out of the sky. She landed heavily in an ornamental rose hedge and, crawling free, realized that it hadn't been just *any* hunter who'd attacked her.

It had been Sonny.

The beautiful Faerie girl tumbled through the air and crashed to the ground in an explosion of leaves and petals. She would make a handsome trophy kill.

No! the voice in his mind protested, louder now. *She's not to be hurt!*

The Rider snarled and shook his head. Beneath his knees, the Roan Horse sensed his confusion and whinnied, bucking angrily.

Kelley!

Above them, the rulers of Faerie fought gallantly to subdue the dragon. The Rider would let them worry it and wear it down, like hounds after a stag, and then he and his hunters would finish the dragon off.

In the meantime, he would have his pretty quarry.

The Rider charged at the shining girl again, but suddenly a tall blond warrior ran in front of her, knocking the Faerie girl aside as the Rider charged harmlessly past.

"*This* was your great idea?" the Rider heard the man ask. "The Wild Hunt? Do you suffer short-term memory loss or something?"

The Rider wheeled his mount and charged again.

"Fenn—look out!" the girl shouted a warning.

Too late.

The Roan Horse thundered past. The flat of the Rider's fiery sword hit the Janus Guard across the shoulders, scorching the leather of his jacket and sending him sprawling. As he struggled to rise, the Rider spun his mount into a rearing turn and charged once more, knocking the Janus to the ground again—with a blow from a hammering hoof. This time, the blond warrior was slow to rise. He pushed himself to his hands and knees, and the Rider raised his sword high.

"No." The Faerie girl stepped in front of the downed man.

Kelley . . . The Rider hesitated and then raised his sword again.

"Sonny."

The name was familiar. So was the voice that said it. He had heard it in the music of the war horn's call. . . . *Kelley*.

She pointed at the sky, where the dragon belched flame. "That's why I summoned you. That's why you're here. Not to hunt us, but to save us."

He stared down at the girl. She would be an easy kill. . . .

"Sonny," she said again, very quietly. "I know you're in there. Where are you?"

The remote creature that used to be Sonny Flannery stared down at her, his face a stony mask. He leaned forward, reaching out a hand toward her, and Kelley froze, wondering if he would snap her neck right there. But then he plucked a rose petal from the tangles of her hair and held it up between them. His lip twitched in the ghost of a smile.

"Sonny . . ."

The petal quivered and multiplied until he held a perfect bloom in the palm of his hand. He looked at it, as if seeing a rose for the very first time. "I remember . . . I only wanted to give you this," he murmured. "You looked as though you could use something . . . nice. . . ."

"You were right," Kelley said, remembering, too, the moment they'd first met in the Shakespeare Garden. Her voice broke. "Sonny?"

Sonny's silver-gray eyes shone as he gazed down at her.

"I'm right here, Firecracker," he whispered.

He held out the rose. She took it and he reached for her, swinging her up behind him onto the back of the Roan Horse. Kelley wrapped her arms around Sonny's chest and they leaped into the sky.

"Hold on tight," Sonny said over his shoulder. "Let's finish this together."

They thundered through the air, the Roan Horse galloping madly toward the dragon—who was beset by a Faerie king and two Faerie queens—and Kelley unfurled her diamond-bright wings. As she did so, she felt the sleek red coat of the Roan Horse ripple and bunch beneath her. Sonny shouted in amazement as his mount's hide suddenly shivered and paled, turning from crimson to white to pure silver. The shape of his muzzle and limbs altered. The long neck grew thicker with muscle and a shaggy mane . . . and a white-fire corona blazed about his head, branching out into the most magnificent rack of antlers.

They no longer rode on the back of the Roan Horse, but astride the silver King Stag, monarch of the forest. And together they were more than a match for the monster before them. The sword in Sonny's hand blazed like a sun, and Kelley's light flared nova-bright, spreading out before them to shield them from the dragon's flame. The King Stag lowered his antlered head and charged like a silver meteor streaking through the black-velvet sky.

They hit. Sonny drove his blade straight into the dragon's heart, and the force of their impact blew Gwynn's new-made enchantment to pieces. The magick that had held the dragon shape together exploded outward in a burst of black feathers and bilious green lightning. The sky rained down the bodies of the demon birds, and the Faerie King of Spring dropped through the night, hitting the surface of the Reservoir with a tremendous splash before sinking beneath the dark waves. The enchanted birds turned to smoke as they hit the ground and drifted away to nothing, all of the Green Magick sinking back into the soil of North Brother Island.

Gwynn ap Nudd did not reappear.

The Wild Hunters let out a savage howl, celebrating their leader's kill. They surrounded him, their bloodlust high as they longed for more sport.

"Free!" they shouted, wheeling their mounts through the night sky. "We are free to ravage this realm!" They turned and beckoned to Sonny. "Lead us in the chase, noble lord. Lead us to the kill!"

Kelley felt Sonny's muscles tense within the circle of her arms and she waited for how he would respond.

"No," he said finally. "We will kill no more. *You* need kill no more."

The hunters hovered in a half circle in front of him.

"We will kill so long as the Wild Hunt rides," one hunter said. "It is our curse. It is our way."

"Ways change; curses can be broken," Sonny said quietly. He took the black talisman from his neck and closed his fist tightly around it. When he opened it again, the jewel was nothing but a handful of sparkling black dust. Sonny opened his hand wide, and the dust blew away on the night wind.

Beneath them, the island began to shudder wildly. The remaining Fair Folk fled for the birch Gate that would take them back to the Otherworld.

"Sonny . . . ," Kelley said, but he had already wheeled the stag and was heading back to the island. Auberon and the queens, too, descended, and they scrambled to get the survivors to shore before the magick holding Gwynn's island together imploded completely, taking them with it. As the last of them waded out onto the shores of the Reservoir, there was a thunderous crack like the world ripping asunder. North Brother Island vanished into the Between as if it had never existed, and the Green Magick with it.

They'd won. Or, at least, Gwynn had lost.

It was over. Almost.

Kelley was helping Carys tend to Maddox and the rest of the crew that had come with them to the island. Percival had, for lack of a better word, surrendered, but they could not find the other rogue Janus—Aaneel had vanished, along with Selene and Camina. Sonny and Fennrys were discussing what to do about it, even as they avoided making eye contact. Fennrys hadn't spoken to Kelley since she and Sonny had taken on the dragon together.

"We need to get out of here," she said. "I'm surprised an entire anti-terrorist unit and several SWAT teams haven't descended on the park yet."

"Outside of the Gate itself, I doubt if anyone even noticed anything strange, Daughter." Auberon put a hand on her shoulder. "Such is the way of magick for a people who have remained hidden in plain sight for thousands of years. But you are right. We should make some haste, in any case. The sun will rise soon, and the mortal populace will return to this place."

That was when Kelley noticed a pale gleam in the distance, growing larger. It resolved into the shape of a shining white carriage drawn by a snowy charger. The carriage sped toward them; gathered Fae and mortals stared as Belrix thundered down the jogging path, his hooves clattering on the gravel as Olrun drew him to a stop. Kelley was shocked to see Emma sitting in the carriage, white-faced but determined. Her arms were wrapped protectively around the shoulders of Herne the Hunter, who lay half-prone on the bench seat beside her.

Olrun stared down at the band of Fair Folk and changelings gathered there. "The Hunter's time draws near," she said in a voice like winter fog. "The woman begged of me to bring him here so that you may bid him farewell."

"Make haste," the carriage driver said.

Beside Sonny, Kelley was rigid with emotion. "No!" she said. "You can't!"

Sonny felt a wave of despair wash over him as he glanced at where his father lay in the carriage. He knew that there was no bargaining with a Valkyrie—no deals to be done with death. . . .

But there *was* bargaining with the Fae. And Sonny had the best bargaining chip of all. He turned to where the three remaining monarchs of Faerie stood.

"Mabh," he said.

The Queen of Autumn inclined her head without taking her gaze from the white carriage.

"My lady . . ." Sonny stepped toward her, tense, respectful. Determined. "You have told me that you are in my debt."

"And so I have." Mabh looked like she was having a hard time holding it together. The sight of Herne, pale and barely breathing, had hit her like a thunderbolt. The queen stared at her one-time Hunter, a shine of tears in her eyes.

Sonny took another step toward her and went down on one knee, bowing his head, before looking up into her face. "I know now what boon I would crave of you."

"Do you?" Mabh asked, glancing at him, her brow creasing faintly.

Sonny nodded. "Forgiveness."

The queen regarded Sonny shrewdly.

"Not for me." He gestured back to the carriage, but his eyes never left the queen. "For my father. For Herne. I know

350

you have never forgiven him for hurting you."

Mabh's features twisted with suppressed emotion.

"Please, lady." Sonny's voice was quiet, but it carried clearly in the still air. "He deserves such a thing before . . ." He couldn't bring himself to finish that sentence. "He deserves it. So do you."

The Autumn Queen drew herself up tall and stared down at Sonny. Their gazes locked, and held, and then Mabh's eyes narrowed. "I would . . . ," she said slowly, "I *would* grant you this thing, were it not the waste of such a gift upon one who isn't going to be around to appreciate it."

Behind him, Kelley drew in a gasping breath of protest, but Sonny reached back and squeezed her hand.

"I'll take that as a yes," he said, rising, and spun around, beckoning to the tall, goatish Fae standing beside Carys. "Webber. The queen of Faerie requires a healthy Hunter in order to grant my boon."

"I'm on it!" the Fae said, leaping into the carriage before Olrun could do anything about it. He laid his large, webbed hands over the Hunter's wounds and sank almost instantly into a healing trance.

Mabh moved swiftly toward the other side of the carriage, stepping up into it to sit on the bench seat opposite Emma. She inclined her head gracefully to the other woman, who stared at her with hopeful eyes. Webber's hands moved in slow circles over the bloodstained bandages that wrapped the Hunter's broad chest. Sonny tried to take deep, even breaths—silently willing Herne to breathe with him.

Finally, after what seemed like an eternity, Webber's large eyes rolled back in his head, and he slumped almost to the floor of the carriage.

The Autumn Queen looked down at the man she had once loved so much that she had made him a monster. "I forgive you," she said. "But *only* if you don't shuffle off this mortal coil anytime soon. It is my boon to your son." She turned to Emma. "And yours."

Herne lifted a hand to touch Mabh's cheek, and she held it pressed there for a moment. Then Mabh put it back down on his chest and, taking Emma's hand, covered Herne's with hers. Herne sat up, the color already returning to his cheeks. Sonny watched as he gazed down at Emma, his smile lighting his handsome face from within.

As Emma and Auberon gently helped Herne climb down from the carriage, Kelley felt like her heart would burst with joy.

It was a short-lived sensation.

A rumble of thunder startled her, bringing her attention back to the woman who sat on the driver's seat of the carriage. Olrun the Valkyrie stood, seeming to grow taller, more majestic. Kelley could see the ghostly shimmer of a long shirt of scale armor covering her towering form. The shadow of a winged helmet gleamed on her brow, and a phantom shield and spear glimmered in her long-fingered hands.

"This is not a thing that can be undone," she said in a voice like smoke over a battlefield. "I will take the Raven's

Tribute. I will take the Hero to the Hall. My carriage shall not leave this place empty."

Mabh turned a baleful glare on her. "You would gainsay a queen of Faerie? Have a care, Shield Maiden."

Olrun did not waver. "You have no governance over the Beyond realms, Mighty Queen." The tone of her voice was respectful, polite . . . and utterly implacable, the words chipped from ice.

This was not a fight they would win, Kelley thought, despairing. After all they had done. After all they had just gone through, Herne was going to die and be taken, and there was nothing they could do to stop it.

She had to look away from the raw hurt in Emma's eyes.

"I am a Chooser of the Slain," Olrun said. "I can do nothing else but this."

And then—

"Choose another," Fennrys said, walking forward, limping from his encounter with the Rider. "Choose me."

"Fenn—no!" Kelley put out a hand to pull him back. He ignored her.

"Hey, blondie," he called to the Valkyrie. "Did you hear me?" Fennrys approached the white carriage as if he was about to ask how much for a ride through the park. "You need *that* hero in particular, or will any one do?"

Olrun didn't answer him with words, but a chilling blue fire kindled in her gaze and she inclined her head. An invitation. A life for a death.

"Fenn—," Kelley tried again.

The Fennrys Wolf shook her off. "Because I have a sudden hankering to see the place where my ancestors hang their shields."

"Fennrys . . . what are you doing?" Sonny asked in a low voice.

"C'mon, Irish." The Wolf turned to him and grinned a bit madly. "I'm a straight-up hero, remember?"

"Fenn . . . don't be an idiot," Kelley said, alarmed.

"Hey." Fennrys smiled at her. "If there's anyone who can find a way back from that place, it's me. And if I don't . . . honestly, Princess, where else d'you think a guy like me should spend eternity anyway? The Faerie realms have never been my style. Not really."

Kelley blinked back tears and took a step toward the Wolf. Then she pulled his head down and kissed him gently on the lips. Sonny would never need to know that it wasn't the first time she'd kissed him. Because, in her heart, Kelley knew it would be the last.

She whispered, "If this is what you really want . . ."

"This is the destiny I *choose*, Kelley. Just like you said." He turned back to Sonny. "Take care of her."

"Like you did when I was gone?" Sonny asked, striving for lightness.

"Better than that."

"It's a deal."

Kelley gripped Sonny's hand hard. Sonny put his arm around her, and together they watched as the Fennrys Wolf

354

leaped lightly up into the carriage to sit on the front seat beside Olrun—who glanced at him with mild astonishment—and put his feet up on the front rail.

"Right then," he said, and leaned back, hands behind his head. "Let's see what this thing can do."

A hint of a smile touched the Valkyrie's lips, and she snapped the reins. Belrix surged forward. The carriage turned to a blur of ice fog . . . and was gone.

Tears rimming her beautiful green eyes, Kelley turned to look up at Sonny.

"Forgiveness, huh?" she said softly. "That was pretty smart thinking."

Sonny nodded. "Sometimes people who do very stupid things—things like telling lies—deserve that."

Kelley blinked at the wetness on her lashes. "I—"

"That was a *very* stupid thing you did, Kelley."

"I—"

Sonny's lips crushed against hers, and his arms wrapped her in a fierce embrace. He didn't know if the tears on his cheeks were his or Kelley's. It didn't matter. She threw her arms around his neck and melted into him, and he knew that she would never let go of him again.

OPENING NIGHT

CLOSING NIGHT

The gala performance of *The Tempest* was an absolute smashing success. The audience gave the Avalon Players three standing ovations. One night only, but the place had been sold out, the weather had cooperated marvelously, and no one had seemed to notice the collection of Otherworldly beings who'd sat just across the Turtle Pond, enjoying the play from a distance.

Quentin was over the moon. Especially when word reached him that there was an anonymous benefactor with, apparently, a rather impressive portfolio of real estate holdings who'd sent word that there might be a new home for the company—in an empty turn-of-the-last-century dance hall not quite as far off Broadway as the old theater had been.

The cast was in a highly celebratory mood at the after-party. Hugs flew fast and furious. Bob had shown up for the performance and seemed to be successfully ingratiating himself back into Quentin's good graces. Even Mindi and Dame Barbara couldn't stop embracing and laughing with each other long enough to drink the champagne they were spilling everywhere. Everything was as it should be. There was only one cast member who was acting a bit strangely toward Kelley—had been, in fact, ever since the one rehearsal where Tyff had done her "stand in" favor—and Kelley had been meaning to ask her roommate about it. She finally got the chance when Tyff showed up backstage, arms laden with flowers for the whole cast.

"Oh . . . yeah . . ." Tyff fiddled with an arrangement of blooms. "I meant to mention that."

"Tyff." Kelley crossed her arms and pegged her roommate with a look. "What exactly happened between you and Alec?"

"Between *you* and Alec, actually."

"Oh God . . ."

"It was just a kiss—"

"Tyff!"

"No—it's cool! Everything is fine!" Tyff put her hand up to forestall Kelley's outrage. "I sort of *convinced* him to . . . well . . . to convince *you* that it would be better if you just stayed friends. You know—that it would be tragic if a romantic entanglement were to screw up such a great friendship, you have too good a working relationship, yada yada. . . ."

"He *bought* that?"

Tyff grinned wickedly. "He thought it was his idea. Got all noble and self-sacrificing and everything. Really let you down gently."

"Oh *gawd* . . ." Kelley put her head in her hands.

"Don't worry about it," Tyff reassured her, smiling brightly. "You also told him that you had a totally hot roommate you would introduce him to at the cast party."

"I did?"

"Uh-huh. And you *will*."

"Why?" Kelley asked.

"Why?" Tyff's expression went a tiny bit dreamy, and she said, "Because I haven't been kissed like that in over a thousand years. That's why."

Like most cast parties, this one seemed as if it would never end, and—just like always—Kelley really wished she could be in two places at once. Gentleman Jack, coffee cup in hand, finally came to her rescue. Just like always.

"You look exhausted, kiddo," the old actor said, just loud enough for the others to hear. "Must be all that climbing about in the rigging."

"Something like that." Kelley grinned.

"You did a hell of a job, you know." Jack hugged her tightly. "I'm proud of you. But . . . maybe you should get on out of here."

"Oh, gosh, Jack"—she stifled a fake yawn—"I don't want to miss anything. . . ."

"'We are such stuff as dreams are made on,' Kelley Winslow," Jack said, quoting Prospero's most famous line. "I imagine you've got at least one dream waiting out there for you tonight. Go on. I'll cover for you. And give your old man my regards next time you see him."

Kelley smiled her appreciation, hugged Jack once more, and slipped away.

Outside in the darkness, a shadow detached itself from the outer wall of the theater. Four long steps and she was in his arms.

"Sonny . . . ," she sighed, and he shushed her with a kiss.

"You were wonderful tonight," he said, gazing down at her with his beautiful silver eyes. "Don't you want to stay at the party?"

"I don't want to be anywhere you aren't."

He smiled. "I'm sorry I'm not one for crowds."

"I don't need a crowd. I don't need anything but this. I don't need anything but you."

"Just plain old Sonny Flannery? All out of magick? Are you sure?"

Kelley nodded up at him. "Positive."

"Good." He took her by the hand, and together they started walking south toward the Ramble. Kelley didn't have any reservations about being in the park at night anymore. Sonny and Carys had gathered the remaining loyal Janus Guards and combined them with those of the Lost Fae who wanted to help. Together, changelings and Fair Folk patrolled the Gate, keeping an eye on the random cracks that still appeared. The Samhain Gate, the portal to the Otherworld, would never truly be closed again.

"Now that your father is back in control in the Otherworld, sorting out the Courts," Sonny said, "I thought you might want to see some of the places where I grew up. I could take you there. You know, sort of like a . . . a . . . ."

"A guided tour?"

Sonny stopped and looked down at her. "I was going to say, 'a date.'"

Kelley felt herself blushing to the roots of her fiery hair. She was suddenly very glad that Tyff had talked her into wearing something nice for the party. Sonny laughed at her expression and, putting his fingers to his lips, whistled a long note. There was an answering sound from the trees, and then the magnificent silver King Stag trotted into view.

"Lucky?" Kelley said, and laughed as the regal creature threw his head up and down, nodding in a familiar, unmajestic fashion. His form may have altered, but Kelley saw that the gleam of personality in his liquid brown eyes was still Lucky the kelpie, through and through. He trotted up beside them, and Sonny cupped his hands to give Kelley a leg up onto the stag's back. She gripped the shaggy silver ruff as Sonny vaulted up behind her.

Kelley felt a shiver of excitement thrill through her veins

as Sonny's arms tightened around her waist. Together, they climbed into the sky, and over the song of the wind whistling past, Kelley heard Sonny whisper in her ear. . . .

"Magick time."

ACKNOWLEDGMENTS

It's funny how this never gets old. This moment when I get to sit down at the end of a book and thank the people who have made this possible. It has been said that writing is a very solitary profession. I strenuously beg to differ. None of what you've just read, be it this book or the two that preceded it, was created solely in the vacuum of my skull. And for that, I roll out the gratitude and offers of goodly libations to the following: as always, Jessica Regel and Laura Arnold—my agent and my editor, two women so wonderful, I don't even mind that they're both taller, younger, and smarter than me. Seriously. I adore you. Thank you again to Jean Naggar and the staff of JVNLA for continuing to take excellent care of me. Thank you to the wonderful, wondrous crew at HarperCollins: my ever lovely editorial director Barbara Lalicki for her continued support; Maggie Herold, my terrific production editor, for making me seem—for the third time—as if I know what I'm doing; and Sasha Illingworth, my stellar designer, for making the whole thing look even better than it did the first *and* second time around (and I *really* didn't think that was possible)! Thank you again to my two Melissas, publicists extraordinaire—especially Melissa Zilberberg, who has cheerfully sent me hither and yon, always making sure I got there and back again. Thanks to editor Lynne Missen and everyone at HarperCollins Canada for making me feel like part of the family. Thank you, Mark and Danielle and Racquel, for turning me into part of the family (and for random gifts of shiny things that kept my head from exploding utterly). Thank you, Cecmonster, for continuing to be my ultimate target reader (even after all these years). Thank you, Adrienne, for the friendship and kind of understanding that comes from shared experience. Thank you, Joanna, for all your hard work. Now, as ever, I send massive love and gratitude out to my family: Mom, Ward, Shelley, Janna, and Dayln—thanks for the tremendous support and continuing to think that what I do is cool. And for the third time running, thank you, John: from "What if?" to "What happens next?" to "Aha! So *that's* how it all turns out!" . . . you were there with the map at every bend in the road and, just like in real life, you never ever let me get lost.

And speaking of that journey . . . the last thank you, as before, is for you, Dear Reader! Thanks for trusting me to tell this story. And thanks for believing in it alongside me as I did.

Turn the page for a sneak peek at the first book in
LESLEY LIVINGSTON'S
thrilling new trilogy,

STARLING

"C'mon, Mase! Where's that killer instinct?"

Calum Aristarchos bounced lightly on the balls of his feet, the tip of his fencing saber tracing tiny, taunting spirals in the air.

"*En garde* . . ."

Mason Starling's gaze narrowed behind the wire mesh of her cage mask, and she sank lower into her stance, thigh muscles searing with fatigue. She shook her head sharply to clear her mind as the sweat dripped, blinding, into her eyes. *Concentrate* . . .

The blade in her hand wavered, dipping as if in uncertainty.

She retreated a half step. . . .

And Calum Aristarchos made his move. Feet crossing over each other in a blur, he ran at her and thrust for her heart, his left arm flung back, spine arching like a dancer's, only *slightly* overextending himself. . . .

Mason dropped into a deep, leg-punishing lunge, scooped her blade back up and—

"A hit!"

"No!"

Toby Fortier—fencing coach drill sergeant, and *not* someone to argue that kind of point with—snorted and marked the practice score sheet. "She tagged you good, Aristarchos. Which also means she wins, again. Whining about it just makes you look like a girl." He glanced up at Mason as she pulled off her headgear and grinned. "A girl who can't fight like Mason."

Calum took off his own mask and flipped his practice foil around in the air, catching it by the blade, just under the guard. He sauntered back over to where Mason stood, his green eyes flashing and a wry smile bending his mouth up at one corner. Mason noticed that his face still glowed with the remnants of a deep summer tan. Part of what made him look like a magazine model.

"Okay," Calum said, nudging her with his elbow. "I guess you found that killer instinct."

"Sure," she agreed. "Or you just got cocky. That lunge left you wide open."

"Not for everybody, Mase." He winked and plucked the sword out of Mason's hand. "Just for you."

Mason felt her heart flutter for an instant. "Does that mean you're gonna help me prepare for the Nationals qualifiers?"

"You bet." Cal wrapped one arm loosely around Mason's waist and whispered in her ear, "I always back a winner."

Mason's cheeks grew warm as she blushed fiercely. Then she felt another kind of heat—like a laser beam focused on the back of her head—and she glanced over her shoulder to find Heather Palmerston staring at her from across the gym. The tall blonde turned away when Mason's eyes met hers, and she slapped her fencing glove into the palm of one hand, the sound of the leather cracking like a whip. Mason was reasonably certain that Heather had only taken up fencing to stay close to Cal, even though the two of them had recently broken up.

Heather was an indifferent fighter—not bad, just not committed—and she really didn't seem to enjoy it all that much. Unlike Mason, for whom fencing wasn't a pursuit so much as a passion. *She* was shooting for a spot on the national team. And after that? Maybe even the Olympics. Heather . . . not so much. Even less so after she and Cal had broken up. Mason wondered why Heather hadn't dropped out of the fencing club then, but for Heather, everything was about appearances. And quitting would have made it look like she'd lost something. The thing she *did* seem to enjoy about it, though, was the way all the guys looked at her as she walked by dressed in her tight fencing whites.

Like Rory Starling, the younger of Mason's two older brothers, who was gawking at Heather that very moment. As she sashayed past where he was working out, punching the heavy bag in the far corner of the gym, Rory's jaw went so slack he was almost drooling. Mason rolled her eyes.

"She'd be a decent fighter if she gave a damn," Toby rumbled from right beside her. Mason hadn't realized he was standing there. "Couldn't hold a candle to you, of course, but she'd certainly hold her own." He grunted and ran a hand over his face, smoothing his finely trimmed goatee.

"D' you want her on the competition's team?" Mason asked. She'd meant the question to be a neutral one, but that wasn't how it came out sounding. Across the gym, Heather said something that made Calum laugh . . . and Mason felt an envious twinge in her chest.

Toby looked down at her and shook his head. "No, Mason," he said. "And you *know* your spot on the team is locked up."

"That's not what I meant—"

"I know. Just understand that it's not something you have to worry about. Not if you keep fighting the way you have been." Toby's gaze drifted back to where Heather stood shaking out her wheat-gold hair from its ponytail. It fell across her shoulders like spun honey. Lookswise, she was the exact opposite of Mason, with her black hair, winter-pale skin, and blue eyes. "Anyway," Toby was saying, "Palmerston's too high maintenance. I just hate wasted potential, that's all."

Mason nodded silently as Toby wandered over to where a couple of boys from the wrestling club were seeing just how hard they could peg each other in the head with a volleyball. Mason fished her aluminum water bottle out of her gear bag and took a long swallow to quench her thirst brought on by the long practice. She was tired, but not exhausted, and that was a good sign. Cal was a tough opponent—the toughest, in fact. He was still better than her, in spite of what Toby had said, and Mason was inwardly thrilled that not only had she been able to hold her own against him, but he'd actually seemed to appreciate it. She liked the idea of being appreciated by Calum Aristarchos. A lot.

Trying not to glance over to see if he was still chatting with Heather, Mason stuffed her water bottle back in her bag and gathered up the rest of her gear. As she did so, she became aware of a subtle shift in the quality of the light streaming in through the high, arched windows. Mason peered up through the construction scaffolding that had been erected all along the south wall of the hall that housed Gosforth Academy's new athletic center, startled to see that the previously clear blue vault of the sky had descended like a dark, heavy blanket, blotting out the sun.

Through the windows, Mason saw thick, bruise-black clouds boiling over one another, moving with a swiftness that was almost frightening. She glanced at her watch. It was only early evening—just before dinner—but it suddenly seemed much, much later. The light outside dimmed to an ominous purplish wash.

If the sky was going to open up, Mason thought, at least it wasn't anywhere near as far to get back to her dorm as it had been when the fencing club had had to use the Columbia University gym. That was a good six blocks away. Now she just had to run the length of Gosforth's quad in order to get home. It was one of the perks of the new facility. The building used to be the academy headmaster's residence, but the old gothic structure had recently been gutted and redesigned, turning it into an multipurpose center to be used by the gymnastics club and for dance classes and wrestling and—most importantly, as far as Mason was concerned—the fencing team. The sprung wooden floors had been installed only the week before, and the whole place smelled of lumber, varnish, and paint.

It was a gorgeous facility, with state-of-the-art equipment wrapped in the antique charm of the building's gothic architecture. There was even a little raised stage at one end for dance recitals and presentations, and the old stone walls had been left exposed along one side. Midway down the long north wall, double doors set into a high glass partition led to a soaring vestibule. It was an oddly extravagant feature for an athletics facility, but it was triple-glazed safety glass and probably could have withstood even a hard-flung basketball. It was there to showcase the high stone arch that had once housed a plain leaded-pane window, which Mason's father, as a benefactor to the school, had ordered replaced with a magnificent stained-glass masterpiece. Even on the dullest day the window caught the sun and shattered it into a million shards of rainbow-brilliant light, casting it across the dark wood-paneled foyer of the new gym, where glass cases stood displaying an abundance of sports championship trophies.

Mason smiled as she stared up at the stained glass. She was proud of her father and his commitment to the school, but sometimes she wished he would choose *slightly* less ostentatious ways to commit.

Outside, she saw that the shadows cast by the branches of the old oak tree in the school's quad had begun to wave wildly in the gathering storm. The tree was enormous—it had been planted when the school's original buildings had been constructed in the late 1700s on Manhattan's Upper West Side—and the gusting wind sent showers of leaves, twigs, and acorns clattering against the window and the old slate roof. The overhead fluorescents hanging from the hall's exposed beams flickered and dimmed. When they returned to their normal brightness, the gymnasium seemed to have taken on a slightly sepulchral air.

"Whoa," Mason heard Calum say.

She turned to see him gazing up at the gathering storm, his eyes wide and forest green in the uncertain light that filtered down through the tall windows.

"Hey, Toby?" he called. "Maybe we'd better head back to the dorms—that looks like some pretty serious weather rolling in."

"Sure," Toby agreed. "We've done enough work today. And it'll save *you* from getting your ass handed to you again by your partner." His mouth quirked upward, and he slapped the folder with the scoring sheets inside closed. Then he picked up his travel mug—his constant companion; the guy was a total caffeine junkie—and turned, bawling to the other student athletes to pack it in. He barked at the fencing club members to hand in their gear to Mason so that she and Cal could check the weapons for loose hilts and burrs and then return them to their proper places in the storage cabinets.

"Hey, Mouse, catch," Rory said as he tossed an extra practice foil carelessly at her, and Mason had to dodge or risk getting the tip through one eye.

Damn, he's annoying, Mason thought. She hated it when he called her Mouse. He knew it, too.

Heather, of course, just strolled right past Mason and handed her foil directly to Calum. They were still cordial, but since their breakup, Cal had been pretty clear in his intentions to keep it that way—cordial. Not that Mason had made a point of noticing that or anything. . . .

"C'mon, Mase," Cal said, smiling at her.

He handed Heather's foil to Mason, shrugged out of his fencing jacket, and threw it over onto the pile of his own gear. Underneath, he wore only a thin T-shirt with the school logo stenciled on the back. "We should hurry to beat the storm or we're gonna get drenched on the way back to the Res," he said to Mason over his shoulder.

Calum in a wet T-shirt wasn't such a bad idea as far as she was concerned, but he had a point. She hurried toward the storage cabinet at the far end of the gym, but it became suddenly apparent that they weren't beating anything. Through the windows, she saw a blaze of lightning fork across the sky with a sizzling, ear-shattering crack that made her jump.

Is it a bad sign when you can actually hear *lightning?* she wondered. But she didn't really have time to ponder the physics of it because the sound was drowned out almost immediately by a cannon-roar boom of thunder so loud it felt as though it had come from inside her head. The air in the hall quivered with the shock wave, and the new gym floor felt as though it had actually heaved upward. Mason yelped and ran for the cabinet. Outside, the rain started to fall in fat, splattering drops and the wind moaned loudly.

Mason juggled her armload of whip-thin aluminum blades, trying to open the metal door without actually having to stop and put anything down. She was surprised when Heather appeared at her elbow and pulled the door open for her.

"Thanks," Mason gasped, struggling to untangle herself from the forest of swords.

"Hold still," Heather said. "You're gonna stab one of us." Together, the two girls struggled to disengage the weapons and stow them on the rack on the cabinet wall.

"Be careful with that épée!" Mason warned. "You're gonna snap the tip!"

"Yeah, yeah. Let *go*, Starling. I've got it."

By the time they got everything stowed, the sky had turned to shades of deepest midnight and lightning lashed the underbellies of black clouds. The lights flickered again, and Mason felt the breath stop in her throat for an instant.

"Jeezus." Cal snorted. "Who ordered the apocalypse?"

As if on cue, another magnesium-bright flash of lightning blazed, and the lights in the hall flickered and died. The entire gymnasium went suddenly, completely, dark. Mason sucked in a sharp breath, and her heart started to rabbit in her chest. She quickly grabbed her gear bag and hurried toward the door.

"Let's get out of here," she said.

She thrust through the double glass doors into the foyer and leaned on main door's push bar—and nothing happened. She shoved it again, harder, but the heavy carved-wood door remained shut.

"What's wrong?" Heather asked from behind her.

"It's jammed or something," Mason said, and tried again.

"Let me try." Calum nudged her over to one side. He used both hands to push against the bar. He kicked the door's brass footplate and tried shouldering it open, but it wouldn't budge.

"Hang on, Cal," Toby called. They could hear him walking across the gym floor toward them. His worn, heavy combat boots made a steady *thump-thump* in the darkness. His bulky form suddenly loomed up in front of them, and he jiggled the door bar and pushed sharply on it a couple of times. Then he stepped toward an alcove at the side of the door. "Hunh," he grunted. "Weird."

"What's going on?" Rory asked, showing up with his gym bag slung over one shoulder.

"I think the power outage screwed up these new electronic locks," Toby answered. "The control panel's dead."

"Shouldn't there be a backup system or something?" Calum asked.

"Yeah." Toby punched at the panel and jiggled the door bar again. "But there should also be emergency lighting, and I don't see that's come on, either. Could be that they just haven't got the bugs worked out yet. . . ."

Outside, it sounded like the world was coming apart. Mason could hear the old Gosforth oak creaking in protest at the punishing winds.

"I'm gonna go check out the fire exit door," Toby said. "Sit tight until I get back. Don't wander—there's still construction equipment lying stacked near the walls and I don't want any of you accidentally kicking a circ saw and amputating a toe."

Even in that pitch dark, it didn't take the fencing master long to travel from one end of the gym to the other and back again. And Mason knew, just from the sounds of his measured tread, that they weren't leaving anytime soon.

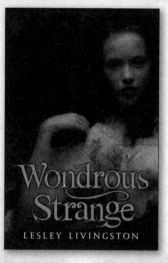

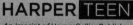